'A compelling combination of political drama and lethal action. There are echoes of Michael Dobbs's *House of Cards* but there is more derring-do in Kent's twisty tale, which has all the makings of a bestseller'

– Daily Mail

'Let's hear some applause from thriller fans! Yes, a new star has arrived with a humdinger that could keep you up all night. I was hooked from the start. The first chapter drips with cold sweat ... packs a storytelling punch, rather like early Jack Higgins'

– Peterborough Evening Telegraph

'*Killer Intent* is not only considered but cleverly layered, unpredictable and best of all really great fun to read ... My advice: Put it on your "must have" list'

– Liz Loves Books

'A fast-paced thriller that packs a punch'

– Crime Fiction Lover

'Wow! Wow! WOW! This book has everything ... A #TopReadof2018 – what a superb story by an author who is well and truly on my radar!'

– Crime Book Junkie

'I cannot recommend this book enough, definitely one to watch for 2018, this will be BIG'

– AMW Books

KILLER
INTENT

KILLER
INTENT

TONY KENT

First published 2018 by
Elliott and Thompson Limited
27 John Street
London WC1N 2BX
www.eandtbooks.com

This paperback edition first published in 2018

ISBN: 978-1-78396-382-9

9 8 7 6 5 4 3 2 1

A catalogue record for this book is available from the British Library.

Typesetting: Marie Doherty
Printed by CPI Group (UK) Ltd, Croydon, CR0 4YY

For Mum and Dad
for everything . . .

And for Victoria
for everything else . . .

ONE

Joshua felt a rush of adrenaline as he looked down into the square. He was 200 feet up, on the edge of the spire of a Regency-era church. From here he could see every crowded inch below. It caused the familiar sensation of controlled adrenaline to rise in his gut. This was the stress point of any assignment. The moment he could no longer walk away. It was what he lived for.

Every detail was visible through his rifle's telescopic sight. Joshua drank in the information, taking just moments to spot the obstacles that could still stand in his way. A less skilled professional would have taken longer to weigh up the evidence. Joshua was nothing if not efficient.

He moved away from the scope. It had told him all it could for now. Instead he viewed the crowd below with his naked eye. The numbers were immense. He wondered – not for the first time – at how unsuitable the location was. Joshua could see the political thinking. Where else for a ceremony to honour the British heroes of the recent Middle Eastern wars than Trafalgar Square, London's monument to military glory? But historical resonance made it no less of a security nightmare.

A grim smile threatened the corner of Joshua's mouth, brought on by the chaos below. The area might be policed by the world's finest security agencies, but any problems they faced were to Joshua's advantage. Right now those problems were legion.

Joshua's hands returned to his rifle.

With the slightest movement, the barrel swept upwards, his eye back behind the scope. He scanned the surrounding rooftops and spotted nineteen sharpshooters in less than a minute. It was rare that he was able to do this so quickly. It might even be unique, but then this was a unique contract. Every other assignment of Joshua's long career shared a common feature: the need to stay hidden in order to achieve the shot. Not today. Today Joshua *had* to remain in sight. If he did not, every one of those nineteen marksmen would wonder where their twentieth man had gone.

TWO

Joe Dempsey stood at a window, less than four hundred yards away. His view from here was every bit as good as Joshua's. His mood was not.

For half his life Dempsey had been employed to identify and neutralise threats. To expect the unexpected. The unthinkable. Eighteen years of that would affect any man and Dempsey was no exception. He saw danger everywhere. Dempsey sometimes wondered if this was thanks to his training, or if it was just paranoia. But such doubts did not worry him today. Today the threat was very real.

'It's not looking any better down there, I take it?'

A soft voice with a distinct Edinburgh lilt interrupted Dempsey's thoughts. He turned towards the speaker.

Callum McGregor sat at the only table in the room. The director of the Department of Domestic Security was a colossus of a man. Six foot six and 270 lb. He over-crowded his empty desk.

Dempsey walked towards the director without a word. Dempsey was a big man himself, but he moved lightly. He pulled a chair to the other side of the desk and sat without waiting for permission.

He looked McGregor in the eye.

'It won't get better, Callum. We can't control a space this big and this public.'

Dempsey's voice was harsher than McGregor's. It was less refined, more intense. This was to be expected. McGregor's was the voice of a diplomat. Dempsey was the diplomat's threat.

'You know you're preaching to the choir, Joe. But it changes nothing. We'll do the best we can with what we have.'

'What we have isn't enough.'

Dempsey's reply was blunt but not insubordinate. McGregor was the senior of the two, but mutual respect cut through rank. He continued.

'It's not just numbers. There are seven different agencies out there, Callum. All working independently from one another. Christ knows why we need that many. If we'd kept it to a single agency this thing could be properly coordinated.'

'The Americans were never going to pass President Knowles' protection to us, Joe. That one was a given even *before* the threat against Thompson.'

McGregor was telling Dempsey nothing new.

'And *we* weren't letting *them* do it alone. No way we risk losing either of the ultra VIPs – president *or* ex-president – on British soil. Which means too many chefs in the kitchen already, even before *our* individual agencies start squabbling to be here. All things considered, this isn't the mess it could be.'

Dempsey leaned back in his chair. It irritated him when McGregor was right. Which the director usually was. But knowing the 'why' did not make the facts any easier to swallow. An event this public, with US presidents past and present in attendance? Even without the British politicians on hand – and they *would* be on hand, thanks to the publicity it would bring – it was nothing short of a nightmare.

If there is a terrorist attack today, Dempsey thought, *it'll take a miracle to stop it.*

The thought was banished as his earpiece flickered into life.

'POTUS has left the Music Room. Bamboo to move in nine minutes. On my mark. Three, two, one, mark.'

The United States Secret Service had been protecting its presidents for over a century. And its former ones, too. In that time they had honed their techniques to perfection. Four short sentences were all it took to put every agent on notice.

The countdown had begun.

Dempsey synchronised his watch as the voice in his ear declared 'mark'. McGregor did the same. Between them the two men had seen more action than the average infantry platoon. They had run covert missions from one side of the world to the other. Today's assignment was a walk in the park in comparison. But still Dempsey's instincts were screaming.

Dempsey got to his feet. His ramrod-straight military bearing took full advantage of his six feet two inches. That height, combined with a powerful physique discernible even under his suit, made him an intimidating presence. His dark, piercing eyes, set deep in a face that carried the damage of a life lived dangerously, completed the picture. He was not an unattractive man. Far from it. But when it suited him, Joe Dempsey could be terrifying.

Those dark eyes now met McGregor's, and no words were needed. The concern on the director's face said enough.

Perhaps Dempsey was not the only one with a bad feeling after all.

THREE

'POTUS has left the Music Room. Bamboo to move in nine minutes. On my mark. Three, two, one, mark.'

Joshua could not place the American accent in his ear. It was East Coast, but where? The failure irritated him more than it should. Joshua's obsession with detail – with control, with ritual – was shared by millions across the globe. To most it was debilitating. Obsessive Compulsive Disorder, capable of ruining lives. For Joshua it was something else. His was a career where attention to detail could be the difference between life and death. In that world, Joshua's condition had helped create the perfect killer.

Joshua synchronised his watch on the speaker's 'mark'. He felt his synapses fire as he did so, fuelled by another surge of addictive adrenaline. The transmission had come from the Presidential Protective Division, bringing complete focus to Joshua's mind. In exactly nine minutes the presidential motorcade would leave Buckingham Palace. It would then make its way along The Mall before arriving in Trafalgar Square in just under thirteen minutes' time. As always, the Secret Service was running like clockwork.

And so was Joshua. The effects of adrenaline differ from person to person. In most it leads to fight-or-flight. In others – fewer – it leads to paralysing terror. And in fewer still it leads to a cold clarity of thought. Where time seems to slow. Where every action is considered. Calculated. Lethal. Most would call it sociopathic – or worse. Joshua called it professionalism.

It was that professionalism which now took hold. With one sweeping movement he scanned the rooftops for the seventh and final time. A number that had long given Joshua comfort. Seven reviews of his surroundings. Seven confirmations that the team was in place, that every one of the sharpshooters was where he or she should be. Between them the team covered Trafalgar Square from every angle. But none of *their* angles mattered. One single line of sight would count today.

It was already Joshua's.

It was another perfectly planned detail from his employer. By now Joshua expected nothing less. The twenty-man team of marksmen and women had been cobbled together from a political tug of war. Half had come from the US Secret Services' Counter Sniper Support Unit, which left a ten-man British contingent. Five from Protection Command. Five from Counter Terrorism Command. Or at least that had been the plan.

Joshua had replaced the senior CTC operative at the eleventh hour. He had not allowed himself to ask how this had been achieved. Sure, he was curious to know. And someday he might even find out. But for today it was enough that – somehow – he was a part of the very team assigned to stop him. In a decades-long career Joshua had found many ways to get close to his targets. None had been so steeped in irony.

He turned his scope back to the square. It had been thirty minutes since he had first looked down. The crowd inside the hoardings – the temporary barrier between invited guests and the massing public – had tripled in that time, to full capacity. Two thousand men, women and children. All patiently baking in the unseasonable October sun.

As far as Joshua was concerned there could have been ten thousand. Or just ten. He was interested in only one.

A small, wiry man, dressed in ageing tweed and sitting in an aisle seat twenty-three rows back from the stage. Exactly as Joshua's instructions had predicted. The motorcade was still minutes away but Joshua's target was in place. From this moment that target would not leave his line of fire.

FOUR

'You're sure we'll get a clear view from here?'

Sarah Truman asked the same question for maybe the tenth time in as many minutes.

'As good as anyone inside the hoardings,' replied Jack Maguire. 'You want better, you have to go higher. That means going outside the square.'

Maguire nodded towards the nearby rooftops. Sarah followed his indication. For a moment she seemed to consider their options. A marksman was visible on a nearby church spire. It was a reminder that all raised buildings were off-limits.

Sarah turned back to Maguire.

'It just seems a bit side-on. Wouldn't we get a clearer shot if we were directly in front of the stage?'

'I'm sure we would. Of the back of everyone's heads, mainly.'

Maguire's brisk words were said with a smile. He could understand her worries. For Sarah – much more than for him – today was a big deal. The first major story the network had given her. Maguire would have been concerned if Sarah had *not* been a little neurotic.

'You almost ready for a run-through?' Maguire asked, focusing his lens.

'As I'll ever be.'

Maguire could tell that Sarah's grin was forced. That she was hiding her apprehension. *Her stomach must be churning*, he thought. *But she can handle it.*

Sarah quickly proved him right. She pulled her long brown

hair free of the band that had secured it in a neat ponytail and scrunched her fingers through its thickness. It was something Sarah did before every take. A transformation from 'behind the scenes' to 'front of house'. A superstition that was almost as pointless as a rabbit's foot or a four-leaf clover.

Sarah placed herself in the centre of Maguire's shot.

'Let's do it.'

Maguire's smile widened. He had worked with TV reporters and actors for years. He was used to their narcissism and had lost count of the shots wasted while 'the talent's' make-up was re-touched. But the last two years had been different. Not because Sarah was nothing to look at. In her own way the tall, slim American was as attractive as anyone Maguire had ever partnered. Sarah was not a classic beauty, sure, but she was somehow better for that. And, unlike the others, she was utterly lacking in vanity. At least as far as Maguire had noticed.

With her ritual complete, Sarah seemed reinvigorated, her pre-shot jitters now hidden by her honest smile and sparkling green eyes. Maguire beamed with pride.

'What are you grinning at?'

'Nothing. Come on, get started.'

Maguire refocused his lens one last time before giving Sarah a thumbs-up. The signal for her to begin:

'We're here in London's Trafalgar Square, where the great and the good will soon arrive to commemorate the thousands of British men and women who have taken part in over a decade of conflicts in Afghanistan and Iraq. As the armed forces of Great Britain and her allies are preparing to rethink their priorities and their deployment, we are here today to say thank you to those who are already home. And to those who have made the ultimate sacrifice in defence of our way of life.

'With the War on Terror shifting its focus in the Middle East, the time has come to take stock of what has so far been achieved in the years of brutal conflict. And to pay our dues to those brave soldiers who have fought so hard and for so long. And now, as we wait for . . .'

Sarah's words trailed off, interrupted by the sound of cheers from the south-eastern end of Trafalgar Square. It could mean only one thing. The presidential motorcade had arrived.

FIVE

'Bamboo is breaching the Arch. Stagecoach at three, Maverick, Mercenary, Footprint and Falcon aboard. Snapshot and Snow at four in Half Back, with Wallflower and Warrior.'

Dempsey glanced at his watch. It had been twelve minutes since the transmission in McGregor's office. That message had set the timetable. So far it had been accurate, almost to the second. Dempsey shook his head in admiration.

The Americans are damned efficient.

But Dempsey could not allow the effectiveness of the Secret Service to make him comfortable or complacent. They had impressed him so far, but he had to stay vigilant. To do otherwise could cost lives. Bitter experience told him that.

Dempsey glanced towards his own nine agents. The DDS team. Handpicked men and women, every one of them outstanding in their previous lives. Soldiers. Police officers. Spies. They had been the best of the best. Exceptional enough to catch Callum McGregor's eye. Tough enough to make it through DDS selection. Dempsey did not trust easily, but every member of this team had earned it.

The nine agents were exactly where they should be. Lone figures at the end of each aisle, in the no man's land between crowd and stage. Each wore a crisp black two-piece suit, a pristine white shirt and a slim black tie. Regulation black sunglasses completed the image. Individually they could pass for extras from a Hollywood movie. Only the conspicuous bulge between the left breast and the armpit of their jackets said otherwise. These guys were the real thing.

Not that Dempsey doubted that. He had complete confidence that each would do his or her duty. That they would act just as they had been drilled over the past forty-eight hours. There were ten aisles in the square today, the only routes through the sea of chairs that temporarily filled a vast space usually open to the public. Of those aisles, nine were covered by Dempsey's agents. The tenth – the only one not currently manned – was different. This was where the VIPs would enter. Their route to the stage. If anything was going to happen it would most likely happen *here*. Which was why it was Dempsey's aisle.

It demanded more from Dempsey than he expected from his agents. *Their* brief was simple. To stand in place. Motionless but aware. Their eyes everywhere. Dempsey's was more complex. Eventually he would do the same as his team, but first he had to get the VIPs from the gate to the stage.

It sounded easy enough. These things always do.

Dempsey's earpiece buzzed again, the continuing commentary of the presidential motorcade's movements. It was the American way: 'Intelligence Is Everything'. If you know every detail, every movement, then nothing can go wrong. Dempsey thought otherwise. It was never that simple.

Dempsey moved to the security entrance at the north-west end of the square and took his place. From here his view was limited. The fence that surrounded the square saw to that. That fence was a necessary security measure. But in politics even the necessary is sometimes hidden. Two thousand guests were lucky enough to be inside the square. Millions more were not. It was the job of the barricade to keep them out. But every one of that unwanted number was a registered voter, which made the sham necessary. Hundreds of metres of blue velvet drapes had been stretched along the hoardings. Combined with the heavy-duty carpet underfoot, the stage at the north end and the thousands of chairs that faced it, they made Trafalgar Square look like the biggest conference room Dempsey had ever seen. All of it intended to fool the public. To hide the fact that only the great and the good were allowed inside.

The deception worked. That was clear from the noise. Dempsey could see one thing through the magnetic security arch that marked the access point from out to in: the arrival of the presidential motorcade. Ironically it was the one thing he did not *need* to see. The cheers of the crowd were deafening. The enthusiasm real. Dempsey knew of only two politicians who received that kind of adulation. Visible or not, the sound alone told him that both had just arrived.

Dempsey fixed his sight on the framed scene visible through the arch. The view was limited but sufficient. It seemed impossible that the crowd's cheers could grow any louder. But somehow they did, just as Dempsey saw the motorcade – codenamed 'Bamboo' by the Secret Service – crawl to a final halt.

'Bamboo' had made the short journey from Buckingham Palace at a jogging pace. Eight agents from the Presidential Protective Division had run alongside each car. Not one of them had broken sweat. An example of superb physical conditioning. This alone should have left Dempsey feeing safer. Should have, but did not.

The voice in his ear told Dempsey that the president's car – codenamed 'Stagecoach' – was the third vehicle in the motorcade. Dempsey knew that already. He had watched it stop closest to the entrance, where it sat for barely an instant before its passengers began to emerge.

The obvious weight of the rear doors only hinted at the extent of the 2009 Cadillac presidential limousine's modifications. This was the first time Dempsey had seen the legendary vehicle so close. Nothing about it seemed too unusual. If Dempsey had not known better he could not have guessed how well it lived up to its nickname: 'The Beast'. Weighing more than the average dumper truck, the vehicle sported five-inch-thick military-grade armour that could repel a direct hit from a hand-held rocket launcher. Run-flat tyres that allowed the driver to hit top speed regardless of the condition of the wheels. Assault-proof glass so thick that barely any natural light could penetrate the car's interior. It was almost a nuclear bunker on wheels. A place where the president was completely safe. If only the same could be said of Trafalgar Square.

The Secret Service team swamped 'Stagecoach' before its wheels stopped turning. Once again Dempsey's view was blocked. But once again sight was unnecessary. The roar of the crowd was enough to tell him that US President John Knowles and his First Lady Veronica – codenamed 'Maverick' and 'Mercenary' – were now in public view. Dempsey knew that Britain's Prime Minister William Davies and his wife, Elizabeth, would be with them. 'Footprint' and 'Falcon'. Their Secret Service handles.

All four were now in the hands of the Presidential Protective Division's best. They would remain so until they passed the threshold of the square. Only then would they become Dempsey's responsibility.

That time did not come right away. Minutes passed as Knowles milked his applause. As Davies – a much less popular leader – basked in the reflected glory, Dempsey could only wait and watch as the Secret Service did its job.

To see the Americans in action was a lesson in how it *should* be done. Unlike the oversized gorillas employed in celebrity protection, whose eyes never seem to leave the star paying their wage, President Knowles' agents were the opposite. Nondescript and efficient. *Their* eyes were where they should be. Constantly scanning the crowd, never resting on Knowles. The agents' job was to spot threats to the president. Barring suicide, those threats were unlikely to come from the man himself.

Minutes more went by with no sign that the cheering would end. It bothered Dempsey. It bothered him a lot. As long as the VIPs were outside they were not under his protection. Which meant that – for now – there was nothing Dempsey could do for them. For a man whose life had been built around self-reliance and complete control, that feeling of impotence was ordinarily unbearable. And there was nothing ordinary about today. The ragged six-inch scar that ran the length of Dempsey's left cheek throbbed. A sign that his blood pressure was spiking.

Dempsey's moment came without warning. While the crowd continued to cheer, President Knowles turned on his heel and strode into the square. Dempsey took a step back. Standing bolt upright, he ripped off a crisp salute. Knowles – a former US Marine and now his country's commander-in-chief – returned the gesture. William Davies – Britain's unpopular prime minister – did not.

Dempsey turned and began to walk towards the stage. He had frozen at coming face to face with Knowles. The US president was a man he deeply admired, but still Dempsey had not anticipated the effect meeting him might have. Even so, the distraction lasted no longer than a heartbeat. Dempsey tore his eyes away from the most famous face on the planet. He had a job to do, at the head of the entourage.

The distance to the stage was no more than a hundred yards. It took a full three minutes to cover it. The crowd was on its feet. Pushing. Reaching. Cheering. Two thousand of them in total. It was all Dempsey could do to keep them at bay as the entourage inched its way forward. The Secret Service escort that surrounded Knowles helped. But Knowles himself did not. The president seemed to shake every hand he passed. It made every step an effort and every yard an achievement. The ordeal only ended when they reached the staircase that led up to the raised platform. Only then could Dempsey step aside.

Dempsey watched as the VIPs climbed the eight short steps and took to the stage. Every one of them was getting off on the adulation of the crowd, with no consideration of the dangers that could be out there. Not even from ex-president Howard Thompson who, Dempsey knew, *must* be aware of the specific threats that had been made against his life.

But then politicians never seemed to worry about such things. Their safety was someone else's responsibility. Dempsey's responsibility.

Dempsey took his place at the head of his aisle. His first task was a success. He should feel better. Should feel more confident. But for some reason the anxiety continued to rise. Something was not right. Something Dempsey could not quite place.

SIX

Joshua's wristwatch sat in front of him, in his immediate eyeline and beside his rifle's barrel. It was wedged face up, readable at a glance. Convenient but unnecessary. Joshua had been counting off seconds in his head since the first Secret Service transmission. Another symptom of his obsessive nature. One thousand, seven hundred and forty had passed.

His expensively engineered Rolex Submariner agreed. Twenty-nine minutes.

It had been time well spent. Joshua had moved through his ingrained pre-shot rituals without a conscious thought. The circumstances of the assignment might be strange, but the fundamentals were always the same. Load the mag. Chamber the round. Settle the line of sight. Identify the obstacles. Seven times over to satisfy his compulsion. Each time done with absolute precision.

Joshua knew his target's name. He knew his face. And he knew where Eamon McGale would be found. McGale had been in Joshua's crosshairs since taking his seat. If everything went to plan, he would not be leaving them alive.

It was an easy statement to make, and sometimes a harder one to fulfil. But not for Joshua. Joshua had been steeped in violence for as long as he could remember. There were, no doubt, many other men who could do what he did. But it took a rare man to do it so well. One who combined physical ability, cold obsession, professional training and an absolute lack of remorse in one lethal package. Joshua possessed all of these qualities in abundance, making him more than a match for the ageing, slightly ragged man who sat in his sights.

McGale had looked out of place from the start. Not physically. He wore aged clothing and looked in need of a good meal, yes, but there was nothing particularly unusual about his appearance. No. What Joshua noticed were his emotions. Or, more precisely, his lack of them.

Even from a hundred yards outside and two hundred feet above the square, Joshua could feel the effect of President Knowles' arrival. The wave of goodwill was like nothing he had ever seen. Yet McGale had stayed rooted to his seat. An oasis of calm within a storm of hysteria.

Nor had McGale reacted to what had followed. William Davies had spoken from behind a two-inch-thick sheet of glass. A combination of teleprompter and bulletproof screen. Davies was a short, plain and unpopular man. Unused to enthusiastic applause. But today, with two thousand handpicked spectators caught up in the euphoria of the moment, even he received it.

Davies had started the event with a short thank you to Britain's armed forces. The crowd had roared its agreement. All except for McGale. McGale had again remained static. Only the beads of sweat that trickled down his neck and brow were proof of life beneath the tweed.

But this changed when President Knowles took the centre of the stage. That was when McGale reacted. When he began to fidget. To repeatedly touch the underside of his chair. To the untrained eye it might look like an itch. To Joshua it was a starter's pistol. He knew the effects of nerves when he saw them. And he knew what would follow.

SEVEN

Sarah Truman had noted her president's every word. She had been living in London for two years. In that time she had seen much more of Britain's prime minister than of her own country's leader. It was inevitable that she would compare the two, and it was hardly a fair contest. Unlike William Davies, the leader of the free world was a very impressive man.

John Knowles certainly impressed Sarah. He seemed to have it all, she thought. Tall, athletic and handsome. A Hollywood president. Because of this he was sometimes underestimated, which was a mistake that was never made twice. Knowles' intellect exceeded even his looks, making him more than a match for any political challenger.

Sarah glanced across to Maguire. She was confident that her cameraman had the shot. That trust was well placed. Maguire had a clear view of the stage with no obstructions. Other camera crews had been less fortunate. Or maybe they just were not as good. Either way, the best footage would today come from Jack Maguire's lens.

Sarah had no doubt that it would. She counted herself lucky to be partnered with such a respected talent so early in her career. She was genuinely grateful for Maguire's guidance. But they were friends and so it could remain unspoken. Instead Sarah concentrated on the stage. On the close of Knowles' speech. As always, both his words and his delivery were faultless:

'... no greater friend and closer ally than Great Britain. It is a relationship that has stood the test of history and of adversity, and I could not be happier to pay tribute to the men and women who have stood beside my own nation in these troubled times. Ladies and gentlemen, we are here today to thank those among us – and those who have tragically left us – for a sustained heroism unmatched since the time of the Greatest Generation. I give you a group that can be summed up in a single word. I give you "heroes".'

The crowd erupted at that final word. Knowles had judged his audience perfectly. He always did. The people reacted just as he had intended. The sound of their cheers was deafening. Disorientating, even. Sarah could feel her head begin to spin as she scribbled into her notepad.

The noise continued for what seemed like minutes. It was all Sarah could do to keep her attention on her notes. Only when the intensity began to lessen did she regain some concentration. It was a temporary relief.

In just moments a fresh injection of energy shot through the audience. Just as suddenly as the first. Sarah glanced up from the page. Towards the stage. Looking for the cause.

President Knowles had taken his seat. His retreat had left the podium free, but the space was not vacant for long. Sarah watched as former US President Howard Thompson joined Sir Neil Matthewson – the Secretary of State for Northern Ireland and Britain's most popular politician – as together they approached the centre of the stage.

The reception the two men received was as enthusiastic as it had been for Knowles. It had been almost four years since Thompson's time in the White House. Somehow he remained as popular as ever. Matthewson was just as well loved. So it was no surprise that they were greeted so warmly. Or that the dead-eyed reaction of a single man in the crowd would go unnoticed until it was too late.

EIGHT

The deafening cheers said different things to different people. To Thompson and to Matthewson they were the deserved thanks for years of public service. To William Davies they were proof that the event was a PR success. Cosmetic surgery to cover the cracks under his government. And to Dempsey they were confirmation of his worst fears. He could not police a crowd of this size.

Dempsey's eyes moved behind his sunglasses. Constantly scanning from left to right. Looking for a hint of something. Of anything. But what? A gun? A knife? A bomb? How could he spot a thing in this sea of bodies? His unease was crippling, yet he could not explain it. Dempsey had faced far worse odds. Had lost count of the times it had been *his* life in danger. But today was somehow different.

The interruption of McGregor's voice in his earpiece was welcome.

'We're behind schedule. The first soldier should have been onstage to collect his award by now. These bastards are milking the applause.'

'Then you need to get a message to them. Get them to sit their arses down!'

Dempsey snapped his words into his wrist-mike. His strong London accent broke through. Betrayed his annoyance.

'Is that an order, Major?' McGregor sounded amused.

'It is if *you* say it! We need this crowd seated, Callum.'

'Agreed.'

No more words. Dempsey lowered his hand back to his side, moving his wrist-mike from his lips. His eyes continued to dart across the crowd.

Dempsey knew that McGregor would do his best. That if any man could force the politicians to get on with the job it was the DDS director. But that knowledge did nothing to salve his anxiety. Not this time. Dempsey had survived as long as he had by trusting his instincts. As he caught a glimpse of an unusual movement and a hint of metal from within the distant crowd, those instincts told him one thing. Whatever McGregor could or could not do, it was already too late.

NINE

Joshua was ready. Primed. McGale's body language had pre-warned him. The sudden tightening of his jaw. The stiffening of his ageing muscles beneath his nondescript clothing. The calming, strengthening intake of breath. All signs of a man about to act.

Joshua's eyeball was inches from the scope. He could see every detail. Every movement. Yet even he was surprised by McGale's speed. Joshua had watched carefully as McGale reached his hands to the underside of his seat. They had remained there for a second. Maybe two. As if they had met resistance. Then, just as suddenly, they were free. The right hand now carried a pistol. Its make and model was disguised by the duct tape that had attached it to the bottom of the chair.

McGale had burst into action, moving as fast as a man who was half his age and twice as active. Joshua struggled to pick him out from the still-roaring crowd as he ran, but it did not concern him: McGale had only one place to go and only one way to get there. Instead of following his target's jinking run, Joshua placed his scope at the stage end of the aisle. Which McGale would reach within moments.

Sarah opened her third notebook of the day. In it she scribbled down every word and emotion that came to mind. Not for the first time, she wrote the slogan 'Beatlemania'. She knew why. This crowd was like nothing Sarah had ever experienced. It was a sustained hysteria and it brought to mind footage of The Beatles' screaming fans in the sixties.

It was not a reaction she understood. Sarah knew that both Thompson and Matthewson were well respected by the British public. Together they had led the Northern Irish negotiations that – until recent terrorist atrocities – had seemed to put the faltering peace process in the province back on track. But this alone could not explain the crowd's worship. As an American living in London, Sarah found the whole display a little 'un-British'.

Sarah's eyes fixed on the page, her focus absolute. She saw nothing else as she concentrated on turning her thoughts into words. The deafening noise around her did not make this easy. Sarah closed her eyes and tried to block out the distraction. And so she failed to see the middle-aged man who sprinted past her, in the direction of the stage. Maguire, though, had been paying better attention.

Maguire hesitated for less than a heartbeat before giving chase. Though slowed by the effort of keeping his lens trained upon McGale, it was a short enough distance not to matter. Whatever was to follow would be caught on film. And Sarah, whose concentration had been broken when Maguire moved, was just a few steps behind.

Joshua used his naked eye to watch McGale run. His crosshairs were perfectly positioned. Everything was in place. He wondered for a moment if McGale might actually reach the stage before being spotted.

He had his answer within an instant. Joshua felt a pang of disappointment as McGale reached the end of the aisle and ran clear into the pistol sight of a waiting agent. The agent was ready, her gun aimed at McGale's heart. Just a movement of her finger and he would go no further.

It was what Joshua had been waiting for. What he had been told to expect. He did not hesitate. Joshua pulled the trigger only once and watched without satisfaction as his bullet ripped through the front of the agent's head. The impact slammed her to the floor, removing the only obstacle in McGale's path. Not that McGale seemed to notice. He appeared unaware of how close he had come to death.

In just three more strides McGale had reached the stage. Too fast for anyone else to react.

Six shots. The full load of the weapon McGale had pulled from beneath his seat. Fired into Matthewson and Thompson from near point-blank range. That number meant everything to Joshua; his instructions had been clear. Phase One was to ensure that McGale reached the stage and fired the full number of rounds. Joshua was to assist in that by removing any obstruction from McGale's path. Only then would McGale himself become the target. Phase Two.

Joshua placed his crosshairs back between McGale's eyes and prepared to apply the kiss of pressure that would release the chambered round. It was fast by anyone's standards. But not fast enough.

Both Sarah and Maguire had pursued McGale without a thought. Neither seemed to consider their own safety until Joshua's shot rang out. It was a wake-up call that stopped both in their tracks. They watched in horror as the young agent's head ruptured.

Maguire was a twenty-five-year veteran video journalist.

He had seen more violent death than he cared to remember. He could only wonder at the damage this had done to his psyche, but today he was just grateful it had removed his gag reflex. Sarah had frozen at the sight of the fallen agent, while Maguire had paused for only a moment. Then he was moving again. Sweeping his lens from the floor to the tragedy unfolding onstage. Perfectly placed, Maguire's camera captured every bullet that ripped into Matthewson and Thompson.

Maguire's attention – like his lens – was directed to the raised platform. It made him miss the sight that followed: a DDS agent passing him at speed and slamming the gunman to the ground.

Sarah had seen Dempsey coming. Her eyes had been fixed on the dead agent as she fought off shock. Maguire may have seen this kind of violence before, she knew. But Sarah had not. Sarah had been raised in a wealthy Boston family. Death – even natural death – had played no part in her life. And so Sarah had no idea how to deal with what she had just seen. Luckily for her, Dempsey now provided a dramatic distraction.

The agent moved like an Olympic sprinter. So fast that Sarah had to throw herself aside as he hurdled the body of the fallen agent. Sarah's eyes stayed fixed upon Dempsey as he passed and she marvelled as he tackled, disarmed and restrained the shooter in one smooth movement.

Seconds passed before Joshua reminded himself to breathe.

McGale remained in his crosshairs, but he might as well have been behind bulletproof glass. Joshua could not fire now that his target was restrained. Not without ruining his own cover.

McGale had been tackled with extraordinary speed. It had not been expected. The surprise had made Joshua hesitate. Just an instant. But even milliseconds can change a life.

Joshua had failed for the first time in his career. As the smoke cleared and the teams of paramedics fought to save the life of the men bleeding onstage, Joshua could only wonder what the consequences of that failure would be.

TEN

Daniel Lawrence's heart raced as Michael Devlin cross-examined Richard Dove, the final and most damaging witness in the case against their client.

Nathan Campbell – the man Daniel and Michael were there to defend – stood accused of a financial fraud that had wiped billions off the stock market value of The Costins Group, an investment bank that had employed him as a derivatives broker.

Richard Dove had been his immediate superior. The man who – according to the prosecution case – Campbell had directly deceived in the course of his crimes.

This was Dove's opportunity for payback. To tell the world of Campbell's guilt. And it was his chance to publicly repair any damage caused by his own proximity to Campbell's acts.

So far he had made the most of both.

Daniel's notes recorded every question that Michael had asked in the past thirty minutes. He knew that his friend was doing everything he could. The charismatic barrister always did.

Their only chance of success – the only chance Nathan Campbell had of leaving the court a free man – was for Michael to undermine Dove's evidence. To find and expose any lies the man was telling. Any prejudices he had.

But Daniel was not naive. He had been around long enough to know how the public react to bankers who take risks with other people's money. He and Michael understood the common belief that it was men like this – men like Nathan Campbell

– who cause the recessions that only seem to hit everyday men and women. And so Daniel knew that for Nathan Campbell to be acquitted, his barrister would first have to overcome that natural prejudice.

It was no surprise that the jury already hated the man now sitting in the dock. They had heard the prosecuting barrister's opening speech. It told a damaging tale. A tale of an arrogant man who had played with hundreds of millions of pounds as if it were Monopoly money. Who had used the bank's funds – the savings and investments of the bank's customers – to take increasingly large gambles on the performance of foreign markets. And who had dishonestly used his bank's 'error accounts', designed to protect its customers from unexpected loss, to cover his own massive failings.

The speech had ended with several jurors staring at Campbell with something close to hate in their eyes. Daniel had expected no less. It was only natural that some would take this kind of crime personally. Savers and investors the world over had been hit by what they saw as the risk-taking of men like Campbell. In all likelihood, at least some of his jurors would have suffered.

But worse had followed. As damaging as the opening speech had been, every trial rests upon the evidence that can be called, and upon the testimony of the witnesses. So far those witnesses had played their parts to perfection, each proving beyond any doubt – reasonable or otherwise – that Nathan Campbell had done exactly what the prosecution said.

It was a frustrating experience for Daniel. To watch witness after witness hammering nails into Campbell's defence. But it was also inevitable, because Campbell had already told Daniel – and Michael – that every fact being alleged was true.

London's Central Criminal Court – known worldwide as the Old Bailey – had been extended many times over the years. New courtrooms added, old ones renovated. Court Two, though, was one of the originals. A cavernous, wood-panelled temple.

Both judge and defendant were elevated, facing one another across the centre of the room. They sat above the jury and witness box on one side, and the full set of lawyers on the other. It was a set-up that gave Daniel a clear view of the jurors as they listened to the evidence.

And from where he sat, their belief in Campbell's guilt was unmistakable.

This was the prejudice Campbell faced as the final prosecution witness, Richard Dove, was called. Daniel knew that even Michael would struggle to overcome it.

He also knew that Michael would not try to do so.

Convention dictates that the barrister asks the questions in court. A solicitor's job is more understated. More legwork. Less glory. But this did not mean that Daniel had no hand in the preparation of Campbell's defence. He and Michael had discussed every tactical move and they agreed on at least two things: that any attempt to deny what Nathan Campbell had done would be disastrous. And that, in any event, Campbell was not *really* what this case was about.

Michael had begun his questions carefully. He spoke with camaraderie. An old lawyer's trick, Daniel knew. Befriend the witness. Be amicable. Be understanding. Wait for his guard to slip.

It was always more effective than starting with confrontation. And so it had proved. Michael had scored point after point. Gently encouraging Dove to admit that he had not been fond of Campbell. That Campbell's working-class Birmingham background had not – in Dove's opinion – justified his position within such a prestigious bank. And that he had, throughout Campbell's career, done much to undermine him with their superiors.

These were small successes. They weakened Dove's credibility. But in the face of the rest of the evidence – evidence that Campbell admitted to be true – they were nowhere near enough.

Daniel knew this. He knew that point-scoring did not lessen the impact of the prosecution case. If anything, it looked like clever lawyers playing clever games because they had nothing else. Michael had to go further, Daniel realised. He had to attack.

It was a dangerous tactic. An all-or-nothing gamble. It was also Nathan Campbell's one shot at freedom.

'OK, Mr Dove, let's put your personal dislike for Mr Campbell to one side for a moment, shall we? Because there's something else I want to ask you about.'

Michael's Irish brogue became more pronounced as he spoke. It was a nervous tic Daniel had noticed before. Always there when Michael's questions took a more dangerous turn.

'Fire away.'

Dove seemed confident. As if Michael's questions up to now had achieved nothing. Which suggested to Daniel that the man was not as bright as he seemed to think.

'I will, Mr Dove.' Michael smiled as he spoke, his tone sarcastic. 'But thank you for the permission.'

Dove looked confused. Perhaps wondering where Michael's matey approach had gone.

Michael continued.

'What I want to ask you is this. You've told us that your role was as Mr Campbell's immediate superior, correct?'

'Yes.'

'And of course we know you didn't think he was even remotely up to the job that he had been given?'

'I thought we were moving away from the fact that I disliked him?'

'Oh, we have. But it's your professional opinion we're discussing. I'm sure you see the difference, don't you?'

'Of course I see the difference.'

Daniel smiled. Michael was already getting to him. Exactly as they had known he must.

'And we're agreed that you thought he was pretty much incompetent, right?'

'Right.'

'Then would you mind telling me, Mr Dove, why it was that you allowed Mr Campbell – the *incompetent* Mr Campbell – to settle his own trades?'

'What? Why does that matter?'

'Do I really have to explain this to you, Mr Dove? Because Mr Campbell knows why it matters, and he's apparently incompetent. So surely *you* know?'

'Of course I know.'

'Well then, perhaps you can help the jury to know as well. Because it's right, is it not, that a trader such as Mr Campbell would usually have his trades settled by another member of the team?'

'Team?'

'You know what I mean, Mr Dove. By another trader on your floor. It's a failsafe, isn't it? It means that if a trader has involved himself in a bad transaction – in something where there has been a loss – then it can't be hidden. Because the other trader, the one who has to settle the trade, knows about it. That's it in a nutshell, isn't it? It's peer supervision.'

'That's right.'

'But for some reason Mr Campbell was allowed to sign off on his own trades, wasn't he?'

'You're making it sound like there's something sinister in that.'

'That's your opinion, Mr Dove. As far as I'm concerned, I'm just getting to the truth. So please tell us, is it right that Mr Campbell was permitted to sign off on his own trades?'

Dove hesitated.

'Mr Dove?'

No response.

'Mr Dove, please answer the question.'

The intervention came from His Honour Judge Peter Kennedy QC, one of the most senior judges in the Central Criminal Court.

It had the desired effect.

'Yes,' Dove finally answered. 'Campbell settled his own trades.'

Michael continued without missing a beat.

'And can you confirm that this was in fact highly unusual, Mr Dove?'

'What does *that* mean?'

'Exactly what it sounds like. It was highly unusual – for reasons that must be wholly obvious from what we have discussed so far – that Mr Campbell was permitted to settle his own trades. That's right, isn't it?'

'It wasn't "highly unusual", no.'

'It wasn't?'

'No.'

'OK. Then please tell me, Mr Dove. How many traders are employed under you at Costins?'

'How many?'

'Directly under you, yes. How many?'

'I . . . I can't really remember without—'

'Without looking at the company records. Well, I have them right here, Mr Dove. Shall we take a look?'

'I don't need to take a look.'

'I'm sorry, your voice dropped there. Could you repeat that?'

'I said I don't need to take a look!'

This time there was no chance the answer would be missed. It was almost shouted.

Daniel smiled. The plan was working. Dove was rattled.

Michael continued.

'So you remember how many it is now?'

'Yes.'

'And?'

'It's fifty-six. Give or take.'

'Actually, it's fifty-six exactly, isn't it, Mr Dove? At least according to your records?'

'Yes.'

'That's a fairly specific number for you to not remember without your records, and then to suddenly remember five seconds later, isn't it?'

'My lord, Mr Devlin is veering very much into the realm of comment with questions like that.' The prosecuting barrister had risen to her feet. 'Can he be reminded to keep points of this kind for his closing speech?'

'You've heard what's been said, Mr Devlin. Make sure your questions are just that, please.'

'My lord.'

Michael did not look away from Dove as he responded. Nor did he hesitate before moving to his next question.

'So, fifty-six traders. Now tell me, Mr Dove, how many of those fifty-six traders working under you are permitted to settle their own trades?'

No response.

'Mr Dove, I'm going to ask you that question again. Perhaps this time you will have the good grace to answer it. So, bearing in mind that I have your company records right here beside me, please tell me how many traders currently working under you are permitted to settle their own trades?'

'None.'

The answer was almost spat out.

'And how many when Mr Campbell was working under you? Again bearing in mind that we have the records right here?'

'Just him.'

Daniel's smile widened. He had to keep his head facing his notebook to hide it from the jury.

This is working, he thought. *Michael's got him.*

'So, back then, Mr Campbell was the *only* trader permitted to settle his own trades. And, right now, *no one* has that power. And yet you're asking this jury to believe that such freedom wasn't "highly unusual"? That's just a lie, isn't it, Mr Dove?'

'Why would I lie?' Dove exploded in anger. 'What have *I* got to lie about? Your client's the criminal. Your client's the one who was losing hundreds of millions of the bank's money and then hiding it. What have *I* got to lie about?'

'Perhaps we'll find out.' Michael's reply was completely calm. 'But, before we do, who would have been empowered to allow Mr Campbell to settle his own trades? Who could make that happen?'

No response. Dove was now glaring at Michael.

'Are you not going to answer, Mr Dove?'

No response.

'Is it because the answer is *you*?'

No response.

'Because that's right, isn't it? The fact is that you – as Mr Campbell's immediate superior, as the man responsible for him and for everyone else on your floor – you would have had to authorise a working practice that allowed Mr Campbell, as a trader, to sign off on his own trades. To effectively become his *own* supervisor. That's correct, isn't it?'

No response.

'Mr Dove, you will answer the question.' Judge Kennedy again.

Dove looked up at the judge, to whom he directed his answer.

'Yes, your honour. I would have to authorise that.'

'And you did, didn't you?' Michael was relentless.

Dove looked back towards the barrister before answering.

'Yes. Yes I did.'

'Can you please explain why? Why such unusual treatment was given to this particular person.'

'Because he was successful,' Dove replied. 'He was making more money than half of the rest of the floor combined. So when he asked for that freedom I thought it would speed him up. That it would make even *more* money for my section.'

'But, Mr Dove, you've already told us at length that Mr Campbell wasn't up to the job. You didn't think he even deserved his place on your floor. But now suddenly he's your best trader?'

'I didn't say he was my best.' Dove seemed to be floundering. 'I said he was the most successful. There are many reasons that could be.'

'Yes, there are. But the only one of them that doesn't justify even greater supervision than usual is that he *was* the best, isn't it? Because if he *isn't* the best but he's still getting results above and beyond everyone else, then there's probably something dodgy going on, isn't there?'

'Well we know something dodgy was going on, don't we?'

The anger was back. Dove seemed to have chosen his battle. A battle Daniel could not wait to see.

Dove continued.

'That's why we're here. Because he *was* up to no good.'

Michael smiled. When he spoke his voice was gentle.

'Mr Dove, if an incompetent trader was doing so well you would have assumed that he was either lying about his success, or that he was achieving it through dishonest means, wouldn't you?'

No response.

'And in either case you would have *increased* your supervision over Mr Campbell, wouldn't you?'

No response.

'And yet what you actually did was exempt him from even the standard supervision that applied to all other traders. You gave him free rein to do exactly as he pleased. Why is that, Mr Dove? Why did you do that?'

Once again there was no response. This time Michael allowed the silence to settle.

Daniel looked at the jury. They seemed confused. Baffled by where Michael had taken Dove's evidence. Questions seemed to be forming in their previously certain minds. It made Daniel smile again. But not over what had happened so far.

No. Daniel was smiling because of what he knew was coming next.

'Is there a reason you've stopped answering my questions?'

Michael's voice was still gentle, and all the more disconcerting because of it. He continued.

'Are you refusing to answer because you've been lying?'

It was a red flag to a bull.

'I've already told you, I've got bugger all to lie about. What have I lied about, eh? Go on. Tell me.'

'The same thing you've been lying about for a long, long time.' Michael's voice was beginning to rise. 'Because you didn't sign off on Mr Campbell settling his own trades, did you?'

'What?' Dove seemed taken aback.

'You didn't sign off on that because it never happened. Mr Campbell *never did* settle his own trades, did he? He never was free of the supervision that applied to everyone else. Because he had someone else settling his trades throughout the entire period that he was supposedly hiding his actions from the bank. And that someone was you, wasn't it?'

Daniel watched as the jury registered the question. They were hooked.

'What sort of absolute bullshit are you trying to peddle?'

Dove's response was angry. It was also immediate. Far too fast if Michael's suggestion was something he had not heard before. Far too fast if what was being put to him was untrue.

'Answer the question, Mr Dove. Did you act as Mr Campbell's supervisor on the transactions that have brought him to court today? Did you take on the role of settling his trades?'

'Of course I bloody didn't.'

Dove's anger seemed to be gone. It was as if they were now

on ground he had prepared for. It was the wrong impression to give, but he carried on.

'Look at the records you've got there. Every single one of the trades are recorded as having been signed off by Nathan himself.'

'Oh, I know that,' Michael replied. 'But that's fairly meaningless, isn't it, Mr Dove. Because as his immediate superior you could have appointed yourself to the role, and you could have easily signed off *as* Mr Campbell without him being any the wiser. Because the only person who would be looking at the trades across your floor – from everyone, not just Mr Campbell – was *you*, wasn't it?'

'Oh, I get it.'

Dove's voice was now arrogant. Daniel could tell that he had been prepared for these last few questions. But he doubted that Dove would be prepared for the next ones.

Dove continued.

'You've sat down and worked out the only way that Nathan could have been overseen without that being recorded. Very clever. But it doesn't really help you though, does it? Because Nathan *did* carry out the trades. He *did* use the error account to hide his losses. And he *did* lose hundreds of millions of bloody pounds. So even if I were settling his trades – and I wasn't – it doesn't make him innocent, does it?'

'It does if he was making the trades under the orders of his boss,' Michael replied.

'That's another comment.' The prosecutor was rising to her feet again.

'I'm moving on,' Michael responded, before the judge could intervene.

He turned back to Dove.

'Mr Dove, it is correct, isn't it, that Nathan Campbell made each and every trade for which he is being tried under your direct supervision and guidance, and that every trade made was made upon your order?'

'You've got to be joking.'

'And isn't it true that throughout that period, at least as far as Nathan Campbell was aware, *you* were settling his trades in accordance with good practice?'

'This is pathetic. It really is pathetic.'

'And isn't it true that, having told Nathan Campbell that you were settling his trades, you manipulated the records to which you had access and presented the settlements as if it were Nathan Campbell settling his own trades?'

'Desperate,' Dove replied. 'Absolutely desperate.'

'So are you denying what I've asked?'

'Of course I'm bloody denying it! Behind the trades? Ordering Campbell to make them? What do you take me for? I'm *good* at my job. No one with an ounce of expertise or experience would have made those trades. Guaranteed losers, every one of them. So this little conspiracy you've put together, why would I do it? Why would I have involved myself in something that was bound to fail?'

It was a good question. And exactly the one Daniel had hoped Dove would ask.

As ever, Michael did not miss a beat.

'You've been with Costins for what, eighteen years?'

'Why are you changing the subject? Come on, tell me what I had to gain from that picture you've painted.'

'Answer the question, Mr Dove.'

'Not until you answer mine.'

'That is not how this works.' The judge sounded impatient.

'Mr Devlin asks the questions, Mr Dove. And you answer them. So please do that.'

Dove looked at His Honour Judge Kennedy QC, his irritation obvious. Still, he did as ordered.

'Yes, eighteen years.'

'For which you have been paid a very, very respectable salary.'

'No more than I'm worth.'

'Heaven forbid.' Michael's response raised a laugh from the jury. 'But still, your salary is, by most standards, a very high one.'

'I suppose that it is.'

'Thank you. It is also correct, is it not, that you are paid an annual bonus.'

'Yes.'

'A bonus that is never less than six figures?'

'So what?'

'Never less than six figures?'

'No. Never.'

'And one which, in addition, always includes shares in Costins itself.'

'That's correct.'

'Every year for eighteen years.'

'Yes.'

'Tell me, how many shares in Costins did you own on the day that Mr Campbell's disastrous trades came to light?'

'I'm sorry?'

'The shares, Mr Dove. The ones that had been building up every year for eighteen years. You must have had quite a few in your possession by that time. How many?'

Michael pointedly tapped a file next to him as he spoke. A clear message that he had the answer right there beside him.

From what Daniel could see, Dove got the message.

'None.'

'I'm sorry, Mr Dove. Your voice has gone all quiet again. Did you say none?'

'Yes. None.'

'Well that's a surprise. Because Costins was doing very well, wasn't it? Or at least it seemed to be. It must have been very irritating to know that but to have none of your shares left.'

No response.

'And, out of interest, Mr Dove. When did you sell your shares?'

Michael tapped the file again. The same message.

'The previous month.'

'The previous month?'

Michael sounded amazed. The part of the act that always amused Daniel most.

'Yes.'

'What, all of them? At once? Or had you been selling them off over the years, a bit here and a bit there? Which was it?'

'All of them at once.'

Daniel shook his head. It was a pleasure to see Dove so uncomfortable – so helpless – as he reached the questions he had not expected.

'So by some stroke of luck, you sold all of your shares when the market was at its highest, just a month before Nathan Campbell's trades almost destroyed the bank?'

Dove did not respond immediately. And nor did the prosecuting barrister rise to her feet, despite the fact that Michael's last question broke all the rules.

It seemed that everyone was stunned by the turn the case had taken. Everyone but Daniel and Michael.

It was an outcome more common than it should be. Something Daniel knew all too well. When the police are presented with a clear-cut case – all the evidence wrapped up in a nice neat package and pointing at an obvious offender – often they don't think it's necessary to look any further. Human nature is human nature, after all, and so the prosecution tend to pursue the obvious suspect, even when just a little digging – a little legwork – would point to the real culprit. And so that legwork was left to Daniel.

It had not taken long for him to uncover the truth behind Campbell's account. And now Michael would reap the benefits.

Michael opened the file that had threatened Dove and removed a single sheet of paper.

'Mr Dove, have you ever heard of a company called Red Corner Inc., registered to the Cayman Islands?'

Dove did not respond. But this time he did not need to. The speed with which the colour drained from his cheeks said enough.

Michael continued.

'Red Corner Inc. is the company which purchased over ten million shares in Costins on the day after Mr Campbell's losses were revealed. Were you aware of that, Mr Dove?'

No response.

'And they did so for just a quarter of what *you* were paid by another buyer for your five hundred thousand shares, less than a month before. Were you aware of that, Mr Dove?'

No response.

'And, of course, since the apprehension and prosecution of Mr Campbell, and the revelation that the bank will survive this little "blip", the Costins share price has risen again, with those ten million shares now being worth ten times what Red Corner paid for them. Were you aware of *that*, Mr Dove?'

No response.

Michael fluttered the sheet of paper in the air as he continued.

'OK, let's try some questions that you *must* know the answer to, shall we? Can you tell me, Mr Dove, the name of the man who set up Red Corner Inc. in the Cayman Islands? The name of the man who is its only shareholder and only director? The name of the man who thought he could hide behind the Cayman Island rules on anonymity and never be revealed as the controller of Red Corner? The name of the man who intentionally tanked Costins? Who offloaded his own shares at full price just before the losses came to light? Who then used his offshore company to mop up millions of Costins shares when they hit rock bottom? And who thought he could get away with all of this by setting up a man he regarded as being below the class that should be employed at Costins in the first place?'

No response. But Dove's head was now in his hands.

'I'll give you a hint, Mr Dove. It's the same answer to all of them.'

Still nothing.

Michael turned to the prosecuting barrister. Even she looked desperate. Worn down by the combination of blows Dove had just received. She indicated to the sheet of paper in Michael's hand. He passed it across.

A certificate of incorporation in Grand Cayman. The company was Red Corner Inc. The director and sole shareholder? Richard Dove.

Daniel smiled a final time as he watched Michael lean close to the prosecutor's ear and say, 'I think that's your case done, isn't it?'

ELEVEN

Daniel watched Michael exit one of the six elevators that opened onto the Old Bailey's ground floor. Nathan Campbell had left the building twenty minutes earlier. Daniel had been waiting for the tall Irishman since then.

Michael's destruction of Richard Dove had forced the prosecution to abandon its case. With Dove behind all of Campbell's actions and with his motives exposed, it had become hopeless. What then followed had been inevitable. A fixed process. The judge had directed the jury to find Nathan Campbell 'Not Guilty'.

Daniel was sure they would have done the same even without the direction. Still, that extra guarantee was always welcome. The Devlin/Lawrence partnership had won. It was becoming a habit.

Michael glanced towards the top of the building's main staircase as he stepped out of the lift. The spot where Daniel always liked to wait.

He had stayed upstairs while Daniel saw Campbell off the premises. Only once the client was gone did the barrister reappear.

It was a practised routine. Michael had always lacked the patience for the 'social work' side of their job. Struggled with the handholding. Not that it mattered; working with Daniel meant there was always a compassionate colleague to pick up the slack.

'It takes you an hour to look respectable these days, does it?'

Daniel glanced at his watch. Tried to fake annoyance. He was no actor.

Daniel might have been joking, but he could not have chosen a better description. Everything about Michael screamed 'respectable'. His impeccable black pinstriped suit and starched white shirt complimented his six-foot-one athletic physique. He was every inch the TV idea of a barrister, which could not be more ironic. Not just because so few barristers actually resembled the clean-cut actors who played them, but because so few came from a background as unprivileged as the boy from the wrong side of Belfast.

'If I didn't know better I'd think you didn't want to speak to Nathan,' Daniel continued. 'He says "thanks", by the way.'

'So he should!' Michael laughed. 'C'mon, let's get going.'

The Old Bailey's ground floor was not at street level; an oddity caused by the building's expansion over the course of a century. So there was a final flight of stairs for Michael and Daniel to walk down before they could exit the building.

At the top of this staircase – embedded in the wall, far above head-height – was a lone piece of shrapnel. A morbid reminder of an IRA bomb that had exploded in the street outside in 1973. Daniel watched as it drew Michael's eye. It always did. Michael had been raised in the more sectarian part of Ulster, where acts of terrorism could be tragically commonplace. He had long ago walked away from that past, but Daniel knew that he had never forgotten it. Now, every time Michael set foot on the staircase his eyes darted to the shrapnel. And every time it made him think of how far he had come. Of what he had left behind. A reminder that always seemed to stir mixed emotions.

No words were spoken as they left the building. They

passed the ever-present paparazzi. Turned left and walked the short distance to Ludgate Hill.

It was one of London's most iconic locations. Left out of Old Bailey – the road that gave its name to the court – was St Paul's Cathedral. Old London's dominating landmark. To the right were Ludgate Circus and Fleet Street. The historic home to Britain's printed press. The journalists had moved on decades ago. The lawyers, who had been there even longer, remained.

Daniel wore his shirt unbuttoned at the collar. Michael – who wore a tunic shirt in court, in line with tradition – had no collar at all. Both carried their jackets slung over the shoulder. It was a relief to be free from the formal dress of Britain's courts. Especially for Michael, Daniel thought. The eighteenth-century outfit still worn by criminal barristers did its job. It made the advocates stand out. Gave them a status that put witnesses at a disadvantage. But that did not make it any more comfortable, particularly in courtrooms built before the invention of air conditioning. It was no doubt a welcome respite that Michael could now enjoy the rare October sunshine in fewer layers.

They made their way west, down Ludgate Hill. Neither spoke. The comfortable silence that can only exist between the closest of friends. Minutes passed as they pushed their way through the crowds. These pavements were always busy. Bustling. Like everyone familiar with the city centre, both Michael and Daniel were accustomed to being jostled as they walked.

'That was a hell of a closing question.'

Daniel's face broke into a grin as he finally spoke. They were already halfway along Fleet Street.

'What's that old rule about only asking one question at a time, Mike? God knows how Kennedy let you get away with it.'

'Don't see why you're surprised.' Michael's smile was just as wide. 'I've asked worse questions than that without getting into trouble.'

'Bullshit! If you had I'd have heard about it. Especially with your big mouth! You'll be calling everyone you know to brag about this one tonight!'

'You're the only one who still lets me boast, Danny. The others just hang up!'

'Then you're calling the wrong people. I'm sure my dad will want to hear all about it.'

Daniel did not mean to silence Michael. But he'd managed it anyway.

Daniel's father was Hugh Lawrence QC, one of England's most eminent barristers. Hugh had been disappointed to see his son become a solicitor instead of following in his father's footsteps. And Michael had been his consolation for that decision. Hugh Lawrence had taken the interest he would have had in Daniel's career and invested it into that of his son's friend. Daniel had long accepted this. But it was not something they ever discussed.

Whatever his pedigree, Daniel had always felt unsuited to a career at the Bar. It was a doubt that had remained unspoken. Until it was confirmed by a young man with every attribute he lacked. Michael Devlin.

They had met as students. Luck had placed them in the same university group, but their backgrounds had been poles apart. Daniel had always been wealthy. A privileged rich kid with the best education money could buy. Michael had come from a very different world. He had fought tooth and nail to break free from his upbringing. To build a better life away from a family he never discussed.

They had been equals from the start. The outstanding students in a law class that was quickly a two-horse race. But their approach to their subject differed drastically.

Crucially, Michael was capable of the one thing that Daniel was not. He could argue in favour of *anything*. Michael's feelings on a subject never affected his ability as an advocate; he could deliver winning performance after winning performance, regardless of the moral rights and wrongs. In this way Daniel could not compete. Daniel could fight a cause as well as anyone. But only when it was a cause in which he believed.

Which was going to be a problem. A barrister must accept any case offered, regardless of personal feelings. It is an ancient rule that guarantees a person will have someone to defend him, no matter how terrible the allegation. But, to be effective, the rule demanded Michael's ability to argue any case. Daniel lacked that talent and he knew it.

It led to the choice that had disappointed Daniel's father. Daniel's ability was bound to his morality, meaning he was more suited to the life of a solicitor. It gave him the freedom he needed. Freedom to champion good causes. And freedom to turn away cases that offended his sense of justice.

It was this life that Daniel had chosen fifteen years ago. A decision he had never regretted.

'Any plans for lunch?' Michael asked, breaking the short silence that had fallen between them.

'A fat sandwich and a fast car. It's Harry's sports day. I promised I'd be there for his race if his Uncle Mike got us out in time. You want to join us?'

'I think Uncle Mike's done enough by getting *you* there,

don't you? Besides, I'd only be watching him lose if he's anything like his old man!'

'Bollocks!' Daniel laughed in mock outrage. 'I never had any trouble outrunning you!'

'Yeah, but that was then. I'll give you a head start any time these days, you chubby bastard!'

Daniel laughed aloud, conceding defeat. Michael was right. They had been equally athletic in their university days. But Daniel hadn't kept himself in the same shape as his friend. That was natural. Daniel returned home each night to the comfort of his wife, his son and – more often than not – a big family meal. Michael did not.

Daniel sometimes envied that his friend's life was entirely his own, but he ultimately knew which of them had the better deal. Even if it *had* caused some softening of his body.

'So what's more important than watching your godson on the road to Olympic glory?'

'Just the usual. I've got a murder trial starting in two weeks. I thought I'd pick up the papers, head home and get some work done.'

'Work? After today? You're joking, right?'

Daniel could not keep the tone of incredulity out of his voice.

'Mike, you need to get out more, get a work-life balance. Come to sports day. Come and cheer on Harry. You can check out his English teacher while you're there.'

'I'm out enough,' Michael said. He seemed a little offended. 'And don't go thinking that you need to set me up with women. I'm not past it yet.'

Daniel laughed in reply, but behind the amusement was concern. Michael's preoccupation with his career was becoming a worry, especially with the impact it was having on his personal life. Or at least what *had* been a personal life.

It was all a far cry from their university days. Or even their twenties.

Back then they had made the most of their freedom. Both of them young, fit and successful. Michael was the more handsome of the two, Daniel knew that. And this had become *more* true as they had entered their late thirties. Michael was tall and strong, with classic good looks, thick blond hair and piercing blue eyes.

Daniel was four or five inches shorter. Dusky-haired and, at least in his youth, a much more wiry build. Though not handsome in the traditional sense, the difference between them had done nothing to dent Daniel's confidence. He was quick-witted and charismatic, a personality that more than made up for anything average about his features.

Their youthful success at charming a stream of beautiful women had been enviable. But those days were long gone. Both had settled down. Daniel to a happy marriage, a contented family life and – he had to admit – to early middle-age spread. Michael had just as committed a relationship, but his was with his career.

Daniel worried that this obsession would prevent his friend from ever finding the right girl. But now did not seem the time to voice those concerns.

It was not long before they had reached the bottom of Chancery Lane, the point at which they would go their separate ways.

'Wish Harry luck for me.'

Michael stopped walking as he spoke.

'Get him to give me a call at home if he wins. And you can get me that teacher's number too.'

Daniel laughed a final time. He was happy to see that his friend's raw nerve did not run too deep. Already walking along Chancery Lane, his own farewell was shouted over his shoulder.

'I will do. And maybe Claire can invite her to dinner at our place! Don't work too hard.'

TWELVE

Joshua flicked from network to network. The image on every channel was identical but the ritual was still necessary. Only on the seventh change could Joshua relax.

Every station's broadcast schedule had been abandoned within minutes of the Trafalgar Square shooting. Even now – five hours later – there was no escaping the horrors of the day.

Joshua settled on CNN and sat back against the oak headrest of his hotel room's double bed. He lit a Marlboro and inhaled deeply, relishing the relaxing hit of the nicotine. Then he turned up the television's volume and fixed his eyes on the screen.

The CNN cameraman had reacted quickly. Fast enough to capture almost every detail at close range. The recording had become the definitive footage of the day, played endlessly across the globe, regardless of the network.

The picture was at first nauseatingly shaky, caused by the cameraman chasing the sprinting gunman. But the lens came under control in time to capture the bullet that bit into the female agent. It was a graphic sight. As shocking as anything ever shown on television. Joshua, though, felt nothing.

He had the same numb reaction to the bloodbath that followed. He did not so much as shudder as Howard Thompson was flung backwards by the first shot. Nor did he flinch at the sight of Sir Neil Matthewson taking five bullets to the chest. The rest of the world mourned the violence that ended with Matthewson slumped in a blood-drenched heap. But not Joshua.

The fate of these men meant nothing to him. He was watching – he was waiting – for something else.

The attack had taken five seconds. Maybe less. Yet it seemed to last much longer in replay. Repeatedly paused and rewound, the footage was dissected and analysed on every channel by supposed experts, all dug up at short notice.

All opinions that mean nothing, Joshua thought; *because it always ends the same way. It always ends with Joe Dempsey.*

The sound of Joshua's cell phone interrupted his thoughts. It came as no surprise. He had been told to expect a call at 7.15 p.m. As always, the caller was punctual to the second.

Joshua stubbed out his cigarette. He answered the call without even a glance at the caller ID.

'Why wasn't Joe Dempsey on the list of agents you gave me?'

Joshua neither offered nor waited for a greeting. There was no anger in his voice but he was demanding an answer.

'Straight to the point as always.' The response was smooth. Even through the obvious electronic voice modulator, Joshua could tell that the speaker was calm. 'I appreciate that. The omission was a misjudgement on my part. Just something I thought it best to leave out.'

'A misjudgement? A misjudgement? You can't hire me for an assignment with full access to intelligence and then withhold information. That's not how this works, Stanton. Your misjudgement cost me my second shot and it saved McGale's life. It's *my* good name at stake here. I don't fail my contracts.'

'That's certainly your reputation, yes. It's a shame you didn't live up to it today.'

The reply was at the same unflustered pace. The voice of a man in control, Joshua thought. Of an arrogant man. It was an attitude that coloured everything Joshua's employer did.

Stanton continued without pause.

'But then nobody's perfect. Not even you. That's why we have contingency plans.'

'What's that supposed to mean? Don't you even think about putting the blame on me.'

Joshua matched Stanton for calm. He had spent his career under fire. Under threat. He was not about to lose it now.

'*You* screwed this up, Stanton. How did you expect me to react when Dempsey showed up out of nowhere? I should have been told that he'd be there.'

'Major Dempsey wasn't meant to show up at all. At least not until your job was done. So I thought it best to avoid the distraction his presence could cause you.'

Stanton's deep, metallic voice betrayed no hint of emotion. He continued.

'He was positioned to cover an aisle some distance from where Mr McGale was sitting. He should not have had time to get anywhere near your line of sight. We had no reason to believe that he would spot Mr McGale so early, or that he could cover that distance in the short time he had.'

'Then you don't know Joe Dempsey.'

Joshua was amazed by such a simple mistake. On a normal assignment he could understand it. But not this one. Not when every other detail had been perfectly planned. Joe Dempsey was peerless. The most effective field agent out there. Joshua knew that. It stunned him that his employer did not.

And then – suddenly – something far more concerning found its way into his mind. He had been so distracted by Stanton's mistake that he had missed the chilling meaning behind the man's earlier words.

'Wait,' he said, the feeling of nervous energy rising from

his gut. 'Why did you think knowing about Dempsey would distract me?'

Stanton did not answer immediately. When he did, the metallic voice somehow sounded even more soulless.

'I think you already know the answer to that, *Sergeant*.' The final word was emphasised. A message not lost on Joshua. Stanton continued. '*I* don't know Joe Dempsey. But I am aware that *you* do. And if I know *that* . . .'

He paused for effect, inviting Joshua to fill in the blank.

'Then you know who *I* am.'

Joshua's heart thumped as he spoke. He could feel the blood as it pumped through his temple. The pressure spiking. Somehow, by some means, his identity had been discovered.

'Yes, Joshua. I know who you are. In fact, I've made an effort to know absolutely everything about you, including your family and those few lonely individuals you call friends. It's a little insurance policy I took out. Just in case you failed to pull off the easiest shot anyone in your profession could wish for.'

A change in pitch hinted at emotion within the disguised voice. It added a little colour but did nothing to lighten the menace. Stanton continued.

'It turns out that it pays to be prepared. Today's misadventure might have left some loose ends. If it has, well, you're going to tie them up. Do that and you'll receive the remaining fifty per cent of your fee.'

'And if I refuse?'

Joshua dreaded the answer. Stanton's mention of family had made it clear that it was not Joshua's safety he was now threatening.

'I'm disappointed that you even need to ask. I'm sure there

are a number of undesirable people in the world who are just itching to pay you, your wife and your son a visit. Particularly the boy, I imagine. After all, there are all manner of accidents that could occur on an American university campus, aren't there?'

Joshua was silent. Helpless. It was an alien feeling.

How had this happened? he thought. *How could this man know all this?*

It did not seem possible. But neither did anything else Stanton had already achieved.

'OK.'

Joshua's word limped out, even as his mind raced. For now his choices were limited.

'Whatever you want. But I'm going to need help. It'll take some kind of miracle to get me access to McGale in custody. What have you got in mind?'

'Nothing that involves you.'

The reply was businesslike. As if Stanton's threats had never been made.

'Plans are already underway to deal with him. Your role is something else entirely. You're to be my trouble-shooter, if you'll pardon the pun. There to clear up any loose ends. There may be none, in which case you can enjoy your pay and the rest of your life. On the other hand there may be a good many. And if there are, I recommend you deal with them more professionally than you managed today.'

Stanton's statement required no reply. He continued.

'A secure mobile telephone has been placed in the Land Rover you parked downstairs. The handset on which we are currently speaking is not to be used again. You are to dismantle and dispose of it at the conclusion of this conversation. You are then to go downstairs, collect the new telephone and keep it on you at all times.'

Still no reply needed.

'Only I have the number. Only I will ever call that number. It is in the interest of your loved ones that you answer that telephone when it rings. You can expect to hear from me before the end of the day, to inform you of our next move. Do you have any questions?'

Joshua did not know what disturbed him most. Was it the level of planning that had anticipated every possibility? Or that Stanton's surveillance team were good enough to have tailed him to his hotel? There was silence as Joshua considered this. Eventually he found his voice.

'Just one. If any loose ends *do* turn up, how do you want them dealt with?'

'Be creative. Expect my call.'

Joshua heard the phone line clear. He waited for five seconds. Just to be sure. The last few minutes had caught Joshua off guard, but he was a professional. He heard no telltale click. No sign of telephone surveillance cutting off. Joshua disconnected his end of the line.

He sat back again against the oak headrest. Shaken, he lit another Marlboro.

The same images still flickered on the screen. Silent. The sound system muted. Joshua paid them no attention; other thoughts now occupied his mind. He ran his fingers through his thick jet-black hair. At the same time the fingers of his right hand tapped out north, east, south and west on the bedside table. The routine calmed him. Helped him think.

Joshua was rarely at a disadvantage. Rarely not in control. It had happened only once before. He had dealt with it then. He would deal with it now. Joshua would do Stanton's bidding. He would fulfil his contract and he would walk away.

And then later, when the time was right, he would make Stanton regret that he had ever heard the name Joshua.

THIRTEEN

Cabinet Office Briefing Room A fell silent as William Davies strode through the open door. The heads of Britain's various security agencies had been around the table for close to thirty minutes already. Little had been discussed. The meeting could not begin until the prime minister was present.

Davies walked to the head of the table and took his seat. All eyes were upon him. His own remained downcast.

Davies knew that he looked worn out. Mainly because he *was*. It had been five hours since the shooting. Some leaders thrive on the pressure. On the stress. Davies did not. The events of the day were a threat to his very survival as prime minister. It was not a situation that played to his political strengths.

He placed his files on the table ahead of him, then glared wordlessly around the room. All eyes looked back at him. Most belonged to men and women who had risked their lives for their country. Together they made up the COBRA Committee, the fast-response body convened in times of crisis and named after the room they now occupied. These were not individuals who were easily intimidated by an angry politician.

Davies' gaze moved from one operative to the next. He knew them all, but in his tired, increasingly paranoid mind each was a blank canvas. Faceless proponents of a world he neither understood nor welcomed. Davies wanted as little to do with these people – with their secrecy and with their espionage – as possible. Just being among them irritated him.

But today it was unavoidable.

'I don't need to tell you what a disaster this is.'

Davies kept his tone soft; an intentional effort. It would help no one to begin with blame or conflict. There would be ample time for those.

'But I *do* have to explain the situation to President Knowles. The Americans of course have their own investigators all over this already, so whether this blows up into an international incident could depend upon what I tell him. Now let's see what spin we can put on this. What do we know?'

Davies watched as each pair of eyes swept around the table. He could tell that no one wanted to be first. They all knew the risk. Trafalgar Square had been a disaster. Millions – by now billions, even – had seen the UK's most popular politician shot dead. That former President Howard Thompson had escaped with just a shoulder wound was no mitigation. Britain's security services had been humiliated in the eyes of the world. And their American equivalents were circling, ready to strike at whoever had put their president at risk.

If Davies were to have any political future he could not allow that humiliation to stand. He could not allow an American investigation to get to the truth before his own agencies. The urgency of the situation demanded a scapegoat. Davies knew it. And so, it seemed, did the men and women in the room.

Finally his question was answered.

'You probably know as much as any of us, Prime Minister.'

Davies turned to face the speaker. It was a courtesy. Nothing more. Davies was interested only in the information. Not in its source.

'Why don't you run me through it anyway? It will be helpful to hear as complete a version of events as we have.'

'As you know, sir, the shooter was apprehended by a

member of the Department of Domestic Security. This undoubtedly saved the life of President Thompson. It was, tragically, too late for Sir Neil Matthewson. The assassin has been taken to Paddington Green police station for questioning. This is ongoing as we speak.'

'And we believe, do we, that this attack was the execution of the threats our intelligence services had uncovered against President Thompson?'

'Yes, Prime Minister. We do.'

'I'm sorry, but what threats?' The voice came from the back of the room.

Davies turned to face the new questioner. It was one of the room's informal occupants, an assistant commissioner of the Metropolitan Police. Officially present as just a witness, the man seemed surprised at this new information.

'It was a direct threat from the True IRA against the life of President Thompson,' the original speaker explained, turning to face the Met officer as he spoke. 'Specific enough that the former president's continued involvement in the event was questioned.'

'Questioned by whom?'

'By both the UK *and* the US. With Thompson under threat, his involvement became an additional security factor. One we could have done without.'

The assistant commissioner took the answer and did not pursue the enquiry. Davies, however, wanted to know more.

'Assuming this is right – that President Thompson was asked to reconsider his attendance in light of the threat – who overruled it? Who insisted on his continued presence?'

'The White House did, sir. We were told that they would increase the Secret Service presence and that this would be sufficient.'

'And my office?'

'Your office directly deferred to the White House on the decision, sir.'

A smile crept across Davies' face. This information had somehow passed him by – an oversight he would be looking into – but, for now, it was exactly what he needed to hear. The decision had been made by the Americans. That made it very difficult for them to criticise the British government.

Difficult, but not impossible. The full picture was needed.

'How sure are we that what happened today was connected to this specific threat?'

'We cannot be absolutely certain as of this moment.' A second speaker. Another face Davies knew. Another recognition he resented. 'Not until we have a verified claim from the True IRA themselves. But circumstances suggest that our assumption is correct.'

'Meaning?'

'Meaning that as Thompson was the target of the threat and as Thompson was one of today's victims – albeit he was not the one fatally injured – then the logical supposition is that the threat made was the threat carried out. In addition we now know the identity of the shooter. His name is Eamon McGale, a native of Belfast. In the current climate McGale's nationality alone would suggest involvement with either the UVA or the True IRA, as they are currently the active paramilitary organisations in the province. When combined with the specific threat from the True IRA, the conclusion rather writes itself.'

Davies nodded in agreement.

'And has this McGale person not assisted by confirming his motives?' he asked. 'Or even just his loyalties? Surely that would negate the need for any verified confirmation from the organisation?'

'Yes, it would. But I'm afraid we haven't been able to get anything at all from him. He won't say anything beyond confirming his identity. At least until he has seen a lawyer.'

'Then we'll have to do something about that.'

Davies had seen an opportunity to shift at least some of the blame to the White House. It put him in a hurry to see it happen.

'If he won't speak without a lawyer then we need to supply one.'

'That's been dealt with already.'

It was the original speaker again. Davies turned to face him.

'It was urgent and so your office made arrangements in your absence, Prime Minister. Of course they had to be very careful in selecting the *right* person. An establishment lawyer wouldn't look right in the left-wing press, while a lawyer with known terrorist connections would be wholly unacceptable to the Americans.

'As such they decided – in consultation with the Ministry of Justice, MI5 and the US Secret Service – to use an independent lawyer with an unimpeachable reputation. This man has been contacted and in all likelihood he will attend Paddington Green to advise McGale and represent him in interview first thing tomorrow morning. After which we'll hopefully know a lot more.'

'*In all likelihood* he'll be there in the morning? You'll *hopefully* know a lot more after that?'

Davies could not hide his irritation. With political survival within his grasp, he was becoming desperate.

'This all sounds very uncertain. We're not operating purely on wishful thinking and good intentions here, are we?'

The speaker opened his mouth to respond. He was stopped by a dismissive wave of Davies' hand. The prime minister had more questions.

'And who is the lawyer in whom we are placing so much trust?'

'His name is Daniel Lawrence. He's a very well-known human rights lawyer with a reputation for utter integrity. We felt—'

'I know who Daniel Lawrence is.'

Davies could hear the change in his own tone of voice as he interrupted. The identity of McGale's lawyer was *not* happy news.

'Daniel Lawrence is the godson of Anthony Haversume. For the purposes of maintaining civility, I'm going to assume *that* wasn't the reason he was chosen for this task. But other than that unfortunate connection, yes, I suppose Mr Lawrence is a good choice.'

No explanation was needed for Davies' comments. His difficult relationship with Anthony Haversume MP was common knowledge.

Haversume had been a minister in Davies' cabinet until resigning his position with the stinging criticism that Davies had surrendered to terrorists in Northern Ireland as part of the renewed peace process. Since that time Irish terrorist activity had surged, both Catholic and Protestant. It had cost hundreds of lives and strengthened Haversume's argument, making him Davies' most vocal critic. If the prime minister had a nemesis, it was Haversume.

Davies continued.

'And, as you say, hopefully we will know more once McGale has been interviewed in the morning. In the meantime, let's focus on what we *do* know. Firstly, how on *earth* did McGale get a gun into Trafalgar Square when we'd restricted entry?'

A third speaker answered. Another practitioner of the dark arts, as far as Davies was concerned. Another face he resented knowing.

'His pistol had masking tape around it. There was no sign of tape on him, or any marks on his body to suggest that anything had been taped *to* him. It's a fair assumption, then, that he collected the weapon inside the square. That someone left it for him.'

The final statement hit Davies like a physical blow. The light at the end of his metaphorical tunnel was suddenly receding. There was rising anger in his voice as he spoke.

'Are you telling me that someone with access through our security planted that gun for him to use? That this thing was planned with the help of an insider?'

'That's the only logical conclusion.' The answer was matter-of-fact. 'Someone in a position of trust was involved. McGale could not have done it alone.'

Silence descended as Davies took this in. He looked from face to face. Searched for a different opinion. All he found was wordless agreement. Defeated, his eyes returned to the bearer of this bad news.

Taking a deep breath, he asked the inevitable question.

'Have we got any idea who this insider is?'

'No, sir.' The answer came from the same senior agent. 'I'm afraid we don't. It could be anyone. From any team. We can't even say if it was from the British side or from the American.'

'THAT'S JUST NOT GOOD ENOUGH!'

The sudden increase in volume made even the most experienced operatives jump.

Davies could see his political survival moving further out of reach. It made him desperate. A desperation that manifested as anger. Every shouted word was directed at the latest speaker.

'WHAT THE HELL AM I SUPPOSED TO TELL PRESIDENT KNOWLES?'

'That we are investigating every angle, sir.' The agent kept his calm. 'The Americans had joint responsibility for security, Prime Minister. It's as much their failure as ours.'

'AND YOU THINK THAT WILL MAKE A DIFFERENCE, DO YOU?'

There was anger in every word.

'IT WAS ON *BRITISH* SOIL. WHICH MEANS *WE* WILL BEAR THE BLAME FOR THIS IF WE CAN'T IDENTIFY THE INSIDER.'

'Sir, we *will* get to the bottom of this. We *will* find who was working with McGale. We just need more than five hours to do that.'

Davies did not respond. He could not, because the agent had a point. Five hours was just not enough time. Even the White House would understand that.

The thought calmed him. As did the realisation that, right now, he needed these people. Alienating them with anger and abuse would achieve nothing.

'OK.' When Davies spoke again his tone had lowered. Still strained, but at least his volume had decreased. 'That seems reasonable enough. At least to buy us some time. Which leaves the question of apprehension. Why wasn't McGale stopped before he fired?'

Most eyes turned to the meeting's first speaker, but it was the second who answered.

'Timing, Prime Minister. McGale was seated close to the

stage, twenty-three rows back and in an aisle seat. He waited until the crowd were on their feet and applauding before making his move. When one considers the short distance, and the cover he had by moving quickly among an animated crowd, it's really no wonder that he wasn't taken down sooner. That anyone reacted at all is quite remarkable.'

'Ah, yes.' Davies jumped on the opportunity. 'The reaction of our operatives. I've been fully briefed on this point. It could be problematic. Having broken cover, the gunman ran into the area at the foot of the stage. An area controlled by a team from the DDS.'

The Department of Domestic Security. It was the first agency Davies had mentioned by name. In that moment every man and woman at the table knew that the scapegoat had been selected.

Davies continued, aware that his intention was now clear.

'Of the nine DDS operatives in that area, only two reacted. Of those two, one managed to put her head into the line of fire of the only marksman to get a shot off. The other failed to draw his weapon at all. I'm no expert, but is that the standard I should expect from our premier department of national security?'

'With all due respect, sir, I think you are oversimplifying the situation.'

Davies turned to face the latest speaker. This time it was the head of MI5, the UK's internal security service.

'How so?' Davies asked.

There was no mistaking the prime minister's tone. He would not accept the explanation that was to come. But still the answer was given.

'As anyone with field experience knows, Prime Minister, those agents did more than could be expected of them. How they reacted so quickly is beyond me, but somehow they managed it.'

'Yes, but you're missing the point. Those operatives may well have reacted quickly, but they also did so incompetently. The world saw seven DDS agents do nothing, an eighth get shot by her own marksman and a ninth who seemed to forget that he carried a gun. They allowed a major security operation to descend into farce.'

'I hardly think that's fair, *sir*.'

The last word was spat out. The expression on the face of the MI5 director suggested that it had not left a pleasant taste.

He continued.

'The DDS agents followed protocol to the letter. Sergeant Regis had the short-range shot. In those circumstances Major Dempsey was required to keep his weapon holstered. If he were to draw it he would risk hitting the agent with the clearer firing opportunity. *That* is why he didn't shoot and *that* is why the police sniper should *not* have pulled his trigger. The agents did everything right. If the marksman had done the same we would not be having this conversation.'

The heads around the table seemed to turn as one. Towards the occupant of a seat in the far corner of the room. The same Met officer who had spoken earlier.

The MI5 director addressed the man directly.

'Assistant Commissioner, as you know, you've been asked to attend this committee today as a witness, to deal with the matter that has now arisen. Namely to establish which of the twenty snipers on duty around Trafalgar Square today took the shot which killed Sergeant Samantha Regis. Are you yet in a position to deal with this issue?'

The police officer rose to his feet. He faced Davies rather

than his interrogator. 'Prime Minister, despite the inclusion of multiple agencies in the blanket marksmen coverage of the square we have been able to confirm – albeit unofficially – that the shot was . . .'

'I did not ask you a question,' Davies interrupted, 'and nor am I interested in your answer. Take your seat.'

Davies indicated the same instruction with his hand as he interrupted.

His eyes returned to the director of MI5. Fault had been placed. Davies would not see that changed.

'It was the DDS agents who failed today. No one else. This was supposed to be a celebration of our victory in the war against terror. Instead, the incompetence of our operatives has allowed it to descend into a rallying call to terrorists across the world.'

There was no response. And Davies knew why. He knew the belief that these people held. It was part of why he hated them. They believed that Davies had surrendered in Ulster. That he had gifted power to those who had maimed and killed in exchange for nothing. They regarded Davies' concessions for peace to be nothing less than cowardice. Davies knew differently. He also knew that he would never persuade them from their views. And nor would he try.

'OK,' he finally said, breaking the silence. 'Time to move on. I want to know what steps are being taken to identify McGale's accomplice.'

FOURTEEN

Daniel Lawrence sat in his Porsche 911 and listened to the purr of its engine. It was a low rumble. Just ticking over. Which was about all it ever got to do in the nose-to-tail London traffic.

The short journey from Daniel's office to Paddington Green police station had so far taken twenty minutes. Roadworks, one-way systems and the sheer weight of traffic meant that the last three miles would take just as long again. Not that it mattered. Daniel had a lot to think about as his car crawled along.

The last few hours had been the most surprising of Daniel's life. He had been selected by the British government to represent Eamon McGale; to protect his interests in police interview. It made Daniel a part of living history. It was a privilege, of course. But it was more than that. It was the case that would make his career.

Daniel had reached his office minutes after leaving Michael on Fleet Street. Still on a high from their victory, he had paid no attention to the distant police sirens. Those sounds always filled the central London air. Why should he notice a few more than usual?

The shocked face of Daniel's secretary had been the first sign of something wrong. She had been oblivious to the single tear that had stained her left cheek with a line of black mascara. Her attention had been elsewhere, her eyes fixed on the room's wall-mounted television. Daniel had followed her gaze and immediately understood. The images on the screen had told him everything. Like half the world, he had been unable to look away.

Daniel turned his car left onto the Marylebone Road and joined the snaking westbound traffic. One of the two main routes into London from the west, this stretch of road was always congested, but tonight was worse than usual. The engine that sat at the rear of his car would be lucky to hit 5 mph. A waste of so much power.

Daniel could not now remember how long he had stayed in his office reception. How long he had stared at the screen. Those hours were a blur. He had closed up for the day, but he had no idea what time that had been.

He could also remember telephone calls. One to Claire. One to Michael. One to his father. These conversations had occurred but, like everything else, the details now escaped him. The entire afternoon remained a confusing haze. At least until the call that would change his life.

There had been no reason to expect it. Sure, his public profile was growing. But Daniel had not dared to presume he would be in the running for such a major case. Every crusading lawyer in the city would be chasing it. Yet somehow it had been handed to him. It begged the obvious question: why?

All of these thoughts had raced through Daniel's mind after the call. But they had not slowed him down. Determined to grasp the opportunity, within minutes of the call ending he had activated the security system, converted the office switchboard to its voicemail setting and left the building.

The request had been that he attend to represent Eamon McGale at Paddington Green police station the next morning. It was the first time he had heard the name, and a name was all it was; he would not receive any more information until in the presence of the man himself. But the location was enough for now. Only one man would be held in Paddington Green tonight, and that was Neil Matthewson's killer.

The only case in town.

The knowledge had made Daniel impatient. Unwilling to wait until morning, he decided he would grasp this opportunity and not let go.

He would meet McGale tonight.

The traffic, though, had been in no such rush. It was typical of London. The only downside to the city Daniel loved. As his car crawled past Baker Street station, he knew that the last half-mile could be covered faster on foot. But the delay did not matter. Nothing could start without him.

FIFTEEN

'The thieving weasel bastard!' shouted Sarah Truman.

Her raised voice startled Jack Maguire. He jumped, banging his head on the low roof of their outside broadcast van.

'Jesus Christ, Sarah.' Maguire rubbed his skull as he turned towards the cause of Sarah's outburst. The remnants of a half-eaten cheeseburger were sliding down two of the six screens that sat in the rear of the van. On the upper screen a resilient pickle obscured the face of CNN lead anchor Martin Hone.

Maguire took a rag and mopped up blobs of relish from the monitors. As the screens were cleaned, the images became clearer. And the cause of Sarah's anger.

Hone's face had disappeared. In its place was Maguire's footage of the shooting. But the anchorman's voice remained. His perfect English diction complemented the visuals. A brilliant example of calm and articulate live reporting. It would have been even more impressive if the words spoken had been his own. They were not.

'I can't believe they've done this to me.'

Sarah's Boston accent was more pronounced than usual. It happened when she was irritated, Maguire had noticed.

'Those are my goddamn words and now that stuck-up son-of-a-bitch is reading them out all over the world. Like it's *his* report.'

Maguire shook his head. He was sympathetic, but he was not surprised. There was no way the network would have left *this* story in Sarah's hands. She had been in Trafalgar Square to cover a semi-newsworthy event. A classic safe assignment, somewhere for a promising reporter to cut her teeth. No one could have guessed it would become ground zero for the biggest story of the year.

Sarah's on-the-spot performance had been impressive. That much was undeniable. Her live commentary had been average at best, but then that was expected; no one assigned to Trafalgar Square that afternoon had been prepared for the carnage they had witnessed. But Sarah's main report, made literally moments later? Now *that* had demonstrated her talent.

Maguire had long recognised Sarah's potential. Today she had proved him right. And in the long term she had likely made her career. But none of that would matter right now. CNN, like any network, paid its main correspondents a serious amount of money. For those salaries they expected airtime and, right now, Trafalgar Square was the only show in town. It had been only a matter of time before Sarah's report was passed to the big guns. That was how things worked. Maguire knew that. He also knew that Hone's co-opting of Sarah's report was a huge compliment. The fact that he had then not changed a word of it? Even more so. But making Sarah understand that would not be easy.

'Look at the upside, Sarah. They know they owe you. They now know how good you are. The public might not connect you with this story but today was the making of your career. It was a big day for you.'

'That's easy for you to say. Whatever voice goes with it, those are your pictures. I'm the one who's being screwed to justify Hone's salary.'

'You need to put it behind you.'

Maguire could understand Sarah's anger, but he also knew how futile it was. Their profession had ups and it had downs.

Sarah would have to learn to live with them. Or to find her way around them.

'It was a great story,' he continued, 'but it fell in your lap. Yes, you did a fantastic job. Yes, I'd rather be listening to your voice than Hone's. But that's life. Complaining about it won't change anything. If you want to keep a story you can't just stumble into it. You have to go out and *find* it. *Make* it. They can't take those ones away from you, Sarah.'

Maguire rarely spoke so bluntly, but it had to be said. Sarah had to understand the realities of their business if she was going to make it to the top. And Maguire felt it was his responsibility to teach her those realities. Even when she did not want to hear them.

Sarah did not respond. Maguire knew why. He could understand her frustration. The truth was sometimes hard to hear, especially when that truth was so unfair. Aware that his words had hit a nerve, Maguire turned away and gave Sarah her privacy.

Sarah sat in silence for a few moments, as Maguire returned to the van's editing equipment. She stared at the vehicle's rear doors as she ran his words through her mind. Every one of them was true. She knew that. And yet they were hard to accept.

Difficult as it might be, Sarah would not be the professional she thought she was if she could not take a little constructive criticism from the man she trusted the most.

Annoyed with herself, she turned to face Maguire and opened her mouth to apologise. No words came out. Instead she just watched as his expert fingers manipulated the van's high-tech editing equipment. And she marvelled as he skilfully improved and refined his footage. Maguire was a man who had his priorities straight. Who took his job seriously, but who never let it interfere with his humanity. Sarah knew that. And she knew he was someone she could – someone she should – aspire to emulate.

'Tell me again why we're sitting here, Jack? When everyone else is around at the front of the station?'

Sarah's tone made it clear that her question was also an apology. An attempt to move past her outburst. Maguire seemed to understand that, and he answered as if the exchange had never taken place.

'It's *because* everyone else is around the corner. Whatever happens at the front of the building will be covered by every network. There's no exclusive there, Sarah. But if *I* were cleaning up this mess I wouldn't be coming in through the front door, fighting my way through the press. I'd come in the back way. If they do that, well, they'll have to get through us.'

The building was Paddington Green police station, the most secure police holding area in the mainland United Kingdom. It was an ugly, grey, concrete tower block whose location next to the similarly unattractive Marylebone Flyover saw it greet millions of motorists a day as they travelled towards London's more picturesque architecture. Since its construction it had seen the interrogation of almost every terror suspect arrested on English soil. It was here that the Trafalgar Square gunman was being held.

A mass of the world's press was camped out at the front of the building. They were waiting for the first crumbs of information to be thrown their way. None knew when that first briefing would come. They would wait for as long as it took.

But they would wait without Maguire and Sarah. Following

Maguire's logic, the CNN van sat alone at the rear of the building, in the empty darkness beneath the overpass. Only the constant sound of overhead traffic reminded them of where they were.

'So how long are we going to be sitting here?'

'Get some patience, girl. The guy's a terror suspect. They can hold him for twenty-eight days without charge. It could be ages before we hear something.'

'Twenty-eight days? You're kidding? We're not sitting here that long, are we?'

'It'll take as long as it takes.'

Maguire's response sounded impatient to Sarah's ear, but when he looked up from his editing decks he was smiling. Any hint of irritation was gone from his voice when he continued.

'Don't worry. I'm sure we'll hear something quicker than that. The government can't let this drag on without comment. But there'll be plenty of coming and going from here before then, and we're the ones who'll see it. It just takes a little patience.'

Sarah was visibly relieved. The prospect of spending twenty-eight days cooped up in the back of the van had not been attractive. But there was more she wanted to ask. The next question was about to leave her lips when she noticed something through the van's windscreen.

'What are you looking at?' Maguire craned his neck to follow her gaze.

'A way to grab hold of this story.'

Sarah burst into a flurry of activity. She grabbed a Dictaphone, tied back her long brunette hair and smoothed down her suit.

'Give me a cigarette.'

'What? What are you talking about? I thought you were giving up?'

Maguire was now thoroughly confused. He reached into the breast pocket of his jacket for the ever-present pack of Marlboro Lights.

'I'm always giving up. Doesn't matter now. I'm about to go and make a story, just like you said.'

Sarah pointed in the direction of a shadowed area close to the station's rear entrance. Maguire's eyes followed her finger towards a glimpse of movement within the darkness. For a moment it meant nothing, until the tiny but unmistakable burning head of an inhaled cigarette illuminated the shadows.

'Oh, I get it.' From where they were parked the figure in the shadows could only be a police officer from inside the station. 'Smoking-break solidarity. Clever girl.'

Sarah responded with a smile. She took the cigarette, turned her back on Maguire and walked towards the shadowy figure.

As she drew closer, Sarah's eyes were becoming more accustomed to the darkness. She could make out more detail. The shape that had been hidden in the shadows took a form. A tall black police sergeant in his late thirties. Sarah smiled as she approached. It was not returned. She needed another way to break the ice.

'They don't let you guys smoke in there now, huh?'

Sarah was obviously a member of the press. The police sergeant could clearly see that. His attitude remained hostile.

'Not many places we *can* smoke these days,' he replied. He seemed intent on minimal response.

'I know how you feel. My cameraman won't let me smoke in the van either. It's getting worse than it is at home.' Sarah put the cigarette to her lips. 'Would you mind?'

The sergeant took a lighter from his pocket. He held it out and watched as Sarah inhaled deeply, for the first time in three weeks. He had no idea how welcome she found the nicotine hit.

'No need to ask what story you're here for, I suppose?'

Sarah laughed as she exhaled a thin flume of smoke.

'No, I guess not. There's a whole lot of us cluttering up the place, right?'

'Right. Reporters do have a knack for getting in the way.'

The sergeant's words gave away his dislike for the press, but his tone suggested that an exception could be made. It was an opening Sarah took.

'I can't argue with that,' she replied, careful not to seem overly flirtatious. 'My name's Sarah, Sarah Truman. I'm with CNN.'

He took Sarah's outstretched hand. Shook it with delicate care.

'Nice to meet you, Sarah from CNN. I'm Trevor Henry.'

'And it's nice to meet you, Trevor. It's the only upside to them persecuting the smokers, right? At least we get to meet new people.'

Henry nodded and smiled as his eyes scanned Sarah from head to toe. She could not tell if this was supposed to be subtle. Not that it mattered. The look on Henry's face as his eyes returned to her face said all that it had to. He liked what he had seen.

'So I've got to ask: are you involved with the case?'

'Of course I am.' Henry gestured his head towards the building as he spoke. 'Who isn't?'

'And you can't talk about it, I'm sure.'

'I can't, no. Shame, though. I can't think of anyone else I'd rather go on the record for.'

Henry put his cigarette to his lips as he spoke. His mouth broke into a flirtatious grin as he held Sarah's gaze.

We're getting there, Sarah thought.

'What about off the record?' she asked. 'Nothing that'll be broadcast. Just enough to put me on track, ahead of the rabble?'

Henry stared for a moment. Smiling. As if he was considering the consequences of granting Sarah's request. They did not seem to worry him.

'OK,' he finally answered. 'Ask me what you want and I'll answer if I can. You won't be getting much, though. And if anyone asks, we never spoke.'

'Goes without saying. So who was the guy? Irish, right? I saw him pretty close and he didn't look Islamic.'

Henry nodded his head.

'Yeah. He's Irish.'

'His name?'

'No chance. You'll have to wait for that one with everyone else.'

'Right. Why'd he do it?'

'I couldn't tell you if I wanted to. He won't tell us anything but his name. Not until he's seen a lawyer.'

'Who's his lawyer?'

Sarah was already growing frustrated at how little Henry seemed to know. She hid it well.

'No clue. No one's shown up yet. Someone's been called but I don't know who.'

'What about Neil Matthewson? It's been suggested that he wasn't the target. That he was actually going after Howard Thompson. Is that true?'

Henry shrugged.

'Well, has he at least shown any remorse about Matthewson then?'

'Hasn't said a word about it. He hasn't apologised, at least.'

Henry looked at his watch. His body language told Sarah that break-time was over. He dropped the butt of his cigarette onto the floor. Ground it out with his foot.

'Time's up, Sarah. Sorry I couldn't help you more. But if you ever want a longer chat, over a few drinks maybe, you know where to find me. Take care.'

Sarah smiled back. It was the look of someone intrigued by the offer. Designed to disguise her irritation as Henry walked back towards the building.

Three weeks, Sarah thought as she dropped her cigarette to the floor. *Three weeks without touching one, and I break it for that.*

Sarah turned back to face the van. She knew Maguire would be watching and so she shrugged. Her conversation with Trevor Henry had told her next to nothing. That in itself was frustrating. But what it could mean was worse; that the twenty-eight-day wait was still a possibility.

She began to walk back towards the van. As she did she saw a pair of car headlights approaching from the distance. There was only one place the car could be heading.

At the same moment the automatic doors of the station's rear entrance began to open.

Sarah stepped back from the kerb and into the shadows. From there she had a perfect view of the approaching car. It slowed as it passed her and turned into the station entrance. In seconds it was gone.

Those few seconds were long enough for Sarah to get a good view of the driver. It was a face she recognised. Like any junior reporter, she had paid her dues on the crime beat. Which meant she could recognise a handful of high-profile lawyers at a glance.

She was rushing back to Maguire before the building's rear gate had even closed.

'Jack, you are a genius!'

Sarah was almost shouting as she jumped into the front passenger's seat.

'Why? What did he tell you?'

'Who, the cop? Oh, screw him. He doesn't know anything we don't. I'm talking about your idea to sit here. If we were out front I wouldn't have seen who was driving that car. We've got a lead, Jack. Now we can go build our story.'

Maguire laughed along with Sarah's enthusiasm, but he still looked confused.

'Slow down, would you? It helps if we *both* know what you're talking about. What lead? Who was in that car?'

'The story was in there, Jack. Well, the start of it, anyway. The police might not want to tell us anything, but now we know who this guy's lawyer is.'

SIXTEEN

Dempsey pulled his DDS identification from his jacket pocket. He was next in a long line of visitors waiting to pass the manned entrance to New Scotland Yard. It was still a world-famous address. Home to the top ranks of the Metropolitan Police and to many of Britain's intelligence agencies. It was one of London's most secure buildings. Few could walk through its doors unmolested. But then few were senior agents in the DDS.

The security door slid aside at the press of a button. Dempsey strode through and headed for the main reception desk, glancing at the clock that sat above it. It showed 9 p.m. Late for a working day. Not that it made any difference. The building bustled with activity.

The reception desk seemed to be a focal point. It was manned by two uniformed sergeants. Tonight it could have used ten. Two lines of visitors were impatiently waiting to be processed and have their questions answered. Dempsey joined neither. He had queued enough for one day.

'I'm looking for Assistant Commissioner Alex Henley.' Dempsey flashed his credentials to the first sergeant. There was a murmur of annoyance from the queue behind. Dempsey silenced it with a glance.

'He's, erm, he's in his office on the fifth floor.'

The desk sergeant seemed disarmed. Few people walked into New Scotland Yard with such purpose. Such authority. Which was exactly why Dempsey had done so. The flustered sergeant continued.

'I can, erm, call up and tell him you're here to see him? Mr . . .?'

'I'll announce myself.'

Dempsey turned without another word. He walked away, towards an open elevator. He stepped inside and pressed '5', staring directly at the desk sergeant as the doors closed.

The sergeant watched in silence, as if hypnotised by Dempsey's confidence. But then that had been the intention all along. Dempsey had many talents. Walking through closed doors was just one of them.

'Who the hell was that?' The second desk sergeant had missed the exchange.

'DDS agent.' The first sergeant spoke slowly, as if just coming to his senses. 'Here to see Henley.'

'Then don't you think you'd better call up?'

The first sergeant seemed to process the suggestion slowly. But then his eyes widened, suggesting that the last few minutes had suddenly sunk in. He grabbed the telephone handset and dialled.

The line was answered before a second ring. He did not wait for a greeting.

'There's a DDS agent on the way up to see the assistant commissioner. He doesn't look happy.'

Dempsey stepped out of the elevator on the fifth floor. A welcome party was there to greet him. Three uniformed officers, all tall and wide, flanking a smaller man in a cheap polyester suit.

Between them they blocked the hall.

'Can I help you, Mr . . .?' Polyester Suit took the lead.

'*Major* Dempsey. I'm looking for Alex Henley.'

'I'm afraid the assistant commissioner is very busy, Major. Perhaps if you could make an appointment for tomorrow?'

'No.' Dempsey's voice was firm. There would be no negotiation. 'I'm seeing him now. Take me or I find him myself. Your choice.'

Dempsey's meaning was unmistakable. Intentionally so. One way or another his questions would be answered. The three larger men tensed. They seemed ready for what would follow. They would know that Dempsey was a DDS operative; that much would have been passed upwards by the desk sergeant. So they would know that he was no easy target, but then he *was* outnumbered. Were they willing to take the risk?

If they were, Polyester Suit was not so reckless. He looked from man to man. One big guy against three bigger guys. They were good odds, but sometimes you go with your gut. Polyester Suit's gut seemed to say that this would not end well for his men.

'OK, Major.' He had made his decision. 'He's down the hall. Please follow me.'

A wave of a hand stood the three men down. They stepped aside. Obedient.

The man has more authority than that cheap suit would suggest, Dempsey thought.

It was a short walk, taking them into the heart of the New Scotland Yard building. Every room they passed was alive with activity. The day had been a propaganda disaster. Security agencies were working overtime to clean up their mess.

They reached Assistant Commissioner Henley's office door

in less than a minute. Polyester Suit knocked once and entered without waiting for a response. This was all the confirmation Dempsey needed that they were expected.

'I'm sorry to interrupt, sir. Major Dempsey of the Department of Domestic Security is here to see you.'

'Major Dempsey.' Henley reacted as if meeting an old friend. 'How are you? No lasting injuries from today, I hope?'

Henley rose from his chair as he spoke. A tall man, he was middle-aged and naturally distinguished. One of life's officers. It was impossible to imagine him in anything other than his perfectly tailored uniform. Some people choose their careers. Alex Henley could have been nothing else.

He strode forward, his hand outstretched. Dempsey thrust his own forward and gripped Henley's tightly.

'No injuries, no.' Dempsey replied. 'Which is more than can be said for Samantha Regis.'

Henley released his grip and took a step back. His surprise at Dempsey's directness was unmistakable.

'Yes. Yes, Major. You have my condolences about Sergeant Regis. Her death was a tragedy.' Henley's voice was sincere. His reaction honest.

'No argument on that here.'

The confrontation Dempsey had been prepared for would not be necessary. He took a different approach.

'I need your help.'

'Anything I can do, Major.'

'I want to know who fired the shot.'

At first Henley did not answer. Dempsey thought he knew why.

Along with the American Secret Service, Henley had enjoyed joint control of the full team of marksmen stationed in the buildings around Trafalgar Square. And someone in that team had killed Samantha Regis. Henley could not deny that. Most likely he did not want to. But that changed nothing. Like Dempsey, Henley's acts were governed by strict rules. One of the nation's most senior police officers, he was unlikely to break them easily. This was confirmed when Henley finally spoke, his voice coloured by genuine regret.

'I'm sorry, Major. I really am. But even if we had reached an official finding on this matter I couldn't tell you. The men on my team have a right to absolute anonymity.'

'And mine have a right not to have their brains scattered over a thirty-foot radius.'

The words were harsh, but Dempsey's tone was not aggressive. Dempsey was a professional first and foremost. Just stating a fact to a man he believed could help him.

'Even so. I'll give you any help I can, but identities are protected. You know that, Major Dempsey.'

Dempsey stepped forward. Henley stood his ground. Dempsey's voice was calm but the intensity in his eyes betrayed him. Having witnessed the death of his friend, he was struggling to remain detached.

'I know your rules,' he said. 'I know your procedures. But I also know that Sam Regis did what any agent in her position should have done. She had the clear shot. That gave her precedence. Standard procedure, for your team *and* mine. One of your men disregarded that procedure and Sam died. Now put yourself in my position. What would you do?'

Henley remained silent. He held Dempsey's gaze. A gaze that was not an attempt to intimidate. It was a plea. And it would take a cold heart to leave that plea unanswered.

Henley finally looked away. Towards a pile of papers that

sat on his desk. Dempsey followed his gaze and immediately recognised the papers' importance. Fifteen to twenty manila folders. Each would contain the professional profile of a member of Henley's team. Dempsey knew then that his questions would be answered.

'OK, Major. I'll tell you what you want to know.'

There was an unusual tone to Henley's voice. It was not defeat. Nor the sound of a man forced into a disclosure. Instead it was the tone of a man who was doing what he thinks is right, and doing so in spite of the rules.

'I debriefed all of my men. I was also present when the American team was debriefed. I can say with confidence that the shot that killed Sergeant Regis didn't come from any of them.'

'That can't be right.'

Dempsey believed that Henley was speaking the truth as he knew it to be. But that did not make the information correct. He continued.

'You were overseeing the only units covering the scene from high. Which is where the bullet came from. You've only got to look at the footage to see that.'

'I've seen the footage, Major, and I agree with you.' Henley was making less sense with every answer. 'The shot *must* have come from one of the team. But the shooter wasn't American and he wasn't one of mine. He was an outsider, Major Dempsey. A Sergeant Steven Jones. A specialist who was seconded in when one of my team leaders was taken ill. I can't tell you anything more about him because I don't *know* anything more. *I* didn't debrief him after the shooting. And neither did the Americans.'

Dempsey could not believe what he was hearing.

'Seconded? Who the hell authorises secondment on a job like this?'

'It came from the top. Absolute top-level clearance.'

'Top-level clearance?' Dempsey knew every aspect of security protocol. What he was hearing made little sense. 'I want to see the paperwork.'

'You're welcome to it.'

Henley had made the decision to help the DDS agent. He now seemed determined to see it through.

'But I can't give you Jones's current location because I just don't know it. I wasn't given *any* information about him, other than his name and his regiment. It was all regimental protocol.'

Dempsey's eyes narrowed. What Henley was now saying sounded ominously familiar. Echoes from his own past. Dempsey knew the answer to his last question before he had even asked it.

'Regimental protocol? What are you talking about? What regiment?'

'You of all people should know that, Major.' It was Henley's turn to seem confused. 'I'm talking about his regiment. *Your* regiment. Sergeant Jones was seconded to us from the SAS.'

SEVENTEEN

Daniel Lawrence took in his surroundings as he approached the custody desk at Paddington Green. It would be an exaggeration to call the place quiet. A better description was dead. Daniel had visited countless police stations. Never this particular one. But as London's most secure custody suite it should surely be the busiest of all?

So far Daniel had seen just one man.

'Is it always this deserted here?' he asked.

'First time I've seen it this way.' Sergeant Trevor Henry's answer carried an impatient tone. 'First time I've seen an ex-president shot, too. You do the maths.'

Daniel stopped for a moment. He looked Henry up and down. Ten different responses sprang to mind. All of them would put the rude police sergeant in his place. He chose to suppress them and remain civil.

'But where is everyone? Surely the place should be crawling with spooks? CIA? MI5?'

'They've got their own way of dealing with things. They were all here earlier. Cleared out every police officer but me. Place has got to have a custody sergeant. Even for a case like this.'

'When are they coming back?'

'Your guess is as good as mine. I suppose they're giving you time to speak to him before the interview.'

Daniel nodded. It made logical sense. The security services had twenty-eight days in which to question Eamon McGale before they had to either charge or release him. With that timescale they did not need to hang around while he spoke to his lawyer. Which explained why the place felt like a ghost town. He turned back to Henry.

'OK then, Sergeant. I suppose we should get this started.'

Daniel's eyes stayed fixed on Eamon McGale as the interview room door was closed behind him. McGale looked back. Silent. His gaze firm. This was not a man ashamed of what he had done.

Not a word was said as Daniel took his seat across the table. He took a few moments to study McGale. The man was small and thin. His age was hard to guess. There was little weathering of his face and even his hands seemed youthful, but while his looks suggested a man in his fifties, his eyes were those of a much more aged soul. He wore a paper forensic suit in place of his confiscated clothing. It already looked as if he had been sleeping in it for weeks. The shambolic appearance did not sit comfortably with the determination behind his eyes.

'Mr McGale, my name is Daniel Lawrence. I've been appointed to represent you.'

Daniel's voice was confident. No hint of his uncertainty. He reached out a hand and McGale took it. The older man's grip was firm but not tight.

'It's a pleasure to meet you, Mr Lawrence.'

Daniel was surprised by McGale's cultured Irish voice. He was not sure why. The lack of calluses on the man's hand suggested a professional. Someone more used to an office than a field. It was not what Daniel would usually expect from a terrorist gunman; they were rarely the intellectuals of the cause.

'Obviously you know why we're both here. But before we discuss today's events I want to assure you that I act in your interests alone. As your lawyer it's my responsibility—'

McGale raised a thin hand. Daniel stopped speaking.

'Mr Lawrence, I am very familiar with the procedures and with the criminal justice system. Please don't feel you have to explain them to me.'

'Then you've had involvement with the police before?'

'No, sir. Far from it. But I do lecture on the subject a little. I'm a professor of Political Science. So you can assume I know the basics.'

'You're a professor. And yet—'

McGale raised his hand once again. Daniel guessed it was a throwback from his teaching career. A method to silence his students. He obeyed.

'Perhaps it's best if I just explain myself, Mr Lawrence. Then I can answer any questions you have.'

Daniel nodded. McGale did the same. And then he waited, breathing deeply. To Daniel he looked to be steeling himself for what he was about to say.

When he finally spoke it was a torrent. Fast and uncontrolled.

'Mr Lawrence, I did what I did today because I believe it was the only course of action left open to me and I believe that my actions were the very best thing I could do for my country.

'I have spent my adult life studying, writing and lecturing on Political Science. I believe passionately in the peaceful resolution of political differences. My entire career has been the pursuit of the ultimate solution to the Troubles that have torn my country apart. Thirty years, Mr Lawrence. Thirty years dedicated to teaching future generations that we could bring these Troubles to an end through negotiation and compromise. I taught my own sons that same lesson. I had nothing but hope for the future. But that is a thing now denied to my children. They will never play a part in their country's future. They will never do anything, Mr Lawrence, because not everyone wants to see an end to the hell that blights Ireland. My children and my wife were taken from me. They were killed because not everyone will gain from bringing unity to Ireland. Some people have everything to lose, and those people will do anything to derail peace.

'It took me time and effort to see that, Mr Lawrence. But once I saw it I realised that my approach did not work. Once I realised why my life had been torn apart – and that this would happen again and again without drastic action – I saw that something *had* to be done. What I did today was for myself, my family and my country. I will stand up and say that in any court in which I must appear.'

McGale stopped speaking. He sat back in his chair. And yet he seemed to leave an aura of intensity behind. What he had said took Daniel by surprise. He had never heard such a perfectly articulated explanation for murder. They were not the words of a fanatic. They were the words of an educated man. One who believed in the sentiments he expressed. One who had taken the only course he felt left open to him.

Seconds passed in silence, maybe even minutes, as Daniel tried to take in what he had been told. It was too much information. Too much of a shock. Nothing had prepared him for the rationality of a man he had assumed to be either a fanatic or a psychopath. But McGale was neither. That much was obvious.

'Mr Lawrence, do you perhaps need a moment?' McGale finally spoke again.

Daniel looked up. He had not noticed his own silence. Now he was all too aware of it. He floundered. Forced himself to think on his feet. Every question seemed to arrive at once. When had McGale's family died? What investigations had led him to Trafalgar Square? There were many queries, but only one demanded an immediate answer.

'Eamon, I don't understand. What on earth did Howard Thompson have to gain from derailing the peace process?'

McGale's eyes bore into Daniel's as he spoke. A look of pain – of regret – flashed across them as he listened to the question. The same emotion filled his voice as he replied.

'Mr Lawrence, I can understand why you might think that Howard Thompson was my target today. But please believe me when I tell you this: that he was injured is something I will always regret. He is a great man who tried to do great things for my country. I would not see him hurt, not for the world. I went to Trafalgar Square to kill one person today, Mr Lawrence. And I succeeded. Neil Matthewson was an evil, evil man with a nation's blood on his hands. He deserved to die the painful death I gave him.'

Daniel leaned forward and prepared to ask his next question. A surge of excitement fuelled him. He wanted to know everything.

'Mr Lawrence, are you planning to drive out of my station or are you going to sit there all night?'

Trevor Henry's voice burst through the intercom at the station gates.

'Only it'd be a shame to close the gates on your nice new car.'

It had been an hour and a half since Daniel's meeting with McGale had begun. The longest ninety minutes of his life. Everything he had learned had shaken him. Shock after shock. He had been relieved when Henry had interrupted to tell them that McGale's official interview had been rescheduled to the next morning. He was not sure he could have faced it tonight.

Daniel apologised, then turned his Porsche out of the gate and onto the quiet road outside. The tranquillity was broken by his roaring engine as he pulled away.

Sarah Truman smiled as she watched Daniel's tail lights disappear. Moments later, Jack Maguire fired up their own engine. Both were happy. Maguire's instincts had secured them information unknown to the reporters out front. Which meant their wait here was over.

Neither Sarah nor Maguire noticed the ignition of a third engine. And so, as they pulled onto the eastbound carriageway of the A40 arterial road, they paid no attention to the black Land Rover that headed off in the same direction as Daniel's speeding Porsche.

EIGHTEEN

'If you could get him to call me as soon as possible, I'd appreciate it. It's urgent.'

Dempsey replaced the telephone receiver. For a moment he remained still, contemplating his next step. Then his hand moved across to a slim manila file that sat on the table. With a flick of his fingertips he slid it back towards himself. He picked it up and opened the cover. Not for the first time. Or even the twenty-first.

The file contained a single page; hardly worth the binder. Dempsey's eyes scanned it once more. It contained little information. Certainly nothing he had missed on previous reads. As before, three blocks of text stood out. The first was a name: Sergeant Steven Jones. The second was a location: Credenhill Barracks, Herefordshire, home of 22 SAS. The third was a signature. An indecipherable scrawl that Dempsey would know anywhere. It was the mark of Callum McGregor.

The presence of McGregor's name had been a shock, but any suspicions it aroused were quickly put to rest. Assistant Commissioner Alex Henley had explained that top-level clearance had been needed to authorise a replacement for his team of sharpshooters. This had to come from the operational commander, and that was Callum McGregor. The explanation made sense. It was confirmed by McGregor himself.

Dempsey closed the binder and slid it back across the table. Back towards a telephone he knew would soon ring. When it did he would want the information close at hand. In the meantime, his eyes darted to a second set of papers. Thicker and well-thumbed. They sat on a bookshelf at the far side of the desk.

The room Henley had assigned to Dempsey within New Scotland Yard was small, little more than a cubbyhole. Dempsey's own office was much larger but it was in Vauxhall, ten minutes away in typical London traffic. For now Dempsey was working with Henley to track down Sergeant Steven Jones. In the circumstances, 'close' beat 'comfortable'.

Dempsey had so far paid less attention to this larger file than to the single page that remained by the telephone. The information on that sheet had been more important, but nothing could now be done about Steven Jones until Dempsey's call was returned. This left time to consider Sergeant John Dutton, the man Jones had replaced.

Dutton's file read like a *Boys' Own* special. At thirty-five years of age he was a thirteen-year veteran of the Metropolitan Police. In that time he had done it all. Territorial Support Group. Flying Squad. The Met's dedicated firearms unit, SO19. And now Counter Terrorism Command.

Henley had described Dutton as his best. It was not an exaggeration.

Dempsey's mind ticked over as he flicked through Dutton's file. He focused on what Henley had told him. Dutton had called in sick the previous evening. Not just off-colour but bed-ridden; plagued by crippling stomach cramps and fever. The timing in itself was suspicious. That it should happen to the team leader – the one man who could not be replaced from within – was downright compelling.

A photograph was attached to the top right-hand corner of the first page. Dutton looked just as Dempsey would expect.

Rough and ready. A man of action. Further investigation was needed, of course, but Dempsey was already as sure as he could be that Dutton was a patsy. Taken out of the picture and replaced by someone more compliant. Someone who *was* a traitor: Sergeant Steven Jones.

Dempsey's eyes flicked back to the first file. He was tempted to pick it up once again. But he knew it would still tell him nothing new. Instead he would wait for the call from Jones's commanding officer. Then, when he knew more, Dempsey would find out everything else from Jones himself. Face to face.

For just a moment Dempsey pictured himself confronting Sam Regis' killer. What would be expected of him, in those circumstances? The same as was always expected of him, Dempsey knew. That he would do his duty. Dempsey would be expected to listen to what Jones had to say and to reach his own conclusions. Always efficient. Always professional. But what if this time Dempsey was not? What would happen if, just this once, he allowed his emotions to take over? It would be no pleasure to Dempsey. Violence never was; he had grown to hate that element of his life. But, damn, it would be justified. Sam was . . . had been . . . a friend. Dempsey had few enough of those, and to lose one like this?

It was not something that Dempsey could allow himself to dwell on. So he was happy for his attention to be caught by the small rolling news box in the top corner of his computer screen.

In it was the image of Anthony Haversume.

The politician seemed to be holding a press conference. Dempsey clicked on an icon that enlarged the image and raised the volume:

'I have nothing but good memories. Good memories of a man who had so much more to do, both personally and politically. It is no secret that Sir Neil and I were sometimes at opposite ends of the political spectrum. But I have never worked with someone for whom I had such unfettered respect. I do not expect to do so again. Sir Neil was a great man, a great statesman and an example of what every aspiring leader should be. A man who made one proud to be British. It is my belief that we have today lost the man who should and would have been our next prime minister. He would have enjoyed *my* wholehearted support at the very least. But thanks to yet another act of violence, I have lost a dear friend. The nation has lost the leader it deserves. Most of all, a loving family has lost the most wonderful father. To call what occurred today a tragedy isn't strong enough. I'm afraid that there are no suitable words.'

Dempsey nodded to himself. He agreed with every word. Matthewson had been a great man. One of the few statesmen Dempsey could bear. His death was a loss to the nation and, according to what he had just heard, a personal loss to the man on screen. Dempsey had not known that Matthewson and Haversume were friends. Why would he? But there could now be no doubt that they were. Haversume's eyes had started to well with the first hint of tears. It caused him to pause.

Dempsey sat back to hear what Haversume would say next. He expected it would be another condemnation of William Davies' government and its failure to deal with the fresh wave of Irish terrorism. Every time Haversume had spoken in recent months had been on that subject. They were not views that Dempsey shared. *His* life experiences were real. Raw.

They told him that compromise was rarely less desirable than murder.

It was hard now for Dempsey to recall a life before this. For two decades he had lived with extreme violence and death. His time in the SAS – and beyond – had been dedicated to both. And from the very beginning he had been good. Very, very good. But time and experience can change a man. And now, in his mid-thirties, Dempsey was sure that he could happily live the rest of his years without firing another bullet or throwing another punch.

William Davies seemed to have similar ambitions, only *his* extended to a far larger scale. Davies had risked his political future to bring institutionalised violence to an end, at least in Ulster. Those efforts may have failed but Dempsey respected Davies for making them. He also respected Haversume. Haversume had taken a stand on principle. Whether Dempsey agreed with his beliefs or not, he appreciated what a rare strength that was in a politician.

The press conference continued. But Dempsey would not get the chance to listen. He clicked away from the news screen – silencing the audio feed – the instant his telephone began to ring. It had time to chirp only once before the receiver was at his ear.

'Joe Dempsey.'

'Major Dempsey. This is Major General Arthur West, Director Special Forces. I understand you've been trying to contact me.'

West's voice was clipped. Matter-of-fact.

'I have, sir. I'm trying to locate one of your men. Sergeant Steven Jones.'

'Yes, I'm aware of that. What do you need to know, Major?'

'For now I just want to know where he is. Jones didn't wait to be debriefed this afternoon. Given what happened, it's a process we need to complete.'

'I've been told that. That he didn't wait, I mean.'

A little emotion now began to colour West's voice. It carried more than a hint of disappointment.

'I can only apologise. I don't need to tell you what a highly unusual course of conduct this is, Major. It concerns me.'

West's honesty was blunt. Dempsey knew why. The major general would have been less forthcoming if not speaking to a fellow SAS officer. Dempsey was now firmly ensconced within the DDS, but no soldier ever really leaves the regiment.

'I understand, sir. And *you'll* understand why I'm keen to speak to him. Failure to attend for debriefing is not usual procedure. I can't think he'd avoid questioning just because of a bullet going where it shouldn't.'

Dempsey's comment was intentionally flippant. He could not reveal an emotional attachment to Sam Regis. Important though their friendship had been to him, the investigation came first. Everything else had to be suppressed.

'I agree. He has some serious questions to answer. But as to his whereabouts, I'm afraid I can be of little help. He should have been back in Credenhill over an hour ago.'

'But he isn't?'

'No. We've tried to contact him but have not succeeded. But I am confident that he'll be back within hours, Major. Despite the black mark of today he is an absolute professional.'

'He wouldn't be the first one of those to turn over, sir.'

Dempsey knew what he was talking about. Knew from bitter experience.

'You'll find that times have changed since the era of Sergeant Turner, Major. Our psychologists are alive to these issues.'

'People can always slip through the cracks. Sir.'

Silence followed Dempsey's last comment. Both men knew

who they were referring to. And neither was likely to agree with the other's point of view.

West moved the discussion on.

'The only question then, Major, is what you want done with Sergeant Jones when he finally turns up?'

'I'd like him separated from all contact with others and placed in a holding area. To await my own arrival. I'll conduct the debriefing myself, along with Assistant Commissioner Alex Henley of the Metropolitan Police who had command of the unit to which Sergeant Jones had been seconded.'

'I understand, Major. Continuity in debriefing is obviously preferable. We will await your arrival.'

Dempsey had feared that West would find his request irregular. After all, Credenhill was full of experienced officers well qualified to carry out the debriefing exercise. That fear was misplaced. West was obviously keen to cooperate. Which encouraged Dempsey to push his luck ever further.

'There is one other thing, sir. Could you send me Sergeant Jones's file? It'll help me to prepare his debrief as we travel.'

'Consider it done. I'll have it emailed immediately.'

West was being as helpful as possible. He clearly did not want Jones's failure to reflect upon his regiment. He continued.

'I look forward to meeting you in a few hours, Major. I've heard a lot about you. It's unfortunate that we'll be meeting in these circumstances.'

'It is, sir. Thanks for all your help. I'll see you in a few hours.'

Dempsey placed the receiver down. He glanced towards his computer monitor. Haversume's speech had ended. It did not matter. Dempsey could not have concentrated on it anyway, not after West's call.

His mind was racing. West was concerned by Jones's failure to remain for debriefing. That much was clear. And he seemed just as unhappy that the sergeant had yet to return to barracks. All of this told Dempsey that he was on the right track.

Dempsey sat in silence for several minutes. Every scenario, explanation and excuse raced through his mind. He analysed them all. Strengths and weaknesses were identified. Probabilities assessed. Everything Dempsey had learned in the last twelve hours was compared, contrasted and compartmentalised with a speed that few could match. There was a reason Dempsey was as good as he was, and it was not wholly physical.

Finally, Dempsey turned to his computer and opened his email. West had been true to his word. Waiting for Dempsey was a one-line email with Jones's personnel file attached.

Dempsey opened the attachment and pressed 'print'. It took a full five minutes, and what emerged from the printer was a very different proposition from the one-pager Henley had provided.

Dempsey secured the papers within a ringbinder, then began to read. He had seen countless files of this type. Each a soldier's life, condensed into sound bites and statistics. Cold but necessary, they combined to provide a complete record of twentieth- and twenty-first-century warfare.

Dempsey flicked from page to page. He knew what to look for.

The file was impressive. Jones had spent eight years in the SAS. Which meant he overlapped with Dempsey's own service. Wondering if their paths may have crossed, Dempsey turned back to the file photograph. It was not a face he remembered.

In those eight years Jones had seen service across the globe. The file recorded many examples of medal-winning conduct in well-known war zones. That was to be expected. It also detailed his more discreet activities, in situations that would never make the news. The inclusion of this sensitive material confirmed what Dempsey already suspected: Major General West was holding nothing back.

Dempsey read for five more minutes: longer than it would usually take, but Jones had seen a lot of action. Finally, he closed the file and set it down ahead of him. His eyes settled on the grainy military photograph. Looking but not seeing. Dempsey's mind was elsewhere. It was fixated on one burning question: why would Jones turn his back on his country? There was nothing in the file to hint at a traitor. But what other explanation was there? Unlikely as treachery was, that a professional like Jones would leave the scene before debriefing and then not make contact with his barracks was even more so.

No. Traitor it had to be.

Dempsey had seen it before.

Twenty minutes later Dempsey strode into Alex Henley's office. It was a bigger room than the cupboard he had been given, but still small for such a senior officer. Space was obviously at a premium in New Scotland Yard.

Dempsey threw the file down onto the desk. Henley's eyes followed it, then looked back for an explanation. He did not get one.

'Get your coat. We're leaving in ten minutes.'

If Henley was surprised, he did not show it. He just smiled and shook his head. Dempsey's intensity seemed to amuse him.

'Do you mind if I ask where we're going?'

'Herefordshire. Credenhill Barracks. Your shooter should

be getting back there any minute. You and I are going to debrief him.'

'You're not serious? You want us to travel to the other side of the country for a debriefing that officers there could do?'

'No one else debriefs him.' Dempsey's voice invited no argument. 'He's got a lot of serious questions to answer. You were his commanding officer. You should be there too.'

Dempsey's tone was all it took. It was clear he would not be accepting 'no' for an answer. This was going to happen, whether Henley liked it or not.

Henley got to his feet, reached for his dark raincoat and pulled it over his pristine uniform.

'You first, Major.'

Henley indicated towards the office door. Dempsey looked over Henley's shoulder, towards the desk.

'Don't forget his file.'

Henley followed Dempsey's gaze and looked down at the manila envelope in front of him. It seemed to confuse him.

'Whose file?' Henley asked.

'The file I just gave you. It's Sergeant Jones's military jacket. His personnel records. We need it for his debrief.'

Henley's eyes returned once again to the file. He picked it up. First he looked at the photograph, then he flicked briefly through its pages.

'You're sure this is Steven Jones's file?'

Henley's voice was uncertain. He seemed doubtful.

'Yes. Why?'

'Because I met Sergeant Jones today, Major.'

Henley held up the closed binder and tapped the photograph with his finger.

'And this isn't him.'

NINETEEN

Michael Devlin sat in the living room of his Islington home. A large flat-screen TV dominated, casting the only light in a masculine room. A room built and decked out for function, not effect. Bare wooden floors under black leather sofas that were angled for the best view of the screen. A top-of-the-range stereo. Small wireless speakers on every white wall. A steel and glass coffee table, positioned for Michael's feet. That the space was aesthetically pleasing was a happy coincidence.

He took a swig from the bottle of Mexican lager that dangled from his fingertips. Relished the slight sting of the lime wedged in its neck. The TV remote control was in his left hand, resting across the neck of Cass, his six-year-old pedigree Rottweiler. Originally bought as a guard dog, Cass had proved spectacularly unsuited to the role and had long ago forced his way indoors. He now lay on the sofa with his square head resting on Michael's lap. He should have looked out of place, and yet somehow he was as well suited to the room as everything else.

Not that Michael was giving this any thought. The screen held his full attention. It had for hours. He had reached his chambers in time for the first rerun of Jack Maguire's live recording. It had been early enough to catch Sarah Truman's original report, before she was replaced by Martin Hone. From that point onwards he had been hooked.

Michael was a product of the Troubles. He had grown up around bullets and bombs. It had left him with an understanding of terrorism that others lacked, and an interest in the attacks that had rocked the British government over the past year.

Experience had told Michael that this recent terror was different from what had come before. Harder to read. It was unusual that both Catholic *and* Protestant groups would attack the British mainland. That had not happened in the past. Now it seemed a regular occurrence. One side would bomb, the other would retaliate. Tit-for-tat. It was not the usual way. Michael's instincts told him that something about it was wrong. Those same instincts were at work now. And they left him in no doubt that the horror on screen had its roots in the north of Ireland.

The images had been shocking at first viewing, even to Michael. He wondered how much more devastating they must have been to the general public – to men and women who had not seen such violence up close. But now? After so many hours of replay and repeat, the footage was losing its effect. Its familiarity was numbing the horror. It was a natural human reaction. It just seemed to come that bit easier to Michael.

His eyes had stayed fixed on the screen while his mind slowly closed down. If asked later, he would be unable to recall how long he had sat and stared at the TV. Taking nothing in. Images that should have made him sick to his stomach were now washing over him like so much static. It was almost hypnotic. A trance, broken by the unexpected appearance of Anthony Haversume MP.

The footage that had been replayed throughout the day had been interrupted, replaced by a live press conference. There had been no warning that the screen's cycle would be broken and so the sudden close-up of Haversume hit Michael like a physical jolt. It cut through the last effects of his near-sleep. Swallowing what was left of his neglected beer, he cancelled the 'mute' button on the remote. The room was instantly filled by Haversume's trained voice, lamenting the loss of Neil Matthewson.

A tall, slim and elegant man in his early fifties, Haversume was usually the epitome of professional calm. Not today. Today he struggled with his emotions. Michael understood why. He knew Haversume personally because Daniel Lawrence happened to be Haversume's godson, and so Michael was aware of how close the politician had been to Sir Neil Matthewson. Haversume had lost a 'brother'.

Haversume had paused for a few moments as he composed himself. But the cameras gave him no respite. They zoomed in on his pain, focusing on his eyes. Michael could not understand why the man was putting himself through it. Not when his loss was still so raw. But then he saw something else. He saw fire burning away the threatening tears. A strength that would see Haversume through. Michael knew then that he was witnessing history.

Haversume continued.

'Over the course of the day it has come to my attention that the gunman was an Irishman named Eamon McGale. This is not information the government intends to release to you at this time, but I see no reason that there should be suppression of the facts. You all know my position. You all know the stance I have taken over the past years in response to my own government's approach to terror and violence.

'Knowing that, ask yourself this: how likely do you believe it is that this man was working for one of the Ulster-based terror groups that have been attacking Britain for the past year? I can't answer that question for certain. My contacts only go so far. My belief that Eamon McGale *must* be linked to one of those groups is, therefore, conjecture. Nonetheless, the horrors we have all witnessed today are certainly reminiscent of the cowardly acts those groups have carried out time and time again. I say that enough is enough. It is time to draw a line in the sand and say "no more". It is time to fight back.'

There must be a mass of reporters off-camera, Michael knew. Barely feet from Haversume. Men and women from television, the printed press, even a few from the Internet. Not one of them made a sound. There was not even the flicker of a camera flash. It seemed that no one had expected Haversume to say what he had. And that no one knew how to react. How could they? How could they have anticipated that a member of the British government would publicly name a terror suspect whose identity was still an official secret? Or that he would go even further, and accuse his own leader of ignoring the only conclusion? Haversume had effectively demanded that William Davies put the peace process aside and declare war on Irish terrorism.

Michael's hi-tech sound system could have picked up a pin dropping, and yet nothing came through the speakers but stunned silence. He moved forward in his seat. His keen lawyer's brain was processing what he had heard. Questioning it. He had to wait for the assembled press to catch up.

'What if one of the Irish groups accepts responsibility? How would you expect the prime minister to respond?'

'I expect very little from the prime minister.'

Haversume's eyes were now red. A mix of the tears he had suppressed and determined anger. When he spoke his voice sounded fuelled by outrage.

'I do not expect him to re-imprison the hundreds of convicted terrorists released over the past three years. I do not expect that he will send our Special Forces back into Ulster, to bring those responsible for these attacks to justice. I do not expect him to issue an ultimatum, to Catholics *and* Protestants alike, that they either put their houses in order or face the full re-militarisation of the province. I do not expect the prime minister to do any of these things because they are the things that *need* to be done. He just refuses to see it.'

More silence.

They're not used to a politician speaking so straight, Michael thought.

'Are you saying that the prime minister is no longer up to the job?'

'Yes,' Haversume replied. 'That is exactly what I'm saying.'

The silence returned yet again. This time for good reason. William Davies had been declared unfit to rule by the very man who – with Sir Neil Matthewson dead – was his obvious replacement.

A starter's pistol had been fired on a leadership contest. One with global implications.

Haversume waited unblinking while his words sunk in. He seemed to stare through the screen. Through the silence. As if he were making eye contact with each and every viewer. Michael knew that he was not. That Haversume was actually looking at the blank faces of the stunned reporters barely feet away. He had to admit, though, that the effect was hypnotic.

'Do not misunderstand me.'

Haversume began to speak again. He gave the press no chance to catch its collective breath.

'It isn't that I lack respect for what the prime minister has attempted to do. He took a risk on Northern Ireland. He made concession after concession. He gambled a distinguished career on bringing peace to Ulster. For that I applaud him. But pure intentions are not enough.

'Both the Catholic and Protestant paramilitaries have breached their obligations under the peace agreement. Lives have been lost as a result. And yet the prime minister has lacked the strength to admit that his gamble has failed. He seems unwilling to do what he must to bring the situation back under control. We now need a leader with the strength to protect our country. The prime minister is not that man. He is not up to the job, he is not strong enough for the job and he no longer deserves the job!'

Haversume spoke with rising passion, his words building to a crescendo. His outrage and his sentiments were clear for anyone to see. And they begged a single question of the assembled press, a question that followed as surely as night follows day:

'How can you continue as a member of a government in whose actions you do not believe? In whose leader you have no respect?'

'I can't.'

The answer was unequivocal. This was not a speech that could later be written off as 'misspeaking'.

'The events of the last two years have made my position untenable. Today's attack was merely the icing upon the cake. The position I now take will remain true, regardless of whether or not any Irish terror organisation was involved in today's atrocity.'

'And what exactly is that position, Mr Haversume?'

'I think that is obvious, don't you?'

There was nothing patronising in Haversume's tone. He was too skilled a politician for that.

'I would be doing the United Kingdom a disservice if I were to leave William Davies unchallenged. I therefore announce my intention to seek a vote of no confidence in the government's policies in Northern Ireland. And by implication, in the prime minister's continued leadership of our country.

'If the vote should go against him, I will then stand as a candidate in the leadership contest that will follow the prime minister's resignation. And if elected, I will seek a vote of confidence in this new government. In a government led by someone who will put a stop to the damage being done to this country by a weak, weak man. The time has come, and I for one am ready to stand up and be counted.'

Haversume's last words were a hammer blow, brought down with utter conviction. They were also a final statement. Without waiting for a response he collected his papers, turned his back and stalked from the podium. He had said enough.

TWENTY

Michael stared at the screen.

Haversume was gone, replaced by the sharply dressed BBC News presenter. He nonetheless still dominated. His performance had been note-perfect, every word expertly delivered. Michael sat in its aftermath, an empty beer bottle now barely supported by loose fingertips, his other hand motionless on Cass's thick neck.

A flicker of nervous energy rose up in Michael's stomach. His own first-hand experience of the Irish Troubles told him that Haversume's view was simplistic at best. But still. Daniel's godfather – a man Michael actually *knew* – had just taken his first steps to leading the British government. Michael smiled. He had to admit, the thought of knowing the next prime minister was a rush.

The digitally rendered tune of Bruce Springsteen's 'Thunder Road' broke the silence. It had been Daniel's favourite song for as long as Michael had known him, and so it now served as his friend's personalised ringtone. It was not an unexpected call.

'I can't believe he just said that.'

Michael had not waited for a greeting. Why else would Daniel be calling?

'What? Who?'

The tone of Daniel's voice told Michael that he had not been watching. And the quality of the line told him why. The crackling interference was typical of the hands-free phone system that came as standard in Daniel's car, meaning that he was nowhere near a television.

Michael could always tell how hard his friend was pushing his car's engine by how difficult he was to hear on hands-free. Right now the speed limit was a distant memory. It usually was.

'Your illustrious godfather,' Michael explained. 'He's just been on TV announcing a leadership challenge. Looks like we'll be getting a new prime minister.'

'You're joking?'

'Deadly serious. Plus he's pretty much declared war on half of Northern Ireland in the process. I thought that's why you were calling.'

'Declared war? Over Thompson's shooting?' Daniel sounded troubled.

'Of course it was. Why? What's up?'

'I've got to speak to him, Mike. He's got it all wrong.'

'He's got what wrong? What are you talking about?'

'I'm talking about what happened today. It wasn't as straightforward as it looked. Nothing like it. It wasn't a terrorist attack, Mike. Certainly not True IRA. Or UVA.'

'What? How the hell do you know that?' Michael was confused.

'It came straight from the horse's mouth. Eamon McGale. The shooter. I've just spent the last two hours with the guy in Paddington Green. You're not going to believe what he told me!'

The interference from the hands-free meant that Michael was not catching every word, but he understood enough from what he *could* hear. And it was not McGale's version of events that surprised him most.

'You've got to be kidding, Dan! You've got the case? How the hell did you manage that?'

'*We've* got the case, Mike. You and me! This one's a career maker for us. And it's a career breaker for a lot of others. That's if they're stupid enough to ever let it come to court.'

'What do you mean, "a career breaker"? For who? What did he tell you?'

'I can't say too much over the phone. It's not safe. But I'll tell you this: Tony's wrong. It wasn't a terrorist attack. And it wasn't an attempt to kill Thompson either, whatever the prior intelligence might have been. McGale *intended* to kill Matthewson. Thompson just got in the way. McGale says that Matthewson was corrupt and was even behind some of the terrorist attacks. That's why he killed him.'

The interference was getting worse. It was not helped by Daniel's overexcitement. His voice was breathless, creating more gaps than even the questionable cell-site coverage. But the message was getting through.

'You can't be serious. Neil Matthewson wasn't a terrorist, Dan. This guy's got to be cracked.'

'You *would* think that, Mike. All you've seen is him shoot two people on TV. But you have to *meet* him. You have to *listen* to him. There's so much more to it, there's so many more names. I can't say any more over the phone and it's too late to come to you. But let's meet first thing, yeah?'

Daniel spoke with a tone that Michael had heard before. Many times. His old friend had found a cause.

'Are you sure about all this? Don't go staking your reputation on the word of a lunatic. Who else have you spoken to?'

Daniel could not reply immediately; his excited laugh – almost maniacal – prevented that. It was a few seconds before he could speak.

'No one,' he finally said. 'So don't worry yet. I'll tell you everything in the morning and you can play Mr Sanity. Then we'll decide what we make public and what we don't.'

Michael exhaled a held breath. He was grateful for a small mercy. Daniel had not yet put his hard-earned name at risk by repeating whatever tale McGale had told him.

The frequent gear changes told Michael that Daniel had left the motorway and was now gunning along the country roads that covered the final miles to his Surrey home. He knew how hard his friend pushed his car on this last leg. And how distracted he could be by their discussions. The conversation had to end.

'OK, Dan, let's speak tomorrow.'

'Speak to you tomorrow.'

Michael shook his head as he pressed the disconnect button on his handset and sat back into his sofa. The news had developed throughout the day, before the eyes of the world. It had been tragic. But not for a moment had it touched his own life, and nor had there been any reason to think it would. Not until Daniel's call. But now? Now he felt himself being dragged into a mess they should perhaps both avoid; a political minefield from which any sensible lawyer would turn and run. But Michael knew that he had little choice. Daniel was going to do this. And Michael would be there to support him.

Daniel smiled as he heard Michael disconnect the line. He knew his friend was concerned for him. That he did not want him mixed up in something so controversial on McGale's word alone. But Daniel had no such concerns himself. Everything McGale had said rang true. The man was no liar and, above all else, he needed Daniel's help. Daniel would give him that help, whether Michael was with him or not.

These thoughts came thick and fast as he sped along the country roads that led home. It was a journey he often thought he could complete in his sleep. Which was just as well, as he felt his tiredness begin to engulf him. It had been a long, stressful day. Both Daniel's emotional strength and his analytical mind had been sorely tested. Only now, on the homestretch and with his excitement winding down, did he realise how hard he had pushed himself in the last twenty-four hours.

If he had been more alert – more awake – Daniel would have noticed the speed of the vehicle behind. Instead he had assumed that the black Land Rover bearing down in his rear-view mirror would either slow or simply overtake. If he had known that its driver intended to do neither then the superior engine of Daniel's car could have kicked in, taking him clear of any collision.

Daniel was aware of no such thing. And so his Porsche was no match when the road-legal tank hit him from behind at almost 70 mph.

Even at his most alert Daniel would have struggled to regain control after the impact. The sheer weight of the other vehicle had shattered his rear-axle and sent the back of the chassis buckling into the rear-mounted engine. He had barely time to let out a scream as his car hurtled off the road and into an adjoining field. It flipped four times before coming to a mangled rest. The mechanical soft-top that had significantly increased the car's purchase price offered no protection.

The black Range Rover pulled to a halt by the kerbside. The door opened and a dark-clothed figure stepped out. The man's jet-black hair completed a black-clad image that rendered his body almost invisible in the moonlight. Only his unusually pale skin lessened the effect.

The figure approached the now-smouldering wreck. Once near he crouched and looked inside through the darkness. Daniel was barely aware of him. His focus was on the blood seeping from a deep wound to his stomach as he tried to escape the tangled belt that seemed to pin him to his seat.

There was no pain. That was unexpected. Daniel knew that he was badly hurt. The sensation that his physical strength was disappearing by the moment told him that. But where was the pain? Where was the cold? Was it a good thing that he felt neither? Or did it mean that he was already too far gone?

Daniel's efforts to free himself became weaker and weaker as these thoughts raced through his mind. Finally he stopped moving. There was no energy left to fuel it. Only then, with the distraction of escape gone, did he *really* see the man now so close to his car.

Blood loss had already fogged Daniel's mind, so it took him a few moments to register the sight of his killer.

His eyes bored into Daniel's own. They told him that his life was at an end. He was defeated. Helpless. As he watched the pale, black-haired man step forward, Daniel began to quietly sob for the first time in his adult life. For his wife. For his child. And for himself. A man who deserved better.

TWENTY-ONE

Alex Henley was unused to helicopters. He had been in three in his lifetime, all short distances. Each experience had been worse than the last but none had come close to tonight. It had required all of his concentration to keep his evening meal inside his stomach.

Dempsey had requisitioned an Army Air Corps Gazelle for the journey from London to Credenhill Barracks. It had been waiting for them at a helipad close to New Scotland Yard and they had been in the air within fifteen minutes of leaving Henley's office. That was now fifty minutes and 130 miles ago and, as his feet touched the tarmac of Credenhill's own landing pad, Henley said a silent prayer of thanks.

'Remember to keep your head down,' the pilot shouted over the din of the engines.

As Henley gratefully left the helicopter, he was greeted by a young man in military fatigues.

'Please come with me, sir.'

The young man's uniform was adorned with an officer's insignia that Henley vaguely recognised, and his sand-coloured beret was gripped in the fist of his left hand. His right he placed in the centre of Henley's back, guiding him away from the aircraft and towards a waiting jeep.

Henley glanced to his left and saw Dempsey striding towards the same vehicle. If Dempsey's stomach had suffered as Henley's had, he was hiding it well.

Dempsey reached the jeep first and climbed into the front

passenger seat. A heavily built Fijian with a corporal's double stripe on his arm was behind the wheel. With the front seats taken, Henley and the young officer had to climb across the vehicle's open sides and into the rear.

'Would you like to check in at your quarters first, sir?'

The question came from the driver as he fired up the Jeep's engine. It was directed at Dempsey.

'We won't be staying.' Dempsey's reply was blunt. 'Just take us to General West.'

'Come in.'

A low voice rumbled through a fire door that was marked 'Director Special Forces'. The officer from the helipad did not hesitate. He opened the door and stepped inside, where he stood to attention, his eyes unblinking. Henley was a little taken aback by the formality of the soldier's actions, coupled with the notable lack of a salute. What surprised him far more was Dempsey, who strode into the office and did exactly the same thing. For the first time Henley was reminded that, beneath it all, this was the essence of the man. A DDS agent in name but a SAS officer to his core.

'At ease, Major.'

Major General Arthur West spoke with a quiet, friendly tone as he rose from his chair. An effort to set a non-confrontational mood, Henley assumed. Dempsey responded by doing just as he had been told, adopting a less rigid stance. It was 'at ease', but hardly casual.

'It's a pleasure to finally meet you.'

West continued to speak directly to Dempsey as he moved around his desk. If he had noticed Henley he did not show it. As he approached he put out his open hand. Dempsey hesitated for just a moment before grasping it.

'Yours is a name I've heard a lot since taking this command, Major. It's a shame we have to come together in these circumstances.'

'Thank you, sir.'

Dempsey's response was brisk and efficient. He was in no mood for pleasantries. Henley already knew that. And now West no doubt knew the same. But his higher rank gave him the right to ignore it.

'I trust you'll see no deterioration in the standards of what we do here, Major. Though I've implemented certain improvements, so I dare say things have moved on since you left us.'

'I'm sure they have, sir. But we won't be here long enough to take the tour.'

'More's the pity,' said Henley, keen to cover for Dempsey's briskness. 'I've always been very interested in the training your men receive.'

West looked at Henley, as if noticing him for the first time. Henley offered his hand as he introduced himself.

'Assistant Commissioner Alex Henley, Metropolitan Police.'

West took Henley's outstretched hand within his own and shook. Their respective grips were far from equal.

'It's a pleasure, Mr Henley.'

West's words said one thing but his tone said another. His failure to refer to Henley by his rank told the assistant commissioner all he needed to know. West turned his attention back to Dempsey.

'Speaking of my improvements, how long ago was it that you left us, Major?'

'Four years, sir.' Dempsey's impatience was becoming more obvious. 'I've been seconded to the Department of Domestic Security since its inception.'

'A shame for us.' West seemed determined to keep Dempsey off-subject. 'You've been a very difficult asset to replace. But our loss is the DDS's gain.'

'That's flattering. But if we could move on to Sergeant Jones, General? We're keen to begin his debriefing.'

West did not respond. For a few seconds he was silent. His eyes were fixed on Dempsey but his mind was elsewhere. Finally he let out a deep breath, looked from man to man and then turned his back on both. West walked around his desk to his chair, stopping for a moment to collect a decanter of mahogany liquor and three glasses from a table at the very rear of the room.

Taking his seat behind his desk, West half-filled all three glasses. With a weary flourish he indicated for Dempsey and Henley to take the two seats across from him. He pushed two of the glasses towards them before reaching out for his own. Within a moment its contents had been swallowed. West did not seem to be drinking for enjoyment. When he finally spoke his voice was quiet.

'I'm afraid that Sergeant Jones remains unavailable for debriefing.'

Henley's eyes darted from West to Dempsey. He had been prepared for what West had said. They both had, but they needed their theory confirmed.

'Could you please explain that, General?' Henley asked. 'Why is he unavailable?'

'Because he has still not returned to barracks.' West seemed to struggle with the admission. 'And he still can't be contacted.'

'Seems less than usual, doesn't it, sir?' This time it was Dempsey who poked West with his question.

'You know it's bloody unusual, Major!' West was angry. He probably had been for hours. And now he was no longer hiding it. 'If Sergeant Jones had followed regimental protocol he would have stayed in London for police debriefing. And he would most certainly have then travelled directly back to barracks, which would mean him reaching here at least three hours ago. The fact he has done neither *and* has failed to call in to explain his delay means he is no longer obeying protocol. Which leaves only one conclusion.'

West fell silent. Henley could see that he was struggling with the idea that one of his men could have become a traitor.

'You're saying your man's turned over?'

West's eyes locked onto Henley.

'Yes, Mr Henley. That's what I'm saying.'

'You're not even considering another explanation?'

'This is not civilian life, Mr Henley. My men get on with the job and they follow orders to the letter. Sergeant Jones has not done that, and there is only one possible explanation for that fact.'

'Actually, sir, it might not be that simple.'

Dempsey's words cut through the exchange. Both West and Henley fell silent. Henley knew what was coming. West, however, was in the dark.

Dempsey lifted the manila folder that he had brought from London.

'This is the file you sent me earlier this evening,' he explained. 'I've read through it four times, sir. Looking for some hint of anything in Jones's history. But there's nothing, and for good reason. Sergeant Jones is no traitor, sir, because Sergeant Jones did not step foot in Trafalgar Square today.'

'What?' West made no attempt to hide his confusion. 'What the hell are you talking about, Major?'

Dempsey turned the file so that the text was facing the major general and passed it across the table. West glanced at the front sheet as Dempsey continued.

'Do you see any problem with that page, sir?'

West did not answer immediately. He took a few more moments to study every inch of the page. Finally he looked up and shook his head.

'I don't know what you're talking about,' he said. 'And my patience is wearing thin. So are you going to enlighten me?'

'There's nothing wrong with that picture, sir? You're sure?'

'I've just said that. Now are we going to move on?'

'Not yet, sir. Because if that picture is Sergeant Jones as you say, then Sergeant Jones is not the man who joined Mr Henley's team today.'

'What?'

'It's true, General,' Henley offered. 'I spent time with the man purporting to be Sergeant Jones in London, and there is no way that the man I met is the man in this file photo.'

West's eyes widened, his initial confusion visibly shifting to incredulity.

Henley could see the realisation sinking in. Could see the pieces falling into place as West sat back in his chair and looked up at the tiled ceiling.

It was almost a minute before the major general spoke again.

'So Sergeant Jones was seconded to Mr Henley's team, practically at the last moment,' he said, as much to himself as to his guests. 'Yet someone was already in place to step into his shoes, to impersonate him and for some reason to kill one of your agents? Thereby allowing the shooting to take place?'

'In a nutshell, sir.'

'Major, you must realise the connotations of what you're suggesting?'

'I do. It means that the police officer replaced – a Sergeant Dutton – was somehow made unavailable for service. Dutton may be involved or he may not; we'll look into that. But whatever the answer, there must be conspirators higher up. Whoever did this knew Sergeant Jones's identity. They knew early enough to fake his credentials, which they did well enough to fool every security agency we have. They also wanted someone in place – *best placed* – to make that shot. Sir, we can't say for sure if the shooter was aiming for Sam Regis but, when you look at it, what other explanation is there?'

West did not respond. He just stared into space as Dempsey's theory played out in his mind.

Henley knew from his own experience what he was witnessing. West was trying – struggling – to undermine a theory that could only damage. He was trying in some way to discredit it. Exactly as Henley would do if he were in West's place. Dempsey *had* to be wrong. The shooter *had* to be Steven Jones. Because West's bureaucratic, regimented mind – a mind shared by Henley and by anyone promoted to their elevated positions – could handle a rogue soldier. But a conspiracy that reached high enough to manipulate the world's best security services? One that could put a gunman in place – on the government's own team of sharpshooters, no less – to ensure an assassination? That was a different story altogether. The immediate future would be easier if Dempsey was wide of the mark.

'There's just one thing I don't understand.' Henley's voice broke the silence. 'If this is all true – and it does sound likely – then where is the real Sergeant Jones?'

Dempsey and West's eyes met. Each had spent a lifetime in a more dangerous world than Henley. They knew the lengths to which men would go to ensure success. The price some paid for the ambition of others.

A silent nod from West elected Dempsey to answer.

'Steven Jones is dead, Alex. He was dead from the moment he was put on your team.'

TWENTY-TWO

'I want to know the last person to have physically seen him *and* the last person to have spoken to him. Assuming they're different people.'

There was a new urgency in West's voice as he barked into his office telephone. Dempsey could hear someone on the other line but could not make out the words.

'I couldn't give a shit where the unit is!' Whatever that someone had said was not well received. 'Get every bloody helicopter we've got out there and locate them. Every last one of them.'

West slammed down the receiver without another word. He looked across the desk towards Dempsey, then Henley. He had the bearing of a man who was not about to explain himself to either.

'So what now?'

'Now we look at this from a different angle.' Dempsey's mind was racing ahead. 'We won't know the time frame for Jones's replacement until we know when he deployed. So let's look at this from the other end. What do we know about the shooter?'

Dempsey waited for a contribution.

'We know he had the absolute trust of whoever's behind this.'

Henley had decades as an investigator on his resume. Dempsey was not surprised that he spoke first.

'Right. They did ask a lot from him. Impersonation of

Jones, reliable shot, calm under pressure, leave the scene undetected. That's a lot of trust. But what does it tell us?'

'Nothing one hundred per cent,' Henley replied. 'But it reduces the possibilities down to two.'

'Which are what?'

West's experience was in warfare, not detection. So this exercise was not playing to his strengths. Dempsey was unsurprised as the major general struggled to keep up.

'That he's one of their own,' Henley explained. 'Or that he's freelance with one hell of a reputation. Nothing in between would do. Not for that level of trust.'

'And how does that help us?' asked West. 'If we don't know who "they" are, how does it help to know that the shooter is one of their own?'

'Actually, that's not the possibility with legs.' Dempsey had already weighed the odds. 'We can't discount it, but it's extremely unlikely that someone with this shooter's talents would be on a permanent payroll.'

'Why do you say that?' It was Henley's turn to be confused. 'He didn't do anything out of the ordinary.'

'No, but he didn't have to. Whoever organised this thing, there's no way they go to all that trouble and don't use someone with the skills for *any* situation. We didn't see a tenth of what this guy was capable of. Who keeps someone like that on the books?'

'Apart from you guys?'

Dempsey ignored the comment. He looked towards West and waited for his input.

'So it must be an independent?' West concluded. 'Where does that leave us?'

'Further forward than you might think, sir.'

Dempsey was several steps ahead, explaining one finding while simultaneously analysing the next. He felt energised by the progress his own mind was making.

'If the shooter comes with the kind of reputation we're talking about then it narrows the field. There are only so many guys out there that meet the profile.'

'OK, Major. Perhaps you're right. But that still leaves a hell of a problem, doesn't it? The fact that almost every freelancer meeting that profile has never been seen.'

'This one has, sir.' Dempsey indicated to Henley. 'Mr Henley's seen him.'

'I know that. But what use is it if we can't show Mr Henley a picture of our suspects? With all due respect to him, his contribution is worthless until we've caught the bastard.'

'True, sir. Unless we *do* have a picture.'

Neither West nor Henley spoke. Dempsey was now far ahead of them.

'Remember the question, sir. "Who keeps someone like that on the books?" Well, Mr Henley's right. *We* do.'

West shot Dempsey an angry glare. When he spoke his tone was clear; he did *not* like where this was going.

'Are you suggesting one of my men did this? That one of my men was involved in the murder of an SAS sergeant? Not to mention everything that's followed?'

'No, sir. I'm not.' Dempsey realised that his answer sounded contradictory. 'But then not all of us have been *your* men, have we?'

Dempsey turned to Henley.

'Alex, what did this guy look like?'

Henley must have been surprised by the sudden question, but it did not slow him. He closed his eyes and stayed silent.

Dempsey could only guess at what he was doing, but it was an educated guess; both men had been trained sharpshooters – Henley for the Metropolitan Police, Dempsey for the SAS – and so Dempsey presumed that they shared the stock sniper's skills of attention to detail and absolute recall. It was the latter, Dempsey thought, that Henley was utilising now.

'I can't tell you much about his clothes,' Henley finally said. His eyes remained tightly shut. 'Standard operational gear. All looks the same when it's on. He was tall. Taller than you, Joe. Six foot three, maybe six four. Pretty thin, but with a strong frame. You know, strong square shoulders that belong to a bigger man, but beneath them pretty slim.'

Dempsey nodded and glanced towards West. So far, so expected.

'What about his hair, Alex? What colour was it?'

'Black. Real black, in fact.' Henley opened his eyes. 'Why? What does that mean?'

'Maybe something. I'm not sure yet. Tell me more.'

Henley closed his eyes again.

'He was pale too. Not unhealthy, just very light-skinned. Maybe it's what made his hair seem so dark. Or it might have been the hair that made him look so pale. It's hard to tell.'

Dempsey had heard enough. He turned to West.

'You really think it's him?' West asked.

'It's him.'

'Who? Who are you talking about?'

Henley had opened his eyes. It was as if he had missed an entire conversation in a matter of seconds.

'We'll show you.' Dempsey indicated towards the computer on West's desk. 'Can that thing access extant files as well as live ones, sir?'

'Of course it can. They're under a different programme heading but it's all there. Do I need to ask who we're looking for, Major?'

The two men shared a grim look before West turned his attention back to his computer. It took West a few minutes, but then he glanced up at Dempsey and nodded; he had found the file. Henley got to his feet. Dempsey did the same. They moved around West's desk to get a full view of the screen, which was filled by a digitised military jacket.

At a glance it resembled Steven Jones's file. On closer inspection it was even more impressive. Piercing blue eyes under jet-black hair stared back at them. A distinctive face. Henley did not need a closer look to be sure. He took one anyway.

'Is it him?'

Dempsey was standing at Henley's shoulder. Henley looked up.

'Yeah. That's him. That's the man who said he was Sergeant Jones.'

Dempsey did not respond. Instead his gaze moved back to the screen. It locked on the grainy black-and-white file photo. A face from Dempsey's past.

TWENTY-THREE

The Land Rover door slammed hard. The force with which Joshua had swung it shut saw to that. He reached out with a yellow cloth and rubbed the door panel where his ungloved fingers had touched it. Four days of driving the rented 4×4 before it had become a murder weapon made the exercise necessary.

Joshua's fingertips stung with the pressure he applied. Hard enough that any prints left from closing the door were gone within five seconds. But he continued for another minute.

Satisfied, he stepped back, opened the rucksack he had taken from the passenger seat and placed the yellow cloth inside. It was not alone. Twenty-nine more filled the bag's cavity. All thirty had been used to wipe clean every last inch of the rented vehicle that had crippled Daniel Lawrence's car. The process had taken Joshua more than ninety minutes. Lucky for him he was in no rush.

The collision had all but destroyed the Porsche. The damage to the Land Rover had been superficial. Joshua had easily brought it to a controlled stop as he watched Daniel's car flip into the roadside field. Turning off the headlights, he had waited for the Porsche to come to a rest before getting out.

The instructions had been simple: follow Daniel from Paddington Green police station and make sure that he never reached home. It went without saying that – whatever means he used to achieve his goal – it had to look like an accident. Daniel's choice of car had made Joshua's job easy. The Porsche had all of the advantages in a foot-to-the-floor race, but that was never going to be a factor. What mattered was its size and strength against the Land Rover. In that contest there was only one winner.

What followed was over in moments. On approaching the smouldering wreck he could see Daniel was still alive. Barely, but barely was enough. The wound to Daniel's stomach would kill him; decades spent ending lives told Joshua that. But it would not kill him quickly, so Joshua had helped nature along. All it had taken was careful hand placement and an instant of sudden force to break Daniel's neck. With his corpse pinned into the wreckage of his mangled car, no one would question what had caused the fatal injury.

For all of his compulsions, Joshua felt no need to admire his own work. That was something that afflicted deranged amateurs. Joshua was a professional and all too sane. He knew the feel and the look of a dead man; there was no need to check his victim's pulse for reassurance. Instead he was back behind the wheel in seconds, and back on the road inside of half a minute. It had not been a moment too soon. In the rear-view mirror was the faint flicker of headlights; another car approaching. Without turning on the Land Rover's own lights he had gunned the accelerator and felt the vehicle launch beneath him.

The lack of road lights on the country lane had made driving without headlights difficult but there was little choice: Joshua could not allow the car behind to notice him. Instead he put a clear half-mile between himself and the crash site before switching them on. He had not taken the time to inspect the front of the Land Rover but had expected some damage. The shape of both headlight beams indicated that it was not insignificant: the vehicle could not be driven much further without drawing attention.

Any rental in this price range came with an in-built satellite navigation system, which came in useful now. Just a few quick taps on the machine's touchscreen accessed the 'Points of Interest' menu and the map to the nearest mainline railway hub. A box in the bottom-right corner of the screen stated that Egham station was a three-mile walk, back from where he had just travelled. Virginia Waters station was a mile further, but in the opposite direction. Joshua opted for the longer, safer journey.

It had taken just one minute more to find a narrow lane – little more than a pathway – that led away from the main road. He followed it for another mile, moving further and further to nowhere. His eyes kept returning to the electronic map as he drove. Memorising his bearings. He stopped only when the satnav could no longer register his location.

Once stationary, Joshua had climbed out of the car and looked around. There was nothing to see, just as he had hoped. Still, he had spent five more minutes looking for any sign that the lane had been used in the last few days. There was none. The likelihood that he would be interrupted was close to nil.

So the exercise had begun, with the removal of the satnav's 'brain' from the centre console. With this gone – stored in Joshua's rucksack – there would be no evidence of his recent search and no way to tell where the vehicle's driver had headed. He had then set to work with the first of his thirty yellow cloths.

Within an hour and a half even the most skilled forensic examiner could not have connected Joshua to the Land Rover. Physically there would be no trace. Nor would there be a financial link. It had been rented by one of a hundred stolen identities. An identity he had not used before and would never use again. As always, Joshua was a ghost.

TWENTY-FOUR

Callum McGregor raised his eyes from a pile of papers as Dempsey walked into the office. Dempsey had not announced himself with a knock.

Dempsey had expected to find McGregor exactly where he was: behind his huge desk, working through an avalanche of documents. But he had not expected to see his friend looking so haggard. The day had taken its toll.

'What do you have for me, Joe?'

McGregor's voice was as tired as his eyes. There was no greeting. The two men were beyond that and time was against them.

'A lot. None of it good.' The last words were unnecessary. Dempsey's tone was enough.

McGregor sat back into his chair. He raised a hand to his brow, his fingertips touching the front of his thick, reddish hair. Dempsey's words had prepared him for the worst. When he spoke again his voice was as dejected as Dempsey had ever heard it.

'Go on.'

'McGale wasn't some crank working alone, Callum. There's a lot more to it than that.'

'Tell me.'

'I followed up on Steven Jones, the SAS sniper. All the way to Hereford. I went to debrief him but he wasn't there. He never went back.'

'Then where the hell was he? AWOL?'

'Worse than that. Jones never even got to Trafalgar Square. The Steven Jones who joined the CTC team wasn't the real one.'

Dempsey knew that the director would have prepared himself for what he thought was the worst. It now looked like his imagination had not stretched quite far enough.

'I don't follow. Are you saying I authorised the wrong man?'

'I wish you had, Callum. But no. The guy who joined the unit – the guy who killed Sam – he was a replacement. Someone put a killer on your team.'

McGregor did not answer. Instead he just rose slowly to his feet. His full height loomed over Dempsey. But only for a moment. McGregor was thinking. And when McGregor thought he did not speak. He paced. Dempsey knew that and so he just watched, his backside against McGregor's desk and his arms folded across his chest.

It was minutes before McGregor retook his seat. Now lower in height than Dempsey, his huge width still made the agent seem undersized.

He looked up from the desk. Focus had returned to his eyes.

'You know what this means, Joe?'

Dempsey nodded.

'If you're right it means that whoever is behind this thing arranged it *through* the security services. That they manipulated all of us.'

'No other way to read it.' Dempsey's tone was matter-of-fact. It had been hours since he had reached the same conclusion.

'But the connections it would take.' Dempsey could see McGregor's doubts struggling against the conclusion. 'To force a replacement on Henley's unit. And then to know who that replacement would be, early enough to take him out and put someone else in his place. We're not talking about small fry here. Can we be sure you're right?'

Dempsey just held the director's stare. Neither man blinked. Neither man spoke. It was answer enough.

McGregor got back to his feet. Silent once again as he moved around the room.

'But what's behind it?'

McGregor spoke sooner than Dempsey had expected. This time he had not even retaken his seat. Dempsey looked up as the taller man continued.

'I mean, what's to gain? Thompson's no JFK, Joe. He's an *ex*-president, for Christ's sake.'

'But are we even sure that Thompson was the target?' Dempsey asked. 'It was Matthewson who took most of the bullets, and Thompson survived.'

'We are now,' McGregor replied. 'The True IRA made a verified claim for responsibility less than an hour ago.'

Dempsey took a deep breath. The new information explained McGregor's reaction. Dempsey knew there were holes in his theory that would leave doubts in McGregor's mind. Why go to so much effort for an ex-president when the current one was right there?

Dempsey saw the problem. But he also knew when he was right.

'Callum, there's something else.'

McGregor stopped pacing.

'What?'

'We were able to identify the man who replaced Sergeant Jones.'

At first McGregor said nothing. He just stared. Dempsey

knew what that meant: a hundred questions were filling McGregor's mind.

'You identified the guy? How?' McGregor seemed to change his mind the moment he heard his own words. 'In fact, never mind "how". Who is it?'

'The shooter was James Turner.'

McGregor's jaw slackened as he heard the name. He was visibly shocked. The first time Dempsey had ever seen it. But then how could he be anything else? How could McGregor have expected that Sergeant Major James Turner – probably the most highly decorated soldier in SAS history, and a man whose whereabouts had been the subject of speculation for the best part of a decade – would re-emerge here and now?

Dempsey knew more about James Turner than anyone. That was inevitable. But he also knew that McGregor – like everyone in any branch of British intelligence – was well-briefed on the SAS's blackest mark. So Dempsey did not need to explain who Turner was. And he did not have to explain that the man had specialised in a field open to only the very best military operatives: the termination of persons worldwide when their continued existence was deemed 'contrary to the national interest'. Few knew that the state was involved in such activities. But McGregor's position placed him in that number.

McGregor had been a senior operative with military intelligence during Turner's active years, but he was not then the power he was today. His influence had been more limited, Dempsey knew, and so he had heard the name but had never met the man.

He did not speak as the implications of Dempsey's revelation sank in. Dempsey knew not to interrupt. McGregor was a brain. Smarter even than Dempsey, and so Dempsey had no doubt that the director understood the implications of Turner's involvement.

The pacing began again. The thinking walk. McGregor moved – slowly, this time – towards the full-length window at the far side of his office. Once there he looked out, down onto the deserted Vauxhall Bridge and the Thames running below it.

'You're right, Joe.'

When McGregor spoke again it was as downbeat as Dempsey had ever heard.

'If Turner's involved then this can't be a simple shooting. There must be more to it. Shit!'

His last word was fired out. An expulsion of despair.

'But who the hell's behind it? What in God's name is going on?'

'I don't know.' Dempsey's response was blunt. 'There are a lot more questions than answers right now. But we've made a start. Give me the resources, Callum, and I'll get to the bottom of this. Let me question McGale and I swear I'll find out why Sam died. I'll find Turner.'

The intensity behind Dempsey's words was unmistakable. As was McGregor's hesitation before responding.

'It's not that simple, Joe.'

'What do you mean? What isn't?'

'You know what. I can't be seen to let you run our investigation while you're still in the firing line for what happened. Jesus, for all I know you're still a person of interest in the American Secret Service investigation. And even if you're not, Davies is looking to hang the DDS out to dry on this. Especially you and Regis. Which means I can't stick you in the field, not with that hanging over your head.'

'Then don't let anyone see you do it,' Dempsey said. 'I can do this off the books, Callum. It's probably better to do it that way.'

'Why's that?'

'Because if I'm not on the case then you didn't hear the name James Turner tonight. And you *not* hearing that is the only way you keep control, because as soon as his name is out this whole thing will explode. The Americans will swoop in if the shooter is a man we trained, and you'll lose control of this investigation. But if they don't know about him? Well then it stays *your* show.'

'But the Americans will have to find out at some point. It's not like they'll leave this alone.'

'Of course they won't. But we've got a head start here Callum, and by the time their team digs up Turner's name I'll have dealt with him.'

Dempsey's tone was now neutral. He would take no pleasure in what he was proposing. Dempsey was a complicated man. A trained killer with few equals, but who despised the trade at which he excelled. He was also the best investigator under McGregor's command. The most capable of finding Sam Regis' killer. Both men knew that. And both knew that if that killer *was* Turner, then he could never see a courtroom.

'What about you? You'll have killed a man. When you do that off-duty, Joe, it's called murder.'

'No, Callum. When it's James Turner it's self-defence.'

Dempsey needed to say no more.

'You know I'll have to suspend you from duty to make this look right, don't you? Which will stay on your record.'

'When was the last time I worried about my record, Callum?'

'And resources. They'll be limited. To stop anyone getting wind of what we're doing.'

'That goes without saying. And all I'd need is information, anyway. Just keep my security clearance live and I can get most of that for myself. And anything I can't access, well, I can come directly to *you* for that.'

McGregor was silent for a few moments more. Dempsey suspected he knew what was going through his mind now. When McGregor finally spoke, those suspicions were confirmed.

'What about if it goes the other way, Joe? What if he's better than you?'

For the first time that night Dempsey took a seat at McGregor's desk. He knew from the question that the decision was made.

'If he is, he is.' Dempsey's tone was fatalistic. 'I'm not doing this because I want to find out, Callum. I'd be happier if I never came across that dangerous bastard again. But *we* trained him. The British military. Which means we killed Sam, and we killed Matthewson. So we've got a duty to stop him, Callum. *I've* got a duty to stop him.'

'You? Why?'

'Because I know him. I know how he works. How he thinks. So I might be the only one who can do it.'

McGregor didn't respond. He knew that it was true. British Special Forces had only one active soldier who could be compared to James Turner, and right now that man was sitting on the opposite side of Callum McGregor's desk.

The director looked at Dempsey for a long moment.

Assessing me, Dempsey thought. *Trying to understand me*.

Dempsey had enough self-awareness to know he was a contradiction. A man with such a talent for death and destruction, and yet such a distaste for the same thing. McGregor had spotted that paradox before most. He had even used it to lure Dempsey from the SAS to the DDS, to a life where killing was a less regular occurrence.

He was sure he knew everything about me, Dempsey thought. *But now there's something he doesn't know. He doesn't know if I'll be good enough.*

Finally McGregor spoke. He rose to his full height as he did so. Ramrod-straight and formal.

'Then you can consider yourself suspended, Major.' McGregor's voice was slow, his meaning evident. 'Pending investigation of your actions in Trafalgar Square yesterday.'

Dempsey rose to his feet as he was addressed. He stood bolt upright, his right hand clasping his left wrist behind his back.

'Sir.'

'You of course retain your rank and your credentials, but you understand that you are not to engage in any investigation in your capacity as an operative of either the British Army or the Department of Domestic Security until further notice.'

'Sir.'

'And that you are no longer licensed to carry a firearm of any description within the borders of the United Kingdom of Great Britain and Northern Ireland.'

'Sir.'

'In which case, Major, consider yourself dismissed and therefore at ease.'

Dempsey's stance slackened.

'Because there's something you need to know before you begin.'

Dempsey frowned. A silent question.

'It's about Eamon McGale . . .'

TWENTY-FIVE

The digital clock on the wall twenty feet away read 4 a.m. It came as no surprise. For Sarah Truman this was well beyond the longest day of her life.

She sat in a makeshift cubicle; the closest thing the network had given her to an office. It was cramped when she was in here alone. With Jack Maguire wedged in with her it was practically inhumane.

The space was little more than a well-equipped desk surrounded by three partitions that acted as walls. Anyone over five foot eight could easily peer over the screens, making privacy impossible. This bothered Sarah. Privacy was exactly what she and Maguire needed.

'So what do we know about Lawrence so far?' Maguire asked.

Sarah knew she was being tested. She needed to be in full command of the facts for what was ahead.

'Well, we know he's doing well for himself.'

Sarah replied in hushed tones; 4 a.m. it might be, but the twenty-four-hour newsroom bustled with activity. They risked losing the story if anyone overheard.

'He's been involved in a lot of high-profile cases. Controversial stuff, mainly. It's not about the money with him as he doesn't really need it; plenty of family money to go around. He lives in a big place in Surrey, near the Wentworth Estate. He has a wife and one son, aged ten. He is thirty-seven years old, qualified for fifteen years and for the past eleven he has run his own firm.'

Maguire nodded. So far Sarah had hit every mark. She continued.

'He comes from a long line of lawyers. Father's a top barrister. So were both his grandfathers. He does one case at a time and dedicates himself to it like you wouldn't believe. He really believes in his clients.'

Sarah stopped speaking. Her summary was over. She was confident that she had everything right, but she was still grateful to have that confirmed by Maguire's smile.

'So he seems principled,' Maguire finally offered. 'And maybe he's got good instincts. Like when it comes to picking out the innocent?'

'Then why is he representing McGale?' Sarah asked, her tone derisive. 'It's not like anyone could say *he* didn't do it!'

Maguire did not seem to have an answer. Sarah's point was solid. Instead he changed the subject.

'What about the political angle?'

'Dammit.'

Sarah made no attempt to hide her annoyance. She had left a key slice of the story out of her summary. Now reminded, she sped through what remained.

'Daniel Lawrence's godfather is Tony Haversume himself. Which was important even *before* tonight's press conference.'

'Why?' Maguire asked. 'Why is that important?'

'Because having Anthony Haversume's godson on the case removes any suggestion of an establishment cover-up.'

'Exactly.'

Maguire seemed pleased with what he was hearing. And Sarah was just as happy to be meeting his standards. She was not just remembering the facts. She was applying them like an investigator. Just as Maguire had taught her.

Maguire continued.

'By selecting a lawyer close to the one man who'd want everything out in the open, the government kills any suggestion that they're keeping things hidden.'

Sarah smiled at Maguire's agreement. She knew that the much more experienced cameraman was guiding her. Educating her in the story that would make her career. Sarah could not be more grateful for his help, or more proud that she was learning her lessons well.

It was a short-lived moment of triumph.

A small plasma screen lurked in the corner of Sarah's cluttered desk. Neither she nor Maguire had glanced towards it as they worked through the information they had collected. That changed as its previous multi-screen news stream was replaced by a single live image: the exterior of Paddington Green police station. Ahead of the building, perhaps twenty yards from its front steps, stood CNN correspondent John Crane.

Crane's close-up dominated the HD image.

Maguire noticed the change before Sarah. He reached out and cancelled the 'mute' button on the screen's bottom console. Sarah's tiny cubicle was immediately filled with Crane's East Coast American tones: 'The body of Eamon McGale was found by the custody sergeant during a routine cell inspection at 3.10 this morning. Little has been disclosed at this time but there seems no doubt that he took his own life. How this was done remains a matter of speculation as we await an official statement.

'What we do know is that McGale's death leaves many questions. Since his identity was made public yesterday evening, a complicated picture has emerged of this fifty-six-year-old university don. A Protestant but a political neutral, McGale spent the last twenty-five years as a lecturer at Queen's University, Belfast. This ended tragically, in November of last year, when he lost his wife and two sons to a terrorist attack in the resurgent Troubles. From then on he became increasingly detached from his own life until disappearing altogether just under a month ago. It now seems that in that time his sanity slipped enough to lead to the horrors of yesterday. But exactly how that happened we are now unlikely to ever know.

'More information is expected soon, and we will keep you informed throughout the night. But for now we can summarise the most recent development in this tragic story. Eamon McGale, the man responsible for the death of Sir Neil Matthewson and for the attempted murder of former President Howard Thompson, has committed suicide while in police custody. He died before speaking to a lawyer and before being questioned by police, and so he leaves countless questions unasked and now probably unanswerable. Reporting for CNN from central London, I'm John Crane.'

Crane's image stayed in the centre of the screen for just a moment, until replaced by CNN's unflappable early morning European anchorman Roger Waites. Waites began to speak, his delivery smooth and unflustered; the consummate professional. But Maguire had heard enough. Reaching out, he pressed the screen's mute button. The cubicle was silent once again.

Sarah stared at Maguire as he moved his arm away from the screen. Waiting to catch his eye. When she did she saw a concern that matched her own.

'What the hell just happened, Jack?'

'I don't have a bloody clue,' Maguire replied, shaking his head. 'What do they mean "No chance to see a lawyer"? I thought you checked up on that? I thought you said Lawrence had to be there to see him?'

'Lawrence *was* there to see him. He had to have been; there was no one else in custody. There was no other reason for him to be there. Plus that police sergeant *told* me that McGale's lawyer was on the way. Jack, this is all wrong.'

Maguire nodded but his confusion was obvious. He was as shocked as Sarah. Not just by the news of McGale's suicide, but by the suggestion that the man had died before speaking about his actions and his motives.

'Then that leaves two options, doesn't it?' Maguire finally said. 'Either someone is making a hell of mistake, or there is a lot more to this than meets the eye.'

Sarah had already considered the possibilities. Now she had moved on to their meaning. Her mind was working even faster than Maguire's.

'Jack, if they're trying to hide that McGale saw a lawyer – that he *did* speak to someone – then they must be trying to keep something under wraps . . .'

'. . . and if they want to keep something covered up,' Maguire picked up where Sarah had stopped, 'then we can't just accept that McGale killed himself.'

Both were now speaking in a whisper. They were reaching the same conclusions, and clearly struggling with what those conclusions had to mean.

They sat in silence for a few moments as Sarah allowed their joint reasoning to sink in. She knew that the first option was more likely. That John Crane – or someone briefing John Crane – had made a mistake that would soon be corrected, with the world being told that McGale *had* seen a lawyer after all.

But until that happened option two was still a possibility.

And so it was worth considering the questions that scenario raised. What information did McGale have that was worth killing to conceal? How had he died, if not suicide? And if it *had* been murder, who the hell could get to him within the secure confines of Paddington Green police station, and how did they make it look like suicide? Who could hide the fact that McGale *had* seen a lawyer, and may have already told that lawyer everything? All of these questions hung in the air.

'We know Daniel Lawrence saw McGale,' Sarah finally said. 'But the official story says that he didn't. So does that mean he's in on it? Lawrence, I mean?'

Her tone was confused. Even disbelieving. What Sarah was asking did not sit with Daniel Lawrence's image as an idealistic, crusading lawyer.

'Let's not get ahead of ourselves,' replied Maguire. 'We don't know we're in cover-up territory just yet. It could be a mistake. The official statement might tell us that he *did* see a lawyer, so this could be a red herring.'

'Could be,' Sarah conceded. 'But what if it isn't? What if they say that McGale died before speaking to anyone? If they stick with that, then we *know* there is something going on. No one else knows Lawrence was there, Jack. No one else knows that this might be a goddamn cover-up.'

Sarah could hear the over-excitement in her own voice. She was speaking in breathless whispers, which exaggerated the effect. It did not worry her. Even Maguire, for all of his experience, seemed less than grounded.

'This is Watergate,' Sarah continued. 'This is Woodward and Bernstein. No one else has a clue about any of it. So how about we assume away until we find out we're wrong, huh? How about we say we're in cover-up territory until they prove that we're not? Because we both know that there's no damn story in option one.'

Maguire smiled. A smile of pride. Sarah hardly noticed. She was on a roll.

'So what do we do now?' Maguire asked.

'I say we doorstep Lawrence early morning. See if he can give us some answers when he's not expecting the questions.'

'You want to wait until morning?'

Maguire's tone betrayed him; he was now mocking Sarah's enthusiasm.

'You don't want to head out now? It's not like we need to sleep or anything!'

'Don't try pressing my buttons, Jack,' Sarah laughed. She knew her colleague too well to fall for – or to be offended by – his words. 'The morning's good enough. No one else even knows Lawrence was there, so it's not a race. Plus, I need some sleep. It's been a hell of a day.'

TWENTY-SIX

Michael Devlin sat alone in the empty hospital corridor. A thousand thoughts crawled through his mind. None stayed long enough for an answer. Instead he was numb. Empty.

It had been less than four hours since he had hung up the telephone. Since he had ended his conversation with Daniel, both amused and bemused, with a promise that they would speak in the morning. Since he had feared that his friend was going to make his life more eventful than he wanted. Those fears now seemed prophetic, but Michael had not foreseen how quickly his world could fall apart.

His bedside telephone had barely woken him at 2 a.m.; he was still half-asleep when he answered. It did not last. The sound of hysterical breathing, sobbing and a distorted woman's voice saw to that. Michael could neither recognise the caller nor understand what was being said, but it did not matter. Something was very wrong.

Ignoring his own racing heart, he had called upon his skills as a witness handler to manage the caller. To slow her. To calm her. It took several minutes and, when he succeeded, he wished that he had failed. As the voice of Claire Lawrence finally emerged from the traumatised distortion only one word came to his mind: Daniel.

What followed was a blur and even now, hours later, his memory remained sketchy. He had listened to everything Claire had to tell him. The words had hit like bullets. They should have paralysed him. They almost did, until some primal instinct had kicked in. Somehow, from somewhere, an unconscious sense of responsibility had taken over just as his conscious mind had closed down. A sense that had forced him to act as a brother would. After ensuring that the police officers would remain with Claire until he arrived, he rushed to her side.

The Lawrence property's front gate sat open when Michael arrived barely thirty minutes later. Record time. Not that it mattered now. He had driven the final few hundred feet of the driveway at a safer speed and parked.

The main door to the house had five separate locks. None was secure. Michael did not need to step inside to see why. Before it was halfway open he had been met by the first devastating sight he would see tonight: Claire Lawrence, sitting and sobbing on the lowest step of the main staircase.

Michael had sprinted to her side, past two uniformed police officers stood nearby. His knees had slid the last few feet as he threw his body down, level with Claire's own. As he came to a stop he had wrapped her in his arms. For a few moments she was his world and he embraced her for all he was worth. As if he could suck the pain from her body and draw it into his own. It had no such effect. Instead she had sobbed harder, clutching at the one thing that still connected her to the man she had lost.

The temptation to remain on the floor, to give in to grief, was overwhelming, but Michael had resisted. Daniel's priority in life had been his wife and child. Everything he had done had been for them, and now his friend would do the same. Grief would have to wait.

The next hours had been perhaps the most difficult of Michael's life. Hours in which he contacted Claire's mother and father, telling them of their loss and arranging for them to come to the house that night. He contacted Daniel's own parents and told them, as gently as he could, that they had lost their only son. And he did the one thing that he dreaded above all else. The identification of Daniel's body.

All of this he had done, and it led to where he now sat. On a cold seat in an empty corridor. Just moments earlier he had walked from the hospital morgue with any hope of it all being a terrible mistake erased. He had seen Daniel. So he knew for sure that his friend – the man who'd been like a brother to him – was dead.

Michael stayed seated. This was the third time in his life that he had lost someone he loved. The third time he reacted without tears. They would have been welcome. Any emotion – sobbing; wailing; screaming; even hysteria – would feel better than this emptiness.

'Mr Devlin?'

The voice came out of nowhere. Looking up he saw that the speaker was the police officer who had driven him to the hospital from Daniel's home.

'Mr Devlin, is there anything I can help you with?'

Her voice was gentle. Soothing. Michael found himself enjoying its effect. It gave him something else to think about, if only for an instant. She waited for Michael to respond. He did not.

'Mr Devlin, are you OK?'

'Yeah,' Michael finally replied. 'I'm OK. I'm sorry, I've kept you waiting.'

'Oh no, you haven't,' she replied. 'You can take as long as you like, Mr Devlin. I just wanted to make sure you were, you know—'

Michael smiled. It could not have been more forced.

'No, officer, I can't.'

Michael's words were directed towards himself as much as anyone else.

'I've got my life to grieve, but not tonight. Tonight I have to be there for his family.'

TWENTY-SEVEN

The hotel telephone rang at 7 a.m. It was Joshua's habit to set an alarm call for that time. It was never necessary. This morning was no exception. He had been awake for over an hour already.

It had been less than five hours since he had returned to his Kensington suite. The four miles from the abandoned Land Rover to the railway station had been covered quickly but the early-hours train service had been less efficient. It had doubled his expected journey time. That could not have been helped. Losing the car had been necessary and use of the transport system unavoidable.

The delay was ultimately irrelevant but it had still irked him. Kept him awake too long. So Joshua had hardly slept when his body clock – honed by years of obedience – ordered him up. Rested or not, 6 a.m. would always be his limit.

He had showered before bed and woke up clean. It made no difference. Routine was Joshua's master and so he showered again. Quick and cold. Enough to wash the sleep from his eyes and from his mind. When finished he dried off and pulled on the clothes he had laid out the night before.

Reinvigorated, Joshua turned his attention to the large metallic case that sat by the room's desk. He reached out, grasped it by the handle and lifted. Once it was on the desktop Joshua opened it.

From the outside it looked like any other suitcase, no different to the countless others dragged around the globe by travelling businessmen. Two simple three-digit codes provided the only security. Exactly the impression its makers intended. Once opened it was an entirely different proposition. The second security barrier could only be bypassed by Joshua's unique fingerprint, which revealed an arsenal of weaponry within.

Each weapon was carefully removed and placed onto a sheet he had spread across the floor, between the desk and the bed. When all were in place Joshua lowered himself to the far end of the sheet. Legs crossed for comfort, he reached out and lifted the hunting knife with which he began this exercise each morning. With a sharpening stone in his left hand he spent exactly sixty seconds on the blade, running the stone along its length. Ensuring it was razor-sharp. It always was.

Once the knife was back in place he continued the ritual. Weapon after weapon came to his hands, each one expertly inspected. Modified. Maintained. It was a compulsion. But it went further than that. It gave him absolute confidence. Absolute peace of mind. The closest he could ever come to therapy.

A calm came over him as he worked. It had never been so welcome. His mind had been in turmoil since the first call from Stanton the previous night. Every action since then had been methodical. Perfect. The work of a professional. But always, at the back of his mind, something had been screaming. Only now had that screaming stopped.

Joshua cleared his mind as he reached out for the next weapon. Every distraction was expelled. Every other thought – conscious or unconscious – ejected. It left just one: Stanton.

The man had been an enigma from the start. A disguised voice at the end of a no doubt secured telephone line. The access he had arranged and the information he had possessed had surprised even Joshua. Yet somehow none of this had prepared Joshua for the unthinkable. That Stanton, a man who took such relish in knowing so much, might know even more besides.

But he did. That much was now clear. Joshua was not going to waste time asking how. Instead he concentrated on the meaning of that knowledge. On its effect. It left him helpless, with no choice but to do as he was ordered. It was not a position he was used to. Nor was it one that he enjoyed.

The thought remained for the next ninety minutes. Through Joshua's weapons check. Through a lengthy television news report on Eamon McGale's death. Through his morning bodyweight work-out. Something should have distracted him. Should have replaced the feeling that he was not in control of his own destiny. But nothing did. Nothing could remove the image of his wife and son – the only two people who meant anything – at the mercy of the faceless Stanton.

Joshua pushed himself harder as the clock showed 8.30 a.m. Dug deeper into his well of endurance. He was used to the combination of intense press-up and sit-up pyramid sets. He put himself through them every morning, pushing his core muscles beyond their limits in an attempt to hold back the effects of time. What was not so familiar was the intensity. Joshua would usually have stopped by now. But he pushed on, hoping that the pain would finally replace the misery.

It did not get the chance.

The distinctive ringtone swept every other thought aside. He filed them for later. For now, the alarm bell had sounded.

Joshua leaped to his feet and grabbed the mobile, knowing already who the caller would be.

'Stanton.'

'Congratulations, Sergeant. A job well done.'

There was no need to question the reference. It could only be Daniel Lawrence.

'Thank you.' The reply came through gritted teeth. 'I see you've dealt with your side of the problem. Can I ask how you got to him?'

'Let's keep our exchanges on a need-to-know basis, shall we?'

'If you say so.'

Joshua's position demanded obedience. It did not demand good manners.

'So what now? Are we clean?'

'I think we're very close to spotless,' replied Stanton, 'but not quite. There is one other person I need you to visit for me.'

'Just tell me who.' Joshua was growing impatient. 'Tell me who and I'll deal with it this morning.'

'Not so fast, Sergeant.'

Was there a hint of mockery in Stanton's voice? Joshua could not be sure through the effect of the electronic modulator, but he suspected that there was. It seemed that, despite the stress of the situation, the man was enjoying his dramatic role.

Stanton continued.

'It can't be this morning. This person is currently out of reach. Probably until tonight.'

The word 'probably' felt heavy on Joshua's ear. It was not what he expected to hear from Stanton. It smacked of uncertainty.

'Who's the mark?'

'His name is Michael Devlin. A nobody.'

'Then what's this nobody done to deserve what's coming?'

'I thought we agreed it would be "need to know", Sergeant?'

'I do need to know. Why he's on your radar could affect how I tackle this. So what am I up against?'

'I've already told you. He's nobody. A barrister.' There was a pause. Stanton seemed reluctant to disclose more. Finally, he continued. 'If you must know, Sergeant, I have accessed Daniel Lawrence's telephone records. Between being summoned to Paddington Green police station and arriving there he telephoned no one. But between leaving and his death there seems to have been a call, made from his car. That call was to Michael Devlin.'

'And you're sure it wasn't about something unconnected?'

'Of course I'm not sure.'

Stanton's words should have been spoken with emotion – irritation, exasperation, anything – but the flat metallic tone rendered them as colourless as ever.

'But as they work together on criminal cases, the chances are that the conversation was about Daniel Lawrence's latest criminal client. Which would be Eamon McGale. So no, we cannot be certain but that possibility alone has to be enough.'

Joshua considered Stanton's words. They left him in no doubt about his wishes. But so much was at stake. It would pay to be thorough.

'Then what exactly is it you want?' he asked.

'Surely that's obvious. I want Michael Devlin dead by the end of this day.'

'As you wish. Tonight. Where will I find him?'

'At his home address. It has been sent to your phone already. Along with everything else you need to know.'

Joshua was not surprised. Efficiency had been a hallmark of Stanton throughout. There was no reason that should change now. Joshua took the phone from his ear and opened his messages to find a newly received one that included photographs and information about Michael Devlin.

Joshua read the few contents quickly before returning to the call.

'OK. That should be enough.'

'I would hope so, Sergeant.'

Joshua was irritated by the arrogance in Stanton's words. A less controlled man would have bitten already. But that was not Joshua's way. Those comments would be collected and stored. To be accessed later, when the tables were turned.

Instead he asked the question that most concerned him.

'Surely if I kill this Devlin guy within twenty-four hours of Lawrence, there are going to be questions about both deaths?'

'Let there be.' The response was flippant. 'With Devlin out of the way there will be no one to suggest that Eamon McGale ever saw or spoke to Daniel Lawrence. And without that, what will people see? The murder of a long-standing legal team. Nothing more. They become the unfortunate statistics of organised crime. Your job will have been done, Sergeant. Your wife and your son will be safe, and you will retire a rich, happy man with our paths never to cross again. You have everything to gain from this, so make it happen.'

Joshua heard the line go dead. He waited for a few seconds. Listened as he always did for the telltale 'click' that would indicate a line interception. Nothing came. Satisfied, he reclined and brought the well-defined muscles of his bare back against the cold hardwood bedstead. With his head resting against the top of the headboard he focused his mind.

One more death. One more and he could walk away. One more and he could return to his life with the safety of his family guaranteed. There was a light at the end of this dark tunnel and only one obstacle stood in his way. An obstacle Joshua would remove before the day was over.

TWENTY-EIGHT

'Still no mention of Paddington Green? Or McGale?'

Jack Maguire's eyes bored into Sarah as he spoke. There was excitement in his voice. As if he already knew the answer to his question. Sarah's discovery that Daniel Lawrence had died the previous night had made their cover-up theory much more likely.

'Not a word,' Sarah replied.

She held open the large glass exit door as Maguire struggled through. His hands were full, a camera in the right and a large case of portable sound and editing equipment in the left. Once outside Sarah released the door and watched as Maguire placed his case down, freeing his left hand to reach to his jacket pocket and remove a cigarette packet.

'Back on the wagon today?' he asked, holding the now-open packet out for Sarah.

'Seems like the wrong time for that,' Sarah replied. 'We've got enough going on.'

She took two cigarettes from the packet, gave one to Maguire and kept the other for herself. A few seconds later and they were both set.

They began to walk again, with Sarah now carrying Maguire's case.

'There's not a word in anything I've seen to suggest that Lawrence went to Paddington Green last night,' Sarah observed, returning to the subject. 'It's like he wasn't there at all.'

'So what *are* they saying?'

'Next to nothing, Jack. Lawrence's death isn't on any radar but ours.'

'And they're saying it was an accident?'

'That's what the cop I got it from says, yeah. The way he tells it, Lawrence was in his office till late, ends up driving home too fast. Can't handle the car or falls asleep at the wheel or whatever and "bam". Goodnight.'

Maguire did not answer. They walked on in silence. At least a minute passed, maybe two. Sarah was used to it. She knew Maguire's mind was working overtime. Finally, a few feet from the van, he stopped.

'This stinks,' Maguire announced. 'There's no way that *no one* knows Lawrence was with McGale last night. Shit, we know the name of one copper who *definitely* saw him.'

'Trevor Henry?'

'Yeah. Henry was there when Lawrence arrived. He must have been.'

'No doubt,' Sarah agreed. 'Henry walked through that gate no more than a minute before Lawrence showed up.'

'Which means at least *someone* knows. We can be sure about that. And then the poor bastard turns up dead a few hours later? Just like McGale? And what? We're supposed to accept that it's all a bloody coincidence? I don't think so, Sarah. Do you?'

At first Sarah did not answer. Instead she smiled, dropped her cigarette to the ground and crushed it underfoot. When she looked back towards Maguire her smile widened.

'No, Jack. I don't. What I think is that we're in cover-up territory.'

She counted off points on her fingers as she spoke.

'McGale? Dead. Lawrence, the lawyer they say he never

saw? Dead. Something else is going on here, Jack. Something only we've got a line on.'

Maguire smiled back. But he did not speak. Instead he began to load their equipment into the van. He did so carefully, securing everything into place. When he was done he slammed the sliding side door shut, took what was left of his cigarette from between his lips and flicked it away.

'So what now, boss?'

Sarah hesitated for just a moment. When she spoke she did so honestly.

'I don't know, Jack. That's the problem. I mean, we know we're being lied to but I can't think of a single way to prove it!'

'Then we follow the golden rule.' Maguire's smile grew wider as he spoke. There were still lessons he could teach. 'When you don't know where to start, you start at the beginning.'

TWENTY-NINE

'How can you be sure we'll even be allowed in?' Sarah asked.

The CNN outside broadcast van was parked at the side of Paddington Green police station, closer to the entrance than it had been the previous night. The massed press were no longer out front, and without that disruption the main road had been reopened. Which meant the 'no stopping traffic' rule was back in force.

'They have to let us in,' Maguire replied. 'It's a public police station. They don't have a choice.'

'They seemed to have one last night. No one could get through the front door.'

'That's because last night the station was on security shut-down with a major terror suspect in custody. In those circumstances they can justify it. But with McGale dead? What would a continued shut-down achieve?'

Sarah still looked unconvinced.

'So that's it? McGale dies and suddenly it's not a fortress any more? Suddenly we can just walk in off the street?'

'Pretty much, yeah,' Maguire replied. 'They'll take some precautions, I'm sure. They'll probably have a cop out front instead of the usual civilian police worker. Just as an extra line of protection. But even that could work in our favour.'

'How?'

'Because cops aren't used to handling the front desk and dealing with the press, Sarah. That's what the civilian workers do, day in and day out.'

Sarah nodded. Maguire sounded confident. And he had the experience to back it up. She could only hope that he was right.

The image in Maguire's lens was steady, even as he walked. His focus remained fixed on Sarah's back as she strode through Paddington Green's automatic front entrance. They had agreed in advance exactly how to play this. Sarah did not miss a step. Without checking that Maguire was keeping up, she scanned the room, located the front desk and headed straight for it.

The desk was long, panning from one side of the back wall to the other. It had room to be manned by as many as six officers. Today, with the reception area otherwise empty, there was only one. A young man, barely into his twenties. A baby police officer, just as Maguire had predicted.

'Good afternoon, Constable Mitchell.'

Sarah spoke with an official tone as she read from his name tag. She was playing for the camera. Maguire had seen her do it before, but never on a matter so serious.

Sarah continued.

'Would you mind if I asked you a few questions about last night?'

Mitchell opened his mouth to respond. Nothing came out. The combination of a rolling camera and a striking, confident woman was having exactly the effect Maguire had hoped. The boy was a rabbit in the headlights. Mitchell looked back and forth between Sarah and the camera lens. Twice. Three times. Finally he forced out a reply.

'We . . . I'm . . . there . . . I'm not authorised to speak to the press, miss. And, erm, I don't really think that you, er, that you should have that camera recording in the station.'

Maguire almost felt sorry for him. Almost. But now was no time for sympathy. And Sarah seemed to agree. She played her hand, leaning forward against the counter. Close enough for Mitchell to smell her perfume. The scent and Sarah's proximity seemed to fluster him even more.

When Sarah spoke again her voice was low. Almost seductive.

'Well if you're not authorised, Constable Mitchell, how about you go out back and get me someone who is. Sergeant Henry, maybe?'

Maguire suppressed a flinch. Sarah was pushing her luck. Mitchell should respond by escorting them both from the premises. By force if necessary. The plan relied on this *not* being Mitchell's reaction. It relied on him instead being thrown off his game and thereby getting the attention of the man they were really here to see: Sergeant Trevor Henry.

Maguire had hoped for success, but he had not expected it to be easy. So he was surprised when Mitchell, after just a few moments of confused hesitation, abandoned the front desk and disappeared into the heart of the building.

Maguire's lens remained focused on Sarah. It recorded as she turned towards it for the first time. No words were needed. Her eyes said everything.

The message in Maguire's visible left eye was just as clear. It widened and focused on a point behind Sarah's left shoulder. She followed its gaze and turned. Her confidence – so important to the plan – seemed to falter as Trevor Henry stormed through a security door at the end of the room.

'What the hell are you doing in my station?' Henry demanded. He sounded furious. 'Get out! Now!'

Maguire saw Sarah's feet begin to inch backwards. And then

he saw her stop herself, standing her ground. He was impressed. In twenty-five years he had seen reporters cower from much less. The thought was a moment's distraction. Not long enough that he failed to notice Henry pause for just an instant when he recognised Sarah – a detail captured for ever through his lens.

'What the hell are you doing here?'

Henry hissed the question through almost-gritted teeth. For that moment he spoke quietly, directly to Sarah. Then he seemed to notice Maguire behind her. When he spoke again the volume and the fury were back.

'Get that camera off! Now! You do not film in my station!'

Sarah's natural instinct would be to do as she was told. Maguire knew that. She was the product of a good upbringing, with respect for uniform drilled in. Somehow she forced that instinct down. They had agreed a plan, and Maguire could sense her determination to see it through.

'Sergeant, can you confirm that Eamon McGale met and consulted with a legal representative in this building, just hours before his death?'

Henry glared at Sarah before speaking. Any attraction he may have felt for her the previous night was now replaced by naked animosity.

'Don't be ridiculous, Miss Truman,' he finally said. 'Eamon McGale saw no one yesterday.'

Henry's voice was now formal but authoritative. It gave no hint of his previous anger.

'The suspect committed suicide before any representative arrived, just as has been disclosed. Now leave.'

Sarah did not move.

'Sergeant, when we spoke yesterday you informed me that Eamon McGale's lawyer had been selected. Shortly after that,

Daniel Lawrence, a defence lawyer, arrived at this station. He stayed here for almost two hours. There was only *one* person in custody during those hours, and so only *one* reason for Daniel Lawrence to be here. Mr Lawrence was the lawyer you mentioned and he *did* meet with Eamon McGale. That's right, isn't it?'

The barrage of questions seemed to force Henry onto the back foot. He seemed surprised.

Probably because Sarah knew more than he had told her, Maguire thought. *A regrettable conversation that was now a problem*.

Henry seemed unsure of how to react, and so he resorted to what he did best. Anger.

'That allegation is ridiculous,' Henry barked. 'Now get the hell out of my station or I'll have you dragged out.'

This time Sarah did not move even a little. Maguire could see that she was just warming up.

'Are you aware, Sergeant, that after leaving your station Daniel Lawrence was killed in a supposed car accident? On the very same night that Eamon McGale allegedly took his own life? Doesn't that seem just a bit suspicious to a detective such as yourself?'

Henry visibly started. It was gone in an instant, but not before Maguire saw it. The last piece of information – the death of Daniel Lawrence – had shocked him.

It was quickly hidden. Henry regained his composure.

'Have it your way,' he said. The anger in his voice was missing. The menace was not.

Henry turned his head towards the security door and shouted. The words came out fast but their meaning was all too clear. Within a moment four male officers were in the room.

They did not wait for instructions. Henry took a single stride back to let his men pass, and he watched as they ejected Sarah and Maguire from the building.

No words were spoken as they were manhandled through the building's main door. No threats. No warnings. Once outside the four officers turned and immediately re-entered the building. Maguire watched the officers disappear as the door slid shut behind them.

Neither Sarah nor Maguire spoke. They just shared a smile. What had just happened – and what Maguire had recorded – may have told them little, but it was enough to know that they were on the right track. Eamon McGale had *not* taken his own life, and whoever had killed him had done the same to Daniel Lawrence and then attempted to cover up any connection between the two.

It was the start they needed.

Trevor Henry slammed the security door shut behind him. He was furious and made no attempt to hide it.

'Goddamn gutter press have the balls to bring a camera into my police station and start accusing *us*? Questioning *me*? What the hell is going on in this country?'

A chair unfortunate enough to be in his path was kicked into the air as he shouted. More furniture might have faced the same treatment; if so it was saved when Henry's attention was caught by Mitchell.

'You!' Henry hollered. 'What the hell were you doing leaving those two to film in the station? When the press come in with cameras rolling you throw the bastards out! Simple as! What did you think you were playing at?'

This time Mitchell was not lost for words, but he could have been for all the good they did. They came out in fits and starts until Henry lost patience.

'Stop blooding stuttering! You can't even deal with a woman fluttering her eyelashes at you. Christ, where do we find you people?'

Henry looked around at the silent figures about the room. All had been brought to a standstill by his outburst. He thought about saying more. It did not seem worth it. Instead he shook his head and walked to the room's back door.

'I'm going for a cigarette. If anyone comes in while I'm gone, try to deal with them like coppers instead of horny schoolboys.'

Once outside he moved to the same quiet corner where he had met Sarah the night before. With a glance to make sure he was alone, he took a small, basic mobile telephone from his pocket and rang the only number in the handset's memory.

The call was answered after just the first ring. It always was. The man on the other end of the line demanded such brevity. Just what Henry now gave him.

'We have a problem.'

THIRTY

Dempsey sat alone in an otherwise deserted Westminster bar, nursing his second Guinness of the session. It was the same glass that had sat in his hand for the past half hour. The DDS agent was many things but he was no drinker. For four years he had lived less than two hundred yards from the bar. This was the first time he had stepped inside.

The pub's walls were decorated with inch-thin plasma-screen TVs. It did not take a regular to know what they usually showed: football, rugby, boxing. Anything to keep its customers amused as they drained its kegs and casks. But not today. Today, no TV in London was showing anything but the horrors of the previous afternoon.

The sound of the nearest screen – of all the screens – was muted. Dempsey didn't need it. Even the images were unnecessary. He needed no reminder of what he had seen first-hand.

The sight of Sam Regis falling to her knees, her eyes lifeless and her skull torn apart, dominated his mind. For his whole adult life he had been surrounded by death and by violence. It was the career he had chosen. The skills he had earned. Dempsey had grown to hate them, but never more so than yesterday. Nothing could fuel his distaste for violence more furiously than watching a friend he had recruited and trained die such a death. It was a torment worsened by one sure fact: that only more violence – greater violence – would bring this thing to an end. That much was assured by the involvement of Sergeant Major James Turner.

James Turner was already an established feature of the SAS at the time of Dempsey's arrival. A dangerous man with a reputation for excellence. Older than Dempsey by seven years, Turner had spent longer in his parent regiment before applying for the infamous SAS selection. His time at Hereford therefore predated the younger man by just three years. But he had made those years count. By the time of Dempsey's arrival he was already spoken of in reverential terms.

Dempsey's own situation had been more difficult. As an officer he was under pressure from the start to excel. To be at least the equal of any non-commissioned man who competed alongside him. In the three-month intense period of basic training and selection that had followed, he had more than lived up to that standard.

From the start Dempsey had been the top of his selection group, and by a distance. Before long his scores were rivalling even those of the most recent outstanding recruit. James Turner's own scores had been among the most impressive in the regiment's sixty-year history, and so Dempsey was quickly proving to be something very special.

Whether he would pass selection was a foregone conclusion by the end of his first month, itself a rare achievement in the world's most rigorous military programme. But still his successes had grown and soon the question became whether he would pass out with scores that eclipsed even James Turner himself. It was not a question that concerned Dempsey; no such motivation was needed for him to push himself to the limit, and so he was one of the few not disappointed when he ultimately fell short. While he had surpassed Turner in a number of areas, he could not quite match him in others and – when all accounts were in – the older man had the edge. But coming so close was enough and Dempsey had been earmarked for specialist deployment.

Taken out of the usual stream from the moment he passed selection, Dempsey had found himself assigned to the SAS's most covert wing. A section whose very existence was unknown to even regular members of the regiment. The Chameleon Unit.

The Chameleon Unit included just ten operatives, every one the best of the very best. They specialised in the most dangerous and the most secretive operations undertaken on behalf of the state, deployments where they often acted without a team and, if detected, without the diplomatic support of their government. Selection was a rare honour for any man.

The nature of the work meant that each man usually deployed alone, but still the ten members were a unit. On the few occasions that they acted as a team, their effectiveness was without parallel. This was especially true of Dempsey and Turner.

Each man had heard little but the other's name during Dempsey's selection. It was only natural that they would gravitate to each other after deployment. It was less inevitable that they would become friends, but they did. In the years that followed Dempsey learned more from Turner than he had from his entire military service, making him ever more skilled at what he did. It was a friendship forged on the battlefield, so close that Dempsey's loyalty to his comrade almost matched his loyalty to his country. Until that loyalty was tested.

Seven years had passed but now, as Dempsey let his memories flow, it felt like only yesterday.

Deployed alone, he had arrived in Colombia with a single task: the termination of Nestor Murillo. The country's leading drug producer, Murillo had flooded Britain's streets with high-quality, low-priced cocaine. His disposal was considered a top priority.

Dempsey had found his way into Murillo's secure compound undetected. Once inside, he had set about his business: identify his point of exit; set diversions in place to deter potential pursuers; remote detonation C4; smoke grenade tripwires; concealed head-height razor wire; and, finally, settle upon the ideal location for a single kill shot.

Dempsey knew his job. Knew how to faultlessly camouflage himself and his weapon so a guard just feet away would have no idea either was there. Knew how to wait undetected, without movement, for as long as it took. Days if necessary. These skills could only be honed over time and even then there were few who could perfect them. Dempsey was in that number.

Almost thirty-six hours had passed before the shot presented itself. A shorter time than Dempsey had expected, but he had been ready.

Murillo had been in the compound throughout, but always in crowded company. Such numbers created risk. The likelihood that one of the crowd would wander into the path of Dempsey's bullet was not great, but it was enough. One shot. There would be no time for a second. So he had waited.

The ideal target-point was the side-window to Murillo's own office. Dempsey had to assume that every window in the property was reinforced, which affected his choice of ammunition. To ensure a safe flight path through the window he selected a coated and tipped bullet, designed to rip through Kevlar and steel.

When Murillo had finally returned to his office and took his seat, his head was planted firmly in Dempsey's crosshairs.

This time there had been no crowds. Dempsey had been able to tell from Murillo's movement that there was at least one other person in the room, but now – with Murillo sat behind a desk – the odds on inadvertent interception were acceptable. It had been time for Dempsey to act.

Dempsey had been through his ritual thousands of times before. And yet, unlike Turner, each time his efforts and actions were conscious. He'd concentrated hard, forcing his heart rate to a minimum and bringing his breathing to a virtual stop. The killer was ready.

He'd felt his right index finger caress the sensitive trigger. A movement that had always preceded instant death. But not this time. This time he'd pulled his finger away when he'd seen the movement of shadows across from where Murillo sat, indicating that the second person was approaching the desk. The risk that the room's second occupant would unwittingly enter the line of fire was – for the moment, at least – too great.

Dempsey's eye remained just inches behind his scope. The opportunity could not be missed. As soon as the guest stepped back, and there was no chance of the shot being intercepted, Murillo would die.

It was this determination that would change Dempsey's life. Because, as he took his first short breath in anticipation, he saw a sight that made him choke down the oxygen. There, on the opposite side of Murillo's desk, reaching out to accept a brown A4 envelope from the Colombian's outstretched hand, stood James Turner.

Dempsey's mind was racing before he could consciously register what he was seeing. What was Turner doing in Murillo's compound? And what the hell was in the envelope he had accepted? There was a very obvious answer: Turner would not be the first operative to stray from the path. But Dempsey would not accept the obvious. Not without proof.

These thoughts flooded his mind in an instant. Just as quickly his discipline suppressed them. No matter how unexpected it might be, Turner's appearance could not be allowed to derail his assignment. Dempsey would finish the job. The new problem would wait.

Inching his crosshairs back towards Murillo, he could feel his heart race. It was the opposite of what he would want before a shot, but it could not wait. Not now. The kiss of pressure needed to unleash the rifle's lethal cargo was minuscule; Murillo would never know how little muscular effort went into his death. But then Murillo would never know anything more. The Colombian was thrown from his seat as the glass of his office window shattered around him. No second shot would be necessary; the hint of grey in the blood splatter on the wall behind his seat confirmed that.

Dempsey was not a man who admired his work. In normal circumstances just a glance to confirm the kill was all he took. But this day was far from normal. His eye stayed behind his scope as he took a last look at Turner. His friend – the man he had thought was his friend – was rooted to the spot. The cream linen suit he had chosen to wear in the Colombian heat was stained with the blood of the man who had died just feet away. Turner did not seem to notice. Instead his eyes were fixed firmly upon Dempsey's chosen hiding place. He already knew – perhaps by instinct alone – from where the shot had come.

For a moment Dempsey felt as if their eyes had met. As if Turner could see through the foliage and camouflage. It was hypnotic, broken only when Turner turned and Murillo's office began to fill with men. Those men would shortly be hunting their employer's assassin. A hunt that would perhaps be led by just as skilled a killer. It was time for Dempsey to move.

His preparations did their job perfectly, taking him out of the compound undetected before Turner could even convince Murillo's men that he had no part in their boss's death. The job at hand was complete. Now only one thing mattered.

The next hours were, even now, a blur. Dempsey had made his way to the British Embassy in Bogotá, still struggling to believe what he had seen. But he did not allow loyal disbelief to cloud his judgement. Instead he had made quick use of the embassy's resources. For hour after hour he cross-referenced Turner's periods of leave with killings thought to bear the hallmarks of military sanction. Time and again the dates matched, and finally there could be no doubt.

Turner was no longer killing for Queen and Country. He was killing for money.

The mixture of disgust and betrayal was like nothing Dempsey had ever experienced. Many times he had risked his life for his friend. Had put himself on the line in the name of brotherhood. In that time there had been sides to Turner's character that Dempsey had chosen to ignore. With everything he had learned in the hours since Murillo's death, those traits came rushing back to his mind.

Convinced of what he had found, Dempsey used the embassy's resources to discover both the identity Turner was travelling under and his location. Time was against him. Turner would suspect the worst; that Murillo's professional killer had recognised him. So he would be leaving Colombia in a hurry. Dempsey had hours at best but this was an appointment he would not miss.

Sweat streamed down his brow as he made his way along

the corridor of the run-down Bogotá hotel, a regulation Swiss SIG 226 semi-automatic pistol gripped tightly in his right hand. The pulse in his damp palm was beating fast against the weapon's butt.

Careful to mask his footfall as he crept along the deserted hallway, he moved slowly towards his destination.

Room 26.

As he reached the numbered door he adjusted his grip on the pistol. Felt its reassuring weight. Chambered a round and took a final glance along the corridor. Once he was satisfied that he was alone, he positioned himself beside the closed but insecure door. Usually he would wait to bring his heart rate down but he knew that, this time, it would not drop. The adrenaline was pumping thick and fast. Why had he not waited for back-up, he now thought. He rarely questioned himself. But then he rarely faced an equal, and the man in room 26 was certainly that.

It would not be allowed to slow him. Those doubts and fears would be swallowed. Dempsey was here to act, consequences be damned. A cursory inspection of the room's door told him that it would offer no resistance to his muscled shoulder. With a final determined breath, he exploded into violent movement.

The door was ripped from its hinges by the force of the impact. Its weakness was expected, so Dempsey knew how quickly he would need to move. Years of training took hold at the instant of his first determined movement. He moved into the room at speed, with his sweeping arm covering every angle as his expert eye sought out immediate dangers. They were there, but to his surprise he was not met by violence.

'Didn't take you long, did it?'

The question came from the tall, slim man who sat in a chair at the far end of the room. A semi-automatic weapon sat comfortably on his lap. Turner had made no attempt to move at Dempsey's entrance but he was no helpless target. He knew the intruder would only fire if under threat. A confidence that was well placed.

'What the hell's going on, Jim?' Dempsey could feel his heart race uncontrollably. He needed an explanation. Any explanation. 'What were you doing in Murillo's office?'

'You know what I was doing there, Joe.' James Turner had made no effort to excuse himself. If anything, it had seemed a relief to him that he could finally be honest. 'Don't try to tell me you came here without doing your homework. You've followed the trail. You know about the others.'

'Why, Jim?'

'Money.'

Turner's reply was blunt. It was obvious why. He was in a South American sweatbox, his gun pointed at the one man who might still beat him to the shot. He had reached the most important crossroads of his life.

'A whole shit-load of money,' Turner continued. 'I had a choice. I could keep travelling the world, killing anyone who made our little government uncomfortable. For a poxy sergeant's wage, Joe. With a sergeant's pension to follow. Maybe the occasional medal, you know, to keep the fool happy. Or I could do the same job for a nice big Swiss bank account and enough zeroes to keep me and mine set for life. What would you do?'

A burning lump rose in Dempsey's throat as he listened. Turner was going to try and force his hand, he realised. But he would not believe a confrontation was inevitable. The man was his friend.

'It can't go on, Jim. It stops here.'

'Well of course it can't go on now, can it?' Turner's response was angry. His voice rose as he spoke. 'I was happy just doing this on the side. Making some extra money. But now I've got to make a choice, haven't I? Thanks to you.'

'There *is* no choice. Not after this. Jesus, Jim, these are people's lives!'

'No choice?' Friendship seemed to be giving way to contempt in Turner's voice. 'Who the fuck are *you* to tell me there's no choice, *Captain*?'

Turner expelled the last word with a malice he could not have hidden if he tried.

Dempsey tightened his grip on his pistol as the words hit his ear. Turner's right hand gave the slightest flicker of movement in turn.

'Put down the weapon, Sergeant, and get to your feet.'

Turner did not respond. Instead he glanced at Dempsey's weapon. At his trigger finger. It was almost imperceptible, but not to Dempsey. Their eyes met again. And Dempsey knew then what had to happen. So too, he knew, did Turner. Both had lived this life. And both had survived so far by knowing how to react when bullets start to fly.

The pent-up adrenaline was released in a chemical torrent. Each man dove to his right as they opened fire, to avoid the other's bullets. They both failed.

Dempsey had landed hard beside the king-size bed that dominated the room. Making the most of the cover it provided, he was immediately aware of two very significant facts. The first was that the bed offered no real protection against Turner's weapon; the best it could do was conceal his exact location. The second fact was more pressing: he had been hit. Twice. The first bullet was in his left shoulder, capable of being ignored. But the other had pierced his lung. Without medical attention, it was a wound that would certainly kill him.

The effect of the blood loss came quickly. Dempsey was sure Turner had taken as many bullets himself, but still he had just moments to finish this. Raising himself to his hands and knees, he was poised for one last effort. Only Turner's voice stopped him.

'You still with me, Joe?' It was not the voice of a man in pain. Perhaps Dempsey was wrong. Perhaps the shots had missed. It ripped away his last hope.

The history between the men was vast and so, despite what had passed, Dempsey tried to respond. His pierced lung prevented any sound passing his lips. Ironically it saved his life.

Dempsey opened his mouth. All that came out was blood. The lack of words was unintentional, but Dempsey knew what effect it would have. Turner would think that only death or unconsciousness would stop his former friend from answering.

He might still be right about that, Dempsey had thought. *Just a few minutes early*.

Seemingly confident from Dempsey's silence, Turner had stepped out from the cover of a full-length wardrobe just as Dempsey hauled himself to the top of the bed's mattress.

Their eyes met for a final time. Both men raised their weapons and fired, their injuries hardly slowing their reflexes. Dempsey made no attempt to take cover. It gave him the truer aim, but he received two more bullets for his trouble.

Turner was less desperate than his dying opponent and so he fired his shots on the run. It cost him a kill shot and two bullets to his own back, but it did not slow him down. Even with the impact of lead, he managed to launch himself through his first-floor window and into the alleyway below.

Dempsey had no time to contemplate the fate of the man he had considered a brother. Blood was seeping from his body. His energy was spent. He could do nothing as the room began to spin and the darkness overtook him.

Even now, seven years later, Dempsey had no recollection of the next week of his life. Later he had learned that the military back-up he had not waited for had found him. They had brought him to the British Embassy, where he had drifted in and out of consciousness for five days as his body struggled to heal itself. Dempsey remembered none of this, but at least he had survived. The lack of a body in the alleyway suggested that Turner had, too.

Dempsey had been the only witness at James Turner's court martial two months later. A pointless hearing, held in the man's absence. Turner was convicted and dishonourably discharged, but never punished. And now, after all these years, he was back.

THIRTY-ONE

'Can I buy you another one of those?'

Alex Henley's well-spoken voice broke the silence and forced its way into Dempsey's thoughts.

'Assistant Commissioner.' Dempsey's tone was flat. As yet undecided if the company was welcome.

'Same again?' Henley ignored the unenthusiastic response.

'Please.'

Henley had ordered a further stout – and a pint of bitter for himself – before he even reached the bar. It was hardly a fight for the staff's attention. If Henley had not waited for the Guinness to settle he would have been back at the table in less than a minute.

'I've heard what happened,' he said, placing a full glass next to what remained of Dempsey's last drink. 'With the suspension, I mean. For what it's worth I think they're making a mistake.'

Dempsey nodded. Word of his supposed removal from the case had spread. But he would still need support in what was to follow, he realised. Support that could not come from the DDS. It occurred in that moment that Henley would make a good ally.

And an ally deserves the truth.

'It's actually a little more complicated than that. My suspension, it's not what it seems—'

Dempsey stopped speaking as the nearest TV screen displayed the image of the Houses of Parliament. It was an eye-catching backdrop – less than a quarter of a mile from where they now sat – but it was not what had caught his attention.

'Can we have some volume please?' Dempsey shouted.

The response was almost instant. The sound of a major outdoor press conference filled the room.

Anthony Haversume was standing behind a podium. He was silent. Waiting for the chatter of the crowd to die down. What he had said so far – what Dempsey and Henley had missed – seemed to have been worth hearing.

The man was as impeccably dressed as always. Bespoke suit. Tailored white shirt. Matching silk tie. The last item alone would cost more than a healthy month's salary. But clothes could only tell half a story, because Haversume looked exhausted. He was pale, with a hint of darkness under the eyes. He looked like a man who had not slept.

The surrounding noise slowly disappeared. Dempsey and Henley had missed Round One of Haversume's speech, but they were ready for Round Two:

'There are those who would prefer that I shirk this task. The position I've taken in response to the recent terrorism has made me a target for the very criminals I've opposed. In the last eighteen months I've made huge changes to my life and to the lives of my loved ones, to keep us safe. Those close to me would prefer that these changes were not necessary. If I am honest, I'd prefer that myself. I do not enjoy putting myself at risk. But what would be the price of doing what I prefer, instead of what is right?

'The price is that William Davies will continue on this route. A route that sees this great nation capitulate to terrorism on a daily basis. That sees us freeing those who have murdered our citizens and our soldiers with impunity. That sees us grow weak in the eyes of the world as we are bombed and we are attacked and yet do nothing. This cannot be allowed to continue, and I can do something to stop it. I will do that, risk be damned!'

Haversume's voice had been rising throughout this short section of his speech. By his final words it was close to a shout. Not the calm, considered rhetoric of a typical British politician. These were the words of a new breed. A showman. And they were working. The crowd – made up of experienced reporters – were hypnotised. Once again the politician's words were interrupted by spontaneous applause.

'They're eating this shit up.' Dempsey was speaking to himself as much as he was to Henley.

'Really?' Henley seemed surprised. 'I didn't expect to hear that from someone like you.'

For the first time since taking his seat, Henley had Dempsey's full attention.

'What do you mean, someone like me?' Dempsey asked.

'You know, someone with your background. Army, intelligence, DDS. I thought you guys were all behind Haversume. Or against Davies at least? No?'

'No.'

Dempsey's one-word answer gave nothing away. Henley no doubt wanted more. He cleared his throat to ask a follow-up question. Before he could form it, the sound of Haversume's voice once again fill the room.

'So, as of this moment, I am confirming my position. I will do whatever it takes to protect this country. To fight the evil behind the tragedy of yesterday. I will stand against William Davies' policies in Northern Ireland, and I will challenge his leadership of this country. And if I succeed I will lead us out of these dark times of cowardly appeasement.'

This time there was no raised voice. It was a cold, determined statement of fact. That did not change the response. Once again the crowd broke into a round of applause.

Henley glanced towards Dempsey as the acclaim began to die.

'You don't think that's good news?' he asked.

'What I think is that it's a load of jingoistic bullshit,' Dempsey replied. 'All this criticism of Davies. It's not right. Yeah, the guy's gone about things badly in Ireland. But he tried. Which is more than anyone else was doing, At least he did his best.'

'But you can't think it's worked, Joe? They're bombing us again. Something has to be done, surely?'

'Of course it does. But does it have to be what this guy's suggesting?'

Dempsey indicated towards the screen. Haversume was taking questions from the crowd, but neither man was listening.

'Because what's *his* answer, Jim? Sending our soldiers back in? Going back to war? It didn't work last time. Why's it going to work now? All we'll get are more dead men. Women and children, too. Is that what we want? Is that what these idiots are applauding?'

Henley seemed shocked by what he was hearing. It was unusual that a man with Dempsey's history – a man in his position – would have such distaste for force. To Dempsey, though, it was exactly that history that informed his position. To Dempsey, the cost of war was not theoretical. It was not numbers on a screen. He had seen the death and destruction first-hand. And he knew how little either one of them achieved.

Dempsey turned back to the screen.

Haversume was holding up his hand. The consummate

orator, he was waiting for the noise of the crowd to die down. It did so quickly.

'I know that there are more questions you'll want to ask. Believe me, I am keen to answer. But I ask that you postpone them for the time being. Many of you will already know that last night there was a further tragedy in my own personal life. A further unexpected death. The loss of my godson in the early hours of this morning has left his family devastated. I intend to do what I can to support them in this hour of need and I ask that I can be left to do that. At least for the next few days. I'm grateful for your understanding. Thank you.'

Haversume was visibly upset. The cause of his haggard looks was now clear. This time there was no applause. Instead the gathered press marvelled at the fact that, in the face of such personal loss, the man could have spoken so well and with such conviction.

'Jesus.' Henley's voice broke Dempsey's focus on the screen, just as Haversume turned and walked away from the podium. 'His godson, too. Unlucky chap.'

'Let's hope he's the only one,' Dempsey replied. He took an extra-large mouthful of his fresh Guinness before continuing. 'Because if he gets his way and we go back into Ulster, a whole lot more godsons are going to find themselves on mortuary slabs.'

THIRTY-TWO

Michael Devlin stood at the mirror in his downstairs washroom. He filled his large cupped hands with cold water from the running tap and buried his face in the contents. Next he placed his hands on the square bathroom sink and leaned forward to look closely into the reflecting glass. The toll of the last twenty-four hours looked back at him.

His eyes were red. Not from tears but from fatigue. The damage had come from holding himself together. From being the rock that Daniel's wife had needed. That had taken every ounce of strength he had. The strain showed on his face.

Michael left the bathroom and walked from the hallway to the lounge. The sight of the leather sofa in the centre of the room was welcome. The thought of letting it take his body's weight was almost a physical pleasure, but it was a pleasure banished in an instant. Replaced by the memory of a telephone conversation from less than a day before.

The memory was forced from his mind. Michael would not allow himself to fall apart. Not now. The strength he had shown throughout the day may have left him, but his mind remained clear. Instead he thought through the past hours. The loss of his closest friend was more than painful. As was the need of those Daniel had left behind. Michael had been there for them. They were his responsibility now. What was it Daniel used to say to him? Family doesn't stop at blood? For the first time he really understood what that meant. He would not let Daniel down.

Michael had already taken every responsibility from Claire Lawrence's shoulders. He had made the calls no one would want to make.

Claire's family had come quickly to her side, comforting her as best they could. Michael had played no part in this. Instead he had kept himself busy, scouring Daniel's contacts for details of anyone close to his friend. Those who should hear first-hand.

It had been an unhappy task, but he could not leave it to Claire. Or to anyone else. It was his duty.

The reactions had been varied. Some were stunned, the conversation stopped in its tracks by shocked silence. Others, including Daniel's secretary, simply collapsed. Others still took the news with stoic but no less devastated acceptance.

Tony Haversume had fallen into the third category. He had been the hardest to contact. Michael had finally managed to reach him in the late morning, and when he did the news was taken as expected. No tears. No sobbing. No self-pity. Tragedy was accepted in silence until – in a voice that betrayed the enormity of his loss – Haversume had asked if there was anything he could do to help. Michael had assured him that there was not, but still Haversume had sworn to be with Daniel's family as soon as possible.

This had been Michael's last call. But not his last responsibility. That was something altogether worse. Explaining to Harry Lawrence why his father had not come home.

Michael had sat and gazed at the child for what now seemed like a lifetime. The boy had always strongly resembled his father, but never more than at that moment. Just eight years younger than Daniel had been when they had first met, Michael could not help but see his lost friend in this child's eyes. It had been almost unbearable. The closest he had come to falling apart. Somehow he had not.

The conversation had gone as well as it could. Placing his hand lightly on Harry's knee, Michael had told him in the softest tone that there had been some bad news. At that Harry had begun to sob. The bright ten-year-old seemed to know what was to come. But he still needed to hear it.

Michael spoke slowly. Gently. Explained how Daniel had been driving home late when his car had been involved in a road accident, and what that meant. Harry had taken it in. He had cried pitifully in Michael's arms until no more tears would come. Only then did the questions begin. Questions Michael was duty-bound to answer until Harry knew everything a child in his situation should know.

The next three hours were a blur. Michael could remember long, strained conversations with Hugh and Deborah Lawrence, Daniel's parents, and with Tony Haversume, who was much more restrained but in obvious pain. There had been talk of autopsies, of coroner's inquiries, and Michael could now recall Haversume's promise to Deborah that no one would touch her son's body; he would see to that.

Above all else Michael could remember a family that was torn apart by the memory of Daniel. Parents. A child. A wife. All of them needing to grieve with no restraint. So Michael had left them, returning home at last to mourn privately and in his own way.

THIRTY-THREE

It was almost 8 p.m. as Sarah Truman and Jack Maguire drove the relatively short distance to Michael Devlin's Islington address. Even at this time of night the journey through the congested heart of London seemed to take forever.

Sarah was silent as she reflected on the day that had passed, and as she thought of what might still be to come.

For as long as she could remember she had yearned to be a reporter. A serious journalist. Her entire working life had been aimed at that ambition. She would do anything to achieve it. Right now she was as close as she had ever been.

Sarah knew that they were on the cusp of a huge story. That something big was being covered up. This fact put her ahead of the game, because – aside from her and Maguire – the press were blindly accepting the party line: that Eamon McGale had taken his own life, before having the chance to speak to anyone about his actions. And why wouldn't they?

But Sarah knew better. She knew that McGale *had* spoken to someone. Someone who was now in a morgue. It could not be a coincidence.

The moment her suspicions had been confirmed was the most exciting of her life. The exhilaration of being thrown out of Paddington Green police station had been a rush like no other, but it had all been an anti-climax, grounded by a reality check. That check had come from Maguire. It was well and good, he had said, to know they were being lied to. The problem was, they did not know what that lie was hiding.

It was then that the real work had begun. Following up on the luck that had seen them in the right place yesterday afternoon, and the good judgement that had placed them there last night. It was this work that had led them to Michael Devlin.

Careful research had told them that Michael Devlin and Daniel Lawrence were close friends and habitual work colleagues. It seemed logical to Sarah, then, that if Lawrence had told anyone about McGale it would be Devlin.

'Nearly there,' said Maguire, breaking into Sarah's thoughts. 'So how do we play it?'

Sarah considered her response. She glanced through the van's window. Watched the Angel Underground station pass on her right-hand side as Maguire veered left to take them from Upper Street to Liverpool Road. They were now only minutes away from Devlin's home. A decision had to be made.

'I think we go in without the camera rolling at first.'

'What?'

Maguire's reaction was as Sarah had expected. The suggestion that a doorstep approach should *not* be caught on film went against every lesson he had taught her.

'And how exactly does *that* help us? Anything he says off-camera will be deniable.'

'I just don't think we'll be getting anything that he needs to deny, Jack.' Sarah was keen that Maguire understood her reasoning. 'I don't see this guy being involved. So what's he got to confess? They've been friends for years and nothing we dug up points to Devlin having any other connection with this. They're just buddies.'

'We can't know that,' Maguire replied. 'Devlin could be up to his neck in this. And if he is then we need his reaction on tape. Just like we have Henry's. When you doorstep someone, Sarah, you make sure your finger's pressing Record.'

'Not this time. I know I'm right. Devlin's not involved. He's just some guy who's lost someone close to him, and who might just happen to have the information we need. If we go about this the right way we get him on side. Shit, once he hears what we have to say we probably won't be able to *stop* him from helping us. But if we do it the usual way we might lose him for ever.'

'You're certain you want to go with your gut on this one?'

The cameraman was by far the more experienced of the two. But Sarah was the reporter. The final say was always hers. Maguire continued.

'Because if we blow this then we lose the story. And that's *your* loss, Sarah. Not mine. You know that, right?'

'I know that. And if I'm wrong I'll be the one who has to doorstep Lawrence's widow. I know what's at stake.'

Maguire nodded. Sarah's attitude had hardened over the last forty-eight hours. Her confidence in her instincts had grown. Maguire seemed to recognise this. He returned his concentration to the road.

Moments later, Maguire was driving around the quiet Victorian-era square, searching for a place to park while Sarah read house numbers aloud. For the second time in less than twenty-four hours, neither noticed the black-clad figure whose job it was to stay in the shadows.

THIRTY-FOUR

Michael jerked upright at the sound of the bell, his unexpected sleep interrupted. The movement and sound combined to rouse Cass. The Rottweiler barked loudly in response. Michael shushed him with a stroke of his neck before climbing to his feet. Still half-asleep, he walked through the living room and into the hallway. It was only when he turned on the light – blinding himself for just an instant – that he stopped moving forward.

For a moment Michael just stood there. Questioning if he really wanted to open the door. After the last twenty-four hours, did he really want company? Then again, how could he be sure this visitor was not bringing some important news? Something about Claire or Harry?

'Just a minute,' he finally called out.

He walked into the bathroom, ran the tap and washed his face. Still, any effort to look respectable was doomed to fail after what he had been through. He settled for clean, left the bathroom and opened the front door.

The sight that greeted him would have ordinarily led to one reaction: a charm offensive directed towards the rather attractive woman on his doorstep.

But today was not a normal day. Today Michael was in no mood to flirt.

His first words were muted and empty.

'Can I help you?'

Michael could feel Cass behind him as he spoke. Ignorant

of his intimidating presence, the overgrown puppy was excited to greet visitors. Michael, though, was used to the effect that a glimpse of Cass could cause, and so he kept his own body between the Rottweiler and the door, and pushed Cass away with the back of his leg.

The distraction dealt with, Michael turned back to his visitor. If his mind had been clearer he would have noticed Sarah's awkward silence and her darting eyes. And they would have told him a lot. Michael's profession made him a keen observer of human behaviour, with body language sometimes saying more than words. What Sarah's would have revealed to him was her discomfort with the situation.

But tonight he noticed none of this. Those skills were muted by a mix of tiredness and devastation.

What Michael *did* suddenly notice was a man, standing directly behind the silent woman. Something about him seemed out of place. Out of the ordinary. It caused the fog in Michael's mind to begin to shift.

Who are these people?

The woman spoke before Michael could find his answer.

'You're Michael Devlin?'

'You're standing at my front door, so I think you know that.' The fog was disappearing fast. 'And who might you be?'

'My name's Sarah Truman. And this is my associate Jack Maguire. We're from CNN. If you have a moment I have some questions I'd like to ask about Daniel Lawrence.'

Sarah spoke quickly, as if the clock was against her.

'You've got to be joking!'

Michael felt his heart rate spike. A surge of anger. It infested his voice, becoming more evident with every accented word.

'The body isn't even cold and you're attacking him?'

Sarah attempted to interrupt. To explain. Michael ignored her.

'I'll tell you about Daniel Lawrence, shall I? Daniel Lawrence was the best man I knew. A good man. Better than me and damn sure better than the two of you. There's no dirt to dig so why don't you leave his memory in peace. Now get away from my door!'

Sarah's approach had been disastrous, which made Michael's next action inevitable. She moved her body far enough forward to take the brunt of the impact as he attempted to slam the door closed.

Sarah did not acknowledge the door's forceful contact with her shoulder. Instead she tried to explain herself.

'We're not digging up dirt, Mr Devlin.'

Michael pulled the door fully open, now even angrier after Sarah had prevented its closure. Fury flashed in his blue eyes.

If you won't leave then you'll get the abuse you deserve.

Sarah beat him to it.

'I believe that Daniel Lawrence was murdered to cover up the fact that he spent two hours in confidential conversation with Eamon McGale.'

She somehow managed to get her words out before Michael could say his own. They did not instantly register. Michael was too angry for that. He opened his mouth to launch the furious tirade triggered by the first mention of Daniel, but nothing came as Sarah's words began to sink in.

His mouth closed. The fury on his face disappeared. Replaced by pain and confusion.

'What are you talking about?'

Michael had not glanced at a television screen or a

newspaper since receiving news of Daniel's death. The fact rendered Sarah's words meaningless.

'The authorities are saying that Eamon McGale didn't see a lawyer last night,' Sarah explained. 'But I watched Daniel Lawrence arrive and I watched him leave two hours later. Now Daniel Lawrence is dead, McGale's dead and they're saying that it didn't happen. They're lying, Mr Devlin. We want to find out why.'

Michael stood next to the open door and listened. He did not know what to think. Did not know how to react. Daniel's death was enough, surely? But now this?

He steadied himself. Then he took a single step back, unblocking the doorway.

'I guess you'd better come in.'

Michael turned without another word. With a slow tilt of his head he indicated that he wanted to be followed into the house.

Sarah turned to Maguire.

'You follow him,' said Maguire. 'I'll bring the equipment in and set up for when you're ready.'

Sarah did as Maguire said. She followed in Michael's footsteps. First through the lounge, where Cass had taken his place in an enormous dog basket by the far wall. As large as the basket was, the animal's fully grown bulk more than filled it.

She walked past the dog, towards the back of the lounge, where a visitor would expect to find a wall. Instead there was an open double doorway. On the other side was a large, clinical kitchen. Like the lounge, it was an overtly masculine room.

Michael was inside.

Sarah watched in silence as he took a stool at the room's central island unit. He placed a visibly chilled bottle of white wine and three glasses on the unit's worktop. Then he turned towards Sarah.

'Please, take a seat.'

Michael indicated a stool on the opposite side of the unit. When he spoke again his voice still betrayed his uncertainty.

'Will you join me in a drink?'

'Yes please.'

Sarah took her place on the offered stool.

'Is your friend not joining us?' Michael asked.

'He will. He just needs to bring in some equipment, and to find a space for the van. We're double-parked.'

Michael took a gulp of wine as Sarah spoke. Large enough to drain most of the glass. For a few moments he didn't seem to know where to look, until caught by Sarah's unusually green eyes. In different circumstances he might have found them captivating.

But once again Michael's mind was elsewhere.

'OK, Miss, erm, Truman, wasn't it?' he said, breaking their brief silence. 'Tell me what you know.'

Sarah took a single nerve-assuring sip from her glass and began to explain.

'What I know is this: following the shooting Eamon McGale was taken to Paddington Green police station. He was the only detainee as the station had been commandeered by the security services. The information that's been released is that he refused to answer questions and refused to give the details of his own lawyer, and that he had no legal visit last night before taking his own life in the cells in the early hours.'

'But that's just not true,' Michael interrupted.

He was struggling to pick up the facts as Sarah spoke. Exhaustion was neutering his usually razor-sharp mind, but he knew what he was hearing was wrong. He continued.

'Daniel *did* see McGale last night. We spoke about it after he left the station.'

'That's why we came to you,' said Sarah. 'I saw Mr Lawrence enter the station last night and I saw him leave. We knew he couldn't be there for any other reason, but when McGale's death was announced the official statement denied that he had seen a lawyer. We were going to question Mr Lawrence about it. I'll be honest with you, we thought he might be involved in some way. But then we found out about last night's so-called accident.'

'So they're denying that Daniel went to see McGale, even though we both know he did. And now McGale's dead too?'

Sarah nodded. Michael paused for thought before speaking again.

'How did McGale die?'

'Badly. They say he snapped one of the plastic forks he was given to eat his meal and used the jagged edge to stab himself in the neck.'

Michael was unfazed by the detail. He did not miss a beat.

'And then Daniel dies in an accident.'

Michael's words were spoken mainly to himself. What he was hearing had focused his grieving mind. There was a problem to be solved. Something he could think about other than his own sadness. He continued.

'It all sounds pretty convenient, assuming there *is* something to hide. Have you any theories on what the something might be?'

'We don't,' Sarah replied. 'Not yet. We needed to be sure that there *was* a cover-up. Once that's done we can start thinking about what's *being* covered up.'

'I might be able to give you a leg-up with that,' replied Michael.

He could feel the energy in his own voice. His mind had already run through the possibilities.

'I know a thing or two from speaking to Daniel last night. But I want to be involved in this. Hands-on. I want to help you find whoever killed him.'

'If that's the price, Mr Devlin.' Sarah did not hesitate. 'But if we're going to be partners, we should be on first-name terms. Please call me Sarah.'

'Michael.' He reached out a large, open hand. 'So do we have a deal, Sarah?'

Sarah reached out, took his hand and shook it.

'We do. Michael.'

Their hands were still grasped when a cough from the kitchen doorway made them both turn. Michael looked over Sarah's extended shoulder and saw Maguire. He noticed a slightly quizzical look in the cameraman's eyes.

'Is, erm, is that your Jaguar just out front, Mr Devlin?' Maguire asked.

'It is,' Michael replied. 'Is there something wrong?'

'I was just wondering if you could move it up a little? There's a space behind it where I could fit the van if you edge forward a bit.'

Michael nodded, stood up from his stool and walked to a kitchen drawer. He took a key from inside, turned to Maguire and threw it in his direction.

'Do you mind pulling it up yourself?'

Maguire snatched the keys from the air as Michael spoke.

'Drive the Jag? No problem!'

Maguire closed his hand around the key and headed back outside. Sarah watched him leave before turning to face Michael.

'So what did Daniel tell you?'

'Not much, but it's a start. Or at least a place to start. Daniel couldn't tell me everything; we were on an open line and you've got to be careful about mobile phone calls being intercepted. But what he did tell me is important. He said that McGale wasn't trying to kill Howard Thompson. He was there to kill Neil Matthewson. McGale believed Matthewson was behind the terrorism in Ireland. Behind the people that killed his wife and kids.'

Sarah seemed stunned.

'But that makes no sense. The True IRA have claimed responsibility already, on the basis that Thompson was the target. Plus we've been told there was prior intelligence.'

'Then I don't know what to tell you,' Michael replied. 'Except the IRA might have good reason to lie, and this came straight from the horse's mouth.'

Sarah did not speak for a moment. She seemed to be assessing what Michael had just revealed.

'OK,' she finally said. 'Let's say that's right. Let's say that McGale was after Matthewson all along, on the basis that Matthewson was somehow involved in the terrorist resurgence. Where did he get an idea like that?'

'I don't know. Daniel wouldn't say on the telephone. And, to be honest, my first reaction was that McGale was a crank. But now? With them both dead? Someone was willing to kill him *and* his lawyer, just to keep them quiet. So maybe not so much of a crank after all.'

'Shit!'

It was all Sarah could manage at first. The fresh information was causing the story to spiral even further. She continued.

'If only we knew what else McGale—'

Sarah never finished her sentence. It was not the barely audible sound of Michael's car ignition that interrupted her. It was the deafening explosion that immediately followed it, violently showering them with broken glass from the shattered living room windows.

Michael reacted on instinct. With glass still flying towards them he leapt over the kitchen island in search of cover. Gravity took him down. As it did, he reached out and grabbed Sarah, dragging her from her seat and to the ground with him. He sheltered her beneath him as debris from the explosion bounced across his exposed back.

They lay there for just moments, long enough to be sure that the danger of flying debris had passed. Only then did Michael get to his feet. He pulled Sarah to hers without a word as his eyes reviewed his devastated home.

Michael's teenage years in Belfast had been blighted by bombs and their aftermath. Like anyone with this background, he knew their effect on sight. He could read the detail. The bomb – the damage – came from outside. The black smoke of a petrol fire now snaking through the gaping living room windows served as confirmation.

Sarah had no such expertise. She looked around in bewilderment as she coughed up a lungful of smoke and dirt. She turned to Michael and saw a stream of blood tricking down his neck.

'You're hurt.'

The words were all she could manage before a second coughing fit.

Michael did not respond. He seemed unconcerned by his injury. Instead he was staring in despair into what was left of his lounge. It was not his devastated belongings that paralysed him. They were just things. No. It was the sight of Cass, motionless under a pile of broken plasterboard and glass, with no indication of whether he was alive or dead.

The sight was almost too much. The iron resolve that had seen Michael through the last twenty-four hours was about to break. Maybe it would have, had he not been interrupted by Sarah's cry.

'JACK!'

Michael immediately understood. Maguire had been outside at the time of the explosion.

He was not quick enough to restrain Sarah as she ran for the door. But he already knew what she would find outside and it energised him. It made him run after her.

Michael was faster but the distance was short. He gained on Sarah with every step, but still he only reached her side in time to catch her as she crumpled to the floor by the charred remains of the Jaguar.

The car Maguire had been driving.

Michael could not console Sarah where she had fallen and so he lifted her from the floor. The car was still burning. A second explosion was unlikely, but it was still a risk. They had to move.

The adrenaline was flowing, flushing through Michael's system as his heart beat faster. Sarah felt almost weightless in his arms as he stood tall, her head resting against his chest. He turned to move back inside. Then he heard it.

Maybe it was the over-acceleration of the motorcycle. Maybe it was that Michael was on his guard after what had just happened. Or maybe it was his own instinct for danger, developed so keenly in his youth and still very much alive, though it had lain dormant in recent years. Whatever it was,

Michael stopped on the kerb still close to the burning car, turned his head and saw the motorcycle approaching.

His instincts were returning by the second. Just moments earlier Michael would not have noticed the motorcyclist steering with only his left hand. Or the right arm stretched out towards them. Now Michael saw both. And he knew what they meant. He knew what to do.

Michael threw himself and Sarah to the floor just as the motorcyclist fired five shots into the spot where he had been standing.

The sound of gunfire and the impact with the pavement combined to break through Sarah's stupor. She looked at Michael from just inches away, and her green eyes were alive once again.

Michael pushed his back against the car and pulled Sarah alongside him. Then he listened. Tried to isolate the sound of the motorcycle's engine. To determine where it had stopped.

Twenty yards, he realised. *Better than nothing*.

Michael grabbed Sarah's hand and pulled her up to a crouch. He was careful to keep their heads below the height of the surrounding vehicles. They provided the only cover in the exposed square.

Staying behind the line of parked cars, they edged forward to the rear of the CNN van. It was heavily damaged and still smouldering; it must have been next to Michael's Jaguar at the time of the explosion.

Michael knew that the motorcycle had at least passed this point before stopping. But that was the best he could do. What remained was guesswork, and so protection was vital. Protection best offered by the bulk of the van.

*

As Michael and Sarah moved, hidden from view, Joshua fixed his attention on the spot where they had dived.

Joshua had no way of knowing if his bullets had hit their target. But whether they had or not, where the couple had gone down remained their most likely hiding place.

He dismounted the bike, pistol aimed. Time was limited – he knew that after the car bomb the local police could not be far away.

Joshua reached the spot in moments and was disappointed to find it empty and free of blood. He had missed. It meant that Devlin and Truman were uninjured, and no doubt desperate. They had also been clear-headed enough to move. The question now was to where.

Joshua's attention turned to the remaining possibilities. His mind ran through them methodically. Weighing the likelihoods. Two thoughts dominated. The CNN van, though badly damaged, offered the best cover and so was the most likely hiding place. And his targets were unarmed, which made more haste and less caution acceptable.

Joshua's weapon remained fixed as he approached the van. He rounded its offside to expose what was hidden by its bulk. Nothing. It was disconcerting.

This is where a frightened civilian should be, he thought. *So why aren't they?*

Joshua could not allow the unexpected to distract him. The clock was ticking. He turned his attention to the vehicles parked close by. One by one he checked the spaces between and all around them, with his weapon aimed and his body braced for impact. Neither was necessary; each time he found nothing.

After the fourth car Joshua glanced at his watch. His concern was growing.

There's no time for this, he thought.

Joshua's heart began to race with that thought. Something he knew he could not allow. He took a deep breath to calm himself. To regain control over his blood flow and his adrenaline. It cleared the anxiety that had been rising. Then – for an indication of what time he had left – he took a moment to listen carefully, for the sound of distant sirens.

There were none. But there *was* another sound. A sound Joshua had not considered.

The roar of the motorcycle's engine was unmistakable. And its meaning was clear. Joshua turned towards it and ran.

He needed to cover the forty yards that stood between him and the front of the CNN van as quickly as possible. From there he would have no obstructions. A clear shot as his targets attempted to escape on his own bike.

It was a short distance, yet far enough to concern him. Stanton's displeasure was already bitter. It would only grow worse if Joshua's prey got away on the back of his own vehicle. The thought made him desperate, and with desperation came carelessness.

Joshua reached the front of the van in seconds, confident the bike was still well within his pistol range. Michael Devlin must have come to the same conclusion, which was why Joshua was hit with a crippling shoulder tackle to his midriff the instant he passed the van's front lights.

The loud revving of the engine had been a ruse designed to grab Joshua's attention. Safe escape on the motorcycle was impossible at this distance. Not when facing a man armed with a pistol. Michael knew that. But he also knew that to remain hidden was to invite death; it would take only moments more for Joshua to find them. And so Michael had instructed Sarah to sound the bike engine and then take cover, in order to flush Joshua out and allow Michael the chance to violently blindside him.

It was a desperate plan that had worked perfectly. The follow-up went less well.

Michael hit Joshua with enough force to down a heavyweight. The impact broke the gunman's grip on his pistol, which was thrown to the floor before sliding to a rest underneath the adjacent van, and the momentum drove Joshua into the side of a parked car. Michael could feel the breath forced out of the taller man by the collision with the immovable metal frame.

Surely that broke some ribs?

Michael did not hesitate as these thoughts crossed his mind. He stepped back and immediately threw what *should* have been a knock-out punch. It took much less than a second to travel the short distance towards Joshua's jaw. Which was long enough for Michael to realise he was fighting out of his league.

Michael would later marvel that the impact with the car had not even registered to Joshua. That his own first tackle had achieved nothing. Joshua seemed to see Michael's punch before it was even thrown. He also seemed to recognise its power as, instead of taking or blocking the blow, he used Michael's own weight against him. Joshua moved his body a fraction to his left and, with his left hand, he guided Michael's punch away. The movement effortlessly sent Michael to Joshua's right, chasing the momentum of his own blow. Michael stumbled forward, out of control, and was met by an expertly timed knee-strike to his exposed stomach.

It took the wind out of him. Unlike Joshua, it was not a feeling he was trained to ignore.

Michael staggered backwards. He was struggling for breath. More importantly, he was struggling for hope. Michael was more than capable in a straight fight. He always had been. But he now realised that this was a different proposition altogether. This man was not just capable of violence. This man was trained to kill.

Michael halted the backward movement caused by the knee-strike. He desperately wanted to inhale – more than once – but there was no time. A flick of Joshua's eyes told him that the killer was scanning for his lost gun. Michael could not allow him to find it and so he moved. With no other choice, Michael threw his entire bodyweight at the thinner man. His only hope was sheer force.

For a moment it seemed to work; Joshua was pushed back for a second time. Michael saw an opening as Joshua seemed to stumble. He went for it. A straight right to Joshua's exposed throat, in the space between his motorcycle helmet and his leather jacket.

But once again Joshua was many steps ahead.

Michael's blow was met by a blocking arm that felt like steel. His earlier punch had been parried but this time it was simply stopped dead. It left his body open to counter-attack.

Joshua swung his blocking arm down in a slashing motion, bringing the back of his right elbow first into Michael's left temple and then downwards. The movement both stunned the lawyer and sliced through his eyebrow. It was not an injury he had time to contemplate, as the next blow was worse. Using his own momentum, Joshua followed up with a crushing left hook into Michael's mid-rib section, expelling what little wind he had left.

Michael contorted upwards in agony, which Joshua also seemed to anticipate. It put Michael at the mercy of a straightforward head-butt. After the beating he had already taken and with the extra force of Joshua's helmet, it was enough to send Michael smashing to the floor.

If Michael had not been fighting for his life he could have admired the skill with which he had just been dispatched. Three devastating blows, delivered as a single fluid movement. But now was no time for analysis. Joshua was again searching for his lost gun.

Michael somehow pulled himself to his feet.

It was not a moment too soon. Joshua seemed to have spotted his pistol and was moving towards it. Michael watched as the fitter, stronger man crouched at the front wheel of the CNN van and stretched his arm underneath.

Last chance, then.

Michael drew in as much air as his lungs could hold, steeled himself and ran full speed at Joshua. Just twenty feet. Close enough that Joshua's search for his gun might distract him and give Michael a chance.

Might. But did not.

Michael was two steps away when Joshua span from his crouch and swept out his running knees. Michael's legs gave way instantly. As he began to fall forward, Joshua brought his own body upwards. The top of his helmet collided with Michael's face with enough power to change the direction of his fall.

Michael's world went black, his mind turned inside out by the blow. For a moment he could not move. Joshua stood above him, making no attempt to move down to Michael's level and finish the job. Not that he needed to. Unable to shake off the effects of his skull's second collision with Joshua's crash helmet, Michael knew that he was beaten.

Through his hazy vision, Michael watched helplessly as Joshua reached for his boot and pulled out a knife, sensing that he was moments from death. And that the young reporter he had just met would be right behind him.

Joshua was leaning forward with his knife in his hand, his focus absolute. And maybe it was this – combined with the muffling effect of the helmet he still wore – that made him miss the sound of the growl. That left him unprepared for the impact as a ferocious Cass leaped upon his back.

Joshua called out in pain as the dog's powerful jaws dug deep into his shoulder. The unexpected attack and Cass's sheer weight sent him stumbling forward. The usually docile Rottweiler was already doing more damage than Michael had managed.

Michael dragged himself to his feet. His head was still spinning; his continuing consciousness not yet guaranteed.

For just a moment he watched as his dog attacked Joshua with a fury he did not recognise. Cass was fighting hard, but it was a fight that could only end one way. The protection of Joshua's bike leathers and the knife in his free hand would see to that.

The urge to help Cass had to be resisted. Michael knew he was outmatched. He had to leave the Rottweiler to do what it could.

He had to escape while he had the chance. And he had to take Sarah with him.

Michael turned his back on the struggle and staggered towards the waiting bike. His legs were weak and in pain but he was fuelled by pure adrenaline. It was enough for now.

He climbed onto the saddle without a word. Sarah ran from behind the cover of the closest car and he felt her hands grip painfully around his broken body. The feeling told him that she was ready. Without looking back, Michael hit the accelerator and left both his devastated home and Cass behind.

THIRTY-FIVE

Michael hammered the motorcycle's engine, determined to put as much distance as he could between himself and Sarah and the violent death they had escaped.

The traffic made no difference to their speed. Michael manipulated the bike through the slightest of gaps. Within minutes they had reached Holborn. Islington – and their attacker – were now more than a mile behind. It was still too close for comfort.

Terror could have driven Michael on, but common sense fought back. It asked the right questions. Where would they go? And how long could he last? His injuries were beginning to hurt through the adrenaline. It made his decision easy.

It was less than a minute later that Michael brought the bike to a halt outside Daniel's office building. He carefully dismounted. Pain shot through his body but he had to ignore it. Now was not the time.

Moving fast, Michael jogged to the nearest parked car and pulled off the tarpaulin sheet its owner had used to cover it. He dragged the thick material back towards the bike.

'We've got to get this bike covered,' Michael explained between pained breaths. 'Hopefully he won't think to come here. But, if he does, the last thing we need is for him to see his bike. We won't get away again.'

Sarah did not respond. She did not even seem to hear. Instead she looked on in silence as Michael pulled the sheet across the parked bike, carefully adjusting it to ensure that the job did not look rushed.

When Michael was done he stepped back. The vehicle was well hidden.

Satisfied, he turned and walked towards Sarah. Her eyes did not even seem to register his approach. Michael took her by the arm without saying a word and guided her towards the building's entrance. Once there he took a ring-full of keys from his front trouser pocket, found the one he needed and unlocked the main entrance door.

Neither spoke as they took the lift to Daniel's second-floor office. Michael was in too much pain for small talk. Sarah remained incapable. Only after they had passed reception and entered the staffroom did either say a word.

'You're hurt.'

Sarah repeated the last words she had spoken inside Michael's home. She was still in shock. That much was obvious. But its hold seemed to be weakening. It was Michael's head wound that seemed to catch her attention.

'It's bleeding bad, Michael.'

'I'll live,' Michael replied. 'More than can be said for anyone else who's already been dragged into this.'

Sarah watched as Michael took down a red first-aid kit from the office store cupboard and walked to the staff toilet. He turned on a dim light and stripped down to the waist.

Sarah did not follow. She rested against the nearest desk and stared into space. It gave Michael the time he needed to clean his wounds. He had moved on to treatment before Sarah spoke again.

'Jack's dead,' she finally said, breaking the silence.

Michael did not immediately reply. He was concentrating on the cut above his left eye, resealing the gashed skin with a tube of clinical glue.

'Jack's your cameraman?' he finally asked. He could see Sarah nod in the reflection of the room's mirror. 'Then yeah, he is. I'm sorry.'

Silence fell once again. And Michael made no attempt to break it. Instead he finished tending to his injuries. It took time. When finally done he left the washroom and headed to Daniel's private office. After a few moments he came back through the doorway. In his hand was a t-shirt. Daniel had always kept a stash of clothes in the office for when his workload led to an overnight stay. Michael pulled it on. It clung to his larger frame.

Almost twenty minutes had passed since they had arrived. In that time Sarah had said little. Michael had welcomed that. It had allowed him to do what he could with his injuries. That was now done, so it was time for them to speak.

Sarah was seated, staring at the far wall. She was still in shock, unable to focus. The best approach would be a soft one. Michael knew that. But he also knew that they did not have the time.

'Jack's dead, Sarah.' Michael placed his hands on Sarah's shoulders as he spoke, a move designed to breach her personal space and help break through. 'The bastard that killed him might be just around the corner. We need to decide what we do now, and who we can trust. And that means we need to both be thinking straight.'

Somewhere, in the depths of her mind, Sarah heard Michael's words. She began to fight her way back.

'What happened?' The words came out slowly. 'What . . . who was that man? What did he want?'

'I don't know who he *was*, Sarah, but I know what he *wasn't*. He wasn't an amateur. That guy knew what he was doing and was bloody good at it. A professional killer. That means he came after me for a reason.'

'What reason?'

The conversation was helping to concentrate Sarah's mind. To prevent her from dwelling on what she had witnessed.

'Daniel called me last night, after he left McGale. Whoever killed him must know that. They must be worried about what he told me.'

'But how could they know you spoke to him? I mean, know for sure? Jack and I were just hoping.'

Michael hesitated. He weighed the possibilities. Only one made sense. It terrified him, but he had to accept it.

'There's only one way. Daniel called me on his mobile. Someone must have accessed his phone records. Which led them to me.'

'But it's been a day. How the hell can anyone get that information that quickly?'

'Most people can't.'

Michael's reply was immediate, but no less considered for its speed. His mind remained sharp despite all he'd just been through. He continued.

'Even the police can take months to obtain phone records from the networks. It's a problem in every trial that needs them. The backlog's massive. So if someone's gotten hold of Daniel's in a day then that person's got access to a serious level of intelligence.'

'The sort of access that could cover up Daniel's meeting with McGale.' Sarah continued Michael's thought process. Her mind shifted up a gear. 'And get to a man in Britain's most secure police station.'

'Exactly.' Michael sat back into his chair. Gently, to lessen the pain. 'Which means you have your conspiracy. Someone killed McGale to stop him revealing why he shot Matthewson. To stop him telling the world that Matthewson was backing terrorism. Whoever that is, they murdered Daniel and they tried to kill me. It's a hell of a story for you, Sarah. Now we've just got to decide what we do about it.'

Sarah took a moment to consider her options.

'I think we have to go to the police,' she finally said. 'Then they can get us back to my office and we can file the story. Once it's out in the open we'll be safe.'

'Jesus, Sarah, are you mad?' Michael sprang forward in his chair as he spoke. 'We can't go to the police and we sure as hell can't go anywhere near your office. These people can find us *anywhere*. They've killed people inside a police station. And they've got access to information even the police can't get hold of. And you want to go back to the bloody office? We wouldn't make it through the door!'

'Why the hell wouldn't I?' Sarah's tone was a mixture of indignation and desperation. 'It wasn't *me* they were trying to kill, Michael. It was *you*. It was *your* car that Jack was driving. It was *your* phone that Daniel called. That bomb was meant for *you*. *You're* the one who wouldn't make it through the door, Michael. Not me!'

Michael watched as Sarah seethed. He understood where the sudden anger was coming from. She was beginning to see the danger of her position and would do anything to reject it.

Human nature.

'You haven't thought this through.' Michael's voice remained calm as he spoke. 'Even if they haven't got wind of the questions you were asking, your van was outside my house. They know we're together and they'll assume I've told you everything. Just like they assumed Daniel told me. If you weren't already a target before we met, you sure as hell are now.'

Sarah opened her mouth to answer. Not a sound came out. Michael knew why. His logic was unarguable.

He watched as Sarah looked down at her own hands. They were still shaking as she took a cigarette from a battered pack within her jacket pocket. She lit it with difficulty and inhaled deeply to calm herself.

'So what do I do?'

Sarah looked up at Michael from her seat. Her green eyes bored into him. Fixed him to the spot.

'If they want me dead, Michael, what do I do?'

'There's no "I", Sarah.' Michael's tone was firm. 'We're in this together. They want *us* dead, not just you. And I don't plan to go that easy.'

Michael stood up and moved towards her. He knelt at her feet and put his hand on her shoulder.

'We won't be safe until we know who we're dealing with. Until then we can't trust anyone. Not the police. Not your network. No one. The only way we get out of this alive is by finding out the truth.'

'You can't be serious?'

Sarah stood up as she spoke. She seemed angry. A last-ditch attempt to reject the inevitable. Michael had seen it many times, from clients keen to delude themselves on the evidence against them.

She stepped away from him before continuing.

'These bastards want us dead – they damn near managed it tonight – and *you* want to fight fire with fire? After what I saw that guy do to you? Michael, we're screwed if we try that.'

'No we're not.' Michael needed Sarah to understand. 'Not if we play it right. We get out of London, Sarah. Hell, we get out of England. We follow the trail to Northern Ireland. We find out what McGale knew and then we find out the rest.'

Sarah shook her head as Michael spoke. Her nervous energy made her stride around the room as she listened.

'But how do we even *get* to Ireland?' she finally asked. 'We've no cash, we've no passports and we've no one to help us.'

'We *do* have money, Sarah.' Michael's mind was overcoming every problem. 'Daniel keeps . . . kept . . . cash in his safe. We can use that. And we don't need passports. Northern Ireland's internal.'

'What about the airport? What if they've put out some sort of warrant for us? You say we can't go to the police because we don't know how much influence these guys have. Well, if that's the case, who's to say they won't stop us as we board the plane?'

'It doesn't work like that,' Michael explained. 'They *will* be able to trace us, but it'll take a few hours. By the time they know where we've gone we'll have disappeared into Belfast. With people I know. People we *can* trust. That's a lot more than we can say about London right now, right?'

Sarah listened carefully. Michael could tell that she was still unconvinced. He let silence fall. Gave her time to digest what she had been told.

'There's got to be another way.' When Sarah spoke again her tone was fearful. 'Michael, we can't do this on our own.'

'What choice do we have? All we know is that the more people we trust, the more likely it is we die. So tell me: is there anyone left who you trust with your life?'

Michael's words cut to the point. They exposed their

situation for what it was: a question of life and death. And they left Sarah with no option.

'No. No one.' Her voice was quiet. 'I guess we do things your way.'

Michael slowly nodded, watching Sarah as he did so. He was looking for doubt. For a change of heart. The first was there in abundance. There was no sign of the latter.

Satisfied, Michael stood up and disappeared into Daniel's unlit office. He returned a few minutes later with an envelope that was filled with cash from the safe.

'Time to pull ourselves together, Sarah. We've got to do this now.'

Sarah stood up from her chair.

'Where to first?'

'Stansted Airport,' he replied. 'But there's something I've got to do first. I've got to call Daniel's family. If this guy came after me, they could be next.'

THIRTY-SIX

Hugh Lawrence walked into what had been Daniel's sitting room, to his remaining family members. He could feel how slow his movements were. It was an unconscious delay. He knew that what he had to tell them would not be welcome.

'That was Michael,' he began. He was unsure how best to explain what was to follow. 'He said that . . . well, he said that Daniel's accident, that it might not have been an accident after all.'

For a long moment there was no response. No reaction. Dealing with Daniel's death had already left the family numb. This new information would struggle to gain a foothold.

'What on earth are you talking about?' Deborah Lawrence – Daniel's mother – broke the silence. 'How is it . . . how . . . what?'

'It's a very long story.' Hugh's voice was flat. He took a deep breath and continued. 'Michael says it's related to Daniel's job. Daniel was in interview with the man who killed Neil Matthewson. Now that man's dead, Daniel's dead, and Michael thinks it's all connected.'

Claire and Deborah looked on in confusion. Neither had the knowledge to properly digest what had been said. But someone else did.

'Daniel saw McGale last night?'

Of the few people in the room only Anthony Haversume knew the name Eamon McGale. He seemed to think for a few seconds before continuing.

'I was told that McGale saw no one before his death. Certainly not a lawyer.'

'That's Michael's point. That McGale was killed before he could speak, for fear of what he might say, and Daniel was killed for what McGale may have told him.'

The room fell quiet once again. A hive of shock and disbelief. Once again it was Deborah Lawrence who broke the silence.

'No.' Her voice was firm but full of emotion. 'This is ridiculous. This sort of thing doesn't happen. Daniel died in a car accident and now Michael's making some bloody conspiracy out of it because he just can't accept it. I won't hear of it, Hugh. I won't hear of it!'

Hugh Lawrence opened his mouth to speak as Deborah began to sob. To comfort his wife. The better-informed Haversume beat him to it.

'I'm sorry, Deborah, but Michael *may* be on to something. The official line that McGale saw no one isn't just for public consumption. It's what we've *all* been told. If the powers-that-be thought it necessary to *tell* that lie, they'd think nothing of killing to *preserve* it.'

'That's why Michael wants us to leave.' Hugh joined Haversume's blunt honesty with some of his own. 'Because he thinks we may be in danger from the same people.'

'What?'

Claire spoke for the first time. If anything could break through her grief it was a threat to what was left of her family. She turned to Haversume for reassurance.

'But we don't know anything. Nobody would come after us, would they?'

'They might.'

Hugh answered before Haversume could. His family needed to know everything.

'Because they went after Michael.'

'Michael? Is he OK?' Claire's voice was suddenly fired with passion. 'Where is he?'

'He's OK, Claire. He's been fairly badly beaten but he'll survive.'

'But where is he?'

Deborah's voice this time. No less emotional. Michael was as much a second son to her as he was to her husband. 'Is he coming to join us?'

'I don't know where he is,' Hugh Lawrence replied. 'He wouldn't tell me. But no, he isn't coming. Michael says he's going to get to the bottom of this. He's going to find out who killed Daniel.'

'Michael can't do that, Hugh! He'll get himself killed!'

'He should be with *us*. With his family. Once he's here we can get help. We can get protection.'

'No, Claire. No, you can't.' Haversume rose to his feet. 'Michael's right. If he comes to you he risks bringing this to your door. The way I see it, the less *anyone* knows about any of you the better. There has to be intelligence involvement in this; it's the only reason they'd have lied to the likes of me. If they've killed Daniel and they've gone after Michael then none of you are safe. But I can help. I can arrange somewhere. Somewhere only I'll know about. Where you'll be safe until this is over.'

'Are you joking?' Claire seemed outraged. 'You're telling us to run and hide in the hope this goes away? To hope that Michael can keep himself alive *and* unearth some sort of government bloody spy conspiracy? This isn't a film, Tony. And Michael's not James bloody Bond. He's going to get himself killed, and we're either going to rot in hiding or be murdered ourselves.'

'I won't be leaving this to Michael,' Haversume replied. 'And I certainly won't rely on him playing the hero. There are people in the intelligence community with absolute integrity, Claire. People I know well. I'll contact them and when I do we will have some of the very best operatives in the world on our side. They'll flush out whoever is behind this and you *will* all be safe. Michael too. But for now you're not. For now, Michael can take care of himself. And I can take care of all of you. Please let me do it.'

Daniel's family were united in silence. Just minutes ago they had nothing but their grief. That had changed. Now they had to run.

THIRTY-SEVEN

Joe Dempsey drank in the details of a devastated Lonsdale Square. He could sense the usually tranquil feel to the place, so rare in the heart of London. To see that torn apart was a crime in itself.

A presence at Dempsey's shoulder broke into his thoughts. Alex Henley had joined him. They had managed two more drinks before news of the Islington bomb had broken through the blanket McGale/Matthewson coverage.

The pictures that had appeared on the screen were all too familiar. The smouldering remains of a car, unrecognisable from the violence of the explosion. Surrounding vehicles damaged beyond repair. Nearby homes wrecked by debris and detritus. All typical of the bombings Dempsey had investigated in his career.

Such images had become common in mainland Britain in the last two years with the resurgence of Northern Irish terrorism. But, coming so soon after the Trafalgar Square shooting, Dempsey and Henley reached the same conclusion: two terrorist attacks in such quick succession were unlikely to be unconnected.

Within minutes of the news report they were hailing a black cab on the streets of Westminster. The journey to Islington took little more than fifteen more. An hour earlier the roads had been jammed. Now they were almost empty, as if the traffic had cleared for the urgency.

'What the hell do you think you're doing?' Henley shouted.

Dempsey turned and followed the assistant commissioner's gaze. He knew immediately what had caused the outburst. Three young officers were setting up a cordon to keep the public away from the scene. The purpose was to avoid contamination. But they were doing more damage than they were preventing as they trampled over possible evidence.

Dempsey allowed himself a smile as Henley produced his Metropolitan Police identification and took temporary control of the scene. The shock on the faces of the local police as a senior officer tore into them amused him. But there was no time for entertainment. Instead Dempsey turned to the best source of information at any crime scene. The bystanders.

One person in particular caught Dempsey's eye. An elderly woman at the front of the crowd. Her location told him that she had been one of the first on the scene. If she arrived late she would have been at the rear, too frail to push her way through.

Dempsey approached the crowd and flashed his DDS credentials. Meaningless to a public generally unaware of his agency's existence, but at this point any sign of authority would have an effect. He scanned the crowd. Just for a moment. Then his eyes settled on his target.

'Did you see anything, madam?' Dempsey asked.

'I did, yes. It was horrible!'

The elderly woman replied without hesitation, without asking who her questioner might be. She seemed to revel in the opportunity to tell her tale. Dempsey could tell that it was not for the first time. She continued.

'I was sitting in my flat when I heard the bang. I live over there, on the second floor. Number 28C. The, erm, the green windows.'

'What did you see?' Dempsey moved her along. He had no time for superfluous information.

'Well it wasn't what I *saw*. Not at first, anyway. It was the bang. Deafening. I didn't know what to think. But then I went to the window and I looked out, and I saw young Michael from number eighteen standing there, by the burning car. Next to him, on her knees, was a woman. Then he picked her up but before he could go inside a man on a motorbike came out of nowhere and started shooting. Michael and the girl only just managed to get out of the way.'

Dempsey listened. Every word added to the picture.

A car bomb alone could be a simple terrorist attack, if there was such a thing. A residential square was hardly a typical target, but he had dealt with stranger. A car bomb followed by a motorcycle gunman, however? That was something altogether different.

That was a professional hit.

'Did you see what set off the car bomb?' Dempsey asked.

'No,' she replied. 'Like I said, it was the bang that made me look out the window. Anyway, like I was telling you, Michael went—'

Dempsey stopped the story by raising his hand. He was not yet ready to move on. He turned to the other men and women in the crowd.

'Anybody else see what set off the bomb?'

No answer.

'No one saw?'

Still no answer.

'What about the car itself? Any of you know who it belonged to?'

Dempsey thought he already knew the answer, based on what he had just heard. The same elderly witness confirmed it.

'Yeah,' she replied. 'That's Michael's car. That's why it was parked outside his house.'

Dempsey looked down at the speaker. She was going to be his best source. That much was clear.

'OK. Tell me what happened next.'

Dempsey listened as the woman described what she had seen. None of it surprised him, up until she described the fight between the resident and the gunman.

'Sorry, but this Michael guy? He took on the motorcyclist?'

'For a few seconds he did, yeah. And he got an awful leathering for his trouble. Knocked all over the place until his dog – great big thing – jumps on the fella with the gun. Which is when Michael and the girl ran to the bike and rode off.'

Dempsey did not respond as the story tailed off. He was mentally re-arranging the woman's confused syntax into a coherent account. Only when he had a picture clear in his own mind did he go further.

'And did the gunman follow them?'

'I don't think so.'

The elderly witness seemed conscious of the attention as she delivered her well-rehearsed tale. She also seemed to enjoy it.

'I mean, he fought with that dog for a bit. So I reckon they were probably long gone by the time he got it off of him, poor animal. By then there was a lot of people coming out of their houses or shouting from the windows. And someone must have called the police by then, too, cos he took off in a hurry.'

'How?'

'On a different bike. One of those ones that are always parked on the corner. He done something to make it work and he rode off. But too late to have gone after Michael, I think. Him and his young lady were long gone.'

Dempsey took in all the information the elderly informant could offer. It was a lot, but it still missed much of what he needed to know.

'What do you know about Michael?' Dempsey asked. 'His full name? Job?'

'Nothing, really. He's an Irish lad in his thirties. Good-looking blond fella. Always very pleasant. But that's about it. I don't even know his surname.'

'I do.'

A voice from the crowd cut through the background noise. Dempsey took a closer look. The speaker was a well-dressed, middle-aged man.

'His name's Michael Devlin. He's from Northern Ireland and he's a barrister. Lives alone, keeps himself to himself.'

'So how do you know him?'

'We sometimes speak when we're walking our dogs.'

'Do you know anything else about him?'

'No, not a thing. Like I said, he's pretty private.'

Dempsey scanned the crowd one more time.

'Does anyone else know anything more about him?'

No response.

'Anyone see anything this lady didn't?'

No response.

Dempsey nodded. It was as expected, and it was enough. The two witnesses had told him more in just a few minutes than an undirected examination of the crime scene ever would. Dempsey thanked them, turned his back and headed towards the police cordon.

A flash of his DDS identification took him past the manned perimeter, into the scene. Here he was far from alone. A stream of forensically trained crime scene investigators were moving back and forth, scouring every inch of debris for evidence. Dempsey stopped one of them and took a pair of blue forensic gloves. Put them on and left the examiners to their job.

He edged past a convoy of white suits and walked into what remained of Michael Devlin's ground floor. The scene was strikingly familiar. Interior bomb damage, caused by an exterior explosion. Dempsey had already known that this was the case. Typical of a residential car bomb. Little else could be learned inside. He spent a few more minutes there regardless, surveying the debris. Half-destroyed photographs littered what was left of the room. None seemed to be of value.

Dempsey turned his attention elsewhere.

The remains of Michael Devlin's car were almost unrecognisable as a vehicle. The front was a mangled, blackened mess. Only the remains of its four wheels helped distinguish what the smouldering wreck used to be.

Three white-clothed forensic investigators were in and around the car. Dempsey flashed his credentials to the closest.

'What do we know?' Dempsey asked.

'No doubt it was a bomb. No car goes bang this bad without one.'

'Any idea what started it?'

'Best bet is the detonator was connected to the ignition and that it went up when the engine turned over.'

'You mean there was someone inside?'

'Still is. Only now he or she is melted into the driver's seat.'

Dempsey was surprised by the information. He leaned down and looked inside. The forensic investigators were better than him. Dempsey could not make out a driver's seat, let alone that it had been occupied.

He looked up.

'What about the other seats? Anyone in them?'

'Doesn't look like it. Driver only, as far as we can make out.'

Dempsey responded with a nod. A gesture more confident than he currently felt. Someone had been driving Michael Devlin's car at the time of the explosion, but it had not been Michael Devlin. That much was clear from what the neighbour had told him. But if it was not Michael Devlin, who was it?

And what, Dempsey thought as he glanced up from the car and towards the damaged CNN van that was still next to it, *has that thing got to do with this?*

He returned his attention to the car. The same forensic examiner was standing by.

'Have you found any sign of the bomb mechanism?' Dempsey asked.

'Not from the portion of the vehicle we've been able to examine.'

'Where's left?'

'Just the underside. We can't go under until the chassis has been secured. Health and safety regulations.'

'Is it solid?'

'Seems to be. But that's not the point. We still have to wait for the engineers.'

'I don't,' Dempsey replied.

Dempsey dropped to the floor by the vehicle's side. From there he checked the integrity of what was left of the frame. It seemed unlikely to collapse. Satisfied, he turned onto his back and edged his way underneath the chassis.

The under-frame of the car seemed strong. More intact than the devastated upper body. The damage was still catastrophic, but from here Dempsey could make out a number of important details. Details that should not have been there. The remains of a two-inch-square sheet of magnetic metal carried the telltale scars he was looking for.

The confined space between the car and the road made it difficult to manoeuvre. It took Dempsey the best part of a minute to reach into his front trouser pocket and remove a small utility lock-knife. It took longer still to slide the knife between the car body and the magnetic plate. Dempsey had no choice but to take care. Too much force and he could find himself pinned to the floor by a two-tonne wreck.

Minutes passed as he prised away with the lock-knife. Finally the plate broke loose, its magnetic force now clinging it to the blade. With no room or light to examine the sheet more closely, Dempsey had no choice but to inch his way out from under the vehicle.

He gripped the knife in his hand as he got to his feet. The light in the square was artificial but blinding. More than enough to reveal the details that Dempsey had expected to see on the recovered item. It was not a lengthy examination. The first glance had been enough.

'What have you found?' Henley had seen Dempsey climb back to his feet and had watched as he examined the metal plate.

'Mercury tilt switch,' Dempsey replied. He handed the knife to Henley with the magnetic strip still attached. 'Have your guys examine it.'

Henley held the knife up. Took a few seconds to consider what he was looking at. Finally:

'This is military ordinance, right?'

'It is.'

'Then what the hell is it doing at a civilian crime scene?'

'Because this isn't a civilian crime scene, Alex.' Dempsey's voice was low. What he was saying was for Henley's ears only. 'We were right. This *is* Turner.'

'You really think that?'

'I don't *think* anything. I *know* it's him.' Henley looked around at the devastation that surrounded them, before Dempsey spoke again. 'It's best if it's recorded that *you* found the tilt switch, Alex.'

'Of course.'

Henley had no need to question why. Dempsey had already explained that although he was officially barred from the investigation, this was just a front to allow him to continue unimpeded. A necessary political lie.

Dempsey's attention returned to the van.

'You know anything about that yet?' he asked, pointing towards it.

'Only that it shouldn't be here,' Henley replied. 'And that there's no sign of whoever was driving it.'

Dempsey nodded.

'Then let's see what we can find out.'

The driver's door of the van had been welded shut by the heat and force of the nearby explosion. Dempsey looked through its shattered window to the passenger's side. It was damaged too, but had been spared the brunt of the blast. If there *was* a way into the van it would be there.

Dempsey made his way to the left-hand side of the vehicle and tried the door. It was difficult to move, but he felt some give. With enough force it would open. Dempsey gripped the handle and the frame and, with considerable effort, he ripped the door ajar.

A short examination of the cab area revealed nothing of

interest. There were no ID cards. No useful correspondence. Nothing that told him anything about the van's occupants or the story they were chasing.

Dempsey wasted no more time with the cab. Instead he moved to the sliding door that guarded the rear. It slid open with little effort; its mechanism had been spared significant damage. What it revealed was an Aladdin's Cave of information.

The rear section of the van was unsurprisingly cramped as Dempsey climbed inside. It was also well equipped and virtually undamaged. A khaki survival jacket rested on the back of a chair that was bolted to the centre of the floor. Dempsey riffled through the jacket's many pockets. It contained batteries, notepads, cigarette packs and a CNN photo ID card in the name of Jack Maguire.

The thumbnail photograph looked back at him. A photo that could be of a dead man, Dempsey realised. Someone had been driving Michael Devlin's car at the time of the explosion. And it had not been Devlin himself. With no sign of Jack Maguire and no other obvious reason for the CNN van to have been abandoned here, the odds were fair that it had been Maguire in that seat.

Dempsey put the identity card aside and searched the rest of the van's interior. The vehicle's official paperwork was filed in a compartment close to the sliding door. It revealed that the van was allocated to cameraman Jack Maguire and reporter Sarah Truman. There was no photograph of Truman. But the name was enough. Dempsey now counted three missing people. Michael Devlin, Sarah Truman and Jack Maguire. Devlin could be accounted for. Last seen fleeing the scene on a motorcycle, with an unknown woman behind him. It would be a leap to assume that woman was Truman, but with the abandoned outside broadcast van in the equation? It was a leap Dempsey was willing to make.

And one which made it ever more likely that Maguire was still just feet away, charred within the burned-out Jaguar.

The remaining paperwork told Dempsey nothing of value. Most was procedural, recording the use of official broadcast equipment. A small amount was more specific, including several short files of information on people of interest. There was nothing in the files to suggest what was so interesting about them, and so they were of little use. Putting them aside, Dempsey turned his attention to the state-of-the-art broadcast equipment. Perhaps Maguire and Truman had left recordings of what they had been working on.

The master console of the electronic board meant nothing to Dempsey so he began to randomly press buttons. This continued for almost a minute until every screen suddenly buzzed into life. The sharp rise of static electricity lifted the hairs on the back of his neck. The sensation barely registered; his attention was on the silent screens. The image of an angry sergeant in what was obviously a British police station dominated.

Dempsey hit every button, dial and lever that might be related to the vehicle's volume control. Nothing worked. His life and training had prepared him for many things. Raising the sound on possibly damaged, high-tech video machinery was not one of them.

Finally he accepted the inevitable and stopped. Opened the sliding door. Looked out. A young, white-suited forensic specialist stood nearby. Not the same guy as before.

Dempsey summoned him into the rear of the vehicle.

White Suit seemed nervous. Made worse when Dempsey

forcefully slammed the sliding door shut when he was barely inside.

'Are you any good with electronics?' Dempsey cut to the chase. His voice bristled with intensity.

'I'm not sure. I . . . I . . . it depends on what—'

'The video equipment,' snapped Dempsey. Surely an explanation was unnecessary, given the screens now surrounding them? 'I need the sound on this equipment up and running now. And you look like a bloke who's spent more time playing with wires in your bedroom than playing football. So can you do it?'

'Yes, sir.' White Suit's confidence was returning as he realised he wasn't being taken from his comfort zone. 'I don't think that will be a problem.'

'OK. Do it.'

Dempsey shifted himself to the van's second seat, to make way for White Suit. He watched as the pale young man began to connect loose wires at a remarkable pace. At first he was interested, but that quickly wore off. It then became a test of patience.

His mind wandered as White Suit worked. The timing of the attack. Its details. The military-grade detonator. Even Devlin's nationality. It could not all be coincidence, Dempsey was sure of that. It *had* to be related to Trafalgar Square. To Turner. But how? How was it all connected? And if Dempsey was right – if the gunman *was* Turner – then how the hell had some lawyer escaped the most efficient killer Dempsey had ever met?

The sudden explosion of sound brought Dempsey's musings to an abrupt end. The speakers were working.

And then some.

Dempsey turned, his ears ringing from sheer volume. He saw that the images on the screen were now perfectly accompanied by their audio recording. His earlier amateur tinkering must have set the now-working volume to its highest level.

Dempsey ignored the pain in his ears as White Suit fought to reduce the sound. Instead he concentrated on the monitors. The footage was coming to an end, taken as the camera was lowered to face the pavement. It was shaky. And it meant nothing without what had come before. But, as the volume came down and the image disappeared, Dempsey could make out a single word, spoken with a soft American accent:

'Perfect.'

The screen went blank and immediately White Suit took the recording back to the start. He selected automatic playback and vacated the central chair. Dempsey replaced him without a word.

The footage onscreen was an obvious rough cut. There was no 'to camera' address to put the footage into context. Instead the scene began with the rear view of a tall brunette as she strode into a police station reception area.

The first minutes of footage were impressive, dominated by the attractive young reporter. Dempsey was as certain as he could be that he was watching Sarah Truman.

Truman had a soft American accent – the same voice Dempsey had heard say 'perfect' moments before – and she used her body language to devastating effect. Her manipulation of the young police officer at the station's front desk was played out onscreen. Truman toyed with him like a predator. Little more than a boy, he was helpless to do anything other than her bidding.

Dempsey continued to watch. Nothing was said or done after the young officer's disappearance. Truman was waiting for something. She did not have to wait for very long.

A single figure suddenly dominated the screen: the same sergeant who had appeared when the footage had first flickered into life.

'What the hell are you doing in my station? Get out! Now!!'

The shout from the apoplectic police sergeant filled the van. It was exactly the reaction Dempsey would expect from an officer whose premises had been invaded by the press. It gave Dempsey no cause for concern.

Unfortunately for the man on screen, his next reaction was a lot less acceptable.

'What the hell are *you* doing here?'

The way the words were delivered. The way the sergeant looked directly at Sarah Truman as he spoke. The way his tone switched from outrage to annoyed recognition. They all rang alarm bells in Dempsey's mind.

These people knew each other.

The telling lapse ended as soon as it had begun. The sergeant turned his attention to Jack Maguire. Loudly demanded him to leave, as if he had no idea of who either reporter was. But Dempsey knew what he had seen and heard.

The footage continued in the face of the officer's anger. Ignoring his orders to leave, Sarah forced a question. A question which injected life back into Dempsey's tiring mind.

'Sergeant, can you confirm that Eamon McGale met and consulted with a legal representative in this building just hours before his death?'

The question hit Dempsey like a shockwave.

The official line was clear. McGale had seen and spoken

to no one before taking his own life. That a reporter thought otherwise would not usually convince Dempsey that he had been misled. But these circumstances were far from usual. In all likelihood the cameraman behind this piece was dead, while the reporter who had asked the question was last seen clinging to the back of a motorcycle as she fled a gunman. That alone made it a query that demanded an answer.

Dempsey's surprise distracted him from the next few lines. But his attention returned in time to hear what came next:

'Sergeant, when we spoke yesterday you informed me that Eamon McGale's lawyer had been selected. Shortly after that Daniel Lawrence, a defence lawyer, arrived at this station. He stayed here for almost two hours. There was only *one* person in custody during those hours, and so only *one* reason for Daniel Lawrence to be here: Mr Lawrence was the lawyer you mentioned and he *did* meet with Eamon McGale. That's right, isn't it?'

The familiar name pricked Dempsey's ears. Daniel Lawrence. It was a name he knew. Or at least recognised. A name connected, in fact, to something he had seen in the last few minutes. His mind searched through its own internal files as his eyes returned to the screen.

'Are you aware, Sergeant, that after leaving your station Daniel Lawrence was killed in a supposed car accident? On the very same night that Eamon McGale allegedly took his own life? Doesn't that seem just a bit suspicious to a detective such as yourself?'

The sergeant had been unable to hide his reaction. At least at first. The news of Daniel Lawrence's death had been a shock. That much was clear, and alone would have been interesting. It was made all the more so by his obvious effort to then hide his shock and feign outrage.

Dempsey had looked many guilty men in the eyes over the course of his career. None had been more transparent than the man he now watched.

As telling as the image was, it did not remain for long. The camera wielded by Jack Maguire instead took in the details of the floor, ceiling and walls as he was roughly escorted from the building. With pavement now filling the screen, Dempsey again heard the word 'perfect' as the monitor went black.

The light cast by the footage died. But Dempsey did not move. His mind was in overdrive considering the meaning of what he had seen. White Suit squirmed in his seat under the agent's apparent stare. It was unnecessary. Dempsey was not even seeing him. His mind was much too busy.

And then it stopped.

After minutes of motionless thought, Dempsey became a flurry of activity. He moved away from the screens and back to the paperwork he had earlier dismissed. File after file was thrown aside as he scanned for the name he had just heard. His trained eye quickly found what he was looking for.

Sarah Truman had used the name 'Daniel Lawrence', the same name as had appeared on one of the manila envelopes that had been strewn across the floor of the van. In just seconds that paperwork was in Dempsey's hands. He opened its outer jacket. Scanned the front page at a glance. He was interested in only one thing. The photograph of Daniel Lawrence that was attached by a single paperclip.

Dempsey tore it from the folder.

'Can you make a copy of that recording using the equipment in this van?' Dempsey asked.

'Well that's exactly what this van's for, so yeah,' White Suit winced at his own sarcasm. He seemed to instantly regret it.

Dempsey had not noticed.

'OK. I want you to make me a copy, and then bag the original up as evidence. Exhibit it as having been retrieved by you. Make no mention of me.'

Dempsey turned to look at White Suit before continuing. His intense gaze made it clear that his next words were no request.

'Don't speak to anyone about what's on that recording, or anything you've seen in here. Just get me a copy, bag the original and then forget all about the last ten minutes.'

These final words echoed in White Suit's ears as Dempsey exited the van and closed the sliding door behind him.

Henley noticed Dempsey step out and walk back towards the house. Henley followed into the blackened lounge. Dempsey was already there, crouched over a small pile of charcoaled items that were heaped together near the corner of the room. He watched as Dempsey flicked away the broken remains of a smouldering wooden frame to expose the photograph that had recently sat inside it.

Henley moved closer, to Dempsey's shoulder. From here he could see the photograph. It showed two young men in full morning dress. The dazed look in the eyes of the shorter man suggested that, of the two, it was *his* wedding day being recorded.

Dempsey held the picture carefully with his left hand and raised his right alongside it. The photograph he had taken from the Lawrence file was undamaged and the comparison was obvious.

Dempsey looked from one image to the other. A perfect match. The shorter man in the burned picture – standing next to a taller blond man who matched the description earlier given of Michael Devlin – was undoubtedly Daniel Lawrence.

It was the connection Dempsey had been looking for. A connection he would not share. Dempsey had had no choice but to include Henley in his illusory suspension. If he had not then he would have been denied access to Lonsdale Square. Henley had proved himself worthy of that trust, but it had its limits. As always, Dempsey would disclose only what he had to. And right now, the picture in his hand was for his eyes only.

THIRTY-EIGHT

Joshua stood bare-chested in the marbled bathroom of his hotel room. The artificially lit mirror highlighted every blackening contour of his battered body.

Michael had been wrong in thinking that his efforts had not had an effect. Few had the ability to disarm a man of Joshua's skill. Fewer still had the strength to put him on the back foot. Michael had managed both. Joshua *was* hurt. But what made him special was the ability to ignore pain and injury. They were for later. Now he was dealing with the consequences.

A dark circular bruise prominent on his pale torso hinted at a broken rib; the result of Michael Devlin's opening body-charge. The pain had been significant but it had not slowed him down. The same was not true of what had followed. Thanks to the protection of his bike leathers the gash that had needed five stitches between his right wrist and forearm was the most visible injury caused by Devlin's dog, but not the worst.

Using a pair of medical scissors he snipped the remaining length of the stitch. This was not the first time Joshua had put himself back together. He could rival most ER doctors with a needle and medical dressing. It did not need his full attention. Nor would it get it. His mind was on something a whole lot more important.

Doubts had set in from the moment he had failed to kill McGale. Doubts made all the worse by his honest assessment of himself. Joshua could not have expected Dempsey's appearance in Trafalgar Square. But was it an excuse? Would it have stopped him in the past?

It was not a question Joshua could answer, but he suspected he knew the truth. Especially now, after tonight. The opportunity had been there to tie every loose end up in one go. To pull himself out of this mess. Yet he had managed to kill just one of three unarmed targets. Poor statistics for even the most inexperienced assassin; for him they were nothing less than unacceptable.

With his medical dressing in place, Joshua moved from the bathroom to the bedroom. The feel of the thin carpet replaced the cold stone on the soles of his feet. The relaxing effect of alcohol beckoned.

Joshua removed a single glass tumbler. A bottle of forty-year-old Bruichladdich whisky sat on the nearby table. One of the few tastes he had developed in the course of his lucrative career was for costly liquor. It was to a bottle of one of the world's most expensive malts that he now turned.

He added the slightest dash of water to a large measure of the Scotch, to open the flavours. Any more – or, God forbid, ice – would be sacrilege. Done, Joshua tapped the glass north, south, east and west before picking it up. Another compulsion, another small price to pay for the advantages his condition had given him.

Lighting a Marlboro, he sat back into the room's single lounge chair and faced the panoramic sixth-floor window. The pain in his shoulder as it pressed against the stiff back of the chair only reminded him of his failure. Of how the second part of his plan – the murder of Michael Devlin and Sarah Truman – had gone so badly wrong.

Devlin had clearly heard the bike's engine. But the man

was just a lawyer. How could he have possibly recognised what was happening in time to prevent it? And how the hell had he disarmed one of the world's most highly trained killers?

The fight that followed had put things into some perspective. While Devlin had shown more heart than almost anyone Joshua had ever faced, he had still been outclassed. But still, an amateur had caught Joshua off-guard. Had met him head-on. Disarmed him. Broken his rib. And, worst of all, he had done all this and he had escaped alive. It meant one of two things. Either Joshua was losing his touch or there was more to Michael Devlin than met the eye. Joshua hoped it was the latter, and feared that it was both.

The ringtone had become the bane of his existence.

It rang out at an hour that was much the wrong side of midnight. Far later than Joshua had expected, it interrupted his disturbed sleep. Too groggy to question why Stanton would call so late, he detected an unfamiliar pace in the usually measured speed of voice. It suggested something, but what? Anger? Fear? Excitement?

Whatever it was, the speaker was not in complete control.

'What the bloody hell happened?'

'I messed up.'

It was all Joshua could offer. An evening of lonely reflection had lowered his reaction to criticism to the path of least resistance.

'I'm sorry.'

'You're sorry? You're sorry?' Even through the electronic interference of the voice modulator, it was clear that Stanton's pitch was rising. 'I contracted you on the basis that you are the best at what you do, Sergeant. I put arrangements in place that would have made your target accessible to an adolescent, and yet you have consistently failed in almost every task. Now you're saying "sorry"?'

'There's nothing more I can say,' replied Joshua. The contrition was genuine. 'I caused this mess and I should have cleaned it up tonight. Believe me, I tried. I just can't explain what happened.'

When Stanton spoke again the pace of his voice had levelled. The rage simmering under its surface, though, was more evident than ever.

'You can't explain it? You've created carnage on the streets of London, by all accounts coming off second-best to a bloody barrister, and all you have to say is that you can't explain it? Just what the hell am I paying you for?'

Stanton's words made his fury unmistakable. But they had also made an allegation against Joshua's hard-earned reputation. That would not stand.

'You listen to me,' Joshua began. 'You might hold the cards but you're not pinning this all on me. I've made mistakes and, yes, this should have gone better. But you've played your part too. First with Dempsey and now with Devlin. There's a lot more to that guy than you've told me. If I'd known that, I'd have taken more care. So you can point the finger all you want, but this isn't *all* down to me.'

'What are you talking about?' For the very first time Stanton seemed to hesitate. 'I told you everything you needed to know about Devlin. He's a lawyer, nothing more.'

'Oh, he's something more. I don't know what, but that guy didn't react like any office boy I've ever seen. I suggest you go back and take another look at this one.'

Joshua could not picture his words wiping the smug smile from Stanton's face. Not when he had no idea what Stanton looked like. But that did not diminish the pleasure he felt from the uncertainty he had detected.

'I will review it, Sergeant.'

No hesitation this time. Only the clipped metallic voice remained.

'But you still have a mess to clear up and this is your last chance to do it. I want Michael Devlin and Sarah Truman dealt with, and dealt with quickly. Find them, kill them and erase any trace of what they may have found. Is that understood?'

'It is,' Joshua replied. He was already back in his subordinate position. It was a place he found far from comfortable. 'What's the timescale?'

'Minimal.' The answer was curt but firm. 'This cannot be allowed to drag on. You will be swift and you will be efficient. The price others will pay if you are not will be a heavy one.'

Joshua felt the hairs on the back of his neck rise at the threat against his family. It gave him the urge to argue. An urge he suppressed. He had no way to get to Stanton, which left just one thing that could free him from this nightmare.

The silence of Devlin and Truman.

'I understand. What about the other potential loose ends? Am I to deal with them too?'

'Which others?'

'The Lawrence family.'

There was a pause. Stanton seemed to ponder the question. Finally he spoke.

'Yes, they're a threat. Devlin spent the entire day with them, so we have to assume that he passed on what he knows. But *I'll* deal with them. I wouldn't want to overburden you, Sergeant.'

Joshua ignored the intended insult.

'OK. I'll be packed, ready to go and waiting for your call. And this time I won't be underestimating anyone.'

THIRTY-NINE

The persistent ring of the doorbell finally broke through Trevor Henry's sleep. As he woke he glanced across at his bedside clock. 3.46 a.m. The bed was empty except for his own large body. Still it was heavily ruffled. A sign of a disturbed slumber.

'Alright, alright, I'm coming.'

The late-night caller had abandoned the doorbell and was now knocking loudly.

Henry rose to his feet. An iron spiral staircase led from his bedroom to his lounge. It was a space-saving measure, its eye-catching design making the most of the living area in his undersized one-bedroom apartment.

The hallway between his living room and his front door was minuscule, filled to capacity by just one. Henry stepped inside and unlocked the single security latch. He did so without looking through the spyhole that was built into all entrances in his apartment block. It showed a confident disregard for his personal safety; that even at this hour he was little worried who might be on the other side of the door.

The sight of a focused Joe Dempsey would take most people aback. A reaction he was used to. The visible strength in Dempsey's muscular frame combined with his weathered, damaged features hinted at his capabilities. It was an impression only heightened by the intensity of his deep-blue eyes.

On this occasion the impact seemed to have been lost. Trevor Henry had not failed to notice these things. He just did not seem to care.

'And you are?'

'Major Joe Dempsey, Department of Domestic Security. I apologise for the hour, Sergeant Henry, but I'm afraid I have a number of questions that can't wait.'

Dempsey saw the slightest change in Henry's demeanour. While unaffected by his guest's physical appearance, the mention of the DDS was another matter entirely.

'Then I guess you'd better come in.'

Henry stood aside and ushered Dempsey into the lounge.

Dempsey passed through both the first and the second doors, which placed him in the apartment's narrow open-plan lounge and kitchen area.

He took in his surroundings with the briefest turn of his head. His trained eye memorised every detail of significance within an instant.

'So what's so important that you're banging on my door at four in the morning?'

Henry's belligerence was not unexpected.

'As I said, Sergeant, I'm sorry for the hour.'

Dempsey took a seat as he spoke. He then placed a portable DVD player on the table before continuing.

'But I'm sure you'll understand the urgency when I explain the situation. Two CNN reporters attended your station yesterday, enquiring into the death of Eamon McGale. Is that correct?'

'You're serious? There was nothing *but* press there yesterday. McGale was the biggest story of the year.'

The answer was designed to appear dismissive.

Unconcerned. Henry took a seat as he spoke, and reclined the chair as he finished. It did not take an investigator of Dempsey's skill to see through the facade. The man was now wide awake and thinking fast.

'These two were a little more specific, Sergeant.' Dempsey gave nothing away. 'They came into your station unannounced. They spoke to you directly and you had them ejected from the premises. Does that ring any bells?'

Henry nodded silently for a moment before speaking. An obvious attempt to make his answer seem natural.

'Yeah, yeah, that does. I know who you're talking about now. A guy and a girl. She came in shouting the odds, making some ridiculous allegations about McGale having seen a lawyer the night before. So yeah, I had them thrown out.'

'*Did* McGale see a lawyer?'

'Of course he bloody didn't.' Henry's feigned belligerence was well acted. 'You've got more access to intelligence than the likes of me, Major. If you're involved in this investigation then you know there was no visit.'

'That's certainly what I've been told, Sergeant. I just wanted to hear it from you.'

Dempsey was an experienced interrogator. He was carefully guiding the accused to the point where Henry had no choice but to tell either the truth or an easily disproved lie.

'These reporters? Had you ever seen them before?'

'I don't know. Maybe I've seen them in the crowds out front. Saying that, though, the girl was a looker. If I'd seen *her* before I'm sure I'd remember. So I guess not.'

It was an attempt to appeal to some shared masculinity. It was ignored.

'As I understand it, Sergeant, the young lady claimed that

she had spoken to you the night before. You're saying there's no truth in that?'

'That's what I just said, wasn't it?'

Henry lost all pretence of civility. The questions were loaded. Dempsey was out to prove what he already knew.

'I hadn't met the woman before that minute!'

'And the other suggestion? That you told her a lawyer had already been appointed? Do you deny that too?'

'What the hell is this?' Henry rose from his chair as he spoke. 'I just answered that question. I didn't speak to that woman and so I couldn't have told her anything, could I? Just what are you getting at?'

Henry's anger was now front and centre. If it was intended to intimidate it had failed. Dempsey continued as if there had been no change. As if Henry were still sitting calmly. He opened the DVD player. Pressed the power button. Waited for the screen to flicker into life.

'Please look at the screen.'

'I don't need to take this shit!' Henry shouted.

The net was closing. Its weight was affecting his rationality.

'I've never . . .'

'Please look at the screen, Sergeant.'

Dempsey's voice remained emotionless. He turned the portable DVD player to face Henry. Dempsey gave nothing away but he could detect that Henry was approaching boiling point. He subtly repositioned himself, poised to react in an instant.

Henry glanced at the screen and saw himself. It was a perfect image of the previous day, when he had burst into Paddington Green police station's reception. Everything was as he remembered. Including the moment he saw Truman and hissed in recognition.

Dempsey froze the scene.

'Still say you'd never met Sarah Truman before, Sergeant?'

It was the classic interrogator's enquiry. Henry could either tell the truth or maintain what was now a very obvious lie. Either way, his honesty was completely undermined.

Henry faltered. Dempsey knew why: he was undecided on his next step. The hesitation was a moment too long for his next burst of outrage to be genuine.

'That means nothing!' Henry began to stalk the table like a cornered animal. 'Everything she accused me of was bullshit.'

'The only bullshit here is coming from you, Sergeant.'

Dempsey knew that Henry was close to the edge. He intended to tip him over.

'You'd met Sarah Truman before, just as she said. That much is obvious from your reaction on the footage. But the fact you're now lying about it means more, doesn't it? It means that she's telling the truth about what you told her. It means that McGale saw a lawyer before he died.'

'Get out of my house.'

Every ounce of fake outrage was gone. Replaced by cold, murderous fury. The sign of a man who knew when the game was up.

Dempsey ignored it.

'So what about the rest, Sergeant? Did Daniel Lawrence turn up? Did he speak to McGale? Because you know Lawrence is dead, don't you? You know they both are?'

'I've told you to get out, Major. Now. Before I throw you out. NOW!'

'They're *both* dead, Sergeant. And if you were involved in any way then you are culpable for their murders.'

Henry said nothing.

'What you don't know, though, is that others are dead too. One of those reporters? He was killed tonight. There was also an attempt on the life of the other, *and* your friends tried to kill a colleague of Daniel Lawrence.'

Dempsey paused for just a moment before continuing.

'I don't know if you were directly involved in any of that but it's all part of the same conspiracy, and you know the law on that as well as I do. If you're a part of some of it then you're part of all of it. These people are on a rampage, Sergeant. And, right now, you're the one in the frame.'

The fresh information was intended to overwhelm Henry. To hit him with the truth of a situation in which he had surely played only a small part. Dempsey intended for it to push Henry beyond breaking point.

It worked.

In one moment Henry was hesitant. Unaware how best to act. In the next the decision was made.

The sudden movement would have surprised most, but Dempsey had expected the reaction. His only uncertainty was the direction in which Henry would move. Would it be towards Dempsey or towards the exit? Either way, the agent was ready.

When Henry burst into a sprint in the direction of the living room door, Dempsey was out of his seat and kicking it shut with a speed the fleeing man could not have expected.

The sergeant's own reaction was almost as impressive. Dempsey's speed would have caused many to be paralysed by shock. Not Henry. Henry's response was to attack.

Their bodies were positioned so that only Henry's left hand was placed to strike with any force. With the options so limited, Dempsey expected the left hook before Henry even thought to throw it. One step ahead, he used the sergeant's own force to guide the fist safely past its target.

As Henry stumbled after his own weight, Dempsey's left hand locked onto the sergeant's wrist. Moving against Henry's momentum, Dempsey threw him off balance and left him exposed. Just a fleeting moment, but it was long enough. With a twist of his hips and torso for power, Dempsey sent his right elbow crashing into Henry's prone jaw.

Henry had no time to feel shocked as the room went black. He hit the floor with a bang. His mind returned quickly, and with it came confusion. Dempsey had seen it before. Hard men, bewildered that they had been taken down so easily. The reaction to being outclassed was never a helpful one.

'At least we both know where we stand now.' Dempsey stepped out of reach of Henry's outstretched legs as he spoke. 'Tell me who you're working for?'

Henry did not answer. Instead he staggered to his feet. Once upright he spat out a mouthful of blood. Unsteady on his feet, he looked Dempsey in the eye.

'Fuck you!'

Henry's words were spat out as he launched himself into a dive, his full bodyweight thrown behind a head-butt that was aimed at Dempsey's face. It would have been a devastating blow if it had landed. It did not even come close.

Dempsey's reaction was almost casual. He kept his left foot rooted to the spot, acting both as an axis from which to spin out of Henry's path and as an obstruction to his trajectory.

The trip unbalanced Henry just as Dempsey used his own spinning momentum to deliver a knee-strike to the lower back. The blow sent Henry careering head first into the living room door. As he did so Dempsey brought his foot crashing into the back of Henry's knee, bringing him halfway to the floor. Stunned, Henry could do nothing as Dempsey grabbed him by the head and twisted his neck, sending him crashing across the room and through the glass dining table.

Dempsey was in no hurry to approach the now-unconscious Henry. He had done what was necessary to win. No more. No less.

He stepped over the unmoving sergeant and went to the kitchen sink. Picking up a small tumbler from the draining board, he filled it with water from the tap and returned to where Henry still lay unconscious. Dempsey used his foot to turn the man's heavy frame onto its back. An overturned metal chair lay nearby. Dempsey picked it up and placed it across Henry's chest.

With his full weight on the seat, Dempsey took the tumbler and dribbled cold water onto Henry's face. He watched it contort as Henry slowly regained consciousness. The sergeant took a few seconds to remember where he was and what was happening. As his memory came back his rage came with it.

'Get this fucking thing off me!' Henry shouted, fighting against the weight that held him down.

'Stop struggling.'

Dempsey's voice was as calm as it had been throughout, but with a menace and an authority that had been lacking. It seemed to work. Henry did exactly as ordered.

'And, while we're at it, enough bullshit. I know there's more to Trafalgar Square than we've been told. I know it wasn't just some madman or a terrorist attack. I also know you're my one living link to whoever's behind this. There've been murders and there's been a cover-up. I don't care why. I only care about *who*. So again: who are you working for?'

Henry met Dempsey's intense stare. He was caught and he was not getting away. But that did not mean he had to talk. The constriction on his chest and the blood running into his throat were combining to make speech a chore. The words came out like spit.

'I'm not denying anything,' he finally said. 'But I ain't telling you a thing, either. If I'm going inside I don't need those bastards looking to do me harm. You want information? Find someone else.'

'There is no one else.'

Dempsey had expected the response. He knew that Henry would have more to fear from his employers than he ever would from the British government. But there was one factor Henry had not considered.

'If you don't talk then these guys will disappear. I know that doesn't bother you, but you've forgotten that I'm not the only one looking for them. If you don't answer *me*, other people will have questions.'

'What other people?'

'Think about it, Sergeant. The shooting happened in London, but who got shot? A Brit, yeah. But also the ex-president of the United States. Think about that for a moment. Do you really think the Americans are going to leave you in a British prison if they think you know something about this? Or do you think that maybe you're going to disappear?'

Henry's eyes widened. It was not just the weight on his chest that was now causing him to swallow fearfully.

'You wouldn't allow that to happen.' The certainty of his words was betrayed by his faltering voice. 'You'd never hand me over to the Americans. I'm a British citizen.'

'So are half the orange suits in Guantanamo. And how do

you think they got there? You really think we don't jump when the US tells us too? Believe me, I've seen it.'

'But I . . . I can't . . .'

'There are no "buts". Either you speak to me or you speak to them. Your choice.'

This time Henry listened to every word. And to the obvious truth behind them. Rumours had circulated for years about the British government's complicity in 'extraordinary rendition'; the process of taking enemies of the United States to neutral countries not bound by inconveniences like the Geneva Convention. It was clear to Dempsey that Henry was terrified of betraying his employer. But that fear could not compete with the prospect of a hood and God-knows-what torture in a secret US prison.

Henry's gaze moved up from the floor, towards Dempsey.

'OK. OK. What do you want to know?'

Dempsey needed just one word.

'Who?'

FORTY

'I don't know. You've got to believe me, I don't. I just know that he calls himself Stanton.'

'If you don't know him, how did you become involved? How do you get paid?'

'I don't get paid. It isn't like that.'

Henry reached out and took a mouthful of water from the glass Dempsey had provided. He was a beaten man. Dempsey had removed the chair from his chest and allowed him to get to his feet. They now sat across from one another, surrounded by what was left of the shattered glass table.

Henry continued.

'They – he – contacted me about three years ago. I was in trouble. My wife had left me, I was gambling and I got in a lot of debt to some very heavy people. Real debt. Nearly a quarter of a million. It just spiralled, and then suddenly these guys were asking for favours. Asking for evidence to disappear. For other officers' details. I had to do it. I had to do what they asked or I'd have lost my job and they'd have come for me.'

Dempsey did not respond.

'Then suddenly they stopped. They stopped contacting me. They stopped chasing their money. They just disappeared and I tried to put it behind me. I tried to get on and rebuild my life. Then he called. Stanton.

'Stanton told me that he had taken over the debt and that he would want one favour in return, then we'd be square. I was over the moon, you know. A bit worried about what the favour

259

might be, but one and gone? It was more than I could hope for. So I asked him what the favour was and he said we'd discuss it when the time came. That was that. I didn't hear from him again until a month ago.'

Dempsey stirred in his seat. What he was hearing was troublesome.

'This was three years ago?' Dempsey asked. 'This Stanton guy bought your debt three years ago but didn't call it in until last month? Were you working as the custody sergeant at Paddington Green three years ago?'

'I was. I've been there five years.'

'So what did Stanton say when he contacted you last month?'

'Just that I had to make sure I was working on the day of the event. Nothing else. Just make sure I was on duty. Then, as the day came nearer, he contacted me again and he told me to make sure no officers had access to any prisoners that night. To keep the prisoners away from anyone else. I told him it was impossible but he said it would be easy enough on the night. Well, actually what he said was that it almost certainly wouldn't come up and that he'd contact me on the day if it became necessary, and that either way we'd be square if I did just as he asked. So I did.'

'What did he ask?'

'Nothing at first. The only contact we had between then and the day of the shooting was when I came home and found a phone on my kitchen table. He called it and explained that it was a dedicated line between us. But after that nothing. Right up until the shooting. By then I thought I was off the hook. But then it all went to shit in Trafalgar Square, we were told to shut down the station for everyone but McGale, and I got the call. A few calls.

'First off he told me to stick to the plan and keep every Met officer away from McGale. To clear them from the custody suite. That part was easy enough, like he'd said it would be. McGale was being dealt with by spooks. Two of them. So it was simple. I just kept my boys out the way.

'But he called again and again with more demands. Suddenly I had to keep it quiet that anyone had seen McGale. I had to claim that Lawrence had never been in the building. Then I had to open the rear entrance and turn a blind eye for ten minutes. It just escalated. It got worse and worse, and I was stuck right in the middle. I didn't have a choice.'

Dempsey ignored Henry's attempts to defend his actions.

'You turned a blind eye? You knew what was going to happen?'

'Of course I knew. By then, anyway. There's only one reason anyone would want to get access to a prisoner like McGale. But by then I was in too deep. What could I do?'

'What about when you spoke to Sarah Truman? When you told her about the lawyer? You were supposed to be keeping Lawrence's visit a secret.'

'Not then I wasn't. When I spoke to her all I was supposed to do was keep my own boys out of the way. And for doing *that*, all my problems were disappearing. So at that point I was on a bit of a high. It was only after she'd gone that the demands got worse. Christ, I wasn't even told to cover up the lawyer until the poor bastard was *in* the place!'

'And the two intelligence agents? Were they involved too?'

'I honestly don't know. They didn't know about Lawrence though, I can tell you that much. Lawrence had been and gone in between interview sessions.'

Dempsey looked deep into Henry's eyes as his answers

came to an end. The man had been lying just minutes before, so Dempsey knew what to look for.

None of the signs were there. Not this time.

Henry was telling the truth. Satisfied, Dempsey ran that truth through his mind.

The first conclusion was obvious: someone with access to a high level of intelligence was behind this. Whoever Stanton might be, he had planned this for a long, long time. And he had planned it well.

Stanton had foreseen the need for a tame custody sergeant at Paddington Green police station three years before the killing. Anyone arrested for a terrorist attack in central London would be immediately taken there, and so to have Trevor Henry in place as a safety net was an incredible piece of forward planning.

The fact that Daniel Lawrence had met McGale and was no doubt killed because of that was just as important. Stanton had tried to cover this up by attempting to murder the only journalists to have uncovered the truth, successfully in one case, and the only friend Lawrence would have spoken to. The importance of keeping the conversation between McGale and Lawrence a secret was therefore clear, and that led to the next question: what did McGale know that Stanton needed hidden?

That question would need to be answered in time. Dempsey was sure of that. He was on the right track, and that track only ended in one place.

But right now there were other things he wanted to know.

'If you were officially the only officer in the station when McGale died, how are you not a suspect?'

'I've been questioned,' Henry explained. 'But only routine. Whoever Stanton's guys were, they knew what they were doing. They made it look like a suicide. One you wouldn't even question.'

'Speak for yourself,' Dempsey said, leaning closer to Henry as he spoke. '*I'd* question it. And what about the phone you used to speak to Stanton? Where is that?'

Henry fidgeted. His discomfort was more than just physical, and Dempsey knew why. Henry's next answer would be a watershed. Once given, it would implicate Henry in Stanton's eyes. There were other sources for the things Dempsey had just learned. But the phone? The phone could only come from Henry.

Henry's eyes flicked towards the far corner of the room.

'It's over there.'

Dempsey followed Henry's gaze and saw the handset. He indicated towards it.

'Go get it,' Dempsey instructed, 'and throw it to me.'

Henry did as he was told. He rose slowly to his feet. Inched past Dempsey. There was no effort to renew his attack. The trauma of the last ten minutes had been enough and a further confrontation would end no differently.

Instead he walked painfully towards the handset, picked it up and threw it to Dempsey.

There was no code protecting the phone's content and so Dempsey could immediately access the contact list. There was a single saved entry. The only number it had ever called.

Dempsey weighed up his options.

The handset *could* be submitted to the DDS lab for analysis. *Should*, in fact; it was the right thing to do. But that would leave it in the hands of an agency that Dempsey feared might be compromised. And with his current unofficial status he would struggle to secure its return.

Besides, Dempsey was sure that anyone who had achieved what Stanton had would *not* be traceable by mere telephone use.

The alternative option was to use the number, to gain an advantage that Dempsey could use.

Dempsey dialled the contact number.

It was answered after a single ring.

'Sergeant Henry?'

The voice at the end of the line was deep and robotic.

A vocal modulator, Dempsey thought. *Makes sense*.

When Dempsey did not respond the man spoke again.

'What do you want, Sergeant Henry?'

'Stanton?'

It was all Dempsey said. All he *needed* to say. The difference between his voice and Henry's was enough.

'Who is this?'

'My name's Dempsey, Stanton.'

Dempsey expected no answer. He continued without one.

'And I want you to know I'm coming for you. That no matter what happens, no matter who you've got protecting you – Henry, Turner, whoever – I'll find you. You think you're safe. You're not. Now you sleep on that, because I'll be seeing you soon.'

Once again there was no response. None was needed. After a moment's silence Dempsey heard the line go dead.

Stanton sat alone at his desk. Stunned by what had just occurred. The implications took a moment to clarify in his mind.

Stanton was confident that Dempsey had no way to find him. He had taken every precaution. Phone lines so secure that even the best of Britain's intelligence lacked the technology to intercept his calls. A state-of-the-art voice modulation unit that only the highest military grade equipment could reverse. And a level of message encryption that made even written communication meaningless to anyone but the intended recipient.

No. Stanton was sure that the call would be the closest Dempsey would ever come to him. But he was still shaken. The loss of control over the situation, although temporary, was unexpected. He had believed no one capable of bringing the fight to *his* door. Now, according to the voice at the end of the line, that was exactly what Joe Dempsey intended to do.

Stanton thought back to the first time Joshua had mentioned that name. The force of his words: '. . . then you don't know Joe Dempsey!' Stanton had taken it as panic — an excuse — but perhaps Joshua had been right after all. Perhaps Stanton *had* underestimated Dempsey. Just the fact that the man had somehow identified Joshua as James Turner suggested that.

It was not a mistake Stanton would repeat.

These thoughts still occupied his mind when his telephone rang again just moments later. For the first time he was unsure that, when he answered, it would be the voice he expected. Still, he reached out and connected as quickly as always.

This time the voice *was* familiar. It carried a strong Northern Irish accent.

'You were right, they're here. The two of them just went inside.'

'Go in after them.' Stanton made his decision in an instant. 'Deal with them, but do it discreetly. I don't want any more questions.'

He paused for just a moment as he considered his next thought.

'And one more thing: don't underestimate him. There's been enough of that already.'

FORTY-ONE

The journey from London to Belfast City Airport had been uneventful. The cash Michael had taken from Daniel's safe had been more than enough to cover both the forty-mile black cab ride from London to the misnamed 'London' Stansted Airport, and the cost of the two airline tickets. Neither Michael nor Sarah carried a passport but, as Michael had explained, photo-identity cards were sufficient for what was technically a domestic flight. Michael had also assured Sarah that the three-hour window between buying their ticket and landing in Ulster was not enough time for them to be tracked and intercepted. So far, those assurances had been correct.

Their safe arrival and Michael's confidence had served to quell some of Sarah's fears over the past four hours. Not all of them, but she now had at least a faint hope that they could survive what lay ahead.

That hope had grown upon their arrival at an unremarkable Express Hotel in the heart of Belfast's University Quarter, where Michael's quick thinking had impressed her.

As they had checked in and paid their bill in cash, Sarah had heard Michael's accent become both broad and slightly slurred. Sarah had understood his intention; a few lewd comments to the night porter, designed for the impression that Michael was a local who had got lucky on a night out. It was the only scenario that could explain their late arrival and cash payment without raising suspicion.

Sarah had played along when, to complete the picture,

Michael had grabbed her lustfully and made a show of escorting her to their waiting room. Conscious of the feel of Michael's hand on her lower back and aware of how easily she could have bought into the illusion, Sarah had broken away as soon as they were behind the door.

'Now what?'

It was their first moment alone since leaving Daniel's office. The first time they could not be overheard by a cab driver or other plane passengers. Michael could finally share the plan that had been developing in his mind.

'We go to McGale's office. See what we can find.'

'When?'

Sarah had not wanted to rest. Momentum had brought them this far and she had not wanted to lose it now. Michael, it seemed, had the same idea.

'Tonight,' he had replied. 'It's the only chance we'll get. They'll know we're in Belfast soon enough. Once they do, the office will be the first place they look for us.'

'Have you checked where his office is?'

'Not yet.'

Michael had been sliding his phone from his front trouser pocket as he replied. Thanks to the earlier attack, there was now a crack running across its screen. Battered the phone might be, but it had come out of tonight's violence in better shape than Michael himself.

Michael had spent the next few minutes online looking up McGale.

'The guy was a professor of Political Science at Queen's University. That's about five minutes from here. He's sure to have an office in the faculty building. We just need to find out which building that is, which will be on the university website.'

Sarah had responded with a nod.

'Let's go then.'

It was almost an hour later that they found themselves on the aptly named University Street. Michael had jotted down the directions before taking apart first his handset and then Sarah's. Decades of criminal trials had taught him that mobile telephones are homing beacons for anyone with the right technology. Too much of a risk. He would settle for the old-fashioned way: a scrap of paper, covered in his hasty scrawl.

Located at the heart of the campus among the greenery of University Square, Queen's University was just as Michael had described. Or at least from what Sarah could see of it in the darkness. The expensively maintained grass expanse was almost entirely unlit and so they crossed the square with no fear of detection.

The faculty building was just ahead. A short stone staircase led from the pedestrianised square to the building's stately entrance.

Michael reached the foot of the stairs first. Once there he turned and whispered to Sarah, telling her to step into the shadows as he climbed to the top. Sarah was unused to doing as she was told without explanation, but now was no time to argue. She moved into the darkness and watched as Michael went to work on the secured door.

Sarah could not see what Michael did in the minutes between first shaking the door to confirm that it was locked, and then somehow opening it. Whatever it was, she was surprised. Somehow Michael had bypassed the building's security system and had gained entry to its interior.

How the hell does he know how to do that?

'Wait there.'

She looked back up when she heard the words, just in time to see Michael disappear into the darkened doorway. He reappeared just a minute or two later and beckoned Sarah inside.

Graham Arnold was a well-respected non-uniformed sergeant in the police service of Northern Ireland, but he would always regard himself as being a loyal member of its infamous predecessor, the Royal Ulster Constabulary. It was as a representative of neither that he now sat in an unmarked police vehicle and watched Michael disappear into the building for a second time.

'That was quick,' he said with a smile. 'Looks like they teach some shady stuff in English law schools, eh?'

'Explains how he got away from Stanton's other lads, I suppose.'

The response came from Noel Best, Arnold's friend, colleague and co-conspirator. Best was no doubt as surprised as Arnold to see a lawyer bypass the building's security entry system so easily. It did not seem to affect his confidence.

'Let's see him get away from us. Phone him.'

Arnold nodded, the phone already at his ear. The call was answered on the first ring.

'You were right, they're here. The two of them just went inside.'

There was silence as Arnold listened to the reply.

'Don't worry,' he said in turn, 'we won't be underestimating anyone. Should I call you when it's done?'

There was another brief pause in which Stanton gave his reply. Arnold did not respond, just hung up and turned to his companion.

'Looks like you'll get yer wish. Stanton wants us in there now.'

FORTY-TWO

Sarah squinted in the dim light of the faculty building. The grand entrance hall was illuminated here and there by permanent emergency lighting, installed in the name of health and safety. The light was much too weak to reach the framed list of faculty personnel beside the main door.

It took three attempts to ignite the cigarette lighter that Sarah took from her pocket. Hardly a torch, but good enough. She placed it close to the glass and began to run down the list of names.

The two words Sarah was looking for were less than a third of the way down: 'Eamon McGale'. Tracing her finger to the right she reached a three-digit number that sat across from the name. 6.11.

Sarah turned to Michael, but he'd spotted the number too and was already halfway into the antiquated caged lift that ran through the middle of the building's central staircase. He was wasting no time.

She followed him into the lift and pushed the '6' button as he slammed shut the cage door. She heard the lift mechanism lock before it lifted them with surprising speed to the top floor.

Michael stepped out on the sixth floor. Sarah followed, allowing the cage to close behind her. Michael opened it again without explanation and placed a nearby litter bin between the door and the frame, preventing the cage from fully closing. Before Sarah could ask why, he was ushering her along the darkened corridor, in the direction of office 6.11.

As her eyes grew more used to the darkness, Sarah noticed details of the posters that were pinned to the corridor walls. She could just about make out the larger wording. It would have been enough detail to suggest the political leanings of the university, if Sarah had been seeking it. Michael was Catholic. He would have seen some of these Republican slogans before. Propaganda that had remained unchanged in the forty-year history of the Troubles. Sarah, though, was unused to the sectarian nature of the world that now surrounded her, and so the posters told her nothing. She just concentrated on the door numbers.

Room 6.11 stood close to the end of the corridor. Until a few days ago it would have looked like any other faculty office. Not tonight. Police crime-scene tape criss-crossed the door and frame, telling the world that whatever was inside was now evidence. It was no surprise, then, that the door itself did not budge when Sarah reached out and turned the handle. She signalled this to Michael. He stepped forward and took her place at the door.

This time Sarah tried to see what Michael was doing to manipulate the lock, but his broad back obscured her view. After a few seconds she gave up.

A minute more and Michael was in. Sarah followed close behind.

The same dim emergency lighting from the building's foyer illuminated the room. It was just as weak as the bulbs downstairs, but the fact that the area was much smaller made it sufficient to see.

'This place has already been searched!' Sarah said, her voice a whisper.

'Of course it has.'

Michael crossed the room and was beginning to riffle through the drawers of the office desk as he spoke.

'McGale shot two major politicians in broad daylight, then apparently killed himself before he could be questioned. Did you think they wouldn't at least search his office?'

'I guess so,' Sarah replied, 'but then what's going to be left that can help us? Whoever searched this place was trained to find anything important. And they were here first. So anything that matters will be gone already.'

'Maybe.' Michael's air of confidence did not falter. 'But we've got a big advantage on them. Thanks to the True IRA claiming credit, they all think that Howard Thompson was McGale's target. But we know different. So what might mean nothing to them could mean everything to us. And, anyway, the fact they've searched the place doesn't mean they'll have taken everything away with them. Now help me look.'

For the past few hours Sarah had been increasingly swept away by Michael's determination. By his confidence. It – he – had hypnotised her. She did not understand why. Why was she placing so much trust in a man she barely knew? Whatever it was, it stopped her from questioning him. For some reason she was willing to blindly believe that he could get them out of this mess. Something about him made her feel safe. So she did as he asked.

A heavily disturbed bookcase in the corner of the room attracted Sarah's attention. It had been ransacked in the original search, all except for a line of untouched photo frames on the middle shelf, containing four photographs. They had been ignored by whoever had searched the room before her as they were still standing in the positions McGale must have set them.

Sarah studied the first picture. An image of a young Eamon McGale in his graduation robes, taken many years before. An educated youth with the promise of his future visible in his bright eyes. A world away from the crumpled remnants of a man she had seen in Trafalgar Square just days ago.

The image in the next frame was more recognisable. Sarah lifted it from the shelf. Eamon McGale, accompanied by an attractive wife and two much taller, athletic-looking young men who – from their ages and their similarity to their mother – could only be their sons. The face was now familiar, but even this recent McGale was a different man. Keen intellect and fiery principles burned through his piercing eyes. Eyes that had seemed blank just days ago.

The same impression came from the two remaining photographs. Each showed the same small family. The first featured all four of them on a golf course, happily competing among themselves, presumably with the expensive-looking Spalding golf clubs that still sat next to the bookcase. The second showed the family together again at the college graduation of the elder son.

Sarah stared at the images. The McGales looked a happy, close-knit family. It shone through each and every frame. What McGale would then go on to do made that impression all the more tragic.

'Sarah, come and look at this.'

Michael's voice broke into Sarah's thoughts. She put down the photograph and turned to where he was now standing. He had his back to her, facing a wall that was covered with press cuttings. Sarah walked towards him.

'Looks like motive won't be too hard to prove.'

Michael gestured to the mass of headlines that papered this part of the office.

Sarah took a closer look, confused. The wall was almost

completely covered by cuttings. They came from every conceivable national newspaper, dated from the previous November onwards. She concentrated, looking for a pattern that emerged in seconds: the central headlines – the cuttings from which the larger collection grew outwards – all referred to a single incident. The November bombing of one of Belfast's finest restaurants, James Street South.

A bombing in which nine diners were killed.

It soon became clear why that particular bombing was so important. The first clipping revealed that Elizabeth, John and David McGale had been among the dead. They had been there for the eighteenth birthday of the youngest son. The same clipping also said that the boys' father, Professor Eamon McGale, had escaped by luck alone; he had left the restaurant minutes before the explosion to take a call from one of his postgraduate students, named as Benjamin Grant.

Sarah shook her head as she read on, trying to expel the image of the happy family in McGale's photographs. It was terrible that such a perfect existence could be so easily destroyed by guns and bombs. By religion and politics.

The thought was pointless, she realised. What was done was done. She pushed it from her mind and turned her attention to the cuttings that sprouted from the central headlines. Branches on a tree of information.

They came from the same selection of national newspapers and covered the activities of the Ulster paramilitary groups from the James Street South atrocity onwards. Terrorist attack after terrorist attack. A dramatic history of the Troubles that had rocked Ulster and the rest of the United Kingdom, as the True IRA and the Ulster Volunteer Army used Great Britain as their battleground.

As Sarah read on, another glaring pattern emerged: the growing presence of Sir Neil Matthewson. More and more cuttings referred to the politician. Some of these related to terrorist activity, but many did not. It was the latter that most stood out on a wall otherwise dedicated to violent death. To someone else's eyes they might have seemed out of context, but to Sarah – aware of McGale's belief that the renewed terrorist activity and Matthewson were intimately connected – their inclusion made sense.

Sarah moved from cutting to cutting for a few more minutes, until satisfied she had seen it all. Finally she turned towards Michael, who, having already scanned the information on the wall, had now moved behind McGale's desk and was flicking through a thin leather diary he had found.

She watched as his fingers moved through the pages at speed, as if they knew what they were looking for. Perhaps they did. How else could she explain the moment when they stopped dead, settled on an entry almost halfway through the journal and stayed there?

'That's what we're after.'

Michael moved back around the table as he spoke. He offered Sarah the finger-marked page.

Sarah looked at its content. Four letters – BG and RM – marked in red in the 11 a.m. slot on the entry marked '15 July'. None of this meant anything to her.

'I don't get it.'

'Look at the date,' Michael said, 'then look at the dates on the newspaper cuttings. Remember that, as far as we know, *everything* McGale thinks is important is up there on that wall. From his family's death onwards.'

Sarah followed Michael back to the wall as he continued to explain.

'So we have the James Street South stories in November. Then every single terrorist act from then on. All on the wall. All growing out from the centre. No mention of anything but terrorism, no interest in anything or any*one* else. And then . . .'

Michael thrust his index finger against an innocent-looking headline.

'. . . he starts obsessing about Matthewson.'

Sarah looked again at the cutting. Remembered almost every detail from reading it just moments before. But still it meant nothing.

'I still don't get it,' she said, beginning to lose patience.

'That's because you're not looking at the bigger picture,' Michael replied. 'Until July 15th McGale was obsessing about every terrorist act attributed to either the True IRA or the UVA. Nothing else interested him. He was completely single-minded. Then, out of nowhere, he's suddenly putting up unrelated articles about Matthewson. Mixing them up with the terrorism stories, even when there's no obvious link.'

'And?'

'And *we* know why Matthewson's up there, Sarah. Even if the police don't. *We* know he's up there because McGale believed Matthewson was involved in the attacks in some way. But that's not all this wall tells us, is it?'

Sarah looked again at the cuttings. She took in as much detail as she could before looking back to Michael. Still unsure, she followed his eye-line back to the first Matthewson story. It was only then that she realised the part of the page Michael was staring at.

'The date,' she said. Aloud and deliberately, but almost to herself. 'The first Matthewson cutting is dated July 17th. That's nearly seven months after his family were killed. Seven months after his obsession started.'

'Exactly. Seven months and he doesn't note Matthewson once. Which means he didn't suspect his involvement in that time. But then suddenly Matthewson becomes the focus. Becomes the obsession. With no real explanation. Except—'

'. . . for the date.'

Sarah finished Michael's theory without hesitation.

'Matthewson appears on McGale's radar within days of his meeting this BG & RM. A meeting important enough for him to schedule it in an otherwise empty diary.'

Michael smiled. Sarah was up to speed. Now they needed to put that knowledge to work.

'So whoever BG & RM are,' Michael began, 'perhaps they could be the source of McGale's belief that Matthewson was involved in the attacks. Which, if that's right, would make them the next pieces of the puzzle.'

'Clearly.' Sarah nodded her agreement. '*If* that's right.'

'It's a big "if ", I agree. But it's the most likely lead we have right now.'

'Agreed,' said Sarah. She glanced back at the diary. 'But those initials? BG and RM? They're not a whole lot to go on, are they?'

'Not if they were all we had, no,' Michael replied. 'But they may not be. I've been thinking about the student who brought McGale out of—'

Michael stopped speaking. His eyes darted towards the open office door.

Sarah opened her mouth to speak but was silenced by his raised palm. Michael tapped his ear. An instruction to listen. Then, without making a sound, he mouthed an explanation.

'Lift mechanism.'

Sarah took just a moment to understand. She attuned her own ears to what Michael could already hear, and she knew that he was right.

The unmistakable sound of the ageing lift's mechanism trying – and failing – to engage. Sarah realised now why Michael had obstructed the lift's cage door, jarring it open with the litter bin. Taking the lift out of action would give them both a warning and time to act on it.

Sarah felt her stomach turn with fear. The vivid memory of their recent violent encounter haunted her.

'Who is it, Michael?'

'I don't know,' Michael replied. 'But whoever it is has six flights of stairs before they get to us. So grab something heavy and follow me.'

FORTY-THREE

Graham Arnold climbed each of the six flights of stairs with silent care. He had cursed the noise that the broken lift's mechanism had made. Their instructions had been clear: do not underestimate the target. The ease with which he had seen the lawyer enter a secure building and disengage the alarm had made sure he took that warning seriously.

So it was unfortunate the lawyer had been warned of their presence.

'Of all the dumb fucking luck!'

Noel Best hissed from several steps behind. His lack of breath undermined his attempt to whisper. Best was short, squat and built for explosive power over stamina. The much fitter Arnold would have chosen a different partner if he had known the climb that was ahead of them.

'For Christ's sake be quiet!' Arnold snapped. 'You're making more noise than the bloody lift!'

'Well, this wasn't in the job description.' Best's patience was equally thin. 'And I don't see why we're trying to be quiet. If this guy's really that good he'll already know we're here.'

Arnold did not respond. Best was probably right.

When Arnold finally reached the sixth floor his partner was just half a flight behind him. The noise told him that.

Arnold took his customised Walther PPS pistol from his shoulder holster. With it he covered the length of the corridor ahead of him. A firearm specialist, Arnold had done this a thousand times, both in training and for real. Nothing would step into the corridor and live.

Best was not far behind. At the top of the stairs, he placed his right hand on the corridor wall as he struggled to draw air into his lungs. Looking up, he saw Arnold armed and ready to go. With a deep breath Best reached into his own shoulder holster, drew his weapon and indicated a readiness to continue.

Arnold led the way in silence. Every movement of his body was mirrored exactly by Best. The choreographed efficiency of their progress had been honed over countless hours of practice. Such had been the way in the hardened Royal Ulster Constabulary. Their eyes were everywhere; every angle covered by the sweeping views of their precision-wielded pistols.

Within moments they were either side of the closed door to room 6.11.

Their ability to silently communicate was practically telepathic. No words were needed. They moved into their usual positions. Best stood head-on to the door, with Arnold to his right.

The bigger man steeled himself, ready to open the probably secured door via the precise application of his powerful right boot. Arnold was close beside him, tightening his grip on his weapon as he prepared to enter.

A final glance, a nod of his head and Best burst into action. The power behind his kick was concentrated on the lock and the latch. It sent the door crashing open. Anyone hiding behind it would be in traction for weeks. If they were lucky.

Best used his momentum to take him through the damaged door frame. He regained his footing with a speed that came from repeated execution of the same movement.

The process was so ingrained that Best had no need to

consider his step. Instead his attention was all around him as he viewed the room ahead. Satisfied in an instant that the rear of the office was clear, Best swept to his right, lowered himself to one knee and covered one side of the office with a single sweep of his pistol.

Arnold was right behind him.

Positioned at his full height, he used the same expert technique to ensure the safety of the left half of the room. Within half a second he knew that his side was clear, and so he aimed his weapon in the direction of the room's one remaining hiding place: McGale's desk.

Arnold was certain that the lawyer had heard them coming and so he expected to find nothing. But that would not prevent him from doing his job. He completed the search before turning back to Best.

'Nothing,' Arnold confirmed.

'No surprise there. So now what?'

'Now we sweep the building. They're still in here somewhere.'

FORTY-FOUR

Michael stood at the door to room 6.3. A five-iron golf club was gripped firmly in his hands; the closest thing to a weapon he had found as he had rushed to leave McGale's office. He hoped it would be good enough. With the repeating crash of violently opened doors growing ever closer, he would soon find out.

'They're almost here.'

Sarah stood behind Michael, another snatched golf club shaking in her terrified grip.

'I know.'

Michael was keeping one ear on the corridor. The violent entry into McGale's office and the systematic search of the sixth floor had confirmed that the newcomers were there for them. He turned back to Sarah.

'Just stay calm and do exactly what I told you. Do that and we'll be alright.'

'How can you be sure? We barely survived against one. What chance have we got with more?'

'These aren't the same kind of guys.'

Michael needed Sarah to be unhesitant if they were to survive this. For that she needed confidence. He would do his best to provide it.

'And I only hear two of them. There's no reason we can't take two, Sarah. You just have to do as I've said. Remember, when the door crashes open you hit the first gun.'

'When the door crashes open, hit the first gun. When the door crashes open, hit the first gun . . .'

Sarah was almost chanting to herself. Michael hoped for both their sakes that the mantra would hold. That it would overcome her panic. If it did not then they were dead; Michael could not do this alone.

The sound of the door to the neighbouring office being smashed from its hinges took Michael's mind away from Sarah. The noise that passed through the poorly insulated walls had a welcome familiarity. It confirmed what he had hoped.

Michael listened closely. In his mind he could see the movements he was overhearing. Movements he had witnessed so many times in a hitherto forgotten past. A door being opened with a single boot, followed by a forward assailant covering one half of the room in a single sweeping movement while his partner covered the remaining half. It was the classic technique employed by the Tactical Support Units of the Royal Ulster Constabulary.

Michael had seen it first-hand as he grew up in the wrong neighbourhoods of Belfast. Tried and tested, the system was both devastatingly effective and yet fatally flawed. It worked perfectly against those unfamiliar with it. But when the prey was aware of the formulaic movements involved, that prey could be prepared.

Exactly as Michael intended to be.

Their pursuers stayed true to routine. Just as Michael hoped they would. The sound told him that the office across the hall had been entered with the same degree of terrible force, while the silence that followed indicated another efficient but fruitless search. It was in this silence that Michael turned to Sarah.

'We're next. Get ready.'

FORTY-FIVE

Sarah's blood turned to ice at Michael's words. As she struggled to control her breathing, she could hardly focus on the metal club she held in her shaking hands. She needed to calm herself. Needed reassurance. She found it by looking at Michael. He was calm and controlled, his breathing steady. The taut muscles of his back were visible through the undersized t-shirt he was still wearing. It was the back of a strong man. Which was exactly what she needed Michael to be. This was the man who had fought a trained killer and lived. Most importantly, this was the man who had already saved her life once. And a man who – she believed – would do everything possible to save it again.

These thoughts were going through Sarah's mind just as Michael turned to her and whispered:

'Time's up.'

The door to room 6.3 was torn from its hinges by the force of Noel Best's boot. Best must have expected another secured room as the power was considerable. Too considerable. Exactly as Michael had hoped.

The unlocked door was thrown through its axis with such momentum that it came away from the frame and struck the left-hand wall of the office. It did not slow Best for an instant as he hurtled into the room. Michael made no attempt to stop him; it would fall to Sarah to engage him first. Michael's attention was already elsewhere. Barely a flicker of time was available in which he had to predict where the second man would appear and muster his full strength to swing McGale's five-iron towards that spot.

The swinging club met a fleeting moment of resistance in the same instant that Michael first saw Graham Arnold. Resistance that did not last. The entire shape of the man's face collapsed under the bad intentions Michael had put behind the swing. It was bone versus metal, and bone lost. In a tenth of a second Arnold's nose had exploded, his right cheekbone had collapsed and most of his teeth were now in his throat. Michael had no way of knowing how tough a man Arnold might be, but that did not matter. No one could sustain that level of trauma and stay standing.

Without pausing, Michael turned to Sarah, whose role had been to swing at the first man's pistol. A simple task, but simple is not the same as easy. It had been a big responsibility to give to anyone. Especially someone alien to violence. And yet, as Michael turned, he saw she had risen to the challenge; Best was clutching his hand, his gun nowhere to be seen.

It bought them a much-needed moment, but that was all; Sarah's second swing was much less effective, lacking both the surprise and the momentum she needed. Best caught the club in his good hand as it came towards him and wrenched it from her grip. As Sarah fought to keep hold of it, she was dragged towards Best. Close enough for a vicious left hook to send her crashing to the floor, blood streaming from her mouth.

Michael's adrenaline was at an all-time high. At its limit, he thought. So he was shocked to feel his blood pump even faster at the sight of Sarah's pain. The rage it brought from within him was like nothing he had experienced in decades.

It found an immediate outlet.

With a primal roar Michael ran at Best. Best's attention was still on Sarah, aiming a kick as she struggled to her feet. It was not a blow he would complete.

Michael's golf club had been discarded in unthinking anger. Instead he had just his own body as he took Best at a run. The two men crashed over the room's only table and landed heavily on the floor behind it.

Michael was the quicker to react as they hit the carpet. He did not hesitate. Best, still reeling from the shock of the attack, had no time to think before being pummelled by Michael's fists, elbows and head. But thinking was not necessary. This situation called for instinct and power, and Best had those in spades.

Reacting as an animal would, Best began to match Michael blow for blow, his fists doing damage wherever they could land. It was a dogfight. Raw. Uninhibited. Exhausting.

Both men were waning within seconds. Slowing. Weakening. The blows were taking their toll. Finally Best managed to flip Michael, sending him feet away. It was a moment's respite, long enough for both to struggle to their feet, but over the instant they were standing.

Sarah backed towards a side wall as Michael and Best careered around the room. She had regained her wits and knew that she risked being crushed as the two men slammed from one wall to the next.

Punching. Kicking. Gouging. Biting. Both men knew that they could not keep up such intensity. Each one needed the killer blow, and were beating each other to a bloody pulp as they looked for it.

It is a common misconception that a knockout punch should be aimed at the chin. A strong enough blow to any part of the head will lead to unconsciousness, by sending the brain slamming into the side of the skull that houses it. But if a fighter *has* the skill to pick his spot, nothing beats a well-placed blow to the temple.

Michael found that out the hard way as Best's left fist found its way through his guard. Best's knuckles crashed into Michael's temple with all the power the weaker hand could muster. It was a blow that would put most men asleep.

That Michael stayed awake was pure genetic luck. The ability to take a punch had been a Devlin trait for generations. Even so, the punch left him dazed for too long. By the time his head cleared he was already pinned to the wall, beside the remains of the shattered door. Best had lifted him clear of the floor, an iron grip encasing Michael's increasingly damaged throat.

Michael looked down as he struggled to breathe and saw the determination in Best's eyes. Best intended to end this fatally. There was nothing Michael could do to stop him. He tried. Thrashed weakly at the wounds he had already inflicted to Best's face and head. But his blows had little effect, with their frequency and power decreasing as his oxygen disappeared.

Michael could feel his strength seeping from his body as his life was choked away. But Sarah still had hers.

Michael had claimed all of Best's attention since launching his attack, and so Best did not spot Sarah as she picked up one of the discarded golf clubs, gripped it firmly in her hands, took careful aim and swung. The head of the club connected with Best's right ear, clean and crisp. His grip on Michael's almost-crushed throat broke.

Best turned, angry and in pain. He was determined to pay that pain back, and then some. But Sarah had learned from her previous mistake. She didn't pause, not even to glance in Michael's direction as he crumpled to the floor, gasping for pained but essential breath. Instead she swung again immediately, full force, and struck Best across the face, tearing a deep gash in his skin.

Michael's eyes had cleared in time to see the second blow, and that Best was still standing. Still fighting. Michael marvelled at the resilience. The man just would not go down.

Then history began to repeat itself.

Sarah took a third swing, but she had again lost the element of surprise, and this time Best was ready. He launched his full weight towards her, bringing him inside Sarah's swing circle. With the club no longer a threat, he shoulder-barged her, sending her careering into and then down the opposite wall. This time Sarah stayed down, the last of her fight now knocked out of her.

Michael would play the next moment over in his mind many times. A moment that would make him question his belief in the life he had created. It proved to him that, despite everything, he had never really left the old Michael Devlin behind.

Best had spotted his fallen weapon and started towards it. Even with his mind still struggling to focus, Michael knew what that meant: if Best reached the pistol neither Michael nor Sarah would leave the room alive.

In that instant Michael made a choice. A choice that cost Noel Best his life.

Michael looked to his left at the remains of the office door, smashed against the wall. He reached out and gripped a single shard of glass that hung limply from what had been the door's upper half. Climbing to his feet, he rushed towards Best without a sound. It was a short distance, and he covered it fast. So fast that Best did not notice him until it was much too late.

Just as Best reached the spot where his gun had fallen, he half-turned. It may have been a sound that alerted him. Or perhaps just that feeling of presence when another human being is so close. Whatever it was, he never had a chance to react. He felt nothing as he saw Michael's arm swing past his throat, sending deep-crimson droplets shooting through the air.

Full realisation took a few seconds more. It coincided with both the knowledge that the guttural choking sound that Best could hear was coming from his own throat, and with a sudden loss of strength throughout his body.

The dying man fell to his knees, blood seeping from the gaping hole that now ran the width of his neck. Then he looked up into his killer's eyes just as life disappeared from his own.

FORTY-SIX

The distant chimes of Big Ben marked 7 a.m. as Joe Dempsey strode through the entrance of MI6 Headquarters. He flashed his DDS credentials and made straight for the elevators.

Dempsey stepped through the open lift doors. He ran his security pass through the scanner that sat just inside and pressed his left index finger to the biometric reader above it. The building's computerised 'brain' immediately kicked in. It sifted through personnel files at unimaginable speeds and immediately granted him entry to the DDS department on the third floor. A destination that required the highest security clearance. Thanks to Callum McGregor, that was something Dempsey still enjoyed.

The short vertical distance was covered in a heartbeat. Used to the sensation, in barely moments Dempsey was striding along a corridor towards Callum McGregor's occupied office. He entered without knocking. A habit.

He was met by the surprised glance of his director. McGregor had not expected the interruption.

'Jesus, Callum, you look like shit!'

Dempsey was taken aback by the first sight of McGregor. The toll the past days had taken upon the man was unmistakable.

'When was the last time you slept?'

'Thanks a lot,' McGregor replied. The heavy bags under his eyes were unusually prominent. 'Some of us have been busy.'

'Bugger busy, Callum. You've got to sleep. You're making yourself ill.'

'I haven't got time for ill, Joe. Or sleep. What do you need?'

Dempsey could detect a strange tone in McGregor's voice. He couldn't place it. On any other man he would describe it as defeat, but not on Callum McGregor. Never on him.

Dempsey pushed the thought from his mind.

'I don't *need* anything. I've come to update you.'

McGregor's eyes narrowed.

'This couldn't have waited until the rest of the world's awake?'

'Only if you want to waste more time chasing shadows.'

McGregor leaned back into a large leather chair that he somehow made look undersized. He took off his glasses and stared Dempsey in the eye.

'OK. Tell me.'

McGregor's debrief took over ten minutes.

He had insisted that Dempsey left out no detail and, with one key exception, Dempsey did just as ordered. The existence of Stanton, however, he held back. It was Dempsey's nature to play his cards close to his chest. To keep key information to himself. Kept even from McGregor, a man he trusted with his life. But on this occasion Dempsey had another reason, too. Because if he shared the existence of Stanton then McGregor would be obliged to disclose the information to Britain's other intelligence agencies. And to the Americans. This would surely take matters from the director's hands, and that in turn could lead to Dempsey's *actual* removal from the hunt for Sam Regis' killer. Dempsey could not allow that to happen, and so he chose to assist McGregor in his duty by not burdening him with the information.

By the time Dempsey was through, he had told McGregor everything else. That – contrary to the official line – Eamon

McGale *had* seen a lawyer while in custody, and that the two men had spent almost two hours together. That the lawyer was now dead, killed in a car accident within an hour of leaving Paddington Green. That the same lawyer's family were now missing. And that someone had tried to kill the lawyer's closest friend – the one person to whom he'd spoken after leaving the cell – just hours later, first with a car bomb and then with a gun.

For the second time in as many days, Dempsey had made McGregor's jaw drop.

'You're telling me that Eamon McGale saw Daniel Lawrence? And now Lawrence is dead? How was it kept quiet? And how the hell do *you* know about it when *I* don't?'

The defeat in McGregor's voice was replaced by indignation. It was no great improvement.

'The same answer to both, Callum. It was kept quiet because the custody sergeant was bought. Trevor Henry was the only one who knew the solicitor was there. He didn't even tell our agents on scene. I stumbled on a lead that took me to him and he told me everything.'

'With only the slightest persuasion, I'm sure,' commented McGregor. 'Where is he now?'

'In his own cells back at Paddington Green. I took him straight there. Someone is going to want him very dead very soon. He'll be best protected by his own.'

McGregor nodded in agreement.

'Safest place for him. Tell me more about the friend.'

'That one's messy. His name's Michael Devlin. A barrister, worked with Lawrence on most of his big cases. Lawrence spoke to him last night after leaving Paddington Green. I checked his phone records. There's a single outgoing call after he left McGale, from his phone to Devlin's. Eighteen hours later there's a car bomb, followed by a shoot-out at Devlin's address. Someone wanted the guy dead, Callum. Do you think that might be a coincidence too?'

McGregor shook his head.

'Of course it bloody isn't. So what happened to him?'

'No idea, except that Devlin wasn't in the car when the bomb went off. It made a mess of the poor bastard's house, though. Someone else was moving the thing for him, I believe a CNN cameraman called Jack Maguire. The car explodes, Devlin rushes outside with the reporter he was talking to, then someone on a motorbike tries to shoot them both in a ride-by.'

'I take it this is the Islington bombing from earlier tonight?'

'It is, yeah.'

'Then why wasn't I fully briefed on that earlier? If it's related to McGale?'

'Because no one connected the dots and put them together, I guess.'

'You mean no one *else* connected the dots. What about the reporters you mentioned?'

'Sarah Truman and Jack Maguire. Both from CNN. They were at Devlin's at the time of the attack. Following up a lead, it seems. They came across the custody sergeant before I did and ended up getting dragged into all this. I believe Maguire died in the car bomb, and that Truman left the scene with Devlin on the gunman's motorcycle.'

'What? They left on his bike? Is this the most incompetent assassin on the bloody planet or something?'

McGregor's incredulity was visibly rising.

'Far from it,' Dempsey replied. 'From what I was told by some of the witnesses, the gunman seems to have been highly skilled. I have a feeling that Devlin and Truman got incredibly lucky. I have a feeling they somehow got away from James Turner.'

McGregor did not respond immediately. He seemed to take his time. To consider what he had been told. For once he did so without standing or pacing around the room. Dempsey found the change a little unnerving. He put it down to tiredness.

When he spoke again the subject had moved on.

'OK. So you've no idea where the lawyer or reporter are now?'

'None at all. They'll have gone to ground if they have any sense. Same is true of Lawrence's family. They've just disappeared. Hopefully with Devlin.'

The room fell silent once again. A silence only broken when McGregor placed his oversized hands on his desk and propelled his wheel-mounted chair backwards, forcibly exhaling as he did so.

'My God, Joe, this is one hell of a mess.'

'It's more than a mess, Callum,' Dempsey replied. 'This department is potentially compromised. All the agencies are. There are things going on which someone in intelligence *must* know about. Turner being placed on the SO19 team. The lawyer meeting McGale without any of us being told. The check on his phone records that must have led them to Devlin. Intelligence *has* to be involved in all of that. This is a full-on conspiracy, Callum. And we're ten yards behind the pace.'

McGregor looked towards the ceiling as Dempsey spoke. He leaned back in his chair, covering both his mouth and chin with a single enormous hand. He stared into space as Dempsey's words sank in. He was considering how he could best regain control of the situation, Dempsey thought.

Finally he took his hand from his mouth and looked back at his agent.

'You're right. Someone in the department has got to be in on this. Maybe more than one. Which means we don't know who we can trust.'

'And?'

'And that makes you the right man at the right time, doesn't it? Everyone else thinks I've kicked you off of this, Joe. So no one is going to question where you are while the main team gets on with the investigation.'

'Makes sense.'

Both Dempsey and McGregor knew that the agent was getting precisely what he wanted.

'But if I'm off the books,' Dempsey asked, 'what are my parameters?'

'At your discretion. We need this cleared up, Joe. And cleared up quick. Do whatever you have to. Just make sure it happens.'

Dempsey nodded and without another word he turned and left the room.

FORTY-SEVEN

The cold of the morning air burned Joshua's lungs as he drank in each mouthful of hard-earned breath. The sights of London's Hyde Park passed him in a blur as he pushed himself ever harder. The unseasonal warmth in which England had recently basked was gone, replaced by the sting of the morning chill. It made Joshua feel more alive than he had in days.

Joshua pushed himself to move even faster. Forced his body to do things that he had previously taken for granted. The speed at which he covered the acres of London's largest park would have been impressive for a man half his age, but as the years advanced he hit that speed through gritted teeth and sheer bloody-mindedness. No one could outrun time. Age was stalking him. Had been for a while. As Joshua drew each tortured breath he found himself wondering, once again, whether his current assignment was a job too far.

Ignoring the park's landmarks, Joshua used his own sense of direction to bring him south. His speed remained constant in spite of the screaming demands of his ageing body. Only his goal mattered: to reach the end of the run in a time that improved upon yesterday's.

The gates at the southern end of Park Lane marked one of the UK's most prestigious addresses; certainly its costliest. Joshua turned left as he reached them and edged onto the straight path that ran alongside the half-mile length of road. With a glance towards the massive bronze statue of Achilles that stood to his left, he prepared to break into his final sprint. This burst of speed would take him the last half-mile to Marble Arch and conclude the torturous element of his morning exercise regime.

Joshua took the first steps with the force necessary to hit top speed in the shortest time. Perhaps today he would have hit his peak, but after just a few paces at his top speed, he was brought to a sudden halt by the sound of the dreaded ringtone.

Pulling up, he cursed to himself, breathing hard. Fumbled through his baggy running clothes for the vibrating handset. Found it. Put the receiver to his ear without looking at the screen.

'I was starting to think something had happened to you.'

'Don't worry about me,' Joshua replied. 'I was jogging.'

'I wasn't worried. Although with your breathlessness from a little exercise, maybe I should be?'

Joshua refused to rise to the bait.

'What do you have for me?'

'Not on this line,' Stanton replied. The answer invited no debate. 'Memorise this number, then destroy your phone. Purchase an unregistered pay-as-you-go handset for cash and call me back. I'll be waiting.'

'Wait!' Joshua exclaimed. 'It's 7.30 in the morning. I won't be able to pick up a handset for another hour and a half at the earliest.'

'Then I'll expect your call at 9 a.m.,' was Stanton's terse reply. It was followed immediately by the sound of the phone line being cut off.

Joshua shook his head at the abrupt disconnection. And at his enforced subservience to a man far from his equal. Not that there was anything he could do about it. For now, at least.

With the number committed to memory, he sat down on the grass leading to the Achilles statue and dismantled the phone's handset.

The established line of communication to Stanton had somehow been compromised. That much was obvious. Joshua wasted no time speculating on what form that compromise had taken. Instead he gazed at the massive bronze Achilles that was still ahead of him.

The statue had been cast from the cannons captured from Napoleon at the Battle of Waterloo and raised to commemorate that victory. One of Joshua's favourites, the sight always brought him to a halt. Today, though, it had a different effect. For the first time he thought of the man portrayed by the statue, rather than the victory it represented. He contemplated the similarities between himself and the mythical hero. Both gifted soldiers whose pride overtook duty. Both warriors who dealt out death as naturally as others took breath. Both giants in thrall to inferior men.

Joshua hoped that his own story would have a happier ending.

FORTY-EIGHT

Joshua was back in his hotel chair as the clock approached 9 a.m. With the new handset's battery plugged into the mains socket, the touchscreen came to life. He punched in Stanton's new number and waited for the ringtone.

A single ring. Same as always.

'Punctual as always, Sergeant. It's a pity you haven't been so reliable in the rest of our dealings.'

'As much a pity as your failure to keep me informed of the necessary details.' Joshua would not let the barbed comment pass. 'But that's not helping, is it? What do you want?'

'I want you on the next plane to Belfast. Michael Devlin and the reporter are both in the city. I want them dealt with once and for all. Do this and you have my word that our relationship is at an end.'

Joshua was surprised by the lack of any threat in Stanton's instructions. He tried not to show it.

'Do you have any idea where I'll find them? It's not that small a place.'

'At the moment I don't, but that will change. And you were right about Michael Devlin. He does seem to be rather more than I had realised.'

'Why the change of heart? I thought you said he was "just a lawyer".'

'Not that it's important, but events have placed things in a different light. Mr Devlin holding his own against you was one thing. That could have been luck. Or a bad day at the office.'

Joshua baulked at the insinuation. But still he held his tongue.

Stanton continued.

'But hours later Devlin encountered two more of my people. Good men. One of them is now in intensive care with a hole where his face should be. The other is in a morgue. Any man who comes up against the three of you in twenty-four hours and walks away needs closer attention. I intend to give him that.'

Joshua processed the information. It caused a number of different emotions. First among them was relief, that his talents had not deteriorated as much as he had feared. Two other professionals had taken a beating at Devlin's hands. One of them fatal. That lessened Joshua's failure.

But the news also raised the stakes. Joshua could feel himself being pulled towards a final reckoning.

'You're clear that this is it for me? I kill Devlin and Truman, plus whatever loose ends they raise in Belfast, and I walk away?'

'Yes.'

'I won't find that I have to deal with the Lawrence family too? And God knows what else?'

'I've told you that you have my word, Sergeant.'

Stanton was becoming impatient. No effort was made to hide it.

'Let *me* worry about what *I* have to deal with. *You* just take care of Devlin and Truman and you're free.'

'I won't fail.' Joshua spoke through gritted teeth. He hated his predicament. 'Just get me the information I need and I'll wait for your call in Belfast.'

'One more thing, Sergeant.' It was Stanton's turn to keep

the line alive. 'You should also know that Joe Dempsey has complicated things.'

The name made the temperature of Joshua's blood drop.

'In what way?'

'In that you were right about him, too. He seems to have come much closer to the truth than I'd anticipated. To the extent that he obtained my telephone number and spoke to me directly.'

If Stanton had been speaking about any other man then Joshua would have dismissed it as a lie. A manipulation. But Joe Dempsey?

Yeah. I can believe that, he thought. *And it explains the panic over the phone.*

'What did he say?'

'That's unimportant. What matters is the fact that he reached me. It means that he has achieved much in a very short time. The man is highly motivated, uniquely talented and he intends to stop us. So you need to be prepared for his intervention.'

'Just prepared? Wouldn't it be safer to take the fight to him? Before he causes any more trouble?'

'Not at this stage,' Stanton replied. 'The last thing we want is to bring that man any closer to us than he already is. If we can keep him at bay, we keep him at bay.'

Joshua listened to every word. He assessed both the content of what was said and the underlying message. The latter was simple. Despite the impression Stanton was trying to give, he was a frightened man.

'Understood?' Stanton finally asked.

'Understood.'

Joshua disconnected the line without another word.

He lay back on the bed and considered what he had been told. The room's panoramic window offered a stunning daytime view, but Joshua saw only his own thoughts. As his mind ran through Stanton's words he allowed himself a wry smile.

This thing now had only one ending. Joe Dempsey was involved, which meant only one of them would finish this alive. It was impossible to tell who it would be but at least one thing was certain: regardless of which one survived, Stanton would not live to see the fruits of his endeavours.

FORTY-NINE

Sarah awoke with a start from a disturbed sleep. Wracked by the trauma of the last twenty-four hours, her exhaustion had been too great to fight. She had fallen unconscious within minutes of returning to the hotel.

She lifted her head from the pillow and looked around. There was not much to see, but still her eyes slowly cleared as she dragged her mind and body into consciousness.

Still half-asleep, she leaned over and reached for the bottle of mineral water on the bedside table. As she did so, she registered two unexpected sights. The first was the makeshift bed she had laid out on the floor beside her own, entirely untouched. The second told her why. Michael Devlin was sat on the chair in the corner of the room, still dressed and bloodstained from the horrors of the early morning.

Sarah raised herself up onto her elbow and faced him.

'Are you OK?'

Michael did not reply. He did not even look up. He made no effort to hide how he was feeling. The effects of the morning were plain.

Sarah pushed herself upright and gazed intently at the man. Had he been broken by what he had been forced to do? It was a thought she could hardly contemplate.

Sarah's mind returned to the horrors of the previous night. She had thought nothing could shock her more than the burning remains of Jack Maguire and the violent escape that had followed. But within hours she had been proved wrong.

What she had seen in room 6.3 was so close – so visceral – that the memory made her gag.

The first thing Sarah had noticed when Michael had helped her to her feet was the blood that masked the left side of his face. It had come from both his existing wound, and from several fresh ones. And it had brought the reality of what she had experienced crashing back in.

With it had come the rush of adrenaline. She had jumped to her feet. To run or to fight? She did not know which, and nor would she ever. Instead she would remember the most shocking sight of her life. The man she had attacked with the golf club, face down and lifeless in a pool of his own blood.

The next minutes were less clear in her memory. Fear and panic saw to that. But she could clearly recall the pain in Michael's eyes. The shock that had overtaken him as his adrenaline drained and the reality of the situation set in.

It was in these moments that Sarah had taken the lead for the first time. She had galvanised Michael, all but dragging him from the office as quickly as she could, out of the building and into the night, where they had begun their short journey through the shadows and back to the hotel.

Sarah shook off the memories. She would not allow them to overtake her. Not now. Instead she pushed herself up onto her feet and shook off the emotional paralysis that had been threatening to grow.

She approached the silent Michael on still-faltering legs. Crouching beside him, she placed her hands on his knees.

'Michael, we need to get moving.'

Sarah gazed upwards into his downcast eyes as she spoke.

'I need to get you some fresh clothes, then we need to leave.'

Michael did not seem to register the words. He certainly did not acknowledge them when he spoke.

'What about last night?' Michael asked. His voice seemed almost nervous, his eyes uncertain. 'Doesn't that matter? After what you saw me do?'

'All I saw you do was what you had to.'

Sarah's voice was firm. Strong. She meant every word.

'You kept us alive when the odds were stacked against us. Somehow you managed it.'

'But *how* I did it, Sarah. You saw. Doesn't it change things? Doesn't it make you want to get away from me?'

'Why would it?'

'Because . . . it wasn't just instinct.' Michael's voice was now even quieter. He sounded ashamed. 'I wasn't jacked-up on adrenaline or anything like that. I was calm, Sarah. And I knew what I was doing. I knew *exactly* what I was doing.'

Sarah took a moment to understand what Michael was saying. To understand *why* he was saying it. The additional time did not help her.

'Does that matter? You saved our lives.'

'I don't know,' Michael replied. 'I just know that what you think – about me, about the depths I can sink to – matters. What you think matters.'

Sarah listened. She noticed the uncertainty in Michael's voice. The loss of confidence worried her. If they were going to survive, the one thing they needed above all else was a fully functioning Michael Devlin.

'Michael, are you worried that you've scared me away?'

Michael nodded slowly. Then he shook his head. He seemed unsure. He took a few moments and a few deeper breaths and then he spoke again.

'I . . . I . . . I think I just, I don't know if you'll want to run. Now that you've seen the real me?'

'What do you mean by that? The real you? Who's the real you?'

'The man you saw last night. The man who picked up a shard of glass and slit another man's throat. I didn't think I was capable of that sort of violence any more. I thought I'd put it behind me. But I *meant* to kill him, Sarah. I *wanted* to kill him.'

Sarah opened her mouth to speak, but no words came out. She was unsure how to respond.

What does he want to hear, she thought. *And what do I want to say?*

The truth was, Sarah was conflicted. Not about what Michael had done. That had been necessary; if he had not killed their attacker then they would both be dead. But what he was saying now was something more. Michael was admitting to a past Sarah had not known about. To a capacity to go to whatever place he needed to. In order to survive. In order to win.

She knew that Michael's admission should concern her. But it did not. And not just because a capacity for violence was useful in their current predicament. It was something more than that. There was something *about* Michael. Something to which Sarah already felt a connection. A connection that, judging by his need for her to accept what she had witnessed, Michael seemed to feel too.

She looked back up into his eyes. She needed to snap him out of it, but she did not know how. In that moment a brusque approach seemed best.

'Michael, you did what you had to do. That's it. It doesn't matter what I think.'

'I understand,' Michael said. His voice was empty, suggesting to Sarah that he did not understand at all.

Without another word he rose to his feet, turned his back, walked into the small en-suite bathroom and closed the door behind him.

The sound of the running shower was almost immediate. It added welcome noise to the room's eerie quiet. Sarah was thankful for that as she took Michael's place in the chair.

Staring out of the near window, her eyes took in nothing from the scenes below. She was once again lost within her own thoughts, trying to make sense of the man she was with. A man to whom she had entrusted her life.

Sarah's internal conflict was fuelled by a paradox. She *had* been shocked by what Michael was capable of, but at the same time she had been comforted by that capability. Michael's charm and charisma concealed a capacity for cold, deliberate violence. But, in the circumstances, that was *not* bad news.

A trail of destruction had followed them from London to Belfast. There was doubtless more to come. They could not go back. They did not know who to trust. All they could do was keep moving forward. Uncover the truth. They would only do that – they would only survive – by staying single-minded. Whatever confusion or connection was going on between them, it would have to wait.

Moving towards the large mirror that sat on the room's small desk, Sarah glanced at her reflection. The last few days had taken their toll; the price paid was visible on her usually fresh face. Her jaw was blackened from the blow of the night before. The skin beneath her eyes was darkened in a way it had never been. Even her usually vibrant brunette hair was matted and messy.

Her clothes were just as worn; her usually pristine white

blouse hinted at what she had endured while her black pencil-skirt had seen better days.

Turning away, Sarah switched on the television and reached into the cheap handbag that Michael had bought for her at the airport. Inside was a basic cosmetic kit. Sarah had little vanity, and what there was had been eradicated by recent experience. But with God-knows-who still searching for her, she could not attract attention by looking like a woman who had just been through hell.

With one eye on the mirror, Sarah changed the television channel to CNN in time for the headlines. She listened to the mid-morning anchor while working to hide the fist-sized bruise on her jaw. There was little on the bulletin relating to the death and destruction she and Michael had lived through in the past eighteen hours. The exception was the report of the Islington car bomb, but even that story lacked several key elements. No mention of her involvement, or even of Jack Maguire.

A feeling of dread grew in her gut as she changed the channel to find BBC Northern Ireland. Sarah reasoned that the murder of a man in a university office would warrant a mention on local news, especially with the connection to Eamon McGale. Wrong. The short report ended with no indication that anything had occurred.

'Anything on the news?'

Michael had a towel wrapped around his waist and was using a second to dry his hair. The confidence had returned to his voice, as if he had forgotten the exchange that had passed between them. It was what Sarah needed to hear.

'Not a thing.'

Sarah noticed the deep black bruises that littered Michael's battered body. She tried to ignore them as she continued.

'Not even on the local news.'

'And what time is it now?'

'They were the 10.30 headlines.'

'Shit!' The development was not unexpected, but it was still unwelcome. 'Then that settles it. We need to go ask for help.'

Sarah nodded. They had already discussed the possibility.

The absence of a report of their attacker's death could mean only one thing: whoever was behind this had enough influence even here to have the body removed and the story suppressed.

What had happened in London made it no surprise that the English press had been compromised. But the silencing of the story in Belfast told them that the tentacles of influence spread further still. Proof that the people behind Daniel Lawrence's death held as much sway in Ulster as in London.

Michael's boyhood streets were, it seemed, no safer than those they had left behind.

'But how do you know he'll help you?' Sarah asked. 'It's been eighteen years.'

'It doesn't matter,' Michael replied. 'He'll help me. He's my brother.'

FIFTY

'I need the 32 Counties Bar on the Falls Road. You going near?'

The broad accent Michael used surprised Sarah for just a moment. Then she remembered the importance of appearing local, to avoid attracting attention. While justified, it did not make the change from soft brogue to 'street' Belfast any easier on the ear.

'No problem, big man. Jump in.'

The driver's real voice was as heavy as Michael's false one. It made the charade even clearer.

Sarah and Michael climbed into the rear of the taxi. A passenger was already inside. Sarah was shocked for a moment, before remembering Michael's explanation of how black cabs operated in Belfast.

Unlike taxis in London and pretty much everywhere else, Ulster cabs did not just go where the passenger asked. Instead the drivers would place a placard on their dashboard, stating the direction in which they were travelling. Any passenger going that way could jump in but they would rarely enjoy an empty cab. The system only worked if the driver picked up as many passengers as possible.

'You've been in the wars, son.'

The third passenger was a woman, elderly, with more bags at her feet than someone of her size could carry. Her attention was focused on Michael's facial injuries. Sarah had purchased a cheap black polo shirt to replace the ripped and bloodstained t-shirt from the night before. But there was little she could do to disguise the damage on his face.

'Oh, that's nothing,' Michael replied, sounding light-hearted. 'Just an accident playing hurling.'

'Ah, that's a rough game. What's a handsome boy like you doing playing that?'

'Glutton for punishment I guess! So are you heading home?'

Michael's feigned interest in the passenger's life and family – and the skilful way in which he deflected questions about his own – made sure that when their fellow passenger later remembered her cab companion, her mind would give no thought to his cuts and bruises.

They reached her home first. Michael helped her inside with her bags. After their conversation it would have seemed strange not to offer. He then returned to the cab, climbed in and forced a smile at Sarah.

Sarah had not spoken at all since taking the cab. This made sense. Just as Michael was speaking with a long-lost accent to blend in, so Sarah had avoided the attention her American tones could draw. But now they were alone and still Sarah did not speak.

'Are you OK?'

Michael had waited a further two minutes before breaking the silence.

Sarah looked at him, meeting his gaze. It was as if she had not registered the question, just the sound. It did not surprise her; she was still caught up in her mixed emotions towards the man beside her.

'I'm fine.'

Sarah did not want Michael to know her thoughts. She looked around, searching for a change of subject.

'I was just, just distracted by the painting on the streets. On the sidewalks.'

It wouldn't take Michael's forensic mind to see through the diversion. But if he knew what was concerning her he did not show it. Instead he played along.

'Have you never seen pictures of the Falls Road?'

He followed Sarah's eyes to the colourful kerbstones they were passing.

'No,' Sarah replied. 'And I don't get it. Why are they painted those colours?'

'Because this is a Catholic area. Very Catholic. Which makes it Republican. The kerbstones are painted the colours of Ireland's flag, alternating green, white and gold. It's the locals' way of saying that they don't regard themselves as British. That Northern Ireland and the Republic of Ireland are one country.'

'That's a pretty powerful statement,' Sarah replied, now genuinely interested. 'What about the other side? Don't they complain?'

Michael laughed at the question. It was a genuine reaction. It lightened the mood.

'Complaining isn't really their style, Sarah. The pen might be mightier than the sword, but a car bomb trumps them both. Besides, they can't complain when they do exactly the same thing. The kerbstones on the next street are all painted red, white and blue!'

'Are you serious? You mean this street is Republican and the next one's Unionist? But they're so close!'

'Belfast isn't a big place. The two sides live on top of one another. That's why things got so bloody.'

Sarah fell back into silence. A more comfortable one this time.

The street passed by as they drove the last mile of the Falls Road, which stretched away from the centre of Belfast. Sarah had heard of the place, of course, but only now did she realise that it was a literal stone's throw from its Protestant/Loyalist opposite, the Shankill Road.

'How far to go?'

'Five minutes in this traffic,' Michael replied.

'Are you ready to see him?'

'No. But I probably never will be, so we might as well get it over with.'

FIFTY-ONE

'You have a package for Mr Francis.'

Joshua's words were a statement rather than a question. They left the receptionist at Belfast's palatial Europa Hotel in no doubt that her guest was correct.

'Here you are, sir.'

The small blonde who manned the front desk was barely out of her teens. She bent down and grasped the handle of a large metallic briefcase, delivered less than an hour before. It was heavy enough to cause her difficulty as she lifted the case onto the desk, but Joshua plucked it up like it contained nothing weightier than air.

'Do you need any help with your luggage, sir?'

The receptionist's words trailed off towards the end. Joshua had already turned and was walking towards the bank of elevators that would take him to his room.

He stepped into a lift half-full with passengers and pressed the '8' button. To those around him he must have seemed the very picture of professional calm. A businessman, probably. They could not detect the emotion that simmered beneath the calm demeanour.

Right now, Joshua was a dangerously coiled spring.

Anticipation was often the most thrilling aspect of Joshua's career. He could visualise every possible scenario that could arise on an assignment. It was an essential skill; the only way to be prepared for anything. It was this visualisation that would usually send Joshua's heart racing with excitement. But this time, uniquely, it filled him with dread.

Joshua had no doubt that Stanton was willing to live up to his threats. That failure would cost Joshua's family dear. This alone would have removed the thrill of the hunt. But it was *not* alone. Not any more. Even now, as he exited the lift and followed discreet signs to his room, one thought continued to dominate his mind.

Joe Dempsey.

The news that Dempsey was closing in on Stanton had been strangely welcome at first. It meant that – should Joshua fail – he would die with the knowledge that Stanton, too, was doomed to a short life. To be hunted by the most gifted soldier Joshua had ever met. But that feeling did not last. Not once Joshua remembered exactly what he was going up against.

It had been the journey to Belfast that had brought the truth home for him. Ulster. The one post to which every British soldier of his generation had been deployed. And the very first place that Joshua had seen Joe Dempsey in the field. It was here that Joshua had seen how good his protégé really was. Looking back, it was a memory that made him fear the worst. That, this time, there would be only one winner.

It was not the thought of losing that concerned him. Joshua had no wish to die, but he was very aware of his own mortality. He had to be, in his profession. No, it wasn't the loss. What worried Joshua was the *consequence* of that loss. Dempsey would find Stanton. Joshua was sure of that, just as he was sure that Dempsey would act with extreme prejudice when he did so. But what Joshua could not be sure of – what he could not count on – was the timeframe. Even the shortest break between Joshua's failure and Dempsey's revenge was a risk for Joshua's family. In that time – however short – they would be at Stanton's mercy. A mercy that Stanton absolutely lacked.

Joshua could not let that happen. He could not expose his family to that risk. And that meant that Joshua could not afford to lose.

The thought continued to trouble Joshua ten minutes later, as he opened the metal briefcase inside his locked room and began another process demanded by his compulsions.

It was a ritual he had followed countless times.

Similar packages had been delivered to him at hotels or deposit boxes or Western Union outlets in every corner of the globe. They contained everything a skilled professional would need to terminate his unknowing target. But by their nature these items were not selected or packed by Joshua, and so upon receipt he would strip them down to ensure that they lived up to his exacting standards.

The ritual – the stripping of the weapon and the detailed examination that followed – had prepared Joshua mentally for decades. Had calmed his fears, calmed his mind. Except this time his mind was on more than the cold steel in his expert hands. This time the monotony of the examination was broken by Stanton, by Dempsey, and by the threat that each man posed to Joshua's own family.

He brought the military-standard Schmidt & Bender 3-12 × 50 PM II telescopic sight to his eye. Manipulated its range to his satisfaction. Continued for longer than was strictly necessary; his obsessive compulsion in action. It should have settled his mind.

Instead it just reminded him of that Ulster mission from long ago.

*

Dempsey had been fresh out of the hellish SAS selection process back then, but still he joined that first mission with an already fearsome reputation.

The young officer had sailed through advanced training with scores that rivalled even Joshua's own. It had been inevitable, then, that they would be matched together for what was to follow. And so months were spent shoulder to shoulder as Joshua strove to raise Dempsey even further, to the level required of the regiment's most elite section: the Chameleon Unit.

But training was no reality. The true test had come in the field.

Joshua had repeated this mantra from Dempsey's first day. He had refused to recognise the rookie's potential. Years of active service in the most dangerous corners of the globe told Joshua that being good on the training ground meant nothing. To win his genuine respect, Dempsey had to prove himself under fire. It was an opportunity that was not long delayed.

Three months of intensive drill-training in the world's least hospitable environments had been cut short by orders to return to Hereford. Joshua and Dempsey had obeyed, arriving in time to join an equipped and briefed assault team as they prepared to leave the base. The two men had collected their equipment and reached the main unit as soon as they set foot on the ground, and received their own briefing in the air above the Irish Sea. It had been an irregular way to begin a virgin mission, but Joe Dempsey had shown no nerves. No fear.

And, for the first time, Joshua had allowed himself to be impressed.

The capital of lawlessness in Northern Ireland at the time was South Armagh, nicknamed 'Bandit Country'. At the start of Joshua's career it had been heavily garrisoned by armoured military installations. By Dempsey's day these were fewer but they were still high in number. It had not seemed to matter. For years the county had been home to the worst of Republican terrorism. To fanatics whose solution to the Irish problem was murder and mayhem. With more violent death per head of population than any other part of the United Kingdom, *this* had been the Ulster where no soldier wanted to serve. And it was where Dempsey's service really began.

The mission had been simple. It was no less dangerous for that. An MI5 informant had passed on word of an upcoming robbery at South Armagh's biggest cash reserve. It was a secure facility close to the border with the Republic; to this day Joshua wondered how it had taken the IRA so long to target the place. Back then it had been guarded by a detachment of the Army's Rifles Regiment and a separate squad from the Royal Ulster Constabulary. That had been a deterrent, but, with enough cash inside to fund an attack of terrifying proportions, not deterrent enough.

The IRA had assembled its best men to carry out the job. Their brief had been a clear one. Overwhelming violence would be the order of the day.

By the time they had reached South Armagh, both Joshua and Dempsey were clear in their own roles. They were to be part of a ten-man unit. All would be deployed outside the facility, with men on either side of the depot's walls. Once there each man would secrete himself in the undergrowth, to await the arrival of the targets.

The team had been stocked for a wait that could extend into days. Each man was prepared to stay hidden – motionless – for up to seventy-two hours. Such early deployment had been deemed essential; the area would be under IRA observation well before the assault. Even a hint of SAS presence would have seen the raid abandoned.

But no such hint had been given. Each man had held his position undetected for over sixty hours. Had ignored the pain and discomfort. And so all had been ready to move when the moment came.

The sudden arrival of the IRA team would have been overwhelming, had it not been expected. Thirty men, hand-chosen to carry out the military-style raid. Half of that number had been divided into smaller groups to cover the depot's exits, while the other half had accompanied a heavily armoured truck as it launched an attack on the front gate.

Only the thirtieth man had remained hidden. Posted to the surrounding hills, from where he would provide sniper cover that very few could equal.

The roar of the lorry's engine had been the unit's call-to-arms. The signal to move had been prearranged: the moment the lorry struck the depot's secure front gate, when the largest number of the IRA team would be committed to the attack. That timing would raise the terrorist death toll to its maximum.

Joshua could still remember the deafening sound of metal upon metal. It had left no doubt that the front gate had been breached. No doubt that it was time to act.

Nine expertly trained soldiers had risen to their feet and moved in unison, flanking the depot from every direction. The tenth man – Dempsey – had remained in place, ready for a very particular role in the counter-attack.

It was Dempsey's clinical execution of this role that Joshua most remembered. And which he now most feared.

Joshua's awareness was as acute then as it was now. So he had been the first of the nine to spot a depot guard falling to a bullet from the hills, a shot that confirmed the presence of a sniper on the IRA side. This had been a worst-case scenario that made the operation much more dangerous. The same threat had been hammered home just moments later, when Joshua saw a member of his own unit fall under the sniper's next shot.

The second shot had sent Joshua diving for cover, into the undergrowth to avoid the sniper's crosshairs. As he hit the floor he had turned his head to where he knew Dempsey was hidden and in that instant had recognised the camouflaged recoil of the young officer's sniper rifle. A single shot in the direction of the South Armagh hills.

It was a shot that Joshua had not expected. At least not so soon. Even now he marvelled that Dempsey could have deduced the IRA gunman's location from just two shots. But back then he had not had time for disbelief. The absence of further sniper fire proved that Dempsey had made a miracle shot. The lone sniper was gone. Only the ground force remained.

What followed was a textbook SAS engagement, ending in the death of all thirty attackers. It was a loss from which the IRA would take a long time to recover. The price was four lives lost. One from the regiment, three from the depot's guards. There had been many reasons for such a one-sided victory, but it was Dempsey's actions that stood out.

Joshua could remember his own reaction like it was yesterday.

He had felt no pride in a successful mission. No sadness in the loss of a comrade. For Joshua there had been only one consideration: the arrival of a soldier with abilities that surpassed his own.

It had been unwelcome then. Now – years later and in circumstances that could cost Joshua his life – it was damn near unbearable.

FIFTY-TWO

Michael and Sarah stood outside the 32 Counties Bar. It was a large street-corner public house. Green-fronted. Just fifteen minutes by cab from the Europa Hotel. The bar front covered an area the width of several shops, and as a weekday lunchtime approached it was beginning to fill up.

'Michael, we have to go in.'

Sarah spoke softly. They had been outside the bar for several minutes. In that time Michael had not moved. He had simply stared at the sign above the door.

Sarah's quiet words broke through. Michael turned. Their eyes met and Michael registered his prolonged daydream. The sight of a childhood landmark had hypnotised him.

A deep breath shook off the feeling. He flashed Sarah a smile.

'I know.' The tone of his voice undermined the smile. Michael was nervous. 'Come on.'

Michael took a deep breath and together they walked through the main doors.

The view that met Michael's eyes was not the one he remembered. The room used to be much smaller, the furniture sparse and low-cost. The bar itself had always been grim. Under-lit.

All of that had changed.

This room was at least twice its former size. The bar had expanded over the years, taking over the shops that had once been its neighbours. It was also now expensively furnished. The polished wood and brass would rival anything Michael was used to in London. Belfast's years of affluence had not passed the place by.

Michael's eyes moved slowly as they took in his surroundings. He was seeing the past, only now in more prosperous surroundings. When Michael left it had been just another rough Catholic bar. His father's bar. Opened at the height of the Troubles, it was where Michael had grown up. And it was from where he had fled.

'Come on.'

Sarah seemed to recognise the effect it was having. She took Michael's arm with her free hand and pulled him forward, towards the long bar that stretched along the room's right-hand wall.

Michael allowed himself to be guided. He enjoyed the feeling of Sarah's hand on his arm. It felt right. But he did not allow himself to be distracted. He signalled to one of the bar staff.

'What can I get you, pal?'

It was the nearest barman. Tall, thin, dark-haired and somewhere in his late twenties. He spoke with the broad accent that Sarah was growing used to.

Michael did not answer. His attention had been caught by a collection of photographs on the wall behind the bar. Sarah followed Michael's eyes.

The faces that stared back were unmistakable. Four photo frames in all. One showed two young boys aged around nine and twelve, dressed in their Sunday best. At least twenty-five years had come and gone since the day captured in the photograph. But the younger boy – the one with the shock of blond hair – could be no one but Michael Devlin.

Michael's eyes, though, were drawn to something different. They had bypassed both the first picture and the frame beside it.

It was an older photograph that had transfixed him. Black and white. It showed a large, powerfully built man, with his gnarled left hand on the shoulder of a blonde girl no older than nineteen. The 32 Counties Bar – the bar as Michael remembered it – was behind them.

Michael felt the burn in the corner of his eyes as he stared at his father, Sean Casey, and the mother he had never known: Katie Devlin. The picture had been taken years before Michael's birth and he had grown up with it on display. He had his own copy, in fact. Kept under lock and key like all his memories of home. Seeing it now? Seeing it here? It was almost too much.

'I asked what I can get you?'

The barman's voice ended Michael's daydream.

Michael snapped out of his semi-trance. He remembered why he was here.

'I'm here to see Liam Casey.'

'Liam's not here.' The barman's tone said that his answer was to be accepted, accurate or otherwise. 'Now, can I get you and your lady friend a drink?'

'Look, mate, I know he's here.' Michael was in no mood for games. 'Now go and get him.'

The thin man's attitude shifted. His previous friendliness disappeared. Replaced by a more threatening presence.

Michael watched as he revealed himself to be more than just a barman.

'I've told you he's not here. Now I think you need to leave before you cause a scene.'

'Listen, mate,' Michael said, his voice low, 'because I'm not telling you again. I want to see your boss so you get your arse behind that bar, go into the back room and tell Liam that Mikey's here to see him!'

'Do you really not know who you're dealing with here?'

The barman's words were plainly the precursor to a threat, but their effect was broken by the words of a woman until now unseen behind him. A woman visibly shaken by the sight of Michael.

'Jesus Christ! Mikey Casey?'

The barman turned to meet the eyes of the speaker, his sneer replaced by a look of shock. He had heard the name 'Mikey Casey' before. Many times. And much more recently than Michael had.

The man's movement to his right gave Michael a clear view of the short, striking redhead who had spoken.

'Mikey, is that you?' Tears welled in her sky-blue eyes as she spoke again.

Michael felt his thumping heart beat harder as he registered a face from his past.

'Anne?' Michael barely managed to choke out the words. 'What are you doing here?'

'What am *I* doing here? Jesus, Mikey, you've been gone twenty years and you want to know what *I'm* doing here? What are *you* doing here?'

Michael's gaze was fixed on Anne Flaherty. Both his oldest friend and the long-term partner of his brother Liam. For some reason Michael just had not expected to see her.

Sarah seemed to sense the history between them. She remained quiet as the two old friends just stared at one another.

'Why have ... what ... what have you come back for, Mikey?'

Anne was the first to speak again. An attempt at formality, but a bad one. Her joy at Michael's return was etched across her face.

'I'm in trouble, Anne. I need his help.' Michael's voice carried no pride.

'Well you look like shite, alright. The other fella's looking worse though, yeah?'

'It's not that simple, Anne. And I can't speak about it out here. Is he in?'

'He's out the back.' A tilt of her head indicated a door at the end of the bar. 'But he won't be pleased to see you, Mikey. You know that, right?'

'I don't want to be here any more than he wants me here. But I don't have a choice. I need to see him.'

Anne nodded her head at Michael's last comment. She accepted it without explanation.

'Well then you two had better follow me.' Anne turned towards Sarah. 'But I think you should introduce me first, Mikey, don't you?'

Michael's eyes followed Anne Flaherty's and settled on Sarah. They lingered, just for a moment. He placed a hand on the small of Sarah's back and guided her forward. A small intimacy; one which Sarah did not reject.

'Anne, this is Sarah Truman. She's, erm, she's a very good friend of mine.' Michael turned to Sarah. 'And, Sarah, this is Anne Flaherty. My oldest friend in the world.'

Sarah reached out and took Anne's hand. The gesture was returned with a warm, genuine smile, and then an indication for Sarah and Michael to follow.

Anne showed them through the door at the end of bar. It led from the large room into a narrow corridor. The corridor seemed to stretch further backwards than the building itself seemed to, at least from the outside. Its walls were lined with photographs of boxing legends from the first half of the twentieth century. They hung at regular intervals along both sides, giving the space a masculine edge as it led to the closed office door at its far end.

As she reached the door Anne put out her hand and gripped the doorknob. Without turning her wrist she looked towards Michael.

'You sure you want to do this?'

'I'm sure I don't,' Michael replied. His heart was racing. 'But what other choice have I got?'

Anne responded with a nod. She turned back to the door, opened it and stepped inside the next room.

'Liam, you've got a visitor.'

Anne's voice seemed distant as Michael's heart thumped ever harder.

The office looked exactly as Michael would have imagined. Sparse and masculine. A reflection of Michael's own style. Something he and his brother shared.

From the doorway he had a clear view of his brother, who was sat behind a desk with just his upper body visible. And not for the first time he thought that no one would ever question their parentage. Liam Casey really was just another version of Michael. Shorter certainly. Bulkier, yes. And with receding black hair in place of his brother's thick blond locks. But for all that they still looked remarkably similar.

Michael did not have long for those thoughts. Liam Casey had glanced up at their arrival and was already rising to his feet. The curiosity that had initially coloured his face had transformed to livid surprise.

Looking at the brother he had not seen in eighteen years, Liam spat out the first words to pass between them in all that time:

'And just what the fuck do you want?'

FIFTY-THREE

Dempsey shook his head at the crowd gathered outside of the Houses of Parliament. It was mostly press, there to hear from the man who would surely be the next prime minister of the United Kingdom. Dempsey was there for a different purpose. But first he would have to endure the inevitable speeches.

As if on cue, Anthony Haversume strode out of one of the Palace of Westminster's many side entrances. The entourage that followed him had tripled in size in the last few days. Hardly a surprise. Parasites always flow in the wake of the biggest fish, and Haversume was the great white shark. A shark that took his place at the makeshift podium erected just ahead of the statue of Oliver Cromwell.

There were many more suitable locations for a press conference. This spot – far lower than road height and with limited standing room around it – left the press packed in, some unable to move, the unluckiest unable to see. But other locations lacked one essential element: the iconic statue now prominent over Haversume's right shoulder.

Dempsey could see the sense in the choice. By addressing the world with the statue of one of England's most famous politicians behind him, Haversume was making a statement. Cromwell had been a committed servant in the history of British democracy. He had also been notoriously ruthless in his dealings with Ireland.

It was a clear message to anyone with a knowledge of history.

The murmur of the crowd grew to a din as Haversume finally took the podium. No individual questions could be heard through the wall of noise. Not that it mattered. Haversume had no intention of answering them.

He took his place and signalled for silence, waiting patiently as voices gradually died. Soon there was nothing but the sound of slowly passing traffic. Only then did Haversume begin.

'As you all know, tonight sees a motion of no confidence in our government's policies in Northern Ireland. You all know where I stand on this issue and what my intentions will be if this vote leads to William Davies' resignation. But this is not a decision for me alone. It is an open vote, taken by all Members of Parliament. By those who represent the British public. By those who represent you.

'Most who hear these words will be familiar with my opinions. And I hope they are sentiments with which you agree. For those unfamiliar with my position, I say this: the Member of Parliament who represents you will tonight have an opportunity to end William Davies' shameful years as prime minister. I ask you to contact that Member's office today and ensure that he or she does their duty. They represent you. They cannot ignore you. Use that power. End this surrender to terrorism. Instruct your MP to vote. To free us of the burden of William Davies.'

Haversume stopped speaking. But his jingoistic plea remained hanging in the air. A round of applause did nothing to shift it. From so close Dempsey could see the domestic press join in only half-heartedly. The podium-thumping style was just not the British way.

After a few seconds of silence, the questions began. Reporters stumbled over each other's words as they fought to be first. They were all ignored. Haversume waved a hand, calling for more silence before he would continue.

'You may well be wondering why I take this view. Why I believe that William Davies has been a disaster for this country and a shame upon us all. Why I believe that he must go, and that he must be replaced by a figure of strength. A figure of resolve. Once and for all, I want to make it clear.

'For many years our country bore the brunt of terrorist atrocity. We stood alone against the longest campaign of terror endured by any Western power. The rest of the world stood by and watched as our streets, our buildings, our very homes were destroyed. Destroyed by Republican fanatics who regarded a disputed border in the north of Ireland as more important than the lives of British men, women and children. We received no help. No support. There was no coalition. No allied military force. We faced this thirty-year threat with no friend alongside us, but face it we did. Generations of young men and women from our armed forces stood as a barrier against this tide of mass murder. They stood together to keep the rest of us safe. They fought this terror, many to their last breath, and they were determined to beat it. They were men and women to be proud of. Men and women to honour. Men and women who gave their youth and, in too many cases, their very lives, to protect you, me and every other citizen of Great Britain.

'And then came William Davies. A good man. An intelligent man. But by no means a brave man. William Davies made it his mission to bring this war to an end. It was a fine ambition, but he pursued it in an unacceptable way. A war is won through strength. Through sacrifice. A war is not won through concession and surrender, and yet this is exactly what our prime minister has done. William Davies met these people around a negotiating table but he failed to negotiate. Instead, he released all so-called 'prisoners of war'. He emptied the prisons of both the mainland and Northern Ireland of their most dangerous inmates. He freed those whose very lives are dedicated to the defeat of this country. Worse still, he has invited the most treacherous of them to join him in the government of the United Kingdom. And for what? What did he receive in return? A promise that the terrorists would lay down their arms. In other words, he gave our enemies what they wanted to stop them attacking us. What is that if it is not surrender?

'But it gets worse. The assurances of peace have failed. Yes, the IRA as it was is gone. Yes, the UVF as it was is gone. But they are just names. Titles. There has been no cessation of terror. It just comes with a different acronym. For IRA, read True IRA. For UVF, read UVA. They are one and the same. They are still attacking us. They are still killing our loved ones. They are still killing our soldiers. And what does William Davies do? Does he eject their political leaders from government? Does he re-imprison those murderers who walk our streets through his surrender, and who are no doubt behind the majority of the fresh attacks? No. He does none of these things. He sits on his hands and makes our once-great nation weaker by the day.

'And so tonight we have an opportunity. Tonight Parliament – men and women who represent you – can say that enough is enough. Tonight they can remove William Davies from power and bring to an end this travesty. They can stand as one and say that their confidence in the government's policies in Northern Ireland is gone. And in doing so they can tell the world that Great Britain is ready for a new form of government. One that *will* stand against those who attack us. One that will *not* be bullied. One that will stand firm and say "attack us at your peril". *That* is the government I will offer and *that* is what Great Britain deserves. Give me the opportunity to provide it. Contact your MP. Instruct him or her to represent you, to say that *you* have no confidence in William Davies' policies. Today is a day of reckoning. You have the power to ensure that reckoning occurs. Thank you.'

Haversume's thanks came with a self-conscious smile. He turned away without another word and walked towards his waiting entourage. He did not look back and he did not respond to the questions that were erupting around him.

A press officer stepped up to the vacated podium. He took almost a minute to bring quiet to the crowd. Only then could the man explain that a question and answer session would be inappropriate until Haversume's nomination for leadership of the government was confirmed. And that could not happen before the result of the vote.

Dempsey's attention was not wasted on the press officer for even a moment. It remained fixed on Haversume.

As the politician walked away, surrounded by his entourage, Dempsey could not help but notice the change. Haversume had been of interest to the intelligence community for several years, since his first public criticism of Davies' policies in Ulster. The military and the security services gave him almost unanimous support. It was no surprise that they would sympathise with the sentiments he regularly expressed; that they would agree with his fierce support for their actions and his powerful tributes to their sacrifices. Dempsey knew more than just the public face, though. He knew the man's history. Things the public could not. And he knew of Haversume's close relationships with people Dempsey trusted. Still he had doubts. Haversume might be making the right noises, but he remained the consummate politician.

Those thoughts were irrelevant today. Dempsey was not here for politics. What he needed from Haversume was personal.

Walking in the same direction as Haversume's entourage, Dempsey made sure to move a step or two faster than its members. His long strides brought him level with the rearmost protection officers within seconds. They turned to intercept him. Dempsey flashed his DDS credentials. They were unnecessary. Dempsey had already been recognised and was permitted further into the huddle.

'Sir, I wonder if I can speak with you?'

Haversume seemed surprised at Dempsey's sudden appearance. He cast his eye around the accompanying officers, seeking an explanation. Dempsey understood. The man was a perpetual target for assassination. Any unknown face could be a threat.

'I'm Major Joe Dempsey of the Department of Domestic Security. If I can have a moment of your time?'

'Ah, that's where I've seen your face before.'

Haversume stopped walking. His entire retinue halted with him.

'You're the man who brought down McGale. That was fine work.'

'Thank you, sir,' Dempsey replied. 'But I'm not here about that exactly. It really is important that I speak to you alone. Is now a convenient time?'

'I'm sorry, Major, but I just have no time to spare. What with tonight's vote. But my staff will make you an appointment for the earliest available opportunity.'

Haversume signalled to a tall, smartly dressed woman stood close by. She stepped forward to take over the conversation as Haversume began to walk away. He did not get very far, halting at the sound of Dempsey's next words:

'It really can't wait, sir. I need to speak to you immediately regarding the murder of Daniel Lawrence.'

FIFTY-FOUR

'I asked you a question.'

Liam Casey was growing impatient. The sudden appearance of his younger brother seemed an unwelcome shock. Every inch of him suggested a man who was just moments from violence.

Michael, in turn, was dumbstruck. He had enjoyed the advantage of time. An opportunity to prepare himself for this, albeit only an hour or so. But Michael also knew that *he* was the one to blame for the bad blood that filled the room. It made his position difficult.

'I'm in trouble, Liam. I need your help.'

Eight small words, they somehow cut through two decades of bitterness and resentment. The look on Liam's face changed from simmering anger to confused concern. He sat back in his seat and poured a large splash of whiskey into an empty crystal tumbler. He drained a mouthful without offering a glass. A pointed omission.

It was half a minute before he finally spoke.

'What kind of trouble? Serious?'

'Serious enough that I've come to you.'

'Bad, then,' Liam replied, his voice still far from friendly. 'That's why someone's worked you over, is it?'

Michael nodded, instinctively lifting his hand to the wound above his left eye: the cut that had been reopened in McGale's office.

'Who was it?'

'I don't know. But it's not just a few cuts and bruises. It's much worse. They tried to blow me up. They tried to shoot me. Some bastard beat me half to death in London last night, then two more tried to kill us in Belfast this morning.'

'You're not serious?'

Liam shifted in his seat. Michael's reappearance had to have more to it than a mere fight, but what he was saying was something else entirely.

'Jesus, Mikey, what have you got yourself involved in?'

There was a subtle change in Liam's tone, a move from animosity to concern. Michael was relieved to hear it. The childhood urge to protect him had not gone.

'It's a long story, Liam. But it's got something to do with Neil Matthewson's shooting. Whoever was behind that is now coming after me.'

Michael glanced at Sarah before correcting himself.

'After us.'

'And what the hell does that have to do with you? You're no politician.'

'It's about my work. You know that Matthewson was killed by a man called Eamon McGale, right?'

Liam nodded.

'Well, after McGale was arrested a friend of mine, Daniel, was appointed as his lawyer. McGale told Daniel a whole lot of pretty revealing stuff, but before Daniel could tell me most of it both he and McGale were killed. Then, suddenly, the bastards are gunning for us.'

Michael's second reference to Sarah finally brought her to Liam's attention.

'And by "us", I suppose you mean you and your woman here?' Liam asked, gesturing in Sarah's direction.

Sarah hesitated, seemingly caught off guard as the discussion had turned to her. Meeting Liam's gaze, she stepped forward, leaned across the desk and offered him her outstretched hand.

'Sarah Truman, Mr Dev ... erm ... Mr Casey. It's a pleasure to make your acquaintance.'

Liam took Sarah's hand and shook it without enthusiasm. He seemed not to have noticed her mistake with his surname.

'I wish I could say the same. Maybe under different circumstances.'

Liam released Sarah's grip and turned back to Michael.

'How did you manage to drag this poor girl into your troubles?'

'He didn't!'

Sarah seemed outraged by Liam's dismissive attitude.

'I'm a journalist, Mr Casey. My investigation raised questions that the same people don't want answered. So I got *myself* into this. And I'm lucky Michael's in it with me.'

Liam's gaze returned to Sarah, considering her more closely. A smile flickered into life as he spoke again.

'Call me Liam, Miss Truman. Only the police call me Mr Casey.' His eyes flicked to Michael. 'And I hear no one calls you that any more, right?'

Michael said nothing. The jibe was the very least he had expected.

Liam shuffled back into his reclining chair. With his whiskey glass dangling loosely in his fingertips he slowly shook his head, just staring at his brother without a word.

The gaze was a confused mix of concern and contempt. Michael knew why. Liam was struggling to reconcile his burning resentment towards the man who had abandoned him with an urge that he could not resist. An urge to harm those who had hurt his brother.

No one spoke until Liam finally broke the silence.

'OK, let's assume this lawyer fella died because of something McGale told him. How does that lead to you? If he died before he could tell you anything?'

'Because they don't know that,' Michael replied. 'Daniel rang me after he left the police station. His phone records would show that. They must know about that call. They couldn't take the risk that he might have told me something over the phone.'

'And had he?'

Liam's question came without the slightest hesitation. Michael's ability for sharp thought and cross-examination ran in the family.

Michael did not immediately respond, unsure that he should burden his brother with more information than necessary. Liam noticed the delay.

'What's the matter, Mikey?' Liam's voice – raised from the start – grew louder with each word. 'I asked you a simple question. And what? You can't tell me? You can't trust me? Is that it? You come to me for help after nearly twenty years and then you want to keep things from me? Jesus, man, I should slap you all around this fucking room.'

The sudden anger took everyone by surprise. Sarah shifted backwards in the face of Liam's fury. A fury that Michael met head-on.

'Of course I trust you!' Michael hollered back.

Both men were on their feet. A current of aggression surged between them.

'I just don't know how much I want to tell you in case it

puts you in danger. Everyone else who knows about this is dead, Liam. Everyone but me and Sarah. Maybe I don't want you to end up that way too!'

Michael meant every word. But it did not matter. His brother was finally venting two decades of frustration. He would not stop now.

'Ah, bollocks, man! You come back here with your English accent and your pretty wee girlfriend and you ask me for help. You expect me to forget that you've been a disgrace to this family for the last twenty years. Twenty fucking years!'

'I had my reasons and you know it!'

This was what Michael had prepared himself to face. Now he was here he did not intend to back down.

'You know I couldn't stay!'

'No, you couldn't stay. But you could've come back.'

There was the barest hint of regret deep in Liam's voice as he said those words. It was almost lost in his anger, but there was enough that Michael could detect it. Enough to breach his own aggressive facade.

'I couldn't come back, Liam. Not after what you did for me. I had to make it worthwhile. You gave me a chance at a life and I had to take it. I had to make a success of it or I'd have been throwing what you did back in your face. I had to stay away.'

'That's shite!'

There was no drop in Liam's aggression. He seemed unaffected by Michael's now calm attempt to explain.

'You abandoned your family when you stayed away. You denied we existed, Mikey. From the minute you left. Jesus, you even changed your name, man. That broke Dad. He could never understand it. *You* broke him.'

'I had no choice, Liam.'

Michael's voice was now quiet. His previous passion gone.

'You know that. Dad was just too big. Too well known. I couldn't achieve what I had to as the son of Belfast's biggest gangster. To succeed I had to separate myself. And I *had* to succeed, Liam. I had to succeed for *you*.'

'Don't go passing the blame on to me.'

Liam's voice remained loud but the animosity of just moments before was missing. Now the anger was a show to cover less acceptable emotions, and Liam Casey was no actor.

'Dad died thinking his golden boy didn't want to know him. Didn't want to see him. What the hell do you think that did to him?'

'And what do you think that did to *me*?' Michael bellowed angrily, his passion flooding back as tears filled his eyes. 'I worshipped that man! Just as much as you did! Walking away was one of the hardest things I've ever done, Liam, but it doesn't come close to *staying* away. I paid a price I'll never be able to live with, to make *your* sacrifice worthwhile. So don't go throwing Dad at me as if I don't care.'

'You *loved* him? You didn't even come when he was on his deathbed, Mikey. You didn't even come back for his funeral! So don't start telling me how you worshipped him because we both know that's bollocks!'

'I didn't know he was dying, Liam. *You* didn't tell me! What do you think I am, fucking psychic?'

The anger between the brothers was beginning to boil over. It threatened Michael's third fight in twenty-four hours.

'And I *did* come to his funeral. I was there!'

Liam opened his mouth just as Michael's final words registered in his mind. They stopped Liam's intended answer in its tracks.

'You were there?' The anger was gone. Liam's voice was quiet.

'I was there.' Michael's reply was simple. His voice as low as his brother's. 'But I knew you wouldn't want to see me, so I kept out of the way.'

Liam was silenced.

He turned his back and walked to the large window behind his desk. It overlooked the whitewashed brickwork of an adjoining building. Nothing of interest there, and yet now it seemed to fascinate Liam, who refused to look away, lost in his own thoughts.

The silence lingered. Michael looked first to Sarah and then to Anne. No one knew what to do. And no one was willing to interrupt Liam's thoughts.

Finally he spoke.

'I'll help you, Mikey.' Liam's voice was now a mix of sadness and resignation. 'And when it's done I want you out of my life again. For good this time. Understood?'

'If that's what you want,' Michael replied, keeping his own emotions firmly in check.

Liam stood with his back to them for several more seconds. Then he turned, retook his seat and looked up at his brother.

'If we're going to do this we do it right.' Liam's tone was now cold. All business. 'I need you and your girlfriend to tell me everything.'

FIFTY-FIVE

Haversume and Dempsey were alone by the time they reached Haversume's office on the fourth floor of Westminster's Portcullis House. Haversume had told his assistant that the two men wished to speak privately, and so his ever-growing team of hangers-on had dispersed as rapidly as they seemed to have appeared.

'This is an impressive place.'

Dempsey took a seat on the guest's side of an ornate, classically designed desk. A glimpse of the discreet brand name etched underneath told him this table alone cost as much as he earned in six months. At least before overtime.

'It's an improvement on the cubby-holes they expected us to work in across the street,' Haversume replied.

The politician's words were an understatement. The growth in government personnel had long ago rendered the Parliament building unfit for purpose. It had been designed when an empire was run by the kind of numbers that might today be trusted with a mid-sized university. And yet it still housed a government and civil service that, since the 1960s, had multiplied in size at a rate that would shame bacteria. This over-population had long required tolerance to hardship from those who worked there. Which was not a virtue held in abundance among Great Britain's politicians.

It was unsurprising, then, that Parliament had tackled the problem with the purchase of a nearby office building, Portcullis House. What was more surprising was how seemingly unlimited amounts of public funds had been thrown at the place. In an age when soldiers die to save the cost of a flack jacket or an armoured reconnaissance vehicle, Portcullis House was proof that the willingness of Britain's political elite to make sacrifices did not extend to their own working conditions.

The thought had troubled Dempsey as they had made their way through the building. Much of his time was spent justifying expenditure. Explaining to bean counters why a surveillance operation was necessary. Or why air support was essential to an off-land terrorist intercept. He suspected that there had been no such interrogation before the purchase of the seventy-inch LCD flat-screens that seemed to be on every wall. Or the millions of pounds' worth of artwork he had seen in the lobby. The hypocrisy disgusted him.

Haversume poured two glasses of what Dempsey assumed to be finest Scotch whisky. He handed one to his guest and took his seat on the far side of his desk. Haversume took just a sip before speaking.

When he did, Dempsey could detect the unmistakable quaver of suppressed emotion.

'You wanted to discuss Daniel.'

'Yes, sir.'

Dempsey knew he was about to bring up what for Haversume would be an upsetting subject. Delicacy was needed.

'I'm sorry for your loss. I'm also sorry if my coming here is going to re-open those wounds, but I have reason to believe that the car crash in which Mr Lawrence died was no accident. Sir, I believe that it was a murder, carried out to ensure Mr Lawrence's silence.'

Haversume held Dempsey's gaze. His piercing eyes gave away no hint of surprise. Or of anything else. He slowly nodded his head.

'Go on.'

'I have evidence that Mr Lawrence attended Paddington Green police station on the evening of his death. That evidence suggests that he was present there in his capacity as a duty solicitor. In that capacity he spent almost two hours alone with Eamon McGale. Whatever conversation passed between the two men in that time we'll never know, but one thing is for certain: both men were dead within hours of that meeting. I believe that their deaths are connected.'

Dempsey stopped speaking. He studied Haversume for a response. All he got was the sight of a tear building in the politician's right eye.

He continued.

'I believe, sir, that McGale had information that someone didn't want to be made public or fall into the hands of the intelligence services. I believe McGale was killed to prevent this from happening. And I believe that the same people killed Daniel because they feared McGale had passed some of this information to him.'

Haversume did not reply immediately. Which did not surprise Dempsey. It was a lot to take in.

'Do you have proof of any this, Major Dempsey?' he finally asked. His voice sounded sad. Again, hardly a surprise.

'I have proof of some of it. The rest is common sense and inference.'

'Never the safest of evidence, Major. So what can we actually be sure of?'

Dempsey hesitated. He did not want to reveal more than

he needed to. Even Callum McGregor had not been told everything. He thought of the best way to move forward.

'Sir, you were Mr Lawrence's godfather. By all accounts you were close, so I'm sure that you know his colleague, Michael Devlin.'

'I do. What do you know of Michael?'

'Not a great deal, but what I *do* know is important. It seems, sir, that Mr Lawrence called him after leaving Paddington Green. This was the only call he made in between his meeting with McGale and his death. The only opportunity he had to pass information on. Following this call there has been an attempt on Mr Devlin's life that carries all of the hallmarks of a professional hit, which Mr Devlin somehow escaped. I think it's safe to say that there must be a connection, don't you?'

Haversume took a few more seconds to consider this. Dempsey could see that this was not a man who jumped to conclusions without careful thought.

'I suppose that there must be,' he finally said. His tone suggested that he would have preferred a different conclusion. 'But that would mean, Major Dempsey, that whoever attempted to kill Michael on the basis of that phone call must have had access to Daniel's telephone records within hours of his death.'

'It does,' Dempsey replied. 'Which in turn means that they have access to intelligence resources, or to someone inside the service. There's no other way they could have obtained the phone records that quickly.'

Haversume nodded his head. With every new piece of information his eyes seemed to grow sadder. More tired.

'Do you know where Michael is now?'

'No. He seems to have gone to ground. As have Mr Lawrence's family. Hopefully they're together and they're safe.'

Haversume seemed unsurprised by the final revelation. Dempsey found that strange, in light of the man's connection to the Lawrence family.

His doubts were quickly addressed,

'I think I can help you with that, Major.'

Haversume pushed himself up in his chair as he spoke. His voice was still quiet, still sad. But its authority had returned.

'You see, not everything you have just said is a surprise to me. I'm afraid I was already aware of the likely truth behind my godson's murder.'

'You knew?' It was Dempsey's turn to be confused. 'But how?'

'From Michael Devlin. Indirectly, anyway. He telephoned Hugh Lawrence, Daniel's father, after the attempt on his life. And he told him very much what you just told me.'

'Then why didn't you stop me?' Dempsey did not like having his time wasted. 'Why did you let me go through everything?'

'Because I wanted to hear it from you,' Haversume replied. 'What Michael told Hugh could have been wrong. My first interest in this is the safety of Daniel's family, and I can best protect them if *I* know what *you* know. Rather than just what Michael Devlin *thinks* he knows. Although, in fairness to him, it seems his instincts were right.'

'What do you mean "best protect them"? Are you saying that you know where the Lawrence family are? Where Devlin is?'

'I've no idea where Mr Devlin is, Major. But yes, I do know where the Lawrence family are. I've arranged for them to be kept in the safest possible place. Where there is no chance that this . . . this . . . whatever this is, can find them. I won't see another member of that family hurt, Major. Not for anything.'

The emotion returned to Haversume's voice as he discussed his loss. And his determination that it would not be repeated. It answered Dempsey's next question before he even asked it.

'I don't suppose you would allow me access to them, sir? There are questions I would like to ask.'

'No, Major. No, I would not.' It was the answer Dempsey was expecting. 'How can I take that risk? You've just told me – confirming what Michael already said – that there is intelligence service involvement in this. If I permit you to see them then I have exposed them to exactly that service. The service we know to be compromised. Would you take that risk? With your loved ones?'

'Mr Haversume, are you suggesting that I might be a security risk? That I'm involved in this?'

'I'm not, Major, no. I'm as confident as I can be, with the little I know, that you are on the right side. I'm sure you know about my friendship with your director, Callum? He and I go back years, and you'll be happy to know that he cannot speak highly enough of you. So no, I'm not suggesting that you're a security risk. But at the same time the fewer people who know, the better.'

Dempsey could understand the answer. But it gave him another option.

'Then what about Callum, sir? Will you allow him to meet with them?'

'Major Dempsey, I trust Callum McGregor more than I trust almost any man alive. But even he will not be seeing the Lawrence family. So please leave this alone.'

'But why?'

'Because we may well have the full apparatus of the intelligence services against us here, Major. We don't know who is behind this and until we do I will not take a risk with the lives of my only family.'

'Your—'

'A figure of speech. But they *are* my family, Major. Maybe not in blood, I realise. But they are the closest thing I have. And if it were your family at risk, would you think any differently?'

Dempsey did not answer. Nor did he need to. Haversume's point was made, and it was a good one. With the intelligence community compromised, he could not criticise Haversume for only trusting himself.

Still, it posed a problem. Dempsey had come to Haversume for one thing: his insight into the Lawrence family. He had hoped that it would help him find them, in the anticipation that Michael Devlin would be with them or that they would at least know where he was.

It was a dead end. But there was something else Dempsey now wanted to know.

'Sir, have you spoken about any of this to Callum McGregor?'

'Why do you ask?'

'Like you said, you go back years. And I know he's a close friend. In the circumstances, if I was you I would have spoken to him.'

'I had wanted to keep that to myself.' Haversume sounded disappointed at what he now had to disclose. 'Because I know Callum should not have discussed this with me. But yes, we've spoken. And yes, before you ask, he had already confirmed what you told me.'

'I understand why you'd want to protect him,' Dempsey replied, 'and he's my friend too. So this won't go any further than this room. But just so I know what you and I can and can't discuss, did Callum tell you anything else?'

'Not really, Major.' Haversume paused. He seemed to be thinking. 'He did mention the name of a reporter too. Sarah Truman. He said that you believed she was with Devlin. But that's about it.'

Dempsey nodded. His curiosity had been answered. He rose to his feet and offered Haversume his hand.

'In that case, sir, I'll leave you to get on with the rest of your day.'

'Was there not something you wanted, Major? Why you came here in the first place?'

'There was, sir. But we've covered it and I don't want to keep you any longer than I need to. Like you said, there's a big vote tonight.'

Haversume got to his feet and took Dempsey's hand.

'Major, I wish you the very best of luck. There's nothing I want more than to see the bastard who did this to Daniel brought down.'

'I'll do my best, sir.'

'How?' Haversume replied. 'I mean, what's next?'

Dempsey thought for a moment. Truthfully, he did not know, and so a plan was only forming in his mind as he spoke:

'I suppose I have to follow the only lead left. Devlin and Truman have gone to ground, and all my other leads are pretty much exhausted. Which only leaves Eamon McGale. I need to know what compels a university professor to become an assassin.'

'So you're off to Belfast, then?'

'I suppose I am. I don't see any other options.'

'Well, then, it's like I said. I wish you the very best of luck.'

'Thank you, sir,' Dempsey replied. 'I just might need it.'

FIFTY-SIX

'Are you sure we've got the right place?'

Liam Casey had asked the same question twenty times in the past hour. The answer would not change.

'I mean, there's no sign of anyone.'

'It's the only address the university had for him,' replied Paddy O'Neil, Liam's longest-standing and most loyal friend. Along with Jack Thornton, he was one of only two men Liam had trusted to accompany him and Michael. All four had been sitting together for over an hour in a Range Rover owned by one of Liam's more legitimate companies.

'Jesus, Liam, it's only been an hour.' Michael's response was snapped at Liam at the same moment O'Neil had spoken. 'He'll be back soon enough.'

O'Neil and Thornton exchanged nervous glances while Liam glared wordlessly at Michael, his eyes filled with malicious intent. He resisted translating that malice into physical action. Instead, a silence descended that carried the live charge of potential conflict.

The barely suppressed resentment between the brothers was making their two companions nervous. With good reason.

Liam's behaviour towards Michael had varied wildly in the hours between Michael's return and now. There had been some moments of levity, when the brothers seemed happy in each other's company. And just as many moments of contempt, when only the memory of their father kept them from each other's throat.

It was their tendency to flip suddenly from one mood to the other that caused the greatest concern. It made it impossible for anyone to tell if and when the obvious tension would erupt into something more.

Michael could see the stress that his return was placing on Liam. He already regretted the irritable comment. He knew he should apologise. Knew that doing so would lighten the mood. But for some reason he could not bring himself to say the words. Instead he avoided Liam's angry gaze. He sat back in his seat and kept his eyes on the small terraced house across the street: the home of a postgraduate Political Science student named Benjamin Grant.

The decision to find Benjamin Grant had been Michael's. It was based on a realisation that had hit both him and Sarah in McGale's office.

Michael and Sarah had recounted everything from Daniel's death onwards, at Liam's insistence. They had left no detail untouched. Only after this, with Liam fully briefed, had Michael set out both the next step and the reason for it.

'So where does this leave us?' It had been Liam's question. 'You don't have much to go on, do you? A set of initials?'

'There *is* something else,' Michael had replied. 'I think there's someone else who can give us a lot more information than we already have. Benjamin Grant.'

'He was McGale's student,' Sarah had explained. 'The one who called him out of the restaurant on the night of the bomb.'

Liam had nodded, understanding. His natural scepticism gave him a healthy head start.

'Someone drags you out of a building just before it blows up, odds are that person knew it was gonna happen.'

'Exactly,' Michael had agreed. 'Too much of a coincidence.

How often does a student track his professor down at that time of the night, interrupting a family event? And it isn't like it was an emergency. They're political scientists. There's no such thing as life or death in that world.'

'Only this time there was,' Sarah continued. 'And so we think that Benjamin Grant was paid to stop McGale getting blown to bits. Which means he can tell us who paid him.'

'And maybe more than that,' Michael had continued. 'If you look at the diary, it says "meeting with BG and RM". Whoever RM is, this first mention of him coincides almost exactly with the beginning of McGale's Matthewson obsession. Which makes it very likely that RM was either the reason for that obsession, or has a good idea what that reason was. And if he met McGale on this date with BG and if BG is Benjamin Grant, then that guy has got to be the place to start.'

Sarah and Liam had nodded as one at the additional reasoning. It was vital that they discover what Benjamin Grant knew.

'You want me to get on the internet and start tracking him down?' Sarah had asked. She had seemed keen to get started.

'Leave that part to me,' Liam had replied. 'I can do that quicker. And then we'll find out what the treacherous little shit knows.'

'. . . and so there I'd be waiting for someone to walk around the corner, on my back, grunting and groaning and doing my best to look like I'd just landed.'

Paddy O'Neil was struggling to get out the words between bouts of laughter.

'Then what would you do?' asked Jack Thornton. He was the only man in the car not familiar with O'Neil's story.

'Well, I'd wait for the person to get real close, then I'd make the noise louder and louder. Make out I was real hurt. They come running over all concerned and ask what happened and I'd say "they threw me off the roof, they threw me off the roof".'

O'Neil paused again as he fought to regain his composure.

'And then I'd point up to the top floor and there they'd be, Liam and Mikey, ready to dunk a bucket of water down on the poor sods as they looked up at where I was pointing.'

'What about you?' Thornton was obviously struggling to see the joke. 'Didn't the water get you too?'

'Sometimes, yeah!' O'Neil showed no signs of his laughter letting up. 'If I didn't roll away in time. But c'mon, Jack. A whole bucket of water, bulls-eye every time!'

'Yeah, sounds like you had a laugh together.' Thornton's tone did not sell his words. 'Great days.'

'When Dad wasn't there.' Michael's reply was wistful. It ignored Thornton's lack of enthusiasm. 'Not quite as wild when he was watching, though. Then we did as we were told.'

'So I've heard.' This was a subject that interested Thornton far more. 'I knew him before he passed, your dad. And even as an aul man you didn't cross him. I'll bet you did as he told you.'

'Not always, but we'd pay for it afterwards!'

Liam heard Michael's voice crack as he spoke about their father.

'He was the best dad you could ask for though. Especially for two boys who didn't have a mum.'

Liam nodded his agreement but stayed silent. Still, both Michael's answer and the sadness in his voice affected him. Liam wiped a tear from the corner of his eye with a flick of his fingertip. He tried to think about happy memories instead.

Funnier memories, like the water prank. One of a thousand stories from their youth, a time when Liam and his younger brother were inseparable.

Liam had endured those memories over the years. They reminded him of happier times that, in Michael's absence, he would have preferred to forget. But they had become less frequent. His life was far emptier without Michael in it, and so he had forced himself to forget the good times.

Liam hated what Michael had done. He hated that his brother had left them all behind. But he hated nothing as much as the feeling he could no longer shake: gratitude that his brother had returned. It was the most unwelcome of emotions and so he was relieved when he glanced in the car's offside mirror and saw what they had been waiting for.

'That's him, isn't it?' Liam asked. 'It looks like him, right?'

Michael stopped speaking. He turned and looked out of the rear window.

A thin, bespectacled man in his twenties was walking in their direction. Michael looked carefully and compared the man against the newspaper article that carried his photograph.

'Yeah, it's definitely him. What now?'

Liam met his brother's eyes. Even in the dark his grim determination was visible.

'Now we grab the bastard and we make him talk.'

FIFTY-SEVEN

Anne Flaherty took a seat across the table from Sarah. The two women sat in a corner booth of the 32 Counties main bar room. They had been here for an hour and a half, since Michael and Liam had left. Other than them the bar was empty. Anne had ordered it closed after the lunchtime rush.

Anne placed two fresh glasses of white wine on the table and slid one to Sarah. Their fourth of the evening. Next she took two cigarettes from the pack next to her and handed one to Sarah. With the bar closed, the smoking ban no longer applied.

Anne sat back into her chair and exhaled a stream of smoke. A smile crossed her face as she considered her new drinking partner.

'Now come on.' Anne's accent lacked the Belfast harshness that Sarah was growing used to. 'They'll be back in no time at all. There's nothing to worry yourself about.'

Sarah smiled back. She had been unaware of her own distraction.

'How can you be sure? What if this Grant guy's dangerous? If he's mixed up in this he might be more than they can handle.'

The honesty in Anne's laugh was enough by itself to settle Sarah's fears.

'Liam's not exactly new to this sort of thing, love. He's dealt with people at least as dangerous as a university student!'

'And Michael?'

'Well, I've not seen *him* for twenty years, have I? But the

Michael I knew? That Michael would've had nothing to worry about either. He can't have changed that much or you wouldn't be sitting here alive now, would you?'

'I guess not. But I can't help worrying about them, Anne. They've got professional killers after them.'

'You get used to that.'

It was the reply of a woman who had grown accustomed to waving her man off to war. Something Sarah hoped she would never become.

Anne did not seem to notice Sarah's discomfort at the thought. She leaned forward, closer to Sarah. Her elbow was on the table, her chin resting on her fist.

'So tell me about yourself,' she said. 'What brings you to Britain and the dangerous Mikey Casey?'

'Really bad luck?'

The mood had been lightened by Anne's description of Michael. Sarah's reply was equally light-hearted. Both women laughed.

Sarah paused just a beat before giving the real answer.

'Just running away from my background, I guess.'

'What do you mean, "running away"? From a man?'

'I guess, but not like you think. It was my dad. I grew up rich back in Boston. Dad's the founder and CEO of his own company.'

'Sounds like a hard life,' Anne laughed.

'Of course it's not,' Sarah replied. 'I'm honestly not complaining. There's a whole lot of upsides to being rich. But it came with a hell of a downside, too. My dad had expectations. He expected me to work for him until I met the right guy. Not the right guy for me. The right guy for *him*. Someone with a bright enough future or from a powerful enough family to interest Dad. Then I'd be expected to be married off like a good little princess.'

'And you had a different idea for your future?'

'Damn right I did! I wanted to be a reporter. Wanted it for years. Even when I was a kid, playing with my brothers and sisters. They'd be Superman or Batman or Wonder Woman. All I wanted to be was Lois Lane. It made me a disaster at fancy dress parties, but that's what I wanted. That's what I decided to become. Eventually I got up the nerve to tell Daddy.'

'And that was something he didn't take well, I'm guessing?'

'Not well at all. At first he tried to talk me out of it. Then he shouted and screamed about how "Trumans don't report the news, Trumans make the news". And then he stopped the shouting and the hollering and instead resorted to cutting me off and stifling my career. No news stations would take me on because he got to them first. I ran out of cash, couldn't pay the rent, could hardly afford to eat. Ended up living on coffee and cigarettes. All because he wanted to break me.

'Then I saw an advertisement for the CNN job in England and I realised it was the way forward. Daddy had no sway there, so I didn't have to worry about him spiking my editors. So that settled it. I moved to England, got partnered up with the best cameraman in the business and the rest is history.'

'That's pretty incredible.' Anne seemed genuinely impressed. 'I don't think I could give up so much to chase a dream. You're a brave girl.'

'Hardly! I've been terrified since this whole thing started, and now here I am, fretting over a man I just met. You're cool as a cucumber.'

'That comes with time, love. I've been with Liam for over twenty years and he's put me through a hell of a lot. But I love him and I wouldn't change him for the world. The downside is that I care about what happens to him. Just like you care about Mikey. Only I'm used to dealing with it.'

'Oh come on, Anne, it's not the same. You've got a lifetime with Liam. Michael and I just met. It's not the same thing at all.'

'Maybe not yet, but it could be. I've seen the way you look at him. And I've seen him looking at you.'

Sarah did not know what to say. Her feelings were mixed. Surprise and embarrassment that her attraction to Michael had been so obvious. And a nervous excitement that Anne – a woman who had known the real Michael Devlin so well – was suggesting he might feel the same way.

It was the embarrassment that ultimately won out. Sarah opted to change the subject.

'So you knew them both as boys?'

'I did.'

If Anne had spotted the subject change – and Sarah was confident that she had – she did not show it. Sarah was grateful for the courtesy.

'And what boys they were, Sarah! Funny, wild and smart. They did everything together. Most of it completely mad. They ran free, back when Belfast was a dangerous bloody place to be. Everyone knew them. Liam and Mikey Casey. The terrible twins!'

'Twins?'

'Just an expression. The Irish never let a fact get in the way of catchy alliteration! But they were *like* twins. Where you found one you found the other. Doing whatever they wanted out of their dad's sight, and whatever he told them otherwise. They were great fun. So much life.'

'But they seem so different from each other?'

'Why? Because one's a lawyer and one's a villain? That could have been very different, believe me.'

Sarah looked puzzled. Anne continued.

'Don't get me wrong, Liam was always ending up where he is. This life's running through his veins. Mikey, though, that's a different story. Mikey was always smart, but he still could have been exactly where Liam is. Or worse.'

Sarah listened intently. She wanted to know all she could about Michael. Good and bad.

'What do you mean? What happened?'

'One day it just all got too serious.' Anne's tone had completely changed. It was flat. Joyless. 'One day it stopped being a bit of fun.'

'How? Did someone get hurt?'

'Worse than that. Someone got killed.'

Anne's words were followed by silence. It made the emptiness of the bar more pronounced.

Sarah found herself looking around. Making sure they were still alone. Happy that they were, she turned back to Anne.

'Who died?' Sarah was now almost whispering. 'I mean, what happened?'

'Do you really want to know?'

'Anne, I think I *need* to know.'

Sarah's meaning was clear and Anne nodded her understanding. She took a large sip of wine before continuing.

'It was a fight in a bar. Not far from here.'

There was a distance in Anne's voice. As if she were there now, at that point in the past.

'Mikey and Liam were rough, Sarah. They were well able to take care of themselves, just like their da. Mikey was seventeen when it happened. Liam was twenty. Still kids, really, but formidable. And the ironic thing? It was Mikey who was the more dangerous of the two. The one who was bright enough to have a future was the one with the temper that could take it away. That night it nearly did.

'We were in a bar owned by one of their da's competition. God knows why the boys made us go there. Probably bravado, but there was no way Sean Casey's boys could drink in a Dave Finnegan bar without something happening. And they knew that, the pair of them. Anyway, the night went on and the atmosphere got more and more charged. All it needed was a trigger to set the whole thing off. And Mikey was happy to provide it.'

'What did he do?'

'Well, Liam was coming back to our table from the bar and one of the regulars barged into him. Tried to make it look like an accident, but we all knew it wasn't. Anyway, Liam let it go. It was a one-off and, believe it or not, Liam's never been that unreasonable. Always gives people a bit of a chance.

'So next it's Paddy O'Neil's round, but Mikey steps up and says *he'll* get the drinks. And before anyone could stop him he's off to the bar, right next to the lad who'd barged Liam. Long story short, Mikey says something, the guy takes a swing and before you know it the guy and a mate of his are on their backs. Then the whole place erupted.

'I couldn't see much; the first thing Liam did was put me out of the way, under a table with Mikey's date. But I did see Liam back to back with Mikey, the two of them fighting everyone who came near, while the other lads we were with were fighting all around the bar. But there were too many of them and the boys were taking a hiding. I mean, they were holding their own for the numbers, but it couldn't last.

'They must have realised that themselves because they all met in the middle of the floor, all five of them back to back, and once they were protecting each other they started to edge towards us. When they got close Liam called for me and Mikey's date to get in behind them. Then they started fighting their way to the door, using whatever they could lay their hands on as weapons. Which was when it happened.'

Sarah was morbidly fascinated. What Anne described sounded like a Wild West saloon brawl. Told after the fact, it was almost entertaining. But not for Anne. Her tone told Sarah that, for her, it was still very real.

'It happened so quickly. So fast. But in my mind it's slow-motion. I saw everything he did. We were next to the door. Two more steps and we'd have been gone. Then out of nowhere a guy comes running at Liam, a knife in his hand. Not big. A butter knife, really, but bad enough.

'So he comes running at Liam and Liam doesn't see him. But Mikey does. I shouted for Liam to look out but he didn't hear me. For a split second I thought he'd be stabbed. And he would have been, except Mikey was so quick. He broke a bottle and threw himself across Liam, sticking it straight into the guy's neck.'

Both women sat in silence. They considered the image. Sarah's version was imagined. Anne's very real. Neither spoke for what seemed like minutes. But Sarah needed to know the rest.

'And the man died?' she finally asked.

'He did. Right there, on the floor of the bar.'

Anne was clearly finding her story increasingly difficult. She lit another cigarette, seemingly forgetting the one still smoking in the ashtray. Anything to calm her fraying nerves.

Her voice was breaking as she continued.

'It was the most horrible thing I ever saw. The whole room just stopped and stared at the guy on the floor, his legs kicking and blood spurting out of his neck, like someone was pumping it. I threw up. I think most of us did. But not Mikey.'

'What did he do?'

'He stayed calm. Like it didn't affect him at all. He was the only one thinking straight, clear enough for us all. He got us out of there. Safe and home. No nerves. No panic. Mikey was cold that night, Sarah. Heartless. And that was the biggest shock of all.'

Sarah was confused. Anne cared deeply about Michael, that much was obvious. And yet here she could have been describing a monster.

'It was Mikey's reaction. It just didn't seem, well, it didn't seem normal. We'd all seen Mikey lose it before. Seen him fight. So we always thought he was a little, you know, psycho. He always went that bit too far. But this time? This time he killed a man and yet he acted like it was just some little thing that needed to be excused. He justified it, Sarah. Said the guy came at Liam with a knife and so he killed him. Simple as that. He meant to do it, he did it and he wasn't about to pretend otherwise.'

Sarah said nothing. She had seen this side of Michael less than twenty-four hours ago. Had heard him make reference to the life he had left behind. So Anne's story did not surprise her. Michael Devlin was a man who would do what he had to do, to protect himself and those close to him. That much was clear. That much had kept Sarah alive.

'The boys were arrested within the hour,' Anne continued. 'They were too well known to just walk away. They only had a little time to talk about it before the police showed up, and no chance to speak to their da. Then they were gone. Dragged out of the flat in cuffs, given a beating along the way. Once the police had them no one could get to them. Not even Sean Casey. We were all here, just waiting for news. And then out of nowhere Mikey walked back through the door of the bar, his face as white as a ghost, saying he'd been released without charge.'

'I don't understand.' This made no sense to Sarah. 'He was arrested for murder and released? How could that happen? They had witnesses.'

'They did. Witnesses who blamed a Casey boy for starting the whole thing. And that the same Casey boy stabbed the dead lad in the neck. But they didn't say *which* Casey boy.'

'You mean the police thought that it was Liam? Why?'

'Because Liam told them it was him.'

Sarah was speechless.

'Mikey was inconsolable. Not because of what he'd done, but because of what Liam had done for him. We had to wait for Liam's lawyer to explain everything. Which he did. He told us that Liam had admitted manslaughter. That he said he'd started the fight and that he'd killed the guy by mistake as it went on. Then he explained that Liam had done it to keep Mikey out of prison.'

Sarah still had no words. She could barely believe the sacrifice that Liam had made for his brother.

Anne's voice grew lower as she neared the end of her story.

'It nearly destroyed the family. Mikey visited Liam in prison and begged him to take it back. To let *him* confess. But Liam wouldn't do it. He said that Mikey was the one with the future. That Mikey had the brains to get away from the life. And so Liam was the one who took the blame. All so his kid brother could make a better life for himself, away from the streets. Away from Belfast. It was a chance that Liam would never have had anyway, as he didn't have Mikey's brains. And that's why Mikey is what he is today, Sarah. *That's* why he isn't Liam.'

Sarah remained silent. But her mind was racing.

Everything she had seen and heard in the last twenty-four hours now made sense. Liam had sacrificed his youth and his freedom for his brother's future, and Michael had spent two decades trying to live up to that sacrifice. To make a life – a man – deserving of what Liam had done for him.

The price Michael had paid for this was separation from the family he loved, a family whose existence – if known – would have cost him the life that Liam's actions had bought him. In its own way it was as high a price as Liam had paid and it revealed to Sarah just how alike the two men really were.

FIFTY-EIGHT

It was 9 p.m. as Joe Dempsey pulled his BMW M6 Gran Coupé hire car into a parking space in University Square. Late, but the place was buzzing.

He stepped out of the car and into the crowd. Young men and women of varied nationalities streamed back and forth. The academic world continued, unhindered by the international drama that had its roots in these very grounds.

The majority of the activity centred on a single building. A classic, imposing red-brick structure. Dempsey watched a swarm of maintenance men come and go through its main entrance. It was the right place.

Dempsey remained in place. Watching. Taking in the impressive view of the six-floor building. His gut told him that this could be where the trail would warm back up. The past twenty-four hours had taught him a lot, but without evidence what he knew – what he thought he knew – was next to worthless. He needed something tangible and he hoped he would find it in the life of Eamon McGale.

Motionless for a few more moments, Dempsey's mind was racing nonetheless. Finally his legs caught up, coming to life as he strode towards the building's entrance. Taking the short staircase to the raised main door two steps at a time, he just avoided a collision with two workmen carrying a shattered office door.

Dempsey ignored their mumbled annoyance. He made his way through the reception, towards the building plan that sat on the far wall. He ran his finger down it and found McGale's name and room number.

The caged elevator was in use on a different floor, so Dempsey made for the ornate staircase. The presence of the workmen had already intrigued him and his curiosity only increased as he climbed the stairs. His suspicion that the men were working on the sixth floor was gradually confirmed.

The sight as he reached the top of the staircase was unexpected. Dempsey had anticipated seeing the workmen gutting McGale's now-empty office. No doubt the university would want it erased from its history. It was why he had been in such a hurry to get to the office before more potential evidence was lost. But as he reached the final step Dempsey found far more than a single whitewashed room.

Serious damage had been done to all but the first two offices on the sixth-floor corridor. Of those rooms that had been hit, not a single door was left standing. Some had been removed by the workmen. Others lay open, badly smashed and almost all free from their hinges. It was a familiar enough sight, but not one he expected to find in these halls.

Dempsey walked into the closest office: room 6.6.

He flashed his DDS credentials as he spoke. It guaranteed an answer.

'What the hell happened here?'

'Bloody vandals by the look of it. Brainless little shites!'

The room's only occupant was in his early sixties. Small. He spoke as he swept up broken glass.

'Probably came to see Professor McGale's office and then got over-excited. Little ghouls!'

'Maybe.' Dempsey was unconvinced. 'Did you know Professor McGale?'

'A little, yeah.'

'What did you think of him?'

The small man stopped sweeping. He stood upright. His body language told Dempsey that he was not used to his opinion being sought. Not here, at least. When he spoke his voice was hesitant, which sent much the same message.

'What I think is that it's a tragedy. You couldn't hope to meet a nicer man than Professor McGale.'

'So it was a surprise, then? What he did in London?'

'God, yes. To us all. Don't get me wrong, I don't doubt what he did but I'll tell you this: Professor McGale must have had his reasons.'

'How so?'

'Well, you'll have never met a brighter man in your life. So clever, and yet a lovely man with it. Time for everyone, he had. Whether you had letters after your name or a broom in your hand. And all he wanted to do was help. Whether it was just helping one of us, one of the staff, even with the smallest thing. Or all the way up to helping Ulster itself with his work. Professor McGale was a peaceful man. So if he tried to kill someone, it was because there was no other way.'

Dempsey nodded. The opinion matched what he already knew. But perhaps more importantly, it was at odds with what Dempsey had seen McGale do in Trafalgar Square.

'What about after his family were killed? Was he the same man after that?'

'With all due respect, sir, of course he bloody wasn't! He wasn't happy. He wasn't chatty. He was darker. But can you blame him? What else did he have left?'

'Did his attitudes change?'

'From the little we spoke after that, yeah, they did. The

optimism was gone. He seemed like he no longer thought the Troubles could be stopped by talking. And I remember something else, something I didn't really understand when he said it. He said that they were different this time. The Troubles. Different to before. Like I said, I didn't really understand it.'

Dempsey thought for a few moments, considering what had been said. Then, with thanks, he walked out of the office. He took a few minutes to look from room to room. Noted the similarities and differences between them. They told him much. Room 6.11 had been ransacked. This was unsurprising; it was McGale's office, after all. Most of the others had seen forced entry, but little else besides. And then there was room 6.3. This one looked *very* different. Like the scene of a pitched battle, with the remnants of a large bloodstain in the centre of its carpet.

A few more moments and Dempsey had completed a moving mental image of the previous night's events.

The small man was still in room 6.6 when Dempsey returned.

'So what makes you think that this damage was done by vandals?' Dempsey asked.

'What other explanation is there? Doors smashed off of their hinges. Offices smashed to pieces. I don't see who else could have done it.'

'Who was the first person to find it like this?'

'Danny McKee. The building's caretaker. I spoke to him earlier. He came in about 7 a.m. and found the place like this; the entry system smashed, the alarm pulled from the wall and all this damage done. Look, I've already answered all of these questions once. I don't see why I have to answer them again.'

'Who were you speaking to before me?'

'The police. They do tend to ask a few questions when

we call them, you know. That's why we're clearing up so late. They wanted everything left until they'd examined it.'

'Right, OK.' Dempsey nodded again. The answer made sense. 'Just one more question: what did Danny McKee say he found in room 6.3? Because there's a hell of a blood stain on that carpet.'

'That's what I thought. I told Danny it was blood but he wouldn't listen. Said it was there when he went in but that there was no sign of anyone bleeding, and that it had been cleaned up a lot before he even got there. He figured Professor Rodgers – that's Professor Rodgers' room – had spilt a bottle of wine or something and had tried to clean it up.'

'Seriously?'

'Seriously.'

'If you don't mind me asking, this Danny guy. Not the sharpest tool in the box?'

'No, sir.' The small man laughed as he answered. 'No, sir, he is not.'

'Doesn't sound like it. But anyway, did he say there was anything unusual in the room? Other than the stain?'

'Not a thing.'

Dempsey stood for a moment and replayed the mental images he had just watched.

He was already fairly sure of what had happened the night before. The damage to the doors bore the hallmarks of a professional area search. Which meant that the otherwise untouched rooms had been empty.

But room 6.3 had *not* been empty. That much was clear. It was the last of the doors to have been hit. Even if it had not been, the bloodstain in the middle of the floor told its own story. What it didn't say – what Dempsey still did not know – was *who* was searching and *who* was hiding. Nor did he know who had covered the whole thing up. There had been no report of a body found in the university, and yet the size of the stain meant the certain death of whoever's body had previously held that blood. No reported death meant that information had been suppressed.

'Is that everything?' The small man's voice broke into Dempsey's thoughts. 'Only I've got more to do and I'd like to get home tonight?'

'Sorry, sorry. Yeah, that's all.'

Dempsey thanked the small man for his time, left the room and walked towards the far end of the hallway.

Room 6.11 looked to Dempsey just as it had looked to Michael and Sarah. It appeared to have been ransacked, but Dempsey recognised the work. The search patterns left by agents of the world's intelligence agencies were familiar.

Unlike Sarah, Dempsey was confident he could find what they could not.

He moved around the room. Slowly. Deliberately. Taking in McGale's personal photographs, Dempsey noted the differences between the man portrayed and the one he had tackled in Trafalgar Square. No more time was spent on the subject than necessary. Instead, Dempsey moved to the desk. Searched the open drawers. Found nothing.

Closing the final desk drawer, he moved McGale's chair backwards and took a seat. From here Dempsey surveyed the office, adopting the view of the room that the professor had created for himself. It was a honed technique which put Dempsey in the shoes of his subject. It rarely failed. Now was no exception. Dempsey had barely settled into the seat before his gaze fell on the newspaper clippings that were pinned to the nearside wall.

Dempsey was up in an instant. He moved towards the clippings, his eyes scanning from one story to another. The pattern told him a story; a montage that extended out from a central core, recounting the death of the McGale family.

McGale's past – the fate of his family – was by now well known. To Dempsey and to the general public. There was nothing to be gained from dwelling upon it and so Dempsey's eyes just skimmed the central headline.

Instead they searched the branches that spread out from the centre. Studying them for extra information. He found it quickly, in the cutting from the 18th November edition of the *Belfast Chronicle*. A news report that contained a detail found nowhere in McGale's dossier; the fact that McGale's lucky escape from the restaurant, just moments before the blast, had been due to a call from one of his students. A student named Benjamin Grant.

Dempsey did not believe in coincidence. Chance, yes. But not coincidence. It was cynical to suspect a person just because they pulled a friend clear of a bomb with moments to spare. But cynical was not the same as wrong. The odds that Benjamin Grant knew nothing about McGale's fate were low. Dempsey had his next step.

A few more minutes were spent surveying the cuttings. The name 'Grant' stayed on Dempsey's mind, but something else was eating at his gut. Something he could not quite grasp. Finally he stepped away from the wall. Unable to pinpoint what bothered him, instead he gave what was left of the office a half-hearted search. There was nothing more to be found and so Dempsey headed for the doorway.

He was halfway there when it hit him.

Spinning on his heel, he rushed back to the wall and

reviewed the remaining clippings. Dempsey had already searched for any mention of President Howard Thompson. For something that might justify the shooting. In doing so he had missed the obvious.

Dempsey read the clippings in a new light. Report after report. The same name appeared in every news article that was not directly related to terror. Dempsey could finally see the pattern. McGale's montage dealt with terrorist attacks *and* with Neil Matthewson. Not because he was an obsessive on two distinct subjects, but because he viewed them as the *same* subject. Intrinsically and inseparably linked. Realisation hit Dempsey like a wrecking ball.

The intelligence had been wrong. The security threats incorrect. And the claim of responsibility from the True IRA? Bogus.

Whoever Stanton was, he was *not* behind the failed attempt on the life of Howard Thompson. No. Stanton was behind the *entirely successful* assassination of Sir Neil Matthewson.

And Dempsey was going to find out why.

FIFTY-NINE

Joshua sat alone at a small table in the Europa Hotel bar. An untouched bowl of honey-roasted mixed nuts rested on the table before him. A large measure of the establishment's most expensive whiskey was clasped in his hand.

As alert as ever, his eyes were incapable of rest. They surveyed the layout of his surroundings. Assessed the room's other occupants. Joshua did not require his skills to place the other patrons. Hotel guests mostly, staying out of business necessity. Men and women whose lives on the road did not interest him. One or two others did not fall neatly into the category. They had taken a little more attention, a second or two extra, but still Joshua had been satisfied of his safety before taking his seat. Constant vigilance was a habit that did not break easily.

'Are you waiting for someone, love?'

Joshua glanced up, at a tall woman standing just feet away. She had approached from across the bar and Joshua knew her intentions at a glance. Assignments across the globe had exposed Joshua to many women of her profession. He was familiar with the telltale signs.

Joshua was many things; a husband of twenty-five years and a father to a twenty-year-old son among them. In those years he had not been immune to the charms of such women. A meaningless diversion to fill the empty hours. It was one of many regrets.

'I'm not interested.'

The words brought the woman to a halt. Her mouth opened to respond but she seemed to think better of it, turned and strode out of the bar. Perhaps it was a strikeout too many for one night.

Joshua sat back in his chair, drained what was left of his whiskey and indicated to the barman for another. While he waited his mind drifted to the subject that had been preoccupying him since his arrival in Belfast. Family.

Joshua was a realist. He knew that he had not been a good husband or a good father. But he *had* been a good provider. A palatial family home. A wife who wanted for nothing. A son who was debt-free after two years at an Ivy League university. Joshua had fulfilled his role as the breadwinner, but he knew that was not enough. In so many other ways he had failed.

The work that paid for so much necessitated frequent absence. For at least two thirds of every year Joshua would be thousands of miles from home, with minimal telephone or – more recently – Skype contact. Joshua had always told himself that it was for the family good. That he was providing financial stability. But never once did he believe his own lie. The money was a welcome bonus. It was not the driving force. Joshua did what he did because he loved it. Loved the thrill of the hunt. The exhilaration of the kill. Joshua loved doing the job and he loved being the best. And for that he had forsaken his family.

His thoughts were interrupted by the barman, who placed his third drink of the evening on the table. A leather wallet sat next to it, a paper invoice inside. Joshua signed to charge the drink to his room, tapped each compass point on the glass with his index finger and took a sip of the brown Irish liquor.

His mind returned to his situation.

The hopelessness of Joshua's position would have been

amusing were it not so deadly. For years he had been a ghost. A rumour. Never even a hint that the death he dealt across the globe would come back to his door. But now it had. Now Joshua's life and his own family were under threat, from a man capable of seeing that threat to its end.

What was left of Joshua's whiskey disappeared in a single gulp. He stood up and left the bar. Striding through the lobby, he stepped into the cold Belfast evening air and lit the cigarette he could not smoke inside.

Barely seconds had passed before the mobile telephone in his trouser pocket began to vibrate, as if on cue. Joshua took it out and lifted it to his ear.

'We have a problem.'

Stanton's voice was disguised as always, yet somehow Joshua could detect his uncertainty. His vulnerability. Joshua liked hearing it.

'You were right about Michael Devlin. There's a lot more to him than meets the eye.'

'Tell me.'

Joshua gave no hint of the satisfaction he felt at being proved correct.

'It seems that Mr Devlin is not the orphan that people have been led to believe. I began to investigate him shortly after we last spoke and he has a family. A family in Belfast. I am as certain as I can be that he's with them now.'

'Well, surely that's good for us? Give me the address and I'll finish the job tonight.'

'If it were that simple, Sergeant, I would already have done it!' The impatience in the snapped response spoke volumes. 'But it isn't. Michael Devlin does not come from any ordinary family, which explains why he lied about them. His only brother, like their father before him, is one of the most powerful gangland figures in Northern Ireland. Which means that Michael Devlin is under the protection of one of Belfast's godfathers.'

'Shit!' Joshua was genuinely astonished at Stanton's bad luck. 'That's a serious problem.'

'I'm well aware of that. It means the man has resources we didn't count on. People who will kill to protect him. It also means that he will have disclosed what he knows to his brother, so now we have yet another target. A very dangerous one.'

Joshua took a few moments to consider the developments. Only the last posed a problem. Joshua had dealt with gangland leaders before. He would do so again. But the likelihood that an ever-growing number knew the same information that Michael Devlin was to be killed for? It would take more than a few bullets to solve *that*.

'You need leverage,' Joshua finally offered. 'You need something they want, just as much as you want their silence.'

'I agree.'

Stanton's metallic voice was flat. As if he remained in control. Joshua did not buy it. He let Stanton continue.

'We need to take something dear to them. Something we can use to ensure their cooperation. And once that's done – once they are where we need them to be – you'll kill them.'

'That goes without saying. But I'll need to know where to find them.'

'I have several addresses; Liam Casey has enemies, which means *we* have friends. They have given me the address of his bar, although that is far too public a venue for a successful operation. But they've also given me a number of other locations where his people do their more, shall we say, nefarious work. You are to search each of them until you find Devlin and

Casey. And once you've found them you are to follow them. Everywhere. I want to know where they go and what they do. Once we know enough we'll be in a position to choose our next step carefully. Is that clear?'

It had never been clearer. The involvement of Liam Devlin – or Casey, or whatever his damned name was – had the potential to derail all of Stanton's well-laid plans. Stanton knew it. And he was losing control because of it. This, Joshua feared, would be when Stanton was at his most ruthless, and therefore his most dangerous for Joshua and for his family.

It was therefore imperative that Joshua dealt with this new threat. That he tie up the ever-growing number of loose ends and protect the lives of his family.

Joshua needed to be as ruthless as Stanton. And he would be.

'It's clear,' he said. 'Give me the addresses.'

SIXTY

Benjamin Grant felt the hard wooden chair viciously bite into the small of his back. Grant was unused to violence. It terrified him to the point of paralysis, and so he offered no resistance as his arms were pulled backwards and his wrists handcuffed together. A painful restriction on his movement, joining the blinding hood and the gag that had already robbed him of his main senses.

Not that sight was necessary. Grant could picture the events that had brought him here without it. Wherever 'here' was.

He had been walking home at the end of a long day of study. His attention elsewhere, there had been no warning before he was grabbed by several pairs of hands. No time had been given for Grant to think through the safest reaction.

Opening his mouth to scream had been a mistake, as it allowed a coarse fabric to be forced past his teeth and onto his tongue. The rag did its job. It prevented Grant from uttering a sound, and had been instantly followed by a near-black hood forced over his head. Next, before he had even noticed his lost vision, he had been dragged a short distance and thrown into the rear of a large vehicle.

The journey that followed was as traumatic as its start. Grant's attempts to call out had been stifled by the rag that inched down his throat. So his only way to communicate was to kick out and punch at the surrounding seats, which had led to injury as he blindly struck at metal with his fists. Soon he had learned his lesson and ended his struggle.

All of this was both terrifying and painful, but it had been the silence that affected Grant the most. Unable to beg for his life. Unable to seek an explanation. That had been bad enough. But it had been made so much worse by the fact that his kidnappers were just as silent. Not a single word had been uttered. No questions asked. It had left Grant with nothing but his own fears. Fears that had grown as the journey ended and the silence continued until, finally, he had convinced himself that tonight would be his last.

The conclusion Grant had reached was the logical one. If his kidnappers had no questions for him then their only goal must be his death.

Grant felt a rope being bound around his chest, tying him to the chair. Next he felt a strong, callused hand make its way underneath his hood. The hand fumbled for an instant before tearing the gag from his mouth. The rag behind it was then ripped out, making him choke as it left his throat.

Grant caught a fleeting glimpse of a damp concrete floor before the hood fell back into place. He ignored it. This was his chance to make some noise. To scream. Grant tried to take it, but he could not. Strong hands grabbed his skull an instant before his first shout. Grant could do nothing to resist as those hands tilted his head backwards.

At the same moment a second person lifted the front of the hood to the level of his mouth and brought a cup of tepid water to his lips. The content was rancid but Grant drank greedily. A coarse gag on the tongue for thirty minutes makes any liquid palatable.

'What, what do you want?'

Grant was spluttering, still suffering the effects of the gag.

'We want to know who paid you to get at Eamon McGale.'

The answer was simple but firm. And it made Grant's blood run cold.

The speaker was a man who knew how to get what he wanted. Grant's current position told him that. But the speaker was also asking a question that Grant could not answer.

'I don't know what you're talking about,' Grant protested weakly. 'I don't even know what that means. I've never "got at" Professor McGale, I just studied under him.'

'That's bollocks, son.' It was the same voice. 'Someone paid you to get at the man. To mess with his head. You're gonna tell me who that was. Either that, or things are going to get painful.'

'Please, I don't know what you're talking about. Professor McGale was a friend. I'd never mess with his head, not for anything. Please!'

Grant doubted his pleas would have any effect, but when they were followed by silence he began to hope that he had underestimated his powers of persuasion. That hope was extinguished the instant it began, by a crushing blow to the temple that sent his chair backwards and slammed his head into the concrete floor.

Blood flowed freely from a cut to the back of Grant's skull. He was dazed. Confused. The same hands that had struck the blow set Grant upright once again, lifting the chair with him.

Once back in place the interrogation continued.

'I'm warning you, Benjamin.' That voice again. 'Every time you lie you'll get that. Each time worse than the last. So there's two ways this ends, son. You tell me the truth and you walk out on your own legs. A bit battered, but you're walking. Keep this shit up, though, and I'll break your legs and throw you off the docks. Your choice.'

Grant hesitated. His head was fuzzy, which made it hard to

make a rational decision in an irrational situation. These people *knew* he had been involved. There was no doubt about that. They also knew he had been working for someone. They just did not know who that someone was.

Denials would get him nowhere. Grant could see that. He also did not doubt that the threats made were serious. But none of this made his choice any easier.

'Alright. Alright.'

The feeling of blood trickling down the back of Grant's neck distracted him.

'What do you want from me?'

'Just what I said. I want to know who paid you to screw about with McGale. To get him out of the restaurant on the night his family died. And to convince him that Neil Matthewson was behind the True IRA.'

Grant was silent. *How do they know so much?* He knew now that he was in the most dangerous position of his life. If he did not answer then he might die. But if he *did* answer then he *would* die.

'You don't understand what you're dealing with.' Grant was too desperate to be anything now but honest. 'If I tell you what I know, I'm dead. I *know* these people. I *know* they'll kill me. I don't know you. I don't know you're not bluffing.'

Michael and Liam exchanged looks. No words. With just a subtle nod, indicating that they had reached agreement.

Liam stepped forward and took hold of Grant's hood. He pulled it from Grant's head, exposing the room and its occupants to his eyes.

Grant looked from figure to figure. At first he could make out only indistinct forms as his eyes focused after the darkness. Gradually his pupils contracted. His surroundings became clear. A large and dirty garage.

More important were the figures around him. As Grant's gaze moved from face to face there was one set of features he immediately recognised.

The sight made Grant's eyes fill with tears. Any hope he had that the speaker had made empty threats was now gone.

'Oh, Jesus Christ.'

'Not quite.' Liam's voice was pitiless. 'But now you know who you're dealing with. You know I'll kill you as sure as whoever you're working for will. Only difference, son, is that *I'm* the one who has you tied up. *I* can kill you where you sit. So now. Tell me the truth and you can go, and if you're lucky you can disappear before anyone else gets to you.'

Grant had lost. There could be no bluffing. There could be no lying. He had grown up on streets where Liam Casey was king. A king who struck fear into braver men than Grant.

'I was told to get Professor McGale out of the restaurant that night.' Grant spoke slowly. 'I was told what time and what to say. But I didn't know what was going to happen. I swear I didn't!'

'I couldn't give a shit what you knew. I want to know who paid you.'

Grant looked at the floor. Did not respond right away as he weighed up his choices. Which killer he wanted gunning for his life. But right now only one of them had him tied to a chair.

'It was Robert Mullen.'

The hush that followed the name spoke volumes. Every man but Michael shifted their bodyweight awkwardly. An identical silent reaction that said more than words.

'Robert Mullen? You're sure?'

Liam's tone betrayed a hope that Grant would answer 'no'.

'I'm sure. I dealt with the man himself. Mullen told me where to go, what to say. The exact time, down to the minute that I was to say it.'

Michael stepped close to his brother, out of Grant's earshot. He spoke quietly.

'Who the hell's Robert Mullen?'

'Later.' Liam turned back to Grant. 'Mullen had you convince McGale there was a conspiracy behind the attacks, did he?'

'Yes.' Grant had crossed the line, offering everything he knew. 'After the bombing I realised what I was involved in. I panicked. I told Mullen I was going to hand myself in. He told me what would happen to my family if I did. And what would happen to them if I didn't do more. He wanted me to use my relationship with Professor McGale to pass on information. Little by little. To get him thinking that the terrorist attacks weren't normal. That they were a cover for something bigger.'

'You've got to be kidding.' Liam seemed to struggle with what he was being told. 'Mullen did all this? Robert Mullen?'

'Yes, Mullen. He wanted me to convince the professor that the terrorist groups – both sides – were being funded by the same person. Someone with an ulterior motive. It wasn't hard. Mullen would tell me when an attack was coming. He'd give me details on the targets and anything else I needed to know. I'd pass it on to Professor McGale after the fact, telling him that I got it from a source. After a few months I had him convinced I was right. That the whole thing was a massive conspiracy. So that in the end he wanted to meet my source.'

'Which was Mullen's plan all along.' Michael's mind now raced ahead. 'Mullen must be the "RM" in McGale's diary.'

'When I took him to meet Mullen, I saw Mullen playing a role. He wasn't himself. Not even close. He came across as a conflicted patriot, dedicated to a cause but unhappy with how it was being pursued. Bloody convincing, too. I almost forgot what a vicious psycho he is during those meetings. Almost.'

'And the meetings? What happened?'

'They would just sit and discuss things, and from the first meeting onwards they were in regular contact. Mullen was careful. He took his time to convince the professor. To indoctrinate him. Basically, he played him until the professor was truly convinced of what Mullen was selling him.'

'And what *was* he selling him, exactly?' Michael knew the answers to most of his questions but some blanks remained. 'That Neil Matthewson was involved in terrorism? Why?'

'Oh, it was much more than that. Mullen wasn't just saying that Matthewson was *involved* in terrorism. No. He made Professor McGale think that Matthewson was *behind* it. That he was the *cause* of *all* of it. He convinced him that Matthewson was bankrolling both sides. Over time Mullen persuaded the professor that the new terrorism had nothing whatsoever to do with politics or with patriotism. That it was all just driven by one man – by Matthewson – and that it could be stopped by the death of that same man. Mullen wanted the professor to think that killing Matthewson was the only way to stop the attackers. And, once the professor was convinced, Mullen showed him how to do it.'

A silence fell when Grant finished speaking. Each man there tried to process what they had just heard. Many questions arose. Some demanded answers more than others.

'Why the hell did Mullen want Matthewson dead?' Liam beat Michael to the punch.

'I don't know,' replied Grant. 'I don't know the point behind any of it. Mullen just told me it was political. That they were doing something that would go down in history.'

'But why McGale?' Michael asked. 'The time and the trouble you went to with the man. To fake a terrorist attack that kills his family and then manipulate him while he's grieving. To turn a good man into a killer? Why didn't Mullen just have someone else kill Matthewson? A professional?'

'Because it wouldn't have had the same effect, would it? If Mullen was going for a big political impact, what better way than to use a well-respected academic whose career to that point had always been so anti-terror? So anti-violence? A man whose life's work was peaceful negotiation? If a man like *that* resorts to violence, what hope is there for anyone else? McGale was chosen because of the message he offered. He was chosen because of who he was.'

'That choice cost McGale and his family their lives,' Liam's voice bristled with anger. 'Did you ever think of that before you turned Judas on a man who trusted you?'

'I told you, Mr Casey. I had no idea there was going to be a bomb. I had no idea the professor was going to be manipulated into what happened in London. I was just doing as I was told. I had no idea of the consequences.'

'And why did Mullen choose you?' Michael's voice carried the same distaste as Liam's. 'Were you just the cheapest?'

'I didn't receive a penny.'

Grant's words were tinged with fear. The atmosphere in the lock-up was turning against him. The words now came out fast as he tried to explain himself.

'I had to do it the first time. At that point I owed Mullen. He'd helped me out and I owed him, and he said that this was how I could pay him back. And it didn't seem so bad, just a message to get him out of the restaurant. I didn't know what would happen. I didn't know what I was getting myself into. And then after that I had no choice. Mullen said he'd kill my family if I didn't help, if I went to the police or tried to warn the professor. I didn't have a choice.'

Liam nodded his head. Grant's reaction was convincing.

The anger in Liam's voice was subsiding when he spoke again.

'Enough, Benjamin. I believe you. Which means you get to live. We're going to take you home. When we do, you need to pack your things and leave. Straight away. Leave Belfast. Leave everyone behind and just go. Do *not* speak to Mullen. Don't tell him that you've met me. Don't tell him a word. You got that?'

'Yes. Yes.' Tears streamed down Grant's face. His answers had kept him alive. 'Thank you, Liam. Thank you.'

Paddy O'Neil reached behind the chair and removed Grant's handcuffs. Next he unbound the rope that tied Grant to the chair.

He helped Grant to his feet and apologised about the cut to the back of his head, assuring him it was 'just a scratch'. The other three men were already walking towards the door.

They came to a halt when Michael stopped and turned back to face Grant. Something had just occurred to him. Something important.

'You said all you had to do was pass McGale details about the terrorist attacks. That Mullen would give you them before and you'd pass them to McGale afterwards.'

'Yeah. That's what happened.'

'But I don't understand. How could Mullen know about

the attacks beforehand? How could he know details of what a terrorist was going to do before they did it?'

'I'm sorry, I thought I'd made that part clear.'

Grant seemed so keen to ensure his own safety that he would now answer any question. He continued.

'Not everything Mullen had me tell the professor was a lie. The terrorist attacks *weren't* real. They *aren't* real. There *is* another agenda behind them. But it's Robert Mullen's agenda. Mullen knew about the attacks beforehand because he planned them. He *was* the terror.'

SIXTY-ONE

O'Neil's black Land Rover screeched to a halt outside Grant's home. The rear passenger-side door opened before the vehicle had come to a complete stop and Grant practically threw himself from the car. The act of a man who wanted to be away from Liam Casey – and out of Belfast – as soon as possible.

'Remember what I said.' Liam spoke through the open window of the front passenger seat. 'Not a word. Now get yourself somewhere safe because he'll be looking for you.'

The final words carried no threat, but they were still an obvious command. The implications for disobedience were unthinkable. Not that someone like Grant would risk testing them.

'Are you going to tell me who the hell Robert Mullen is?'

Michael spoke over the sound of the V8 engine, which roared as O'Neil took off and navigated the streets of Belfast at breakneck speed. With only the four men now present, Liam was free to speak.

'A whole lot of trouble, Mikey, that's what he is.'

The answer carried more than a note of concern, something Michael had rarely heard in his brother's voice.

'He's a villain from North Belfast. Serious player. Robbery, extortion, protection, drugs. The man runs psychopaths and lunatics. No moral compass. No limits. Mullen was mid-size forever. Just a bloody nuisance. Then, a few years back, he took off in a big way.'

'How big?'

'As big as us, but a lot more unpredictable. People are scared of him, and with good reason. If Mullen's involved in this we're up against a whole world of trouble.'

Michael sat back into his seat as he took in the fresh information. Was this the man behind Matthewson's assassination? The man who had the influence to arrange McGale's death in custody? Who had accessed Daniel's phone records quickly enough to lead to Michael himself? Was this the man who had doggedly sought Michael's death from London to Belfast?

If it was, then they had taken a huge step forward by putting a name to the mind that was running things from afar. But Liam's description of Mullen and his first reaction to Grant's use of the name? They both gave Michael doubts.

'What do you think, Liam?'

Michael leaned forward. Closer to his brother.

'Do you think this Mullen guy could be behind this?'

'Not for a second.' Liam answered without the slightest hesitation. 'He's not sophisticated enough. They're a crude lot. No finesse. From what you've said there's serious brainpower behind this whole thing. Mullen's not got that in him.'

'But you don't think Grant was lying?'

'I don't, no. I think everything he told us was true, at least as far as he knows it. Mullen's in this up to his ears. But there's no way he's running the thing. The man's a hired thug. Doing as he's told. Someone else is pulling the strings.'

'What makes you so sure?' O'Neil spoke from the driver's seat. 'Mullen's built up a serious little outfit very quickly. He can't be that useless.'

'I didn't say he was useless. But maybe that's the point.

He pretty much came out of nowhere and suddenly he's almost running Belfast? In a matter of years? All coinciding with the rise of the True IRA, a group no one seems to know about, not even the old-school Provos. It all smacks of a set-up.'

'I don't follow.' Michael rarely felt so off the pace. 'Why do you think the two are connected?'

'Because it fits. Think about what they told McGale. That someone was funding both sides. The True IRA and the UVA. You heard Grant. Not everything they told McGale was a lie. What if that part was true? What if someone *was* funding both sides? What if that's where Mullen suddenly came from? A lunatic who got lucky because he was willing to kill a lot of people for money and make it look like he did it for a cause? It makes sense, doesn't it? How Mullen could afford to expand into the big time? Mullen was being funded from outside. Plus it explains him getting involved in terrorism in the first place.'

'What do you mean? Why does he need an excuse? No one else ever did.'

'This guy would. I've known the man for years, Mikey. Mullen hasn't a religious or a political bone in his body. Money is what drives him. Not a united Ireland or any other principle. Mullen's involved in this for his pocket.'

O'Neil took the left-hand corner that led to the rear car park of the 32 Counties Bar. He brought the Land Rover to a halt before anyone spoke again. Michael was considering what Liam had said. It made sense.

The silence remained until O'Neil had removed the key from the ignition, turning on the interior lights.

'So what do we do about this?' asked Jack Thornton. 'If we go after Mullen it's a war. You know that, Liam.'

'We might not have a choice.'

Michael heard the resignation in his brother's voice and in that moment he realised how far his brother would still go to protect him.

The realisation made Michael's fraternal instincts fire.

'You don't have to do that, Liam,' Michael said. 'I came to you for a little help but this is much more than that now. I don't want you starting a war over me. That's not why I'm here.'

'But if Mullen *is* behind this whole thing? If he is and I don't stop him?' Liam met his brother's protestations head-on. 'What happens to you, Mikey? Do you think he'll just leave you and Sarah alone?'

'I didn't mean—'

'Then what choice do I have? You can't deal with Mullen alone. Which gives me a choice, doesn't it? I can walk away and leave you to run from him for as long as you can, until you end up dead. Or I can risk a war. Which one do you think I'm going to be able to live with, Mikey? Which one?'

Michael opened his mouth to respond but this time his mastery of words failed him. He wanted to tell Liam that he could handle himself. That he didn't need his brother's help. Both would have been a lie.

Michael *did* need Liam's help. And, like it or not, he was going to get it.

SIXTY-TWO

Joshua's eyes narrowed as he watched Benjamin Grant leap from the Land Rover. Sitting in an inconspicuous rented Fiat Brava, he could see everything without being noticed. It was a perfect car for the job and had kept him close to the action for the past few hours.

The early part of the evening had been spent in the darkest corners of Belfast, visiting the many locations associated with Liam Casey. The 32 Counties Bar had been discounted as a realistic possibility. It was an obvious front for Liam's illegal activities and so he would not risk bringing trouble to his one clean door.

Joshua had instead concentrated on the list's murkier addresses.

The last location Joshua had visited was the Craven Street Repairs and Servicing Centre. An innocuous garage that sat down a backstreet in the South Belfast suburbs. The interior lights – still illuminated past 10 p.m. – suggested that it operated unlikely hours.

Those lights convinced Joshua to examine the area more closely. Parking his car in an adjacent street, he made his way through the shadows and into the grounds of the garage on foot. Once there he located the motion-sensitive security lights on the front wall of the unkempt garage forecourt. A closer look revealed that the device was of a very high standard for such a run-down establishment; he had come to the right place.

Joshua flattened himself against the closest wall, to fool

the motion sensors that he was a part of the structure. Safely concealed, he edged his body towards the battered garage doors, never losing contact with the wall. Not even when he reached the doors themselves. Joshua slid his way across their aged, rotting wood. Felt brittle splinters break off and catch on his clothes. His body stayed in contact with the doors, neither he nor they making a sound.

Once at the centre of the doorway Joshua manoeuvred his body for a clear view through the thin and uneven gap where the doors joined. The line of sight was direct but limited. Through the space he could see three men standing, Michael Devlin among them. Liam Casey was nowhere to be seen. All were facing the side. Watching. Listening. Joshua could only assume that it was Liam Casey who was somehow captivating their attention. It was unlikely he was doing so for their entertainment.

Joshua could tell from the movements of the light that there was at least one other person in the lock-up. Or more likely two.

Whatever else was going on inside – whoever else was in there – did not matter. All Joshua needed to know was that he had found the brothers. Satisfied, he slowly retraced his steps, first against the doors and then the wall, and then back to his parked car. Once there, Joshua waited for them to emerge.

He did not have to wait long.

Less than twenty minutes later the dim glow of the interior lighting cast itself across the darkened forecourt. It was followed within seconds by the high beam of the forecourt security light. Joshua held his thin telescopic sight in his hand, ready to catch the details of who emerged. It was not needed. The group of five men who climbed into the waiting Land Rover parked on the forecourt were plainly the lock-up's full complement.

Joshua slid himself down into his seat. The brothers' vehicle had to pass him on route to the main road into Belfast and so Joshua needed to be concealed. Once the Land Rover had passed he waited to allow for a respectable but manageable following distance. The brothers deserved more respect than Joshua would usually allow, and he would not forget that the driver was probably experienced in avoiding both surveillance and pursuit.

The journey to Grant's home took around five minutes. Joshua parked a safe distance from the property, on a long street that led to a small, run-down terraced house. From here he observed Grant's near leap from a rear passenger's door.

As the Land Rover sped away, Joshua mentally noted every detail. Stanton would want them all. He watched Grant run along his garden path before shifting into first gear and – when the vehicle was far enough ahead – he pulled back into the road and continued to follow.

As he passed Grant's house Joshua took note of the door number, invisible from where he had parked. The detail memorised, he returned his eyes to the road and, in doing so, he almost missed the smooth, swift movement on the nearside pavement.

Almost.

Joshua's peripheral vision was just one of the factors that made him so good at his job. Without it he might have overlooked the same sight that had delayed him just days ago. The sight of a stone-faced Joe Dempsey, stalking his prey.

'Shit!'

Joshua weaved through traffic as he watched Dempsey, now in his rear-view mirror. It was no surprise to him to see Dempsey turn from the pavement, onto the path that led to

Grant's front door. If Liam Casey could find whatever had led them to Grant, Dempsey could sure as hell do the same.

'Shit!'

Joshua's mind was suddenly torn between two choices. He could continue after Devlin and Casey, as Stanton had instructed. Or he could go back and deal with the threat posed by Dempsey while the man didn't expect it.

The first choice meant following orders. But the second could save his life.

Ordinarily there would be no dilemma. Stanton would be ignored. The brothers would be abandoned. Dempsey would be dead. But these were not normal circumstances. With Joshua's family at risk, he did something unnatural.

He asked for permission.

'What can I do for you, Sergeant?' Stanton answered on the second ring. He always did.

'Guidance,' Joshua replied, still keeping pace with the speeding Land Rover. 'I'm following Devlin and Casey. I've just seen them interrogate a guy and then watched them bring him home. Which means he must have told them everything or else I doubt he'd be walking. Now they're heading somewhere else and I'm following like you said. But there's a problem.'

'What problem?'

'The man they were questioning, he's about to get a visit from Joe Dempsey. So what do I do? Follow them or go back and deal with Dempsey? I need to know. Now!'

'Calm down, Sergeant, there's no need to become agitated.' Stanton's voice was as flat as always. 'Describe the person they were interrogating.'

'Do we have time for this?'

'Yes, Sergeant, we do. Describe him.'

'He was young. Early twenties. Looked like a bookworm. I don't know other than that. Does that help?'

'It does. I think I know who it is. I want you to stay with Michael Devlin. We don't know what he and his brother have found out so it's important we keep close.'

'But what about Dempsey? What about what this guy tells *him*? We have to keep a lid on that too.'

'We do, Sergeant, and I will. You're not the only asset I have in play. Now, please, stay with them and leave Joe Dempsey to me.'

Dempsey moved along the pavement at speed. Benjamin Grant was in his sights. The young academic moved fast along the path into his house, closing the door behind him.

There are times when it helps to give notice of your arrival. There are times when it does not. Grant was coming home with fresh wounds from a determined interrogation. Dempsey saw these details and knew that, tonight, the second approach was best.

Dempsey increased his speed as he turned onto Grant's path. It grew until he hit the front door, just moments after it had closed. Hard and fast, the force took the heavy wooden structure off of its frame and hinges.

Grant had got no further than his hallway.

Dempsey did not lose a step of pace. He caught up with Grant and grabbed him by the scruff of the neck before he had a chance to run.

'I want to know everything about Eamon McGale.' Dempsey's voice carried no hint of compromise. 'And I want to know what you told Michael Devlin.'

'I, I don't know what you're talking about,' Grant's legs buckled beneath him. 'I don't know a Michael Devlin.'

'Don't lie to me! What did you tell him?'

'OK, OK.'

Grant offered no resistance at all further. The night had destroyed his resolve.

'I told them everything.'

Dempsey moved his face closer. So that Grant could feel the heat of his breath as he spoke.

'Then it's good you're used to the story, because now you're going to tell it to me.'

SIXTY-THREE

Stanton pressed the red disconnect button. The line went dead.

He placed the phone onto the table and sat back into his high-backed chair. Then he began to tap his fingers absentmindedly as he thought through the fresh developments.

That Stanton was at his desk so late proved how out-of-control events had grown. The most meticulously planned operation of his life had become a debacle.

The thought of how well things *should* have gone haunted him.

McGale had played his role to perfection. Better than that, even. And the faked True IRA threat against President Howard Thompson's life had done exactly as Stanton intended. It had caused the world to focus on the former leader instead of Sir Neil Matthewson, the man who had actually died. A focus only strengthened by McGale's wounding of Thompson as he shot at McGale. That was a stroke of luck Stanton could not have hoped for.

Joshua, too, had successfully completed the first of his tasks. A perfectly placed bullet had cleared a path for McGale. But, looking back now, that victory had been their last real success.

All the mistakes from that point could be traced back to Joe Dempsey, and therefore to Stanton's miscalculation. Stanton had recognised that Dempsey's presence at Trafalgar Square could prove problematic. A remote possibility, but a possibility nonetheless. Stanton had dealt with it by keeping Joshua in the dark. To do otherwise risked revealing to Joshua that Stanton knew his true identity. That was valuable information, to be used later if necessary. Just as Stanton had done. But it was also itself a potential distraction, every bit as big – bigger, even – than the sudden appearance of Joe Dempsey. And so Stanton had chosen to keep it from Joshua. To rely upon the odds against Joshua spotting Dempsey in a crowd of thousands, particularly when Dempsey's placement was on the opposite side of the square to where McGale would be.

That decision had been his first mistake.

Luck had also played its part. The plan had been years in the making. Every precaution had been taken. Even McGale's unlikely arrest and detention had been accounted for, by the long-standing purchase of Sergeant Trevor Henry. A failsafe that would ensure McGale's convenient 'suicide'.

But fate had intervened, and even that brilliant contingency had proved insufficient.

Stanton had of course known that McGale might see a lawyer before he could be silenced. The odds against that were significant. Under English Law a terror suspect can be kept incommunicado for days. Denied the right to see or contact anyone. Even a lawyer. It was a long shot that this power of isolated detention would not be used, but Stanton had been prepared nonetheless. And so he had been ready when – with the encouragement of a prime minister desperate to protect his own interests – Daniel Lawrence had spent time alone with McGale.

Any person having one-to-one access with the man was unacceptable. Not that McGale knew anything that could lead directly to Stanton. The professor's knowledge was deliberately inaccurate. But he knew enough to raise questions. Questions that could lead to the truth. This Stanton could not allow. And so Daniel Lawrence had had to die.

Stanton had hoped that Lawrence's death would be the end of it. Somehow it had not, and now it seemed that loose ends were multiplying at an uncontrollable rate.

The resilience – the sheer nuisance – of Michael Devlin had been wholly unpredictable. As for Sarah Truman, Stanton still had no idea how she had stumbled onto the story. Not that it mattered. She was involved. The damage was done. In truth she added little; Stanton still believed that matters would have been resolved quickly if he faced Michael and Sarah alone. But now he faced much more.

Michael Devlin's past presented a host of loyal connections that Stanton could not have anticipated. Problems he could do without. Problems which now posed the greatest threat to the success of his operation.

Stanton took a calming breath as he looked around his home office. The extra oxygen helped his anxiety. As did his surroundings. Stanton's ability to think and act under crippling pressure had brought him this far in life. They had paid for much of the opulence that now surrounded him.

Those same qualities would see him emerge victorious. Of that much he was sure.

Another deep breath. A slow exhale. Stanton's head cleared. His resolve returned. It forced the despondence from his mind. The steps that would deal with Devlin and his brother had been taken. The arrangements made. It would not be pretty, but it would be effective.

Joe Dempsey was a different matter. The DDS agent had disrupted every careful plan. The man's determination and resourcefulness had surprised at every turn. Now the time had come to remove the thorn from his side.

Stanton put the telephone to his ear. Dialled a familiar number. Waited to be answered. For once he did not activate his voice modulator.

'It's me,' he said, as the expected voice greeted his call.

'How are things panning out in Belfast?'

'Mostly under control.'

'Mostly?'

'What do you think? He's getting too close.'

'I did warn you. He's good.'

'I know. I should have listened. It's time to end his involvement. Once and for all.'

'He's *that* close?'

'Getting closer by the minute.'

'And you're sure there's no other way? *Without* tackling Dempsey head-on? He's a dangerous bastard.'

'I'm certain. Do you have the sufficient assets in Belfast to act? Because we need him dealt with quickly and effectively.'

'There's no one there we could rely on. There's no one else that good. I'll have to do it myself.'

Stanton hesitated for a moment. He was surprised by the statement. But he would not turn down the offer.

'OK. Then just make sure it's done soon. I don't want Dempsey turning up at my door.'

The call was ended without the courtesy of a farewell. Stanton sat back in his chair.

For the first time in hours he felt the situation coming back under his control. Michael Devlin and Liam Casey were dead men. Joshua would see to that, once Stanton was ready.

And now his second problem would soon be resolved,

too. It would receive the personal attention of the one man he trusted absolutely. The one man as dedicated to their cause as Stanton was himself.

It was enough to reignite the fire inside him.

SIXTY-FOUR

'You're going after who?'

The fear in Anne Flaherty's voice was unmistakable. It said all it had to about the dangers of Liam and Michael's next step.

'Robert Mullen.' Liam's nonchalant response fooled no one. 'He's behind this, Anne. So we don't have much of a choice.'

'So you're just going to go take him, are you? You're going to go out and kidnap the one person in the whole of Belfast who can bring this back to our door? You do this, Liam, and you'll start a war we might not win.'

'And if I don't, Anne, then I leave Mikey and Sarah to die. I don't see another way. Do you?'

Twenty years at Liam's side had educated Anne in many ways. Her hold over him was not strong enough to change his mind. She knew that.

Instead she turned her attention towards his brother.

'And you?' Anne's finger pointed at Michael. 'You think it's OK to turn up after twenty years and drag your idiot brother into something that'll be the death of him?'

'Anne, I've asked him not to get involved.' Michael explained. 'It's not why I came back. If this Mullen guy is dangerous then I don't want any of you involved in this. I can run. *We* can run. I don't want any of you hurt.'

'You can run?' Liam interrupted. 'And what? You don't think Mullen can chase you, Mikey? For so long that you'll run out of steam? Then what? When I hear that Mullen has caught and killed my little brother? What do I do then, eh? I murder the bastard, that's what. Does no one see this? One way or another I end up killing him. So I might as well do it on my terms. I might as well do it now.'

A moment of silence filled the room. Four people, all considering the logic behind Liam's words.

Only Anne refused to accept it. She spoke fast, her thoughts jumbling out.

'It's not that simple, Liam. Mullen's maybe even bigger than you now. At least *as* big. And he's a ruthless bastard. And how are you even going to lay your hands on him? He's always surrounded by protection. But even if you manage to do that and you come away in one piece, do you think the lunatics that work for him aren't going to come after you?'

'You're telling me nothing I don't know, Anne.'

Resignation made Liam's words sound angry.

'But there's only one way and so I *have* to take it. I don't have a choice on this one. We're taking Mullen tonight.'

The decision was made.

Liam stalked out of the room. Michael, Sarah and Anne were left speechless in his wake.

The silence did not last.

'How the hell could you let him do this, Mikey?'

Anne's anger was now focused on Michael.

'I didn't mean for this to happen, Anne. I didn't even know who Robert Mullen was, let alone that he was involved in this. I begged Liam to step back when I knew. To leave me to it. But he wouldn't listen.'

'Liam never bloody listens, but you shouldn't have put him in the position in the first place. You knew what he'd risk to help you.'

'I wasn't even sure he'd *speak* to me, Anne. Much less *protect* me. Jesus, you saw how he reacted when we showed up this morning. Like he wanted to kill me. How could I know he'd be willing to start a war for me?'

'Of course he'd bloody be willing to start a war, you idiot!'

All of Anne's frustrations poured out as she spoke, her face now a mix of anger and tears.

'He served seven years in the Maze for a man *you* killed. Do you think he could lose that kind of loyalty? That need to protect you? Your brother can preen and posture all he likes, Mikey, but he's loved you like no one else his whole life. He followed everything you ever did. Bought English newspapers to read about your trials. All we'd ever hear from him and from your father was how well Mikey was doing. How he was over in England, beating them at their own game. For Christ's sake, he might have resented the fact that you never came back but he never stopped loving you. And now it'll probably get him killed.'

Michael did not respond. He did not seem to know how.

Anne could see the hurt in his eyes as her words sank in. Words that had crushed him. It had not been her intention. Not that she had one; Anne had simply been lashing out in anger. But now she wished she could take them back.

'Mikey, I—'

'I've no right bringing trouble to your door,' Michael said, cutting off Anne's apology. 'I can't stop Liam going after Mullen if I'm here, but maybe if I'm not? Maybe if we leave now he won't feel he has to do it?'

'That's not your brother and you know it, Mikey.' Anne's voice was softer. Her anger mostly gone. 'If you run, Liam will think about nothing other than what happens if you're caught.

He won't take that risk, whether you're here or not. Which means he has no choice, at least the way *his* mind works. Liam has to take Mullen. Whatever the consequences.'

'You mean *we* have to take Mullen.' Michael's correction offered no opportunity for disagreement. 'If Liam goes I'll be by his side. He's not doing it without me.'

Michael's words hit Sarah like a punch to the gut. The thought of him going up against someone like Robert Mullen was painful to her. The thought of losing him now – before they'd even had a chance to admit their feelings – was a painful prospect.

She wanted to speak. To object. But even if she had had the courage, she did not have the time.

Liam strode back into the room without warning. He threw a small sports bag to Michael. When he spoke his certainty demanded obedience.

'Put that on. We're ready to go.'

Michael opened the bag. It contained a set of dark clothing, complete with gloves, boots and balaclava. The perfect full kit for what lay ahead.

'That was quick.' Michael said.

Sarah noted the tone of his voice. He seemed almost excited now.

'I had Paddy and Jack put a crew together while we were speaking,' Liam replied. 'They're used to doing these things at short notice.'

'You're sure you want to do this, Liam?'

'Of course I don't *want* to do it. But we both know I *have* to. So let's go.'

Liam's words closed the discussion. Neither man spoke

again. Instead they turned away from one another, towards the door.

Their path there was blocked by two women, concern etched across their features.

Anne threw her arms around Liam in a tight hug. She pulled him close with a strength her petite body did not suggest. Liam leaned down and kissed her. As he did this he wiped a tear from her cheek with a gentle brush of his thumb.

'You be careful, Liam Casey,' she said as she let go. 'Come back in one piece.'

'I will. I'll see you after.'

The same moment for Sarah and Michael was more awkward. Neither seemed to know how to say goodbye. But Sarah knew it could be the last time they ever did.

'You'll be careful?' Her voice was quiet.

'I will. And don't worry. I'll be coming back.'

Sarah forced a smile in response, but any effort to hide her emotions was betrayed by the tears that welled in her eyes.

Michael hesitated before placing his hand on Sarah's wet cheek, just as Liam had done to Anne. For a moment they both just stood there and gazed at one another, until Michael leaned forward and placed the softest of kisses onto Sarah's lips, lingering for just moments before he stepped back.

Their eyes remained locked for a second or two more, until Michael finally started towards the door. Once he reached it he turned and repeated the words his brother had spoken just moments before.

'I'll see you after.'

SIXTY-FIVE

Dempsey walked slowly to his car, his mind swimming with the information he now held.

Benjamin Grant had been the most willing informant he had ever questioned. A man already broken by earlier interrogation, his answers had moved Dempsey's investigation forward in a leap. The jigsaw of discoveries was becoming clear. Dempsey was close.

When he reached his car he climbed inside, but made no attempt to start the engine. Instead he used the silence to enhance his clarity of thought. Cocooned from the distractions of the street, Dempsey drew together the information he had collected into a coherent picture.

Grant had confirmed Dempsey's suspicions about McGale's true target. That had been his hope. What he had *not* expected was what else the young man had told him. The manipulation of McGale. The murder of his family. The counterfeit terrorism. All of it had cost too many lives already. And all of it would be brought to Stanton's door.

Dempsey had been told so much. Each part unbelievable in isolation, but it all made perfect sense when looked at as a whole. Dempsey would never have believed that Matthewson had been behind the new Irish terror, but after listening to Grant he could see how Eamon McGale would have bought every word, especially in his grief-stricken state.

Someone *had* provided resources to Robert Mullen's organisation, using it to create the impression of terrorism.

And though Grant did not know it, that someone was Stanton. Any proper interrogation of McGale would have ultimately led to this truth, which was what both the professor and Daniel Lawrence had been killed to prevent.

This knowledge alone took Dempsey no further. But it put him on the right track. Dempsey had the name of Robert Mullen. Of the man who could take him even closer to Stanton.

But first he had another matter to deal with.

Grant had told him about Liam Casey, enough that Dempsey had connected the dots between that man and Michael. Circumstance made the brothers his natural allies, and they were hours ahead of him. They could have much to offer.

Dempsey tapped Callum McGregor's name on his phone screen. The call was answered in seconds.

'Joe.' For once McGregor's greetings went beyond a word. 'I was planning to call you.'

'You sound pretty awake, Callum. Still in the office?'

'We haven't caught the bastards yet, have we? So yeah, I'm still in the office. What do you need?'

Dempsey ignored the tone. He was used to hearing impatience in McGregor's voice. Particularly in the last few days.

'I just need some information, Callum. Addresses. How long do you think it will take you?'

'Well, that depends on whose address you want. I can give you mine right now.'

'Alright, alright.' Dempsey was in no mood for sarcasm. 'I need whatever information we have on two Belfast villains. Robert Mullen and Liam Casey. And I need possible locations for them both.'

'Liam Casey?' McGregor asked. 'I know the name. What's he got to do with any of this?'

'The lawyer from Lonsdale Square,' Dempsey explained. 'Michael Devlin. He's turned out to be Casey's younger brother. And I think that's where Devlin is now. With Casey. More importantly, I think they're following the same leads we are. So it's important we track them down.'

'Something wrong with Google, is there? Or do you think I've nothing better to do?'

'I'm not looking for public addresses, Callum. I need to know the places these people use when they *don't* want to be found. I figure you have better access to that sort of information than I do right now, since I'm off the books.'

'Understood. I'll get you the addresses. Have you found anything else?'

Dempsey struggled again between his duty to answer and his reluctance to add to an insecure stream of intelligence. Anthony Haversume had admitted that McGregor had disclosed information that he should not. That concerned Dempsey. The more links in any chain made a weak link more likely. That was especially true in the field of intelligence.

A compromise seemed prudent.

'Yes. But it's not something I can disclose over an open line. Sorry.'

McGregor did not immediately respond, but when he spoke again his voice suggested agreement.

'OK, if you think that's best. In which case you can tell me face to face. I'll be in Belfast first thing in the morning.'

'What? You're coming here? What I have to tell you hardly justifies *that*.'

'I was coming anyway, Joe. Because for once *I* have information for *you*.'

'What sort of information?'

'We've intercepted a number of calls this evening. They have a bearing on your investigation. I can't go into detail over the line but it's something you need to know as soon as possible. Until then, I need you to stay put.'

'Can't you tell me anything?' Dempsey was perplexed. 'I'm making real headway here, Callum. I don't want to hold things up waiting for you.'

'Sorry, Joe, but that's exactly what you'll have to do.'

McGregor's answer was friendly but Dempsey could recognise an order when he heard one.

'The information covers a few subjects, all of which you'll want to hear. But it also relates directly to you. They know you're in Belfast and they're looking for you. You're at risk, Joe. So I don't want you doing *anything* more until I can tell you what that risk is.'

'You've got to be kidding!' Dempsey was stunned. 'I'm always at risk. It's my job! I can't stop working just because someone's looking for me!'

'You can and you will. This is a specific threat. We know who's behind it and we know how to deal with it. But you need to be in the loop if you're going to protect yourself. It's just a few hours, Joe, and then you can get back to the investigation. It'll hold that long.'

Dempsey wanted to argue but knew it would be futile. McGregor had information that Dempsey did not. He also held superior rank.

Dempsey knew when he was beat.

'OK. I suppose I could do with a few hours' rest. Where will you be?'

'I'm taking a suite in the Fitzwilliam Hotel. Meet me there at 6 a.m. Get yourself some sleep in the meantime.'

'I suppose there's not much point saying the same to you, is there?'

'I'll sleep when I'm dead, Joe. So will you. But let's make sure that's not too soon.'

'You'll still get me my information, right?' Dempsey did not want the reason for his call to be forgotten. 'I'll need it, whatever else you have to tell me.'

'I'll bring everything with me. And once you know what you're up against, you can use the intelligence as you see fit.'

Dempsey heard the line disconnect without a farewell.

He dropped his mobile onto the passenger seat and put his key into the car's ignition. The engine purred into life. Dempsey hated the idea of a delay. He did not want to slow the investigation just as he was gaining momentum. Whatever McGregor had for him, it had better be important.

SIXTY-SIX

Robert Mullen's office was at the rear of a run-down North Belfast snooker hall. Hardly Hollywood's idea of a criminal empire's headquarters, it served its purpose perfectly. Tonight it was full. Six men, all standing while Mullen sat. They were all criminals. Violent. Feared. But each one wilted under the gaze of their employer, a five-foot-six ball of fury.

'There was no sign of Grant?' Mullen asked.

He directed his attentions at one man. Andy Ferguson. A subordinate whose size alone should have left him with nothing to fear. But Mullen could see the dread clearly etched on Ferguson's face.

'No, Rob.' His deep voice lacked any confidence. 'The door was off the hinges. The place was a mess. There was no way to tell where he'd gone.'

Mullen did not answer straightaway, keeping his rage in check. For now. When he finally spoke, he kept his voice calm.

'So his front door was off the hinges, the place was a mess and there was no sign of him?' Mullen spoke slowly. 'Don't you think that sounds like someone took him, Andy?'

'Aye, I suppose it does, Rob.'

'And who do you think that someone was? Have you given that any thought?'

A sing-song tone to Mullen's voice was accompanied by a dangerous look in his eyes, as he dragged the scene out. He was enjoying Ferguson's discomfort.

'I haven't.'

'It didn't occur to you that he might have been paid a visit by Liam Casey? That Casey might have traced McGale back to Grant and started to connect the dots? That there were a few questions the little shit could answer? That didn't occur to you, Andy?'

'No, Rob. I'm sorry.'

'You're sorry? You're fucking sorry!'

The sudden volume and ferocity of Mullen's voice were off the chart. Nought to sixty in a heartbeat.

'I *told* you Casey was involved. You *knew* his brother was back. That they were looking into everything we've been putting together! I gave you one fucking job. To make sure Grant couldn't talk. You couldn't even do that right, you half-wit!'

'I did what you said, Rob. I swear.'

Mullen stared furiously at Ferguson as he desperately tried to defend himself.

'I went to Grant's place just like you said, but I was too late. There was nothing else I could have done.'

Nothing else was said. The pause that followed Ferguson's answer lasted less than a second. Long enough that he would have known what was coming. Not long enough to avoid it. Ferguson remained rooted to the spot as Mullen leaped from his seat, grabbed a heavy glass ashtray from the desk and brought it crashing into the man's unguarded temple.

The first blow alone was ferocious enough to render Ferguson unconscious. A fact that did nothing to save him from what followed.

His heavy body hit the floor with a sickening thud. It would have remained motionless if Mullen had stopped there, but he did not. Mullen grabbed Ferguson's unkempt black hair, pulled his defenceless head from its resting place on the cigarette-marked carpet and hit him three more times with the same ashtray.

Only when the force of the blows caused the glass to shatter did he stop.

Mullen raised himself upright. Breathless. He paused to consider his work. For a moment he seemed to have come back to his senses. For a moment. Then, without warning, Mullen renewed his assault, repeatedly kicking Ferguson in the stomach, chest and head.

Silence filled the room as Mullen continued his attack. A silence born from long experience. No one would ever challenge Mullen. He knew, as did they all, that none was a match for him.

Mullen finished his assault as suddenly as he had started it. He pushed his lank, greasy hair away from his eyes and addressed the room.

'That's what complacency gets you.'

Mullen, breathing deeply, pointed at the heavily bleeding near-corpse in the centre of the office.

'But it's better than what Liam Casey will do to each and every one of us if we lose this.'

A bare murmur of agreement went around the group.

'Are you lot not fucking listening?' Mullen felt his temper beginning to flare again at the lacklustre response. 'Casey has Grant. That little bastard won't hold out for long, and when he cracks, Casey's going to know everything. He's going to know that we're in this up to our ears, and then he's going to realise that there's only one way to keep that brother of his alive. When that happens it's gonna be a fucking war. We need to be ready.'

This time the reaction was the one he wanted. Mullen looked for certain skills in his team. Intelligence did not top that list, but an appreciation of danger helped. That appreciation was finally on the faces of the men present.

'So what do you want us to do?'

The question was asked by Dermot Stephenson, the closest thing Mullen had to a Number Two.

'First I want that piece of shit out of my sight!' Mullen pointed at Ferguson. 'Two of you deal with that. The rest of you come with me. We need to find out what Casey knows and stop this before it starts.'

As the first two men moved towards the barely breathing Ferguson, Mullen stormed off towards the darkened, empty snooker room with the rest of his men.

He had owned the building for over fifteen years. A long time for a base of operations, especially one so well known. But it was the only place he felt completely safe, sheltered from the threats of his chosen career. No one would dare attack him here.

It was a complacent feeling he would soon regret.

It took half a minute to walk through the large hall. Just seconds more to get down the stairs and to the building's main door.

Mullen stepped out into the dark night and immediately felt uneasy. It took a moment to work out why.

It was the absence of the sodium streetlight that did it. Every night for fifteen years the light had lit up the entrance to the snooker hall. That it was missing tonight could mean nothing. Or it could mean everything.

Mullen found out which before his brain even registered the choice.

The impact of a full-sized aluminium baseball bat on Mullen's right knee brought him crashing to the floor. The blow to his head from the same weapon kept him there, struck senseless by the force.

As his head began to clear the pavement around him came into focus. Mullen's men were employed from their size and tendency towards extreme violence, but they had been overwhelmed by the sudden attack. It had lasted fifteen seconds at most, leaving his best men as motionless and damaged as Ferguson had been.

Mullen could not tell if they were dead or alive, and he was given no chance to check. Instead he was hauled up by the hair and dragged ten metres along the street. Finally he was thrown – broken and bleeding – into the rear of a battered Ford Transit van.

Mullen's usual bravado escaped him. Shock will do that to anyone. Still, he tried to struggle to his feet. To escape. A hopeless effort; he was sent crashing back to the floor with a second blow to the head, this time from a fist instead of a bat.

Staggering from the punch, he rolled onto his hands and knees. Involuntary tears ran down his cheeks as he slowly regained his composure. The embarrassment of allowing himself to cry proved more agonising than any blow.

The van began to move, making escape and rescue equally unlikely.

Mullen took a series of deep breaths, bringing his pain under control. Finally he looked up, towards the six masked faces that surrounded him.

Mullen concentrated on the closest silhouette.

'You were quicker than I thought you'd be, Liam.' Mullen had no doubt that his assumption was correct. 'So now what?'

Liam did not hesitate. He reached up with a gloved hand and pulled off his balaclava. The face beneath it was grim.

'Now, Robert?' His tone oozed menace. 'Now we're gonna have a little chat.'

SIXTY-SEVEN

The live images were beamed across twenty-four-hour news networks worldwide. Every inch of the green benches that filled Britain's House of Commons was obscured by braying politicians. All were determined to be a part of history. The noise coming from them drowned out the chimes of the world-famous Big Ben as it sounded the passing of 1 a.m.

It had been decades since British politics had been of interest to the world. Who ruled a faded imperial power held little relevance to anyone outside its borders. But the public shooting of a former US president had changed that.

The UK Parliament operated under a system of conventions. Outdated but eye-catching ceremonies that sat uneasily with modern, televised politics. The introduction of cameras into the chamber had revolutionised some aspects of that system, creating a world in which image was everything. It was a minor miracle that someone as charisma-free as William Davies should have risen to power in such times. It was poetic that the world would be glued to its screens as this anomaly was rectified.

The turnout of Members for the occasion was almost unprecedented. They competed for the few available seats and for the lenses of the cameras. Tonight they would all play a part in ending William Davies' time in power, by voting on their confidence in his government's policies in Northern Ireland. With public interest galvanised, every one of them was determined to be seen.

The two major political parties – Labour and Conservative – were seated on either side of the historic house. A vote on any contentious matter would usually be supported by one side and opposed by the other. On this occasion, there were no such clear lines.

From the moment he had turned his intellectual attentions to the Northern Irish problem, Davies had not just divided the nation. He had split his own party. The Conservatives were the traditional champions of patriotism and strength. Yet here was their leader, negotiating with terrorists and making concessions to end the conflict. Although not welcomed by many members of his party, they had been silenced by Davies' initial successes.

The resurgence of terrorism and the rise of Anthony Haversume as an opposing figurehead had seen those critics return with a vengeance. Tonight would be their ultimate victory.

The vote that was to take place tonight had its beginnings in Haversume's televised comments after the tragedy of Trafalgar Square. He had then taken the decisive step by officially calling for a motion of no confidence in Davies' leadership. This was a point of no return from which neither man could step back.

To the outside world it seemed dramatic. But within politics it was recognised as the finishing line after years of passionate moral dissent. Haversume had walked away from a ministerial career in protest at Davies' policies. It was an unusually principled stance for any politician, one that gifted Haversume a foundation of strength unavailable to any other candidate for leadership.

The vote itself was one of Parliament's oldest traditions, but one that had not been used in decades. The vote Haversume had called for – a motion of no confidence – outwardly concentrated on the government's Northern Irish policies, but in reality it amounted to much more. The fact that a loss for the government would inevitably lead to Davies' resignation made it nothing less than a vote of confidence in his overall leadership of the state.

If this made the question posed to the Members of Parliament more difficult, it was one they proved more than willing to answer.

Haversume felt a knot of anticipation in his stomach as he watched the Speaker of the House rise to his feet. Appointed as a cross between a referee and a judge to keep Britain's rowdy politicians under control, it was the Speaker who would lead the short voting process to decide the future of his country. All eyes would usually be on him. But not today. Today they were on the man of the hour, sitting in what should have been the inconspicuous back benches.

Haversume knew that both the room and the world were watching. He did his best to look professional. Impassive. It was a Herculean effort as the vote for his political future began.

For the first time that evening the House grew silent. All eyes now turned to the Speaker. The hushed atmosphere was maintained as he stepped forward.

Michael French wore the ceremonial robes and ruffles of office, designs that were a throwback to the nation's past. Somehow his authority was not diminished by the absurdity of his seventeenth-century clothing. Nor by the words that followed, as he addressed the House in the language of yesteryear.

'The question is that this house has no confidence in Her Majesty's Government's policies as they apply to the paramilitary situation in Northern Ireland?'

For centuries the same form of words had been the only acceptable preamble to the open-house vote. French continued, 'As many as are *not* of that opinion, say "aye".'

It was the responsibility of the Speaker of the House to count the 'ayes' that followed. He alone would then contrast the number with the 'noes' that would come later. Once done, he would decide which of the two possible answers was supported by the majority. It was a monumental responsibility. But on this occasion it was one the Speaker could discharge without fear of mistake.

French could count the responses to his first question on his fingers and toes. From that moment the result of the motion was beyond doubt. But a thousand years of parliamentary history demanded that the vote be seen to its end.

As the murmur of 'ayes' trickled to silence, the Speaker spoke again.

'And of the contrary, "no".'

French's voice was this time far louder, in anticipation of what was to follow. Still he was drowned out by the response. Almost six hundred politicians from every party spoke as one. French could say only one thing.

'The noes have it!'

Despite the specifics of the vote, those four words brought the leadership of William Davies to an end. His resignation now had to follow. And for Anthony Haversume, it could not come a moment too soon.

SIXTY-EIGHT

Dempsey sat on his hotel bed, bare-chested. His bedsheets had been kicked onto the deep carpet of the floor. An hour earlier he had watched the end of William Davies' premiership with interest, but that had quickly faded. Now his mind had returned to two names: Stanton and Turner.

He was supposed to sleep. It had been an order. But, as 2.15 a.m. flashed on the bedside clock, thoughts and theories were keeping him awake.

The causes of his insomnia piled up, but one fire burned more brightly than all others. The desire to find Sam Regis' killers. Duty was enough to drive Dempsey to any end. Patriotism took him further still. But the will to bring those responsible for his friend's death to justice took his determination and ramped it to obsession.

Dempsey knew his next step. So the frustration at being unable to take it was overwhelming. It was matched only by the fear that this delay could set him days behind the pace. Orders or not, rest was impossible. Instead he got to his feet and paced the room as the minutes ticked slowly by.

Dempsey could understand McGregor's concern for his safety, but it did nothing to lessen his annoyance. Before their call he had been racing from one lead to the next; each time getting closer to finding the mind behind Sam Regis' death. But now? Now he was cooped up in a hotel room. Ineffective. Stagnant.

He moved around the room. Looked for a distraction. Some

way to kill the three and a half hours until his 6 a.m. meeting with McGregor. There was nothing.

His frustration increased by the second. It was only made worse by the lack of anything that could hold his interest. Desperate for an outlet, he stepped into the en-suite bathroom.

It was a luxurious space. Larger than most bedrooms he had slept in over the years. There were two basins. Dempsey filled the smaller of the two with cold water and tipped the contents of the suite's ice bucket into the same sink. He waited for five minutes and then plunged his head into the collected pool. As intended, the shock of the sub-zero temperature focused his racing mind.

Dempsey pulled himself upright. Violently. The force of movement sent the water in his short hair hurtling towards the rear wall. Ice-cold liquid trickled down onto his unclothed shoulders and back. Dempsey barely noticed. Instead he focused on the decision he had finally made.

Sod Callum, he thought, his patience exhausted. *If he'll only help on* his *terms I'll just go elsewhere.*

Dempsey moved back into the bedroom and slid open the wardrobe door. Inside was the same two-piece suit he had worn on his trip to Credenhill Barracks. In the breast pocket of the jacket was a single white business card.

Dempsey was relieved to see that Alex Henley's details included a mobile number. Probably the only way that the assistant commissioner could be contacted so late. To Dempsey the time was of no concern. He did not hesitate before dialling the number.

The telephone rang for longer than expected. Dempsey was preparing to leave a voicemail when he heard the sound of a connection.

'Who is this?'

The grating sound from the back of his throat said that Henley had been unconscious just moments before.

'It's Joe Dempsey. I need you to dig out some information for me. Urgently.'

'Bloody hell, Joe. Do you know what time it is?'

'I know, Alex, and I'm sorry. But it *is* urgent. I'm making headway here and this will help me.'

'Headway where? Where are you?'

'I'm in Belfast. After the bastards who put Turner on your team and had him kill Sam. I'm sure I'm just a few steps behind them now, and I need your help to catch up.'

'Still off the books, I take it?'

'Wouldn't need to ask you otherwise, Alex. But that does mean you'll have to keep this to yourself.'

'That goes without saying. So how's the investigation going?'

'It's growing, Alex. It's growing quickly. That's why I need you.'

'There's not much I know, really,' Henley replied. 'I've been kept out of the loop since the bombing. The Americans weren't too keen on me being involved, not with the shooter coming from my team.'

'That won't be a problem,' Dempsey explained. 'It's just addresses and intel I need. Off-the-book stuff that you'll have in the intelligence database. It's to do with two big names over here. Robert Mullen and Liam Casey.'

'Do you have dates of birth?'

'No. I was hoping that you could help me with that.'

'OK. It's not ideal but I'll live with it. Where are these guys, Joe? What area?'

'They're both based in Belfast. It's a smaller pond and they're big fish. You'll be able to pinpoint who they are real quick.'

'Is there anything else you can tell me that might speed things up? Any historic points or family details, anything like that?'

Henley was playing the role of information gatherer. A familiar skill for a police officer. Dempsey could tell that he was in his comfort zone.

'Not really.'

Dempsey paused for a moment. He considered whether to give Henley the one further piece of information that might help in locating Devlin. In the circumstances, it seemed sensible.

'Actually there is one other thing. The second guy. Liam Casey. It might help to know that he's Michael Devlin's brother.'

'Michael Devlin? The guy whose house was bombed in Islington?'

'That's him, yeah.'

'What the hell does he have to do with any of this?'

Dempsey tried to focus. How to condense so many discoveries into a digestible form.

'I didn't tell you in London, but Michael Devlin was close friends with another lawyer. A guy called Daniel Lawrence. Lawrence was the other guy in the wedding photo I dug out at Devlin's house. He was also the lawyer who represented McGale at Paddington Green police station after the shooting, following which they both ended up dead. I think—'

'Lawrence is dead?' Henley's voice betrayed his shock. 'How?'

'Car crash.' Now Dempsey was confused. 'I don't understand. You knew Lawrence?'

'No, I didn't know him,' Henley explained. 'But I knew *of* him. At least, I knew he'd been appointed to look after McGale.'

'How could you know that?'

'Everyone present at the COBRA Committee knew that, Joe. It was discussed openly, even in front of those of us who were only there as witnesses. They said that McGale was in custody, that he wouldn't speak without a lawyer and that the lawyer appointed was called Daniel Lawrence. Lawrence was supposed to see McGale the next day.'

Dempsey's mind was racing. Henley had knowledge of a fact that had apparently been kept from everyone. What could that mean?

'Alex, I've been told that McGale never saw a lawyer. That he killed himself before speaking to a soul. Now you're telling me you *knew* he'd seen Lawrence?'

'I'm not saying that they definitely *saw* each other, Joe,' Henley explained. 'I'm not part of COBRA so I only know what I heard while I was in that room. But I do know that McGale had committed suicide before the next morning, so they probably *didn't* meet. All I know is that Daniel Lawrence was appointed as McGale's lawyer.'

Dempsey felt an almost physical internal pain as Henley spoke. Something he had not experienced since his time in Columbia seven years before. He was hardly able to ask the next question, but he knew he had no choice.

'I need you to be clear on this, Alex. Are you saying that the whole of the COBRA Committee knew about Lawrence?'

'Of course they did. Everyone at the meeting. The COBRA members *and* the witnesses.'

'And what about Callum McGregor? From my department? Did he know about Lawrence too?'

'He's the one person who *definitely* knew, Joe . . .'

Henley could not know how devastating his answer was to Dempsey. It made all pieces of the puzzle fall into place.

Dempsey did not need to hear Henley's last words to know the truth. About McGregor. About Stanton. And about everything else.

'. . . because it was McGregor who told the rest of us.'

SIXTY-NINE

Fury bristled across Robert Mullen's skin like an electrical charge. He sat, unblinking and motionless, on a rough hardwood chair. Wrists cuffed behind his back. He looked from face to face. The spitting and snarling had stopped. After two hours it had proved pointless. Now he sat in silence, his control of his temper on a knife-edge.

The sudden ambush had been unexpected and painful. But Mullen had regained his composure quickly. For the past hours he had concentrated on what would probably follow.

Stanton had warned him about Michael Devlin and his relationship to Liam Casey, so he knew why they were involved. It was this knowledge that made Mullen sure of how things would end. With the stakes as high as they were, Liam Casey could not leave him alive.

The only question was what would happen in the meantime. In this respect Mullen had an advantage. Long experience of both kidnap and aggressive interrogation left him with little to learn about either. Mullen was not surprised, then, that Liam Casey had so far left him isolated, with nothing to do but dwell upon what might follow. It was an old technique designed to weaken resolve. To encourage him to grasp any opportunity of survival that presented itself. Seeing it for the first time from the other side, Mullen recognised how effective it was.

The urge to offer information in the hope of securing his safety was overwhelming. For most it might even prove irresistible. But Mullen was made of different clay. The irrationality that had guided him to the top of his trade would not submit to inner torment.

Robert Mullen would not be beaten.

The same irrationality – the same streak of madness – had driven Mullen to react in the only way he knew how. To struggle. To scream. To shout. To threaten. It had proved ineffective. The few men left on guard had ignored him. So now Mullen sat in silence, his anger, his resentment and his anticipation of the end ever growing.

Just as Liam intended.

It would not be anticipation for much longer. Mullen heard the roar of an engine outside. It was exactly how Mullen would have played it. Big delay. Big arrival.

The sound of a ringtone caught Mullen's attention.

'I'll be right there.'

They were Jack Thornton's only words as he held the phone to his ear. An unconscious glance told Mullen that the call was about him.

Thornton moved to the garage's main doors and unlocked the four deadbolts that secured them. He opened the small man-sized hatch that sat within the right-hand door. It was designed to allow individual access to the lock-up without opening the main doors. To keep the heat in and the world out.

Thornton stood aside to let the new arrivals enter. Liam. Michael. Paddy O'Neil. And Sarah Truman.

The time between Michael's departure and his return had felt like hell to Sarah. An ordeal made worse by the helplessness of waiting. By the time Michael and Liam had returned, she had made up her mind. Michael would not leave without her again.

It had not been an easy discussion, but Sarah's refusal to spend any more time knowing nothing and fearing the worst had won out. It was an argument strongly supported by Sarah's reminder that her life was under threat just as much as Michael's.

Michael had seemed willing to stand his ground. Sarah suspected – hoped – this was through fear for her safety. But it had been Liam who had cast the deciding vote, agreeing that Sarah had the right to play a part in securing her own future.

Now, as she looked around the lock-up and set eyes upon a bloody figure secured to a chair in the centre of the space, Sarah began to question her own decision.

Mullen looked directly past Liam and Michael towards Sarah. He seemed to recognise her uncertainty. His stare bored into her. The intensity in his gaze caused a shiver to run to the base of her spine.

It made him crack a sinister smile.

'You took your time, Liam.'

Mullen's grin did not fade as his eyes moved to Casey.

'I thought you might have changed your mind about coming back.'

'I was always coming back, Robert. I just thought I'd give you some time to yourself.'

'Time to think about the things you might do to me, you mean? Well, I've had time. And you may as well get started with it, because I'm not telling you a thing.'

Liam did not seem surprised by the statement.

'What makes you think I'm going to do anything to you?' he asked. 'No one's touched you since you've been here, have they?'

'Fucking right they haven't.' Mullen's lack of respect for anything and everyone was absolute. 'Your boys haven't the balls to start without you. Maybe you need to show 'em the way, eh?'

Sarah wanted to look away, yet she could not take her eyes away from Mullen. The man was almost hypnotic. He seemed unfazed at the prospect of torture. It was a mentality she could not understand.

'They didn't touch you because I told them not to.'

Liam's voice was as calm as Mullen's. Even more controlled.

'And I won't touch you either. Because I don't need to.'

The first flicker of confusion crossed Mullen's eyes. A moment of uncertainty. It was gone as quickly as it had arrived. When he spoke again his voice was still calm.

'Don't waste your time playing games. I've been doing this too long to fall for the shite. We both know how this works. You'll offer to let me go if I tell you what you want. I refuse, you torture me and then you promise to stop if I talk. Then you kill me anyway. I end up dead whatever happens, Liam, so I'm not telling you shit.'

Mullen's words were certain. But Liam had very different ideas.

'What makes you think it goes that way, Robert? We're not all unsophisticated psychopaths. There are alternatives to torture. To murder. You just never worked them out.'

'Is that right?'

Mullen was trying his best to sound dismissive, but it was clear that the possibility of survival was impossible to ignore.

'What are they, then?'

'It just takes a little thought, Robert. But then that's something you've never been that good at.'

Liam's tone was becoming intentionally patronising. He continued.

'I only need to kill you if you *don't* tell me what I want. Because if you do, you're finished anyway, and then you're no threat at all. So you get to live. It's simple when you think about it. You've just never been smart enough to see it.'

'Fuck you, Casey!'

Mullen responded with renewed ferocity. And Sarah could see what had caused it.

It was the illusion of choice. Liam seemed to have given Mullen two options, but human nature dictated that only one path would ever be taken, and that made it no choice at all.

Whatever the cost, survival wins every time.

'Fuck you!' Mullen seemed to be fighting his natural will to live. A pointless battle. 'You're all so fucking civilised with your big cars and your posh restaurants and your trendy bars. So what? At the end of the day, you're still in a lock-up with a fella tied to a chair and you're still gonna kill him. We're not fucking different, Liam. We're both murderers. I just don't hide it from myself.'

'Neither do I,' Liam replied. 'I know what I am. But there *is* a difference, Robert. I've killed when I had to. But you? You never see any other choice. You think I *have* to kill you because you're too simple to realise that I don't.'

'What are you talking about?'

The carrot of survival was dangling. For some reason Mullen still struggled to understand the consequences of taking it.

Or maybe he knows, Sarah thought, *but just can't believe it.*

When Mullen spoke again he was ranting.

'We both know what you have to do, Liam. Killing me is the only way to stop a war. If I leave here alive I'll hunt every one of you bastards down. My boys will be on your back day and night. We both know it, Liam. Don't try telling me I'm wrong.'

'But you *are* wrong.' Liam was as calm as he had been throughout. 'You're only a threat to me with your organisation behind you. But once I know about the True IRA and every other dirty little secret you have, you won't *have* an organisation. No back-up for me to worry about. You'll be what you were a few years ago, Robert. A nobody with a bad temper.'

Mullen did not move an inch as Liam's words trailed off. His unblinking eyes stared blankly at Liam's face, the truth seeming finally to sink in.

'You expect me to believe you'll let me walk out of here?'

Mullen's words remained defiant, but his faltering voice betrayed them.

'I don't care what you believe,' Liam replied. 'You'll talk. If you're so stupid that I have to break every bone in your skinny little body to make that happen? Well, that's up to you.'

Mullen did not respond. Instead he glared at Liam. He gave every indication that he would erupt again. A final act of violence before death.

Sarah stepped back. She began to tense, preparing for the fury they all seemed to expect.

It never came.

The phone was not answered on the second ring. Not even on the third. Only on the eighth did the line come to life.

Joshua was met by Stanton's usual empty greeting.

'What can I do for you, Sergeant?'

'Where the hell have you been?' Joshua's annoyance tripped off his tongue. 'I've been trying to contact you for three hours. Why didn't you answer?'

'That's *my* business. Not yours.' Stanton offered no

apology. 'You might be surprised to hear this, Sergeant, but I have responsibilities other than to be at your beck and call.'

'Really? In that case you won't be interested in what Devlin and Casey are doing right now then? Or to know who they've got tied to a chair?'

'Someone else? Already?'

'Yes, someone else. They don't dawdle. They had this guy within hours of the last one. What do you want done about it?'

'Do you know who it is?'

'I didn't catch the name tag, no.'

It was Joshua's turn to enjoy some sarcasm.

'Then tell me what he looks like.'

'He's small. Five foot six. Wiry build, sandy hair. Mean anything to you?'

Stanton's momentary silence was answer enough, but he confirmed it with his next words.

'Yes, it does. His name is Robert Mullen. Where was he taken from?'

'They grabbed him from outside a snooker club in the north of the city. There were men with him but Casey and his boys dealt with them. Pretty brutal stuff. I'll tell you something for nothing, Stanton. These guys are good at what they do.'

There was another pause before Stanton spoke again.

'How good?'

'That's hard to say,' replied Joshua. 'I don't really know what you're asking.'

'What I'm asking is are they too good for you? Or can you deal with them now? Inside the building?'

Joshua had already surmised that the man in the lock-up was important. Now he knew for sure. The answer Stanton wanted to hear was obvious. But realism was safer than bravado.

'Maybe. But maybe not. It'll be messy, and I can't guarantee it'll go our way.'

'OK. Then we can't take that risk. Not now.'

'So?'

'Stay where you are for now. Mullen won't break easily. Which means there's a good chance they'll leave him there to stew a while. If that happens – if Devlin and Casey leave – how confident are you that you can take what's left?'

'They left three last time. And three would not be a problem.'

'Good. Then we wait for now. And if they leave you go in there and you mop up what's left. Starting with Mullen.'

Joshua did not answer.

'I'll take your silence as agreement,' Stanton continued. 'And one more thing: I want the brothers alive if possible. At least for now.'

The line went dead before Joshua could question the last order. It made no difference. He had his instructions.

SEVENTY

'I was working for someone called Stanton.'

The explosion of anger they had expected never came. It seemed that Mullen had accepted the inevitable.

Liam hid his satisfaction that his mind games had worked.

'This Stanton wanted you to carry out terror attacks, and you just did it? Why, Robert? You've never had a cause.'

'I still don't.'

Mullen smiled as he spoke. As if he took pride in the role he had played in global events.

'I did it for money. Lots and lots of money, Liam. Enough to make me bigger than you!'

'But which one of us is tied to a chair?'

Liam's response elicited a scowl from Mullen but no response.

'OK, so tell us, this guy wanted you to pretend to be the True IRA? What's in it for him?'

'I'm sure he had his reasons, but Stanton wasn't one for sharing them.'

Mullen seemed to be warming to his new role. Revelling in holding information that Liam needed.

'I don't buy that for a second.'

Liam picked up a length of thin link-chain from the oil-stained floor as he spoke. Slowly – almost absentmindedly – he wrapped it around his right fist.

'I *know* you spoke to McGale time and again. I *know* you told him the lies that led him to London. *You* were behind all of that. Which means you know more than you're letting on.'

'What, you're gonna hit me now, Liam, is that it?' Mullen's eyes rested on Liam's covered fist. 'That's a bit of a change of plan, isn't—'

Mullen did not finish his sentence. Liam's ironclad hand impacted his face. The teeth on the left-hand side of his jaw shattered. Thick, free-flowing blood poured from his mouth.

'It is, yeah.'

Liam stepped back. He paid no attention to the fact that Mullen was now doubled up in agony.

'But then plans do tend to do that when I don't get what I want.'

Mullen spat out what remained of his shattered teeth. A blood-stained smile broke across his face. Liam could see a hint of his defiance returning. Of his arrogance. But he was confident that Mullen would control it. That he still hoped to leave here alive.

'He wanted to change the world!'

The blood continued to flow as Mullen spoke. It stained his already tattered white shirt crimson.

'The stupid fuck thought the return of terrorism would turn the country on its head. That it would get rid of the government and let us all start again. He'd been waiting for it to happen. Waiting for the IRA to breach the ceasefire. When they didn't, he did something about it. He *made* it happen. He gave me enough money and information to tear the country apart. And that's exactly what I did.'

'So you admit it? You admit that you and this Stanton were behind the True IRA?'

Sarah's soft voice was out of place in the surroundings.

'Not just the True IRA, sweetheart.'

Mullen looked towards Sarah as he spoke. He appeared to be enjoying himself.

'The UVA too. We were behind *the lot*. I did it all and you know what? That stupid fuck Stanton wasn't so stupid after all! The government's been turned on its head. The army *is* coming back. We've changed the country. We're going back to the good old days, Liam. Back to when the likes of you and me ran this city. You should be fucking thanking me for what I've done!'

'We already know you were behind both.' Liam again. 'What I don't understand is why. What's the point behind any of this? What the hell was it all supposed to achieve?'

'And you called me stupid!' Mullen's voice was now mocking. 'If the man wanted a resurgence of terrorism he *had* to play both sides, didn't he? To keep control on things. What's the use if one side is playing a role but the other is running rampant, doing it for real? Or worse, what if the other side stuck to the damn ceasefire? It was both sides or nothing. Which meant double money for me.'

'You heartless bastard!' The disgust in Sarah's voice was unmistakable. 'You killed innocent people for nothing more than money. For your goddamned pocket! How can you live with yourself?'

'Up to now? Very comfortably.' Mullen looked towards Liam. 'Maybe not so much after tonight, though.'

'What about my brother and his friends?' Liam kept the conversation on track. 'Why was it decided they had to die?'

'I honestly have no idea.' The answer was matter-of-fact. Believable. 'Before today I didn't even know you had a brother.'

'You mean you had nothing to do with the bomb in London last night? Or the attack in the university?'

Michael's questions were desperate. Liam could understand that; Mullen's previous answer, if true, meant that his organisation were not the only pieces Stanton had on the board. Whoever had tried to kill Michael and Sarah was still out there.

'All I had to do with that was cleaning up the mess you made there. Good work, by the way. Those RUC bastards had it coming.'

Michael looked away. Towards Liam. They seemed to be reaching the same conclusion.

'Well, if you weren't involved in those attacks, who was?'

'I don't know! Do you think I'm the only gun Stanton's got? I'm just a cog in a machine, boys. Stanton has people and resources from all over. If you think you've got to the bottom of things by getting your hands on me you're very wrong. I'm just the tip of the iceberg, Liam. The tip of the iceberg.'

Liam did not know what to say. The information had been unexpected. Mullen smiled at his uncertainty.

'So if Stanton's the man in control of all of this, tell us who he is.' It was Sarah who spoke, her question filling the empty air.

'I can't do that.' Mullen turned to face Sarah. 'I don't know who he is.'

'You've been working for him for years,' she replied. 'You must have spoken to him countless times!'

'Hundreds. Maybe even a thousand. But that doesn't mean he introduced himself. The man calls himself Stanton. Do you honestly think that's his real name? Of course it isn't, but it's all anyone ever knew. It's all I can tell you about him.'

'I don't buy it.' Liam did not waste any time considering what Mullen had to say. He knew the man too well. 'You're a deceitful bastard, Mullen. There's no way you got into this without making sure you were protected. You know something about him. What is it?'

Mullen took his eyes away from Sarah and met Liam's gaze. The conceited smile crept back across his bloodstained face. It was an answer in itself.

'I may have done a little digging. But it won't do you any good. This guy's set-up is bigger than you and me combined. He's got resources we can only dream of. You start a war with him, you'll lose.'

'Since when did that stop anyone? Tell me what you have.'

'Just a little insurance policy. I've got recordings. Digital ones, of hundreds of conversations. You can hear both of our voices, clear as day.'

'You expect us to believe the guy you're describing would be that careless?'

'Not at all,' Mullen replied. 'He took every precaution he could. Used some sort of top-end voice disguise machine that I couldn't break through for months. But I got there in the end, from the cockney arsehole Stanton used as a facilitator. That eejit used to get me whatever I needed, no questions asked. So one time I asked for the one thing I really needed and what d'ya know?'

Liam looked at Michael.

'That any use to us?'

'If he's telling the truth,' Michael replied. 'Voice recognition is as good as a fingerprint. If we can find someone to analyse the recordings then we might be able to work out who this Stanton is. Or at least use them as a bargaining chip.'

Liam watched as Michael looked towards Sarah. He saw relief and reassurance in his brother's eyes. The look of a man who had ensured the safety of everyone he cared about.

The tapes gave them two choices. Liam knew it. And he could see that Michael did, too.

Michael turned back to face Mullen.

'Where do you keep them?'

SEVENTY-ONE

Joshua slumped into his seat. Michael, Liam and a third man were leaving the lock-up and climbing into the usual Land Rover. The engine roared into life. At the sound Joshua manoeuvred himself into a low position. Only once they had disappeared around the road's first bend did he sit back up.

Joshua considered his next move carefully.

There were three men left inside. A more than manageable number, they posed no real threat to a man like him. But the girl was in there too. Sarah Truman. It was a complication.

He ran through the options. Killing her was easiest, of course. But perhaps she had value. After all she had been through with Michael Devlin it was possible that he would feel at least some loyalty to her. And loyalty could be helpful. It could provide leverage, or even just a distraction. Plus it might help to know what the brothers knew, and she would no doubt be able to tell him that.

He made his decision. Sarah Truman would live. For now, anyway. Unfortunately for every other soul within that building, she would be the only one.

Joshua reached for the glove compartment. Inside was a SIG 226 semi-automatic pistol. He inspected the weapon. Even on this timescale, his obsessive compulsions demanded at least that.

Satisfied, he thrust a fifteen-round magazine box into the gun's handle and chambered a round. He then shoved a second magazine into his belt. With three potential targets he did not expect to use both clips. But he had learned long ago that it was safest to overestimate the odds.

The exhilaration that came before deadly action made Joshua's heart race. It always did. It was partly why he had done this job for so long. What had kept him going.

Joshua forced the thought from his mind and concentrated on what was to be done. This time he would not fail.

SEVENTY-TWO

The best suites in Belfast's Fitzwilliam Hotel were the definition of opulence: luxury rooms equipped for every whim of the privileged residents. They were large enough to comfortably house a medium-sized family. The fact that so grand a space should be reserved for just one man – and a man travelling on the public purse – offended Dempsey's sense of justice.

This had been his first thought as he manipulated the room's entry system ninety minutes earlier. The second was that its size gave him many places to hide.

It was 5.30 a.m.

Dempsey remained motionless and silent as the imposing bulk of Callum McGregor entered the room. Hidden in the air vent that served the suite's separate office space, he could only hear McGregor's arrival. The director of the DDS had no reason to think that he was not alone.

With the suite's main door closed behind him, McGregor walked directly to the bureau in its office. Just as Dempsey had assumed he would.

McGregor placed his leather briefcase on the L-shaped desk that sat in the far corner of the room. He entered a code into its combination lock, opened the case and reached inside.

Dempsey's view was obscured by the case's lid. But once McGregor had re-closed it he saw that a thin pile of papers had been removed and placed on the desk. On top of them was a Walther P99 handgun.

McGregor moved around the table and took his seat on the far side. He reached back across and picked up the weapon. It looked lost in his enormous right hand.

Dempsey studied McGregor's face as the director reached back towards the briefcase. This time he delicately picked up an object inside it. A customised pistol silencer.

A knot grew in Dempsey's gut as he watched his friend screw the silencer to the pistol's barrel. His instincts – his deductions – had been right. McGregor had come to Belfast for one reason, and it was *not* to protect his agent.

The next few minutes would remain with Dempsey for ever.

His eyes remained fixed on a man he had trusted above anyone else. He watched as McGregor inspected the weapon before placing it in an open desk drawer. McGregor then turned back to the pile of papers and spread them across the desktop, creating the impression that he had been working: the perfect scene to lure him to his death. It was almost too much to take.

Only when McGregor rose to his feet, picked up the case and walked back into the suite's living area did Dempsey's mind begin to clear.

He silently removed the air vent's grill, slid his body out of the cold metal canal and lowered himself into the empty office. Taking a seat in a leather armchair that was obscured from view by the open office door, he rested his fully loaded Glock 17 pistol on his right knee, gripping the gun's handle.

Dempsey could feel the sweat on his palm. The result of nervous anticipation. Of spiking adrenaline. He fought to bring his breathing back to a regular level.

McGregor's return to the office area was telegraphed by the sound of his heavy footsteps. He walked through the door without a glance to his right. He was halfway around the desk by the time he realised he was not alone.

Dempsey revealed himself with the sound of his pistol's safety release.

McGregor span on his heel to face the source of the noise. It was with a visible mixture of shock and respect that he saw it came from Dempsey.

McGregor's eyes glanced to the open drawer, now just feet away. The Walther P99 was almost in reach. Close enough that McGregor might have beaten many men to the shot.

But Joe Dempsey was not one of them.

'You're early, Joe. It's only 5.30.'

'Lucky I am. Otherwise I wouldn't have seen where you hid your gun.'

Dempsey's unblinking eyes flitted to the desk drawer for an instant. Long enough to tell McGregor that he knew the weapon's location.

'And now you're going to tell me everything.'

Dempsey fought to keep his voice cold. Calm. It carried no hint of emotion. No suggestion that McGregor's betrayal was ravaging him from within.

The killer – the side of himself that Dempsey despised – had taken over.

'When did you find out?' McGregor's question was more curious than fearful.

'That you're the murdering piece of shit responsible for hundreds of innocent deaths? A couple of hours ago.'

Dempsey's voice was angry. Threatening. McGregor's, though, remained gentle.

'Can I ask how?'

'Daniel Lawrence. You said you didn't know who he was.

But then I found out everyone from COBRA knew he was McGale's lawyer.'

McGregor responded with a rueful sigh.

'A goddamn slip of the tongue and we end up here. I knew I'd made a mistake. I was supposed to stick to the official story: Lawrence was appointed but never saw him. But I was so damn tired and you were moving so quickly. So. Here we are.'

'Don't kid yourself, Callum. You're a murdering bastard who's killed his own people. One way or another, we were always ending up here.'

McGregor nodded his head slowly in response.

'I didn't want it to come to this, you know?'

'I bet you didn't.'

'I mean it, Joe. Why do you think I sent you out on your own? Why do you think I took you off-book? I thought if you were alone I could guide you away from all this.'

'Well, that didn't work out so well, did it?' Dempsey replied. 'And now here we are.'

McGregor exhaled hard at the answer, and waited a few moments before speaking again.

'So what now, Joe?' he asked, sinking into the desk's chair. The pistol drawer was out of easy reach. 'Now what do we do?'

'Now you tell me why. You tell me why you killed those people. Why you killed Sam.'

A hint of emotion had coloured Dempsey's voice. His professional detachment was breaking.

'I didn't want anyone to die, Joe.' McGregor's tone was sincere. 'I want you to know that. But I didn't have a choice. Matthewson had to go. It was the only way to make this work. To make every sacrifice worthwhile. Sam got in the way of that, but that wasn't supposed to happen. Matthewson and then McGale. They should have been the last.'

'The *last*? Are you listening to yourself, Callum? You're talking about mass murder! Why did *anyone* have to die?'

'Because it wouldn't have worked any other way. There had to be a cost. Without that there'd be no outcry, and that outcry was essential. I didn't *want* anyone to die, Joe. I swear that's the truth. But I had no choice. So those deaths were a sacrifice. Those people died for a cause.'

'What the hell are you talking about? What cause?'

'Overturning the government. Making them pay for betraying all of those who died in defence of their country. The cause of replacing William Davies with a leader who'll stand up to terrorism instead of surrendering to it. That's the cause, Joe. That's *our* cause.'

'You can't be serious, Callum?'

Dempsey's mood had swung from determination to confusion. Now it was moving to disbelief.

'You're telling me that you've involved yourself in terrorism to bring down the government? Are you mad?'

'I'm as mad as hell!' McGregor raised his voice to a roar. 'I'm mad that I've spent twenty years sending soldiers and agents to their deaths, Joe. Great men and women. I'm mad that they've been paid back by betrayal. I'm mad that the people who took their lives in cold blood are walking the streets – sitting in Parliament, for Christ's sake – while they're rotting in the ground. Yes I'm mad, Joe, and you should be too. The only difference is that *I've* done something about it!'

Dempsey was stunned. McGregor's opinion of William Davies was not news. The director had long believed that Davies had surrendered to terrorism. But to go as far as

McGregor had? To fake an entire terror campaign to bring down a government and restart a war? Dempsey could hardly conceive of it.

'And it doesn't matter who dies, I suppose?' Dempsey demanded. 'It doesn't matter how many lives are ruined, so long as you get your way?'

'Of course it matters.' McGregor's voice had lowered. His intensity had not. 'I've told you, I didn't want *anyone* to die. If I could have done this without shedding a drop of blood then I would have. But I couldn't. People *had* to die to make this happen. I've had to live with that for two years. Don't think that's not a high price, Joe. Don't think it hasn't haunted me.'

Dempsey studied McGregor's face. It told him the truth behind the words. McGregor *had* paid a price. The man at the desk was not the man that Dempsey knew. He was visibly older. Thinner. Infinitely more haggard. In the past few months McGregor had seemed to be carrying the weight of the world. Now Dempsey knew why.

The choices McGregor had made had taken a heavy toll.

'I know they'll haunt you.' Dempsey's voice had lowered. 'But that doesn't make it right. You've killed a lot of people. Including Sam. What you've done is terrorism, Callum. Whatever your reasons. You know I can't let you walk away from that.'

'I wouldn't expect anything less. I know I'm not leaving here alive.'

The answer shocked Dempsey.

'I'm not going to kill you, Callum,' he said, confused. 'I'm going to arrest you. You're going to answer for what you've done.'

'I can't let you do that, Joe.'

There was finality in McGregor's voice. It set Dempsey on edge.

'I've given too much to this to see it end here. I've done too much. So I'm not going without a fight, and there's only one way you win that. I'm ready to die for my cause. I hope you're ready to kill for yours.'

Both men glanced at the drawer to McGregor's right.

'You'll never get to it in time.' Dempsey's grip tightened on his own gun.

'I know that,' Callum replied.

Their eyes locked. Neither moved. McGregor had no doubt how the confrontation would end. But he was in no hurry to die.

'I'm glad I've had the chance to explain this, Joe,' he said, his eyes never leaving the pistol drawer. 'Why I did these things, I mean. I don't want you to remember me as a monster. If that's possible.'

He was already speaking of himself in the past tense. If Dempsey had doubted the director's willingness to die, those doubts were now gone. But he had one last question to ask.

'What about Haversume?' Dempsey asked. 'How long has *he* been involved?'

McGregor's eyes left the drawer and focused on Dempsey. His certainty seemed to falter.

'What do you mean?'

'You know what I mean. Was he in this before you? Or did you start it together?'

McGregor opened his mouth to respond. And then he closed it. For once, words seemed to have failed him.

'Answer my question, Callum.' Dempsey adjusted his grip. 'I know Haversume's behind this. I know he's Stanton. I just want to know if you cooked it up together or if that bastard somehow talked you into it.'

McGregor could only manage one word.

'How?'

'How? Because he couldn't help boasting about how well connected he is, Callum. That he was your friend and so he already knew everything I'd told him. The arrogant bastard couldn't stand for me to think that I knew something he didn't, and so he admitted that you'd been passing him information from the investigation.'

McGregor said nothing. Dempsey continued. 'It didn't ring any alarm bells then. It was a little off that you'd do it, sure, but it was *you*. I *trusted* you, so I guessed that you had your reasons. But when I found out you'd lied about Lawrence? When I knew you were involved? Then it all made sense. Why would you risk being discovered by passing information to someone who wasn't in it with you? More to the point, who was gaining the most out of what happened to Matthewson?

'And then there's what you told me just now. That the whole plan was to replace William Davies with a prime minister with strength. We both know who *that* is, Callum. So if I hadn't been convinced already, that would have done the job.'

McGregor moved uncomfortably in his chair. It was a few seconds before he spoke, but when he did there was admiration in his voice.

'Tony was in this first,' he said. 'Before me. Before anyone. The idea was his and the money was his. But the vision was *ours*. We *both* wanted this, Joe. We *both* wanted Davies gone and Britain's place in the world regained. The only way to do it was to undermine the government. To replace Davies with Tony. Only then would we have the power to do the rest.'

'You're describing a coup, Callum. Don't you realise that?'

'I'm describing the efforts of two patriots!' McGregor's words were no longer calm. Passion was creeping in. 'You believe the same as we do, Joe. You believe that Davies betrayed us all. The only difference is we did something about it while you all sat and whimpered!'

'What you did was treason and murder!' Dempsey met McGregor's passion with his own. 'You killed the people you swore to protect, and you did it because you're a bloody fool. Haversume doesn't believe what you believe. The man's a politician. An opportunist. He's using this whole thing to grab power, because he couldn't get it any other way. Haversume has used you, Callum. He's used what made you a good man and manipulated it for his own gain.'

'You're wrong.'

McGregor's voice was hushed.

'Tony believes what I believe. What *we* believe. When he takes power you'll see. He'll crush those bastards instead of surrendering. Instead of betraying the memory of the dead.'

McGregor believed every word. Dempsey could see that. It was tragic, but worse was that he believed Haversume shared his cause.

'I've heard Haversume's speeches, Callum. He says whatever the press wants to hear. Sound bites and bullshit. The man doesn't mean a word of it. And he'll never take power because I'm going to stop him. I'll make him pay for what he's done.'

'I can't just let you do that, Joe.' McGregor's eyes moved to the pistol in Dempsey's hand as he spoke. 'I at least have to try.'

Dempsey saw the movement in McGregor's eyes. He knew what it meant.

'Callum, please. You won't make it.'

'Then I'll go out like a man.' McGregor's tone was clear. He would go down fighting, however hopeless that fight might be. 'But I want you to know that if it had to be anyone, Joe, I'm glad it's you.'

McGregor lunged for the open drawer as soon as the final word left his lips. In response Dempsey did what Dempsey did best. Three shots, clustered in the centre of McGregor's massive chest, before he had moved even twelve inches.

McGregor's lifeless body slumped against the now bloodstained wall.

Dempsey stood for what seemed like an eternity, staring at McGregor's motionless bulk. Only the need to breathe – something he now realised he had forgotten to do – brought him back to the moment. With a deep inhalation he moved closer, to look into McGregor's open but empty eyes.

Reaching out, he gently ran his fingers down the length of his friend's face and closed his eyelids for the last time.

SEVENTY-THREE

'Do you think Mullen will tell us anything more?'

O'Neil spoke as he took the right-hand turn that would lead to the forecourt.

'If he knows anything more then he'll tell us,' Liam replied. 'He's given us enough to set Stanton after him already. No point holding out now and getting killed by us. Mullen's crazy but he's not stupid. At the very least he can tell us how to work his recorder, I still can't work out how to turn it on.'

'I'm surprised he folded so quickly,' said Michael. 'From what you said about him. I thought he'd have held out.'

'Like I said, Mullen isn't stupid. He still thinks we might kill him, but he knows cooperating is the only chance we won't.'

'Is he right?'

Michael was genuinely uncertain. After so long apart he no longer knew the limits of his brother's ruthlessness.

'Is he going to die?'

'Depends how much of a threat he still is when this is over. When Stanton's gone. I wouldn't lose any sleep over it if he did have to go, but you only kill when you have to, Mikey.'

'Ah, a lesson every big brother should teach.'

The sarcasm in Michael's voice risked re-igniting the animosity between them. It almost did, until they turned onto the illuminated forecourt.

'What the fuck?'

The small inner door they had exited hours earlier was no longer on its hinges.

Michael was the first to move. His shock was overshadowed by fear for Sarah. He was out of the car and through the doorway in seconds. Liam and O'Neil were close behind.

All were met by the sight of a massacre.

Robert Mullen, still bound and slumped in his chair. Two bullet wounds decorated his unmoving chest.

There were three more bodies. The number included Jack Thornton.

Each body carried a fatal bullet-wound to either the head or the chest. And only Thornton had drawn his weapon before dying. It was a worrying fact. If only one man had reacted before death then the assault must have been incredibly fast.

Whoever had killed these three men with such efficiency was good. And Mullen's body made it clear that it wasn't a counter-attack by his organisation. That left only one option. Stanton. The man so intent on killing Michael and Sarah. Clearly he had decided Mullen had outlived his usefulness and brought in other assets.

'Sarah?' Michael had finally found his voice. He shouted Sarah's name so loudly that it stopped Liam and O'Neil in their tracks. They tore the place apart until it was certain that there was no sign of Sarah. Dead *or* alive.

'She's not here.'

Michael could feel Sarah's absence as a crippling pain in the pit of his stomach. She was dead. He knew it. And it was a thought that he could not bear.

'She's dead, Liam. She's dead. I should have been here. I should have been here.'

'Listen to me, Mikey.'

Liam stepped forward and grabbed his brother in a bear hug. His strong arms pulled Michael into his chest.

'Listen to me. She's not dead, Michael. She's not dead.'

'What?' Michael's voice was desperate. 'How do you know? How *can* you know?'

'Because there's no body, Mikey. If she was dead her body would be here. With the rest of them. Why would they take it?'

Liam's logic pulled Michael back from the edge. He began to regain some clarity of thought.

'They've taken her alive? Why?'

'Because they aren't sure what we have or what we know. She's a bargaining chip. Sarah, for whatever we've got.'

'You mean the recording?'

'For whatever. They don't know *what* we have, Mikey. They don't know what they're actually bargaining *for*. They're just hoping you'll hand over whatever it is to keep Sarah safe.'

'But then they'll kill her anyway. They must realise we know that?'

'Maybe they do. Maybe they don't. Either way, we play along. We wait for them to get in touch.'

'Or maybe you contact them.'

The last words came from a deep English voice. It was out of place in a room full of Irishmen. All three span to face the door. Liam and O'Neil reached for their weapons.

'I wouldn't do that.'

The authority in the voice was backed by a gun in an expert hand. Intense, unblinking eyes rooted all three to the spot.

Michael studied the man. He took in the details. Powerfully built. Smartly dressed. Clipped military hair. One thought occurred to him: the killer had returned. So the newcomer's next words were a shock.

'Were you here when this happened?'

A gesture of his pistol indicated to the carnage around them.

'Were you?' Liam asked. Gun or no gun, Liam was control of the scene.

'You're Liam Casey.'

Liam's response had been all that was needed to mark him for who he was. The newcomer continued, gesturing towards the younger brother.

'Which makes you Michael Devlin.'

'And who the hell are you?'

'I'm Major Joe Dempsey of the Department of Domestic Security.'

Dempsey lowered his weapon and took another glance around the room.

'And I think we can help each other.'

SEVENTY-FOUR

Haversume sat back into the luxurious chair behind his ornate office desk. The familiar chimes of Big Ben announced the passing of 7 a.m. Early for a cigar on a normal day. But today was far from that.

Haversume opened the rich-brown humidor that sat to his left and removed a prohibitively expensive Cohiba Cuban cigar from inside. He cut the tip from its rear end and began to gradually ignite the rolled tobacco leaves. It was a ritual he found calming.

For months Haversume had survived on four hours' sleep per night. Sometimes less. By now he should have been past the point of exhaustion. Yet he felt nothing but exhilaration.

It had worked. So very nearly derailed, his intricate design had come good in the end. He deserved the pleasure of this cigar, but the warmth of success – how close he now was to so much power – was the real reward.

His eyes swept across his office. Soon it would be swapped for the more traditional setting of 10 Downing Street. It was the culmination of decades of well-hidden ambition. And it was no less than he deserved.

Haversume's rise to power was unconventional. A strange route which only strengthened his belief in his own superiority.

Who else could pull off a plan – years in the making – to seize control of one of the world's most powerful governments? Who else could manipulate people from every walk of life? Compel them to put their own lives on the line for his advancement? Who else could mould public opinion to the point where he was one of only two possible replacements for the leader he would displace? And who else would use his only competition – Neil Matthewson – as the trigger for his ultimate coup?

It proved what Haversume had always believed. There was no one better.

But it had been a far from faultless journey. The time and effort had been enormous. The financial cost immense. Haversume had delved into the criminal underworld. He had created his 'Stanton' persona to place him at the apex of a criminal hierarchy, from where he was able to coordinate the attacks that had brought Great Britain to its knees.

At the same time he had cultivated his relationships in the military community. Had manipulated the patriotism of Callum McGregor, the most powerful man in British intelligence, to the point that McGregor had involved himself in the unthinkable. All of these things carried a price.

But the greatest cost had come at the end.

Haversume would have given almost anything to avoid Daniel's death. *Almost* anything. The moment he heard of his godson's involvement was the worst of his life, knowing that it meant Daniel would die. There was no choice. Haversume had reached a point of no return. Daniel *had* to be sacrificed.

As terrible as that loss had been, what followed was almost worse. Michael Devlin's refusal to die had put the rest of the Lawrence family in danger. It had taken every ounce of Haversume's manipulative genius to make their survival possible.

His frustration at Michael's phone call to Hugh had been genuine. He had listened to his friend pass on Michael's message with dread, knowing that if Michael shared too much with them, they would also have to be dealt with. So Haversume had offered them refuge – and isolation. Anything to keep them from hearing what else Michael might discover.

For a time he had been rattled by Michael's success. But not now. Joshua had confirmed Mullen's death and Sarah Truman's capture. That gave Haversume the advantage. Michael Devlin might have turned out tougher than expected, but he still had a weakness. Devlin was an honourable man. And he had already been through a lot to keep this woman alive and by his side. Devlin would bargain for Truman's life. Haversume was confident of that.

And if he was wrong? If Devlin refused? Well, if that happened, Haversume had other leverage. He might be reluctant to resort to it, but he would if necessary.

And what of Joshua? Haversume thought.

A man so well regarded, but whose failure had led to Daniel's death. Joshua's subsequent actions had been impressive. He had shown great commitment, demonstrating the talent for which he was infamous. But it did not change the fact that his failure had jeopardised everything. For that – and for Daniel – Joshua would pay a high price.

But all of this was for the future. For now, Haversume would enjoy his success.

The planning. The sacrifice. The cost. The worry. It had all come to fruition. And it had ended more cleanly, more completely, than Haversume had dreamed possible. The report of two bodies in a hotel suite in Belfast had been passed to every intelligence agency by Assistant Commissioner Alex Henley of the Metropolitan Police, and from there the identities of the deceased had quickly become common knowledge. The apparent victims of a mutual shooting, the men had been named as Joe Dempsey and Callum McGregor.

It was the perfect conclusion. Unthinkably convenient. The scheme's greatest threat *and* the man who could later prove to be its biggest loose end. Each one taking the other out of the equation, and just hours after the release and subsequent 'disappearance' of Sergeant Trevor Henry. The final obstacles, all removed in one fatal morning.

Haversume could not have asked for more.

The feeling of contentment remained for several minutes. Haversume wanted to revel in his victory for as long as he could.

Finally – inevitably – the feeling was replaced by an urge to work.

A compulsive need to occupy his mind with details and strategies had served Haversume well. And it would do so again. As much as his upcoming appointment was a race already won, he would obsessively ensure that his leadership campaign would impress. It had to. The government had fourteen days in which to call a vote of confidence, to avoid an election. It was a vote they would only win if a new leader – Haversume – was firmly in place.

He accessed his computer's contact list and found the email addresses of those Members of Parliament who he knew shared his public stance. They were good men and women, idealists who believed in the policies Haversume had only used for advancement. The likes of Jeremy Ross and Elizabeth Prince would form the backbone of his first government, and for this they needed to be under his spell.

There were seven addresses in all. Satisfied, Haversume began to type a short message that invited each to a House of

Commons lunch. He was halfway done when he was interrupted by his secretary, the only member of staff who kept hours as unsociable as his own.

'Mr Haversume, I have Michael Devlin holding on one.'

Haversume's usual speed of thought deserted him. He had no idea why Devlin could be calling. So he could not react with anything but a false friendly greeting as he lifted the telephone to his ear.

'Michael, thank God you're OK. We've been worried sick. Where are you?'

'You know exactly where I am, *Stanton*.'

Michael's answer brought Haversume's self-satisfaction to an abrupt end and made his blood run cold.

'So why don't you come and get me?'

SEVENTY-FIVE

The feeling was like nothing Haversume had ever experienced. From the height of elation to the pit of despair in an instant.

He needed to take control of the situation.

Without a word he noted down the number on the telephone screen and disconnected the line. Next he reached for his second handset. His secure handset. He entered the same digits and activated his voice modulator.

If Michael had been surprised by the disconnect and then the immediate recall he did not show it.

'Some reason you don't want to speak on an open line?'

Michael's tone was mocking. It did not improve Haversume's mood.

'I just didn't expect you to be so effective, Michael,' Haversume replied. 'You've been quite a surprise.'

'*I'm* a surprise? *You* murdered your own godson, Tony. That was hardly expected.'

'Believe me, it wasn't something I wanted to do.'

'That makes it better, does it?' Michael's voice was raised. Filled with disgust. 'You killed Daniel – a man you claimed was like a son to you.'

'I did what I had to do for the good of my country.' Haversume kept his voice steady. His feigned righteousness was well practised. 'I was willing to lose a son. I was willing to pay that price.'

'Oh, you'll pay a price. You'll pay a price for Daniel and for everyone else you've killed. Believe me on that!'

Haversume listened to the rage in Michael's voice with growing regret, knowing that Michael's determined fury had an inevitable consequence, one he had hoped to avoid. Michael must know that Haversume had Sarah, and yet he had taken an aggressive approach. It suggested that Haversume could not rely on Sarah being sufficient collateral. A fact which made a further bargaining chip – a more certain one – necessary.

Daniel's family.

He made one last attempt to avoid it.

'I think you're forgetting something, Michael.' Haversume's tone was still calm. It hid his desperation. His hope that this final gambit could still prevent the unthinkable.

'I think you're forgetting that I have your lady friend.'

'You think I give a shit about her? We just met, Tony. Do what you want with her. I'm coming after you for *Daniel*.'

It was the wrong answer. The choice was made.

'I don't believe that for a moment, Michael,' Haversume replied. 'But even if it were true, do I need to remind you of the whereabouts of Daniel's family? Of Claire. Harry. Hugh. Deborah. You do know where they are, don't you?'

Michael was silent for a moment before answering. It told Haversume that the additional threat was unexpected.

'Where are they?'

The resentment and anger in Michael's voice had been replaced by fear. It brought a smile to Haversume's face. As did Michael's next question.

'What have you done to them?'

'I've not done a thing. Not the slightest thing. But that could change, Michael. Depending upon what you do from this point.'

Michael was silent again. Haversume could picture the whispered conversation with his brother that was sure to be taking place.

When Michael spoke again his tone was different. Slower. He came straight to the point.

'If you release them all – Daniel's family *and* the girl – this can all still go away. I'll let it go. Daniel. Matthewson. Everything. I'll let it all go and I'll fade away. We *all* will. So please, just let them go.'

'You're making me an offer?' Haversume could not suppress a laugh. 'You *have* nothing to offer. So we'll be doing this on *my* terms.'

'Actually, Tony, I think you'll find I *do* have something to offer. Something you might want.'

'Oh you do, do you?'

Even through the voice modulator the answer was sceptical. Haversume's patience was wearing thin.

'And what might that be?'

'It's a voice recording,' Michael replied. 'Robert Mullen recorded almost every conversation you ever had. A digital record of every call. And you know how this works as well as I do. I can have the recording analysed. I can have it confirmed that it's your voice on there, giving Mullen dates, times and details of terrorist attacks. How do you think that will play out in your leadership campaign, minister?'

'Really?' Haversume was almost amused by the weakness of Michael's gambit. 'And how do you propose to identify the voice when every single call used the same electronic disguise I'm using now? I'm not a fool, Michael. What you have – *if* you have it – is worthless.'

'I thought you'd say that.' Michael's voice remained

confident. Unflustered. 'But Mullen wasn't as dumb as you seem to think.'

'What the hell are you talking about?'

'I'm talking about the fact that whatever kit you're using to disguise your voice, it's not flawless. It's military ordinance, isn't it? And it can be bypassed – reversed – by equipment of the same grade.'

Haversume said nothing. He felt his confidence falter.

'Which is exactly what Mullen laid his hands on,' Michael continued. 'Through your own organisation. Whoever it was you had supplying him with what he needed to fake those attacks, they also supplied him with a recorder that could decrypt your voice modulator.'

'I .. I . . . I don't believe you.' For the first time in as long as he could remember, Haversume was truly scared. 'None of my people would—'

'For now, let's just assume I'm right, shall we? Let's assume I *do* have what you want.'

Haversume could not quite believe what he was hearing. But it was a threat he could not ignore. If it was true? His heart quickened at the thought of another weakness. Another threat to the success that – moments ago – was in the palm of his hand.

He thought quickly before continuing.

'Then it looks like we're at an impasse, Michael. Because if you're telling the truth then you *do* have something I want. And in that case this negotiation is not as simple as I first thought. So what do you propose we do next?'

'We meet. Any deal we do, we do it face to face. I'll bring the recording. You bring Sarah and Daniel's family. We exchange and we walk away. But anything out of the ordinary and I'm gone, and this recording goes to the press. Understood?'

Haversume had no choice. So close to success, the recordings could ruin everything.

'You realise I won't come alone, Michael?'

'Neither will I. Bring whoever you like.'

'Where and when?'

'Somewhere neutral. Eamon McGale's family had a cabin in County Wicklow. I'm sure you know all about it from back when you were brainwashing the poor guy.'

'I'm aware of it, yes.'

'Then we'll meet there. Tonight at 7 p.m.'

'A poignant choice. I'll be there,' he replied. 'Just make sure you are too.'

'You don't need to worry about that, Tony.'

The line went dead.

Haversume sat frozen for a moment. The sensation of his heart racing was unfamiliar; confirmation that things had taken a turn for the worse.

Mullen's recordings would be fatal for the campaign. And for his liberty. So the mere possibility that they might exist and be in the hands of Devlin and Casey left him with little choice. For now he would comply with Michael's demands.

But only for as long as it suited him.

Haversume had already thought of how he would use Michael's conditions against him.

His best asset – Joshua – gave him an advantage with which the brothers just could not compete. An advantage he would bring to bear. The terrain had been chosen by Michael, but it best suited Joshua. It was a place where he would make short work of Haversume's enemies, finally bringing this nightmare to an end.

Haversume smiled. Michael had made the wrong choice.

A choice that would be his last. It was a thought that should have pleased him, but the smile disappeared as quickly as it had come. Because Michael's choice had done something else. It had ensured that, tomorrow night, what was left of the Lawrence family would share Daniel's fate.

And for that Michael Devlin would pay.

SEVENTY-SIX

Michael placed the handset on the table ahead of him and looked around Liam's office. Every pair of eyes in the room looked back at him.

'That's that, then. McGale's cabin, 7 p.m. Haversume will be there.'

'You really think a gutless bastard like that will show up?' O'Neil sounded doubtful.

'He'll be there,' Dempsey replied. 'He can't risk the recording going to the press. Besides, he doesn't think you're a big enough threat to stay away, and he thinks I'm dead.'

An earlier call to Henley had made sure of that. Dempsey had recounted the part he had played so far to the brothers, and they had done the same, each filling the gaps in the others' information. Michael had stared in disbelief at the news that Stanton was none other than Anthony Haversume. And then been filled with a terrible rage that his friend's death had been at the hands of someone he considered family. Having finally calmed down, his face had been set in an expression of grim determination ever since.

Together they had formulated a plan, to draw Haversume into the open, to get him to come to them. To get Sarah back. The first stage of that plan was complete. Now for the second.

'We're going to need a crew,' Liam said.

Michael could see that his brother was already thinking ahead. That he knew what odds they would face at McGale's cabin.

Liam continued.

'The best we have. I want them double quick.'

'How many?'

'If they're good men, ten's enough.'

This time it was Dempsey who spoke, his voice as certain as always.

A nod of Liam's head confirmed the number. O'Neil stood up in response.

'I'll get on it.'

The 7 p.m. meeting and the journey to County Wicklow in the Republic of Ireland made for a tight timetable.

'We'll be ready within the hour.'

'So can we do this?' Michael asked as O'Neil left. 'You think ten is enough to pull this off?'

'Enough to deal with the numbers Haversume will bring?' Dempsey replied. 'In all likelihood. The man's not planning a straight gunfight, so you guys should be a match for them. But they're not the problem. The problem will be in the hills. The man who paid a visit to your garage earlier.'

Those words worried Liam. His memory of the lock-up massacre was still fresh.

'Who is he?' he asked.

'It's a man called Turner. Haversume knows you won't offer up the recording if he doesn't show up in person. That puts him in the line of fire, but he won't risk a gunfight on the ground if he can avoid it. He'll have another plan, designed to take you out of the picture before a fight can start. That's where Turner comes in.'

'What is he, a sniper?' Michael was more intrigued than afraid.

'Oh, he's a lot more than that. He's a professional killer,

and he's already caused you a world of trouble. It was Turner who killed one of my agents at Trafalgar Square, which is what got this whole thing started. And the bomb in your car, Michael? And the guy on the bike? Turner. And, judging by the bodies in the lock-up tonight, I'd bet good money that was him too.'

Now Michael was worried. Shaken by the mention of his first encounter with Turner, which he had barely survived.

'So he'll be in the hills?' he asked. 'Just picking us off one by one from some safe spot in the distance?'

'Exactly,' Dempsey replied.

'But how's that going to protect Haversume?' Michael was not following the logic. 'Surely he knows he'll be the first person we go for, once the bullets start flying?'

'Don't underestimate Haversume, Michael. He ended up an army lawyer before going into politics, but before *that* he was in military intelligence for years. So he knows how people react in a combat situation. The destabilising effect of sniper fire. And, more importantly for you, he knows the importance of target selection.

'Michael, you'll be the first to go. Followed by Liam. Believe me, Turner is good enough to take you both out before anyone can react. And once you two are gone your men will panic. They won't be looking to kill what they can see. They'll be looking to hide from what they *can't* see. That'll give Haversume more than enough time to find cover for himself, after which Turner will take out what's left of your crew.'

'But if he does that,' said Michael, 'then Haversume can do what he wants to Sarah and Daniel's family.'

'Except let them live.'

Dempsey's final words summed up the situation.

Silence fell. Neither Michael nor Liam had anything to add.

What was there? They seemed to be going into a fight that they could not win. And yet they had no other choice.

The quiet was only broken by the intervention of Anne Flaherty. Anne had been outside the office door. She had heard everything. And she did not seem happy.

'Let me get this straight.' She was speaking even faster than usual. 'This Haversume fella, he's got a man hidden in the woods whose only job is to kill the two of you as quickly as he can? A man who can do it so fast that neither of you stands a chance? And you're still going? Have the pair of you lost your bloody minds?'

'It's not that simple,' Dempsey replied, when Michael and Liam failed to speak. 'What I said was that Turner is that good – that quick – *if* he gets the chance. But that's a big "if". And you have an advantage. You have me.'

'And just who are you, Clark fucking Kent?'

Anne did not mince her words.

'Far from it. But I *am* someone who can put Turner down, and that's what I intend to do.'

Dempsey turned to Liam.

'It's what gives us the upper hand. Haversume will be relying on Turner. As far as he's concerned Turner is the deal-breaker; the only one that really matters. The upshot of that is he won't worry too much whether his men on the ground are as good as yours. He doesn't think he *needs* them. But when Turner's bullet doesn't come, then it'll be Haversume's turn to panic. After that, he's all yours.'

'Are you sure you can take this guy?' Liam asked. 'Are you sure he won't be expecting you?'

'I'm sure on the second one. Like I told you, Haversume thinks I'm dead.'

'And the first?'

'Any man who gives you a guarantee on something like that, that man's a liar. What I *am* sure of is that I've got a better chance than anyone else you'll ever meet.'

Dempsey's blunt response was cold but honest. And it was enough for Michael, as it seemed to be for Liam. Which was just as well, because Dempsey did not seem inclined to answer any more questions.

Dempsey got to his feet.

'I need to be at the cabin first if this is going to work. Which means I need to leave ahead of you.'

'You're going? Now?'

'Old habits die hard,' Dempsey explained. 'His *and* mine. Turner will be at the cabin long before 7 p.m. For reconnaissance and to choose his hiding place. So I need to be there first. That means leaving now.'

'But how will we know you've managed it?' Michael asked. 'How will we know if it's safe to hand over the recording?'

'You won't know that until Turner doesn't shoot. I'm sorry but there's no other way.'

The weight of Dempsey's words plunged the room back into silence.

'I'll see you all when this is done.' He was already at the door. 'And trust me. I *will* take care of Turner. You have my word.'

The room remained silent as Dempsey left. Only once he was gone did its three remaining occupants begin to speak among themselves.

'Liam, you've got to think about what you're doing,' said Anne. 'This isn't a few Belfast gangsters. These people are serious. Please stop and think.'

'I have thought, Anne. Long and hard.'

Liam's words were gentle. His hand cradled Anne's cheek as he spoke.

'But I have to do this. Haversume has everyone Mikey cares about and he's gonna kill them because that'll make Mikey come to him. And if *Mikey's* going, *I'm* going. I can't let him do it alone.'

'But there's got to be another way,' Anne said, her eyes welling with tears. 'There has to be.'

'There isn't. You know that. And you know I'd be going even if he *didn't* have Mikey's friends. He's killed innocent women and children, Anne. Murdered babies. And all for power. For ambition! The bastard's gotta be stopped.'

'But what about what's waiting for you? You heard what your man there just said. This Turner fella's going to be there. He's going to be waiting for the pair of you.'

'But he's not waiting for Dempsey. We have to trust the man. We have to trust that he can do what he says.'

Michael could see the tears trickle down Anne's face. And he could see the effect it was having upon his brother: Liam wished he could listen to her. Wished that he could stay. But Michael knew that his brother would do what he must, not what he desired. He was leaving to face Haversume, and there was nothing Anne could say or do that would change that.

'Then I'll be praying that he *is* that good,' Anne finally said, her voice faltering. 'I'll be praying that he gets you home to me in one piece. *Both* of you.'

With her last words Anne glanced at Michael, who stepped forward in response.

'I'll be looking out for Liam, Anne, so don't you worry.'

Michael forced a smile as he spoke. He leaned forward and kissed her wet cheek before continuing.

'But he's wrong about one thing. Haversume doesn't have all of the people I care about. Two of the people I care about most are right here.'

With that Michael turned and walked away, leaving his brother and his oldest friend to say their intimate goodbye.

SEVENTY-SEVEN

Haversume sat in the back seat of his chauffeur-driven Rolls-Royce Phantom. The palms of his hands perspired with nervous anticipation. It was the first time they had done that for longer than he could remember.

Haversume tried to ignore it. He focused instead on his private Learjet 60 as it was refuelled. It was a sight that usually buoyed him, filling him with the pride of accomplishment. A private jet was an achievement – a status symbol – that few could match. So what if he had started out rich? If he had inherited his family business? He had still overseen that empire as it grew bigger and more powerful. And he had managed that while also building a political career *and* creating the Stanton persona. All of which just increased Haversume's feeling of achievement.

Or at least it usually did. But not today. Today he could not shake the guilt of what he would soon have to do.

His first concern had been dealing with Devlin and Casey. A call to a contact in Dublin had secured enough men for the confrontation. And a second call had secured the only man who really mattered: Joshua.

Once the arrangements were in place Haversume had turned his mind to the other consideration of the day. It was this that now caused him such trouble.

'Sir, the jet's ready.'

Terry Barrett was Haversume's long-time chauffeur, confidante and – if such a thing were possible – his personal friend. Barrett's thick cockney accent broke into his employer's troubled thoughts.

'Thank you, Terry. Is everyone on board?'

'They are, sir. They ain't going nowhere.'

The relationship stretched back to Haversume's earliest army days. There was almost nothing Barrett did not know about his employer's business and personal life. Including the truth about Stanton. With McGregor dead and Devlin and Casey soon to follow, Barrett would be the only other person who did. Haversume's man had never bought into his employer's counterfeit principles. Barrett had no doubt that his boss sought power for power's sake. Well paid beyond his qualification and talents, it was an ambition with which Barrett empathised.

'Did anyone see them board?'

'No, sir. They did it while the plane was in the hangar. Nobody would have seen a thing.'

'And how are they?'

'A bit confused,' Barrett explained, 'but they don't suspect nothin'. And I've told 'em you'll explain every'fing when you get 'ere.'

'Good,' Haversume replied. 'Then let's get this over with.'

Haversume took a final deep inhalation of the car's warm air before forcing himself to move. He stepped out of the open rear door and felt the tarmac of the private Denham Airfield underfoot. Next he took the short walk to the waiting aircraft. Barrett was at his shoulder for every step.

Finally he reached the few steps on the underside of the jet's open door. It was one of the shortest journeys of his life. And one of the hardest. He was unsure if he could maintain the deception to follow, and he dreaded its inevitable end.

'Tony!' It was Hugh Lawrence who spoke first as Haversume entered the plane fuselage. 'Thank God you're here. Have you heard anything?'

Haversume looked his closest friend in his eyes. And he began to lie.

'I have. Michael's safe. He's in Ireland and we're going to get him. We're going to bring him home.'

'All of us?' It was Deborah Lawrence who spoke. Daniel's mother. 'You can't just send for him?'

'There's no way he would come, Deb,' Haversume replied. 'Michael has got himself very worked up about all of this, and I don't think he would trust me without knowing that you're all safe and sound.'

'What do you mean?'

'I mean that everything he told Hugh on the telephone, well, I've had it looked into and he was wrong. There *was* an incident near his home, but it wasn't what he described. Not even close. And it had nothing to do with Daniel's death. But Michael convinced himself that it did, and so it now seems he took Daniel's death harder than any of us realised. It, well, it affected him. And now we need to protect him from himself.'

'But he was strong,' Claire Lawrence offered. She seemed hesitant to believe what they were being told. 'He dealt with it better than any of us. He can't just have lost it.'

'He hasn't lost it, Claire.' Haversume was careful not to go too far. 'He's just emotional and confused. So like I said, we need to protect him from himself. And if I have you all with me that will be much easier to do.'

Claire Lawrence did not answer, but she still looked sceptical.

Haversume was concerned he might be losing her. That

he might be losing them all. He had to be more persuasive, he knew. It was still too early for them to know the truth.

'Listen,' he said, addressing them all in his softest tone. 'I've done everything I can to bring Michael home, but he doesn't trust anyone now. Which I have to presume includes me. But we can't just leave him to his own devices. He's paranoid and God knows what problems he is going to cause, to himself and to others. That leaves two options. Either we send people after him who *can* bring him in, but who could well hurt him in the process. Or *we* can go. All of us. So that he can see the people he trusts.'

There was no response. At least not verbally. But Haversume could see the unspoken communication between the Lawrence family. He had convinced them, and so for now he would enjoy their cooperation.

It would not last. He knew that. At some point Daniel's family would learn the truth. But for now the illusion continued. And he was grateful to delay his last – and greatest – betrayal.

SEVENTY-EIGHT

Joshua unclipped his Rolex Submariner and carefully concealed it in the undergrowth ahead of him. He covered it with loose autumn leaves to obscure any hint of metal. The watch face itself was visible only from his position. As it always was when he settled in to await a shot.

His internal clock was exceptional, but confirmation of time at a glance was a crutch he had never left behind.

The time displayed was 5.30 p.m. It would not be a long wait.

Joshua had arrived over an hour earlier and done exactly as Stanton had instructed. Sarah had been secured inside the isolated cabin, bound and gagged.

He had spent little time in there with her. Just a minute or two. Long enough to take a mental note of its layout. The pervasive odour of damp had revealed how long the cabin had been empty; the overall effect suggesting a return to the wild. Maybe it was the deteriorating furniture. Or the moss that grew on happy family photographs.

Not that he had been there to observe nature. There was a job to do, and he would not be distracted.

It was essential to his mission that the cabin could offer no protection to anyone who took refuge inside. With Sarah secured to a chair in the centre of the cold lounge, Joshua had assessed the room. It had not taken long. The open area was surrounded on all sides by windows. It would be near impossible for anyone inside to avoid his line of sight.

It was all Joshua needed to know. Satisfied, he had returned to his newly rented four-wheel-drive vehicle and driven away, navigating the narrow country roads that led to the small village of Avoca at the bottom of the wooded hills.

Joshua parked directly outside of Avoca's dominant feature, a nineteenth-century grey stone church. The car was instantly anonymous in a line of similar utility vehicles, most left by the many fishermen now dotted along the gentle river that ran alongside the single village road.

Joshua had looked around as he climbed out of the car. Once satisfied that he was not overlooked, he removed a leather gun case from the car's back seat. He strapped it to his back and began the return journey to the top of the mountainous hill on foot, moving through the uneven terrain easily. Experience and training made him well suited to the task, and he reached the top of the steep, wooded hills in a time that would have been remarkable for a man in his twenties.

Once there, Joshua had moved silently through the shade of the trees, eyes fixed on the clearing ahead of the cabin. That would be where it happened. Where the confrontation between Stanton's and Casey's groups would take place.

Which meant that the best possible view of the clearing was needed. Taking a pencil-thin, hand-held telescopic sight, he had slowly walked the hillside.

Instinct had already told him the ideal vantage point; the spot with an unobstructed view of both the clearing and the cabin. But Joshua still followed the process. His compulsions had brought him this far. He would not abandon them now. And so he had moved from possible location to possible location. Always stopping to check the scene below through his sight. Always assessing which spot was best.

It had been time-consuming. An hour went by before he finally settled on a location. The spot his instinct had first identified. Inevitable, really. But time spent on diligence was never time wasted.

Next came concealment. A much quicker task. There was abundant foliage. Distinctive ground markings. With these Joshua could disappear completely. Within minutes both he and his Accuracy International sniper rifle had become invisible. So well hidden that even an expert eye would struggle to see him from feet away. It was a skill Joshua had mastered over decades. It required speed and it required confidence. Fear of discovery could not be a consideration. It could not be allowed to distract from the deadly accuracy of his shot.

Joshua glanced at his concealed wristwatch. Time was short, but there was still more than enough for him to align the rifle's Schmidt & Bender 3-12 × 50 PM II telescopic sight. Joshua went through a series of delicate adjustments. After two minutes the scope's calibration and view were perfect, capable of sweeping from target to target with the slightest movement. Ten minutes more – seven separate checks – and even Joshua was satisfied.

With accuracy assured, Joshua removed the rifle's magazine from his inside pocket and locked it into place. He removed two more identical leather cases and placed them within easy reach, carefully hidden by the ample fallen foliage. Each case carried five lethal rounds. Fifteen .338 Lapua Magnum calibre bullets in total. It was more than Joshua could expect to need. Enough to bring Stanton's enterprise to a bloody end.

Joshua was trained to remain motionless for days at a time, in locations far less hospitable than the wet but moderate Irish climate. It should have made the ninety or so minutes that lay ahead seem like barely a pause. But the thoughts that now raced through Joshua's mind made that impossible.

As hard as he tried, Joshua could not stop imagining what his own reaction would be when he first glimpsed Stanton. It was unhelpful. He tried to distract himself by studying the area through his rifle's sight.

The clearing at the front of the cabin was between forty and fifty feet below, and perhaps 500 yards ahead. Far enough that no sound quieter than a gunshot would reach from one location to the other, but still close enough that every shot would be both accurate and lethal.

He took in every detail of what would soon become his killing zone. Scanned from tree to tree. From shrub to shrub. Moving his rifle slowly, he made himself familiar with every object that could be capable of obscuring his view and calculated the clear angles he would need if those objects were used for cover.

Joshua continued his sweep of the area, preparing for every eventuality. Finally he came to the cabin. He had to determine in advance which window gave which unobstructed angle. To ensure that no spot inside was beyond the reach of his bullet. His selection of shooting spot had already ensured that there were available lines of fire for every eventuality. And one of those lines now gave him a clear view of Sarah Truman, who was conscious and fighting to free herself.

Joshua watched Sarah as she struggled. Beads of sweat ran down her cheeks and off her jaw as she fought against her restraints. The woman was still trying to break free, over half a day after her capture. Most would have retired in exhaustion by now. But not Sarah.

Her determination was remarkable.

It was hardly a surprise, though. He had expected Sarah would fight back before he had even entered the lock-up the previous night. She couldn't have come this far without that kind of resilience. But still he had been unprepared for the alley-cat assault that had followed.

The men in the garage had been easily dealt with. Joshua had taken the inner door from its hinges with one well-placed kick. Two head-shots dealt with the first two men. Quick. Efficient. Two bullets in the heart of the third and another two for Mullen should have ended all meaningful resistance.

They had not.

Sarah had frozen in the seconds it took Joshua to dispatch Casey's men. That was natural enough. So she had been rooted to the spot when his gun then turned on her. Then he had lowered his gun and walked towards her. He had put out his hand, intending to take Sarah by the arm. Sure that she would come quietly if it meant that she would live. Looking back, Joshua was amused by how wrong he had been.

Sarah had followed the best self-defence instruction: go for the eyes and the groin. She struck out with her right foot, though far too slowly to come close to its delicate target. Joshua had reacted with his usual sublime skill, unbalancing her with only the slightest movement of his body. A light push. Sarah had fallen back clumsily and struggled to regain her footing. But the effortless defence had not stopped her. She must have known from the outset that she was outmatched, but she seemed determined to not go down without a fight.

Regaining her balance, she had launched herself at Joshua. He allowed her right hand to sail past his own, knowing she would miss his eye by inches and that the momentum would make her unsteady. But those inches could be misinterpreted, and the illusion of success had seemed to encourage Sarah. It made her fight harder, trying to scratch and tear at Joshua's skin. It was as much as Joshua had been prepared to accept, and so he had pushed Sarah's flailing arms aside, lifted her from the floor and threw her across the garage.

Sarah had landed heavily on the hard floor, hurt, but adrenaline had forced her to her feet. And instinct had told her what to do. Taking a lesson from Michael, Sarah had grabbed the nearest thing she could use as a weapon. A four-pointed, cast-iron wheel brace. Metal in hand, she had rushed at Joshua, just moments after she had been tossed aside. It was so fast that Joshua had not yet wiped the fresh blood from his eye. But it was still not fast enough.

Sarah's gender had made Joshua underestimate her. But only at first. By this point he wanted their struggle over, and there was one way to do that without killing her. So Joshua had subtly moved his feet – planting them shoulder-width apart – and waited for Sarah to rush in with the wheel brace raised above her head.

The blow that Sarah ran on to was devastating. Joshua had positioned himself perfectly. His timing was impeccable. A right cross had slammed onto Sarah's jaw as she came within reach. It sent her crashing to the ground. And it kept her there.

Blood had run free from Sarah's mouth while her entire body shook; her nervous system coming alive just as her mind shut down.

Joshua had not even needed to look. Experience had told him that it would be a long time before Sarah regained consciousness. And he wasted none of it. He had immediately bound her hands and feet, picked up the deadweight of her unconscious body and thrown her over his shoulder. He had then stalked out of the lock-up without looking back, leaving nothing but death and destruction in his wake.

As he watched Sarah now – hours later and through the dehumanising distance of his rifle's sight – he could see a blackening bruise covered the entire left-hand side of her face. The result of the punch she had run into. But it meant nothing to Joshua. He had harmed many women in his career. It was no different to hurting a man. To him, anyway.

A sudden intrusion of sound brought Joshua's focus back to the moment. All distractions were immediately wiped from his mind. With the smallest movement he turned his sight away from the cabin and into the clearing.

A small motorcade emerged from the darkness of the tree-lined road. Joshua moved his scope from car to car. He watched as three identical off-road vehicles came to a halt in the open area ahead of the cabin.

Joshua moved his eye away from his rifle sight and relied instead on his own un-enhanced vision. It gave him a full view of the scene ahead of him, too far for real detail but close enough to follow the full movement of the vehicles that was denied to him by the limited focus of his sight.

The vehicles' occupants were climbing out of various doors. Joshua watched their inept attempt to secure the area. He counted eleven men in total and he presumed that all were heavily armed.

Enough to start a graveyard.

Joshua became conscious of his breathing as he watched. It was now an effort. He knew what it meant: that his anticipation was heightening.

Stanton was in one of those cars, Joshua knew that. He

knew that Stanton was waiting for the all-clear from his team before he would climb out.

It amused Joshua that Stanton would trust these amateurs. A smile itched the corner of his mouth. Because none of these men could protect Stanton from the greatest threat that night: Joshua's murderous intent towards the bastard who had threatened his family.

But it was a threat that Joshua could not carry out. Not yet. Not until he knew that his family were safe and that Stanton did not have measures in place to ensure their deaths in the event of his own. Stanton must have known this when he answered to the assessment of 'all-clear'.

Joshua was too distant to hear what words followed. So he moved the scope back to his eye, to observe the response to the 'all-clear'.

Stanton's men responded by returning to the first and third vehicles. Two bound and gagged captives were dragged from each. A man, two women and a child, all marched into the cabin and seated next to Sarah.

Joshua's scope swept then swept back to the middle vehicle and he felt his heart miss a beat as Stanton stepped into view.

SEVENTY-NINE

'No. Fucking. Way.'

Joshua was trained to maintain silence when concealed and awaiting his shot. But this time – for the first time – he could not keep the words inside.

The sight of Anthony Haversume was one of the greatest shocks of Joshua's life. He had prepared himself to discover Stanton's identity. Had steeled himself for any eventuality. Or so he had thought. But Anthony Haversume? The scourge of Northern Irish terrorism? It had not even crossed his mind.

Now he wondered why, because it made perfect sense. The death of Neil Matthewson would clear Haversume's path to high office; Matthewson was the only politician with approval ratings anywhere near Haversume's. But to be *behind* that assassination *and* to make it look like a terrorist attack? That was a new level of wrong.

The shock did not last long. Joshua would not be where he was if he could not shake off the unexpected. But the feeling of betrayal was not so easily ignored. Joshua may have abandoned the army years ago, but he still had military sympathies. He shared the military's distaste over the government's treatment of its soldiers. Hated how they were sent into battle under-funded and ill-equipped. And he despised the way William Davies had struck political deals with terrorists. He had believed that Haversume was the answer. That he was the man to lead his country from the mire. He had put what faith he had in the man.

And now he knew it was a lie.

That feeling – that bitterness – clouded Joshua's judgement. He despised Stanton and had vowed a terrible revenge once this was over. A vow to make Stanton pay for the threats he had made. But Joshua had also determined that it would not happen today. It would not be until his family were safe. Joshua would wait, and he would enjoy his revenge cold.

Except now he was not so sure.

Joshua watched as Haversume strode about the clearing, barking instructions. An occasional glance into the hills was the bastard's only acknowledgement of Joshua's presence. Haversume was obviously unconcerned that his gunman now knew his identity. He had no fear of the man he had repeatedly threatened. It was a dismissive complacency that only angered Joshua more.

That fury grew as Joshua continued to watch. It badgered him. He contemplated ending Stanton – Haversume – with a single bullet. But he could not win. Nothing would override Joshua's duty to his family. He had already calculated the odds the moment he realised that Stanton would show up. And while he enjoyed the thought of taking Stanton's life at this secluded spot, he knew that he could not.

It was Haversume's ability to consider every possibility that protected him. A torrent of bad blood had passed between Joshua and 'Stanton' during their short relationship. Threat after unacceptable threat. It went without saying that Joshua would want his tormentor dead. Which meant that Haversume *knew* the risk of putting himself in Joshua's sights.

It was this fact that held Joshua back. Haversume would not have placed his life in Joshua's hands without arrangements in place for his own protection. Without the 'bargaining chip' of Joshua's family. Both men knew that they were still under threat, and that the threat would only pass if Haversume came away unscathed. It was the ultimate insurance policy. The ultimate incentive.

It was what kept the smile on Haversume's face, and a bullet out of Haversume's brain.

Dempsey looked through his own hand-held telescopic sight. It gave him just the barest glimpse of a face he had not seen in seven years.

James Turner was concealed beneath a duvet of mud, dirt and arranged shrubs. Dug into the hill. The man would have been impossible to find, if Dempsey had not watched him arrive.

Dempsey had travelled alone after briefing the brothers. A police helicopter, arranged by Henley at Dempsey's request, had covered the miles between Ulster and Wicklow at a speed unmanageable by land. It had allowed him to arrive in Avoca hours before Turner. He had then completed the journey with the same fast-paced trek up the hillside that Turner would later take.

All of which had allowed him to reach the McGale cabin by 3 p.m.

Just like Turner, Dempsey had taken time to identify the spot with the best lines of sight. The result was the same; Dempsey had settled on the spot his former sergeant now occupied. And then he had moved away, to a spot with the clearest view of *Turner's* likely location.

It was in this second spot that Dempsey had then concealed himself. Just as effectively as Turner would later manage. The two men had the same training. The same techniques. The same natural talent. For the next ninety minutes Dempsey had lain motionless.

Invisible.

Waiting.

That ninety minutes had ended with Turner's arrival, driving into the clearing in his newest hire car. Sunlight had broken through the gaps in the overhanging foliage, tracing a path from the vehicle's front wheels to the cabin door.

The tall, brown-clad figure had stepped out of the driver's door. It was the first time Dempsey had seen his old friend since Colombia. The years seemed to have hardly touched the man. Turner was as slim and as fit as ever. His pale face carried none of the scars that Dempsey had picked up in the years between. The eyes were as alert as ever.

Dempsey had watched as Turner moved to the car's rear passenger door. Saw him pull a struggling figure from the back seat. Dempsey recognised the heavily bruised face of Sarah Truman.

With Sarah secure in the cabin Turner had climbed back into his car and driven away. But there was no doubt in Dempsey's mind that he would be back.

Dempsey had calculated that it would take Turner a minimum of thirty minutes to return on foot, which would be his inevitable means of covering the distance; parking his car anywhere but in the town at the foot of the hills would risk giving his presence away.

Which would defeat the point of having him here, Dempsey had thought.

That thirty minutes had given Dempsey time, and he had used it wisely. By the time of Turner's return Dempsey's weapons were primed and ready for use. And they remained that way for the next few hours. Just as Dempsey had remained motionless and hidden, watching as his former friend selected the perfect spot for his particular task.

Turner's ability to blend into his surroundings had not been dulled by the years. Dempsey had seen that for himself. After perhaps an hour of careful scrutiny, the older man had concealed himself exactly where Dempsey had known he would. He had done so with a skill that Dempsey shared but rarely witnessed, becoming all but invisible.

Dempsey had observed intently throughout, genuinely fearful that he would not find Turner again if he did otherwise.

Once Turner was settled, Dempsey had used a particular branch – part of Turner's coverage – to mark the spot in his mind before forcing himself to look away.

He had not allowed himself to obsess about Turner. To do so would only heighten his anticipation and release long-buried emotions, both of which were a waste of valuable energy.

Instead he had used the time to survey the distance and terrain that separated them. What mattered today was how he could best protect Devlin, Casey and their men. And for that Dempsey needed to calculate how long it would take him to reach Turner without being detected.

Usually it wouldn't be necessary to deal with Turner face to face. A bullet would make the journey in an instant. But that was not an option today. Dempsey had already determined that it was too much of a risk.

He could not have fired before Haversume's arrival, while it had just been the two of them. Dempsey had no way of knowing what contact Turner had with Haversume, and so he could not have risked taking Turner out in case it had alerted Haversume. And he couldn't fire now either, with the brothers yet to arrive.

Not with Sarah Truman and the Lawrence family surrounded by armed men; they would surely die before Dempsey could finish Haversume's full group. Even once Devlin and Casey did arrive, an immediate bullet would be too dangerous; the sound of gunfire, even a single muzzled shot, would almost certainly start a firefight in the clearing below, perhaps before Liam, Michael and their men were ready for the fight that would follow.

The situation had left him no choice. Turner – the most dangerous man Dempsey had ever met – had to be taken up close. Which meant that Dempsey had to reach him.

Keeping his body flat to the mud and the undergrowth, he began the long, slow crawl that would do just that.

EIGHTY

The road to the McGale cabin was narrow. Tree-lined. It wound around the hill, so closely that in some places its edge was a sheer drop. Surrounded to the sides and above by the wild foliage, shafts of light occasionally broke through the overhanging canopy. In those spots the sun would temporarily blind any driver, a shift from darkness to daylight.

It was a risky enough route to chasten the most confident driver, with Paddy O'Neil no exception. His normally aggressive driving was tamed. Which had its upsides. Michael, at least, was comfortable in the backseat of O'Neil's car for the first time.

The twists and turns seemed to be causing Liam some nausea. His face was unusually white as he turned his body from the seat beside O'Neil and looked back, first at Michael and then the men who flanked him. Michael followed his brother's gaze and observed the determined looks that were etched upon their companions' faces. They had come to play their part, well aware of what lay ahead. It was clear that neither of them was here to lose.

'We're coming up on the clearing now. Is everyone ready for this?'

Liam's question was a simple one. And Michael's simple answer, if he was being truthful, was 'no'. He knew that they could be driving to their deaths.

'We're all ready,' Michael lied. 'Let's just get it done, Liam.'

The view through the windscreen began to change as

Michael spoke, revealing a clearing. The vehicle came to a halt, and all five men saw the same sight at the same time. Three white off-road vehicles, surrounded by a group of eleven armed men.

'I don't see Haversume.' O'Neil was the first to speak. 'Do you?'

'No,' Michael replied. 'But it doesn't mean he's not here. He's probably in the cabin with Sarah and Daniel's family. Let's go.'

All four doors of the Land Rover were opened on Michael's word. Its five occupants stepped out and moved into the clearing, their guns on open display. Five more men immediately joined them. They had followed from Belfast in a separate car, just moments behind.

Michael strode purposefully ahead of Liam's men, towards the group that awaited him. There was no sign of Haversume among them. Instead, in the centre, was a whippet-thin, middle-aged man. The thin man had a certain cockiness. The confidence of someone placed in charge. Michael glared at him.

'Where's Haversume? He's supposed to be here.'

'He's here.'

Terry Barrett's cockney accent stood out. Somehow alien in the Irish hills.

'But you don't talk to 'im 'til I know the recording's real. You could be spoofing for all I know.'

'Tony knows the deal. He shows his face or the recording goes to the press. He comes out here or we walk away.'

'Deal?' Barrett's response was pure arrogance. 'You ain't in a position to talk about a deal, mate. We got your missus and your mate's family and we'll kill the lot of 'em if you don't behave yourself. Now stop being a stupid bastard and show me the tape.'

Michael looked the thin man from head to toe as he spoke. Years of courtroom experience had given him an innate understanding of body language and bluffing.

Michael could smell the uncertainty.

'You'll be killing no one, *mate*.' He placed a condescending emphasis on the last word. 'I've got what Tony needs, which leaves you with a choice. Either you go and get that piece of shit and bring him out, or this place becomes a war zone. And, believe me, if we go down the second route you're target number one for every gun behind me. So it's *your* choice, *mate*.'

'You're threatening me?'

Barrett was as confrontational as he could manage. But Michael could see the fear in his eyes.

'You really think you're in a position to threaten *me*? I've got more men and more guns. Your little lot don't stand a chance.'

'Maybe we don't. But what does it matter? We're dead the second it starts, you and I. Only difference is I'm doing this for my family. I'll die for them if I have to. I hope you're being paid enough to say the same.'

Michael spoke with belief behind every word. And it seemed to have the desired effect. Barrett stood his ground for as long as he dared – a five-second show of bravado – before turning his back and walking towards the cabin.

Michael watched him go and, as he did, he considered what must happen next. Once Haversume was in the clearing Michael would have no choice but to hand over the recording in exchange for the hostages. But once *that* was done the intervention of Turner – if he was alive – would instantly follow.

Michael turned his head, looking for some reassurance from Liam. But Liam was not looking back. For just a moment he had glanced to the hills, fruitlessly searching for a reassuring glimpse of Dempsey. It was just an instant, but long enough for Michael to know what his brother was thinking. And to agree.

Dempsey had better be as good as he seems.

Joshua watched the encounter through his telescopic sight, read lips where he could see them. It gave him a limited understanding of the conversation. Interesting, but incomplete. That was inevitable when all he could see of Michael Devlin was the back of his head.

Restricted though his vision was, Joshua couldn't miss the change in Haversume's lead man. From his initial confidence – arrogance, even – the thin man had visibly wilted. His exposed jugular vein, clear in Joshua's scope, had thumped with fear as Devlin spoke. Joshua had even suppressed a laugh, amused at how easily the man's bullish command had been crushed.

It was a brief moment of humour. It would not last.

With his right eye peering through his lens, Joshua's left eye remained open to scan the overall scene. It was a trusted technique that allowed him to remain aware of happenings outside the tunnel vision of his rifle sight. Things such as the small but vital detail that made his heart suddenly race.

Joshua had paid only fleeting attention to the men with Michael Devlin. Had only half-noted Liam's occasional head movement. He instead concentrated on what he now saw through his lens. Haversume, walking into the clearing with a gun in hand, behind the stumbling cover of both Sarah Truman and Harry Lawrence.

Haversume was taking no chances with his own safety, Joshua could see that. Not content with hiding behind his captives, his eyes kept darting towards the hills; searching for some impossible confirmation that his protector was watching.

It was the eye movement that triggered Joshua's mental alarm. The gaze that swept back and forth. Initially angered by the man's obvious fear, Joshua's heart rate jumped as his subconscious connected the dots. As he realised that Liam Casey – metres behind the action – was doing exactly the same thing as Haversume.

Joshua pulled his right eye away from the scope and looked directly into the clearing. Liam Casey was standing just metres from Michael and from Haversume. Their encounter should have held his undivided attention, but did not.

Liam – like Haversume had – glanced towards the hills.

Joshua returned to the scope. Moved it a twitch to the left. His enhanced vision settled on Liam's head. The close-up view confirmed his instinct. Liam was looking for something. For *someone*. It was subtle, but to someone of Joshua's experience it was now unmistakable.

And it meant one thing. Liam Casey knew that Joshua was there.

The panic and paranoia that came with the realisation overcame him. How could Casey know? Was it Haversume? Was the whole thing a set-up? And, if it was, who else was up here? Questions flooded his mind. Too many. In response he did what he had never done before.

He moved before taking his shot.

Joshua threw off the leaves and shrubs, grabbed his pistol and climbed to his feet. Then he turned to run. And came face to face with a man he had not seen in seven years.

EIGHTY-ONE

It had taken twenty minutes. Dempsey had crawled through three hundred yards of mud, caked to the hillside by Wicklow's almost perpetual rainfall. He had moved slowly. Silently. Giving no hint of his presence.

The plan had played out to perfection.

Right up until Turner rose to his feet.

Caught off guard, Dempsey hadn't yet brought out his gun, still strapped to the small of his back, as Turner turned towards him, a pistol gripped in his right hand and his rifle in his left.

In an instant Dempsey was moving, launching himself at Turner just as their eyes met. The explosive momentum allowed him to tackle Turner before he was steady on his feet, throwing his full bulk at high speed into the older man's ribcage, sending them both crashing into the undergrowth. The impact forced Turner's gun from his grip.

Dempsey leaped back up immediately, reaching for the gun still strapped to his back. But the strapping had been put in place to keep it secure during his crawl, not for a quick-draw contest, and before he could release it Turner had also scrambled to his feet and covered the ground between them at speed.

Dempsey saw him coming, but his effort to free his gun left him open. And Turner took the opportunity. His timing impeccable, he hit Dempsey at a run just as the weapon came free.

Dempsey reeled backwards from the powerful impact, managed to keep his grip on the gun, but was unable to recover in time to avoid the expertly placed knee-strike that Turner then delivered to his ribs.

The air in Dempsey's lungs rushed outwards as he felt several rib bones give way. He was stunned. Only for an instant, but long enough. Turner struck again, this time aiming the back of his fist at Dempsey's exposed wrist. The blow knocked the Glock 19 from Dempsey's hand, into the cover of the nearby undergrowth.

Turner's arm was still swinging away from himself as he switched direction and threw his entire bodyweight into a second knee-strike, this time to Dempsey's solar plexus. Every drop of power he managed to rip through his torso was delivered with pinpoint accuracy. A shuddering blow that took both men back to the floor.

Dempsey hit the ground hard. Disarmed and with ribs already broken, the third blow had sapped his energy and torn up his insides. He did his best to ignore it. To hide it. But he knew he could not fool Turner.

Turner seized the advantage. He pulled himself upright before Dempsey had a chance to move and manoeuvred his body on top of the bigger man. Dempsey felt his arms crushed under Turner's knees. It left his upper body completely exposed for Turner to rain blow after blow upon it. Head. Neck. Chest. None of the blows were the most powerful Dempsey had suffered; Turner was hampered by his position. But they were hard enough. And they were relentless.

Dempsey could feel his strength sapping and his consciousness failing. He could not survive much more of this.

Instinct, experience and skill kicked in.

He ignored the blows. Stopped trying to avoid them and

just allowed them to land. Instead he focused on his right arm. Consciously targeted every last ounce of strength towards it.

At first Turner did not seem to notice as Dempsey slowly pulled his right arm from under the weight of Turner's knee.

When he *did* notice, it was already too late.

As soon as his arm was free Dempsey reached up and grabbed Turner's left wrist. He held it in place. Dempsey was still the stronger man, and his desperation only widened that gap between them. It caused the ferocity of Turner's attack to falter. He hesitated, as if torn between the blows his right fist could still deliver and the vice-like grip on his left wrist. It was all the invitation Dempsey needed.

Seizing the moment, Dempsey freed his left arm, now able to fight back. Much the broader and heavier, Dempsey had always been a powerhouse. It was an advantage he now brought to bear, pulling him closer. From here Turner could cause Dempsey no real damage, and his attack weakened.

With an explosion of power that tore through his abdomen, he brought his legs up high and used them to envelop Turner's body. A further gut-busting thrust and Turner was thrown clear across the undergrowth.

Separated, both men climbed back to their feet.

Dempsey finally had a moment to shake off the blows he had taken. To regain his breath. His composure. He faced the rising Turner as he did so, and for the first time he could see fear creeping into his old friend's eyes.

It was all the encouragement he needed.

'Predictable spot you chose, wasn't it?'

Dempsey's question was delivered with a smirk. It was designed to delay. To give him more time as the breath returned through the pain of his broken ribs.

'Still couldn't get the drop on me, though, could you?'

Turner also spoke through hard-fought breaths. The struggle seemed to have tired him as much as it had Dempsey. Maybe more. And Dempsey now saw why. Turner's hand pressed into his ribcage as he pulled in air; the act of a man trying to restrict the movement of broken ribs. He was carrying an injury as well, Dempsey now realised.

The two men started to close the distance between them, drifting around one another. Slowly, with all of the caution of two natural predators.

Turner moved first.

He feigned a blow with his left hand once they were in striking distance. Dempsey pretended to buy it, moving his right arm up to protect himself. It was the movement he knew Turner's feint was designed for, as it exposed Dempsey's broken ribs long enough for a second knee-strike.

Only this time that strike did not serve Turner so well.

Aware of what was coming, Dempsey used Turner's movement against him. With his parrying arm raised and so able to add momentum, he brought his elbow down with phenomenal force. It caught Turner as he threw himself forward and sent him crashing to the ground, the skin above his eye torn apart in the process.

Turner was down, but he did not stay there.

Though blood was seeping into his left eye and his head was still reeling from Dempsey's blow, Turner struggled to his feet. But it was a slow movement and it left him vulnerable.

Only halfway up, Turner could not defend against the perfectly timed knee-strike that crashed into his face. It smashed into his exposed nose and sent him careering into a nearby tree. His legs buckled beneath him as Dempsey watched, causing short, sharp branches to dig into his back as he slid down the tree's trunk.

This time he was that little bit slower in climbing back to his feet again. More painfully than before. Slow and unsteady.

Dempsey stood and watched. He was now ignoring his own pain as he made Sam Regis' killer suffer.

'You're getting old, James.'

'Maybe,' Turner replied, his breathing now audibly painful. 'But I'll be around long after you.'

Turner launched himself at Dempsey without warning, throwing parried blow after parried blow. Punches that kept coming, but with no clean strike landing. Dempsey blocked or avoided whatever Turner could throw at him, but in doing so he could not switch from defence to offence.

It was a stalemate that could not continue, and it ended when Dempsey lost his footing on an exposed tree root. It was just the slightest stumble, but it gave Turner the opening he needed. He sent a well-timed kick towards Dempsey's chest as the agent struggled to place his feet. It sent Dempsey reeling backwards and to the floor, where he landed heavily on his spine.

He was back on his feet just in time as Turner rushed towards him, and, moving with an unexpected speed, swept Turner's legs out from under him. Bringing himself upright with the momentum, he quickly followed up with a kick to Turner's jaw.

Turner was sent sprawling backwards. Blood was flowing freely from his mouth, but Dempsey could tell that this was the least of his problems. Turner's eyes said it all. The last blow had defeated him. He was done.

All Turner could do was scramble backwards through the dirt as Dempsey walked towards him.

'It's over, Jim.'

Turner did not answer. He just continued to crawl away. To put distance between him and the approaching Dempsey.

And in the next moment both he and Turner spotted the abandoned Glock, laying within Turner's reach.

Dempsey reacted first, but Turner was closer. He moved faster than his physical condition should allow. In a moment the gun was in Turner's hand, just as Dempsey reached him, in time to block Turner's turn and grip his wrist, preventing a clean shot. Allowing Dempsey to grab the gun itself.

Each man had a firm grip on the weapon. And each was determined to be the one who used it. But this was not a battle won by the greater will to win. It would come down to something much more basic. It would come down to physical strength.

Turner gave it his all. Used every ounce of strength he had left. Still the weapon was turning towards him. Dempsey was winning, and he was pinning Turner to the tree behind him as he did so. Its fledgling branches once again dug into Turner's back. Deeper this time.

Dempsey pressed ever harder, wrestling control of the pistol.

The barrel of the gun kept turning, until it faced fully inwards. Towards Turner's chest. His best efforts had not been enough and – as he looked away from the gun and into Dempsey's eyes – he must have known it was over.

He snarled at Dempsey in defiance.

'I should have killed you in Colombia.'

The words were simple, his mouth contorted by blood and bitterness as he spoke.

Dempsey needed just two words in reply. He uttered them as he squeezed the weapon's trigger and sent three bullets into Turner's chest.

'You tried.'

EIGHTY-TWO

All eyes were on Haversume as he strode into the clearing. Sarah Truman and Harry Lawrence walked ahead of him. Haversume kept his gun trained on their backs. He intended to press every advantage he had.

He walked slowly, giving him time to take in the details that were around him.

Eleven armed men in the clearing represented his interests. Nine accompanied Michael. They seemed an evenly matched grouping. Or they would have been, if it were not for Joshua.

It was the location of Joshua that interested Haversume most. He instinctively cast his eyes to the hills. He was not sure why. Haversume knew he would be unable to spot a hidden sniper at a distance of twenty feet, let alone the quarter of a mile Joshua had likely chosen. Still, human nature compelled his gaze to the distant trees.

'You're looking a little beaten up, Michael.'

The sarcasm in Haversume's voice was intentional as he came to a halt, ten yards from where Michael Devlin stood. He placed a hand on Harry's small, shivering shoulder as he spoke. A reminder of the power he held.

'I do hope we can settle this without the need for any more bloodshed.'

'You started the violence, Tony,' Michael replied. His attitude was defiant. 'You're the animal here.'

'I think Sergeant Best would disagree. What you left of him was hardly the work of a civilised man.'

'He didn't leave me a choice. But *you* didn't have to do any of this. You're a murdering piece of opportunistic shit.'

'Opportunistic?' Haversume was annoyed. Michael's choice of words had stung. 'Have you any idea how much planning goes into bringing down a government? Any idea at all?'

'A great deal, I'd imagine. But then you had plenty of time on your hands to plan it, didn't you? What with only being a backbencher.'

Haversume saw the comment for what it was. An attempt to goad him. It would not work.

'I don't have time for silly games, boy. Just tell me where the recording is.'

'The others first.'

Michael indicated beyond Sarah and Harry. Towards the cabin.

'The deal was everyone.'

'I don't have time for more demands, Michael.' Haversume's patience was wearing thin. 'Give me the recording now or people die.'

'You want it, you'll do as I ask. Once I know the other three are here and that they're OK. *Then* we'll talk about the recording.'

'You truly are an intolerable nuisance, Michael.'

Haversume was unsure if he should be angry or amused; Michael Devlin really had proved himself an absurdly determined irritant. He turned to face Sarah, forced down her gag and stabbed a finger in Michael's direction.

'Tell him.'

He grabbed her by the back of her neck and forced her forwards.

'I said, "tell him"!'

'They're in there, Michael,' Sarah spluttered. 'They're safe, they're not hurt.'

'Thank you.'

Haversume spat the words as he threw Sarah aside. She stumbled heavily to the floor, the binding around her wrists preventing her from cushioning her fall.

Haversume turned back to Michael.

'Now where's the recording?'

'It's here.'

'I want to see it. Now.'

Michael hesitated. Haversume thought he knew why. The recording was the endgame. Once revealed, Michael's hand was played and what would follow would be out of his control.

It was understandable that Michael would want more time, but Haversume would not allow it. He trained his gun on Harry as a final threat.

'OK, Tony.' Michael raised his open hands in response. 'I have it here. Take the gun away from the boy.'

Michael reached into his jacket pocket. He moved slowly. With so many armed men around him, a devastating domino effect would begin if his movement caused a shot. Care was needed, and it was with care that Michael now revealed Mullen's recording device.

Michael held the device in his right fist. Still avoiding sudden movements, Michael slowly put out his arm, opened his hand and held it out for Haversume to see.

'This is it. This is what Mullen had.'

'Play it.'

'I'm not your butler, Tony. Play it yourself.'

Michael threw the device to Haversume, who caught it in mid-air.

A single glance at the device brought a smile to Haversume's face. He recognised the technology, and it told him two things. First, Michael had not been bluffing. This equipment *could* reverse the effect of the voice modulator. Whoever was responsible for handing this over to Mullen was going to answer to him once all this was done.

And the second thing? Well, that would depend . . .

Haversume turned the device over and looked closely at its underside.

His smile widened.

'You haven't even listened to this.'

The words were not a question. And they made the colour drain from Michael's face.

'What? Of course I've listened—'

'Don't bother lying to me, Michael.' Haversume's smile lingered as he held up the device. 'This is military hardware. It's designed to be totally secure. There's only one way to make it work and you haven't done it. I can tell from the device. But, more importantly, if you haven't heard what's on this then you can't have re-recorded it, either. Which means *this* is the only copy. I imagine that was another lie you were going to tell me, wasn't it, Michael?'

Haversume made no effort to keep the triumph from his voice. He had won. He had the device in his hand, and the only threat Michael could have made – that there were copies of the recordings, ready to be delivered in the event of their deaths – was gone.

It left Haversume with no need to wait.

He raised his right hand high above his head, opening and closing his fist. A very obvious prearranged signal.

But a signal that achieved nothing. No bullet. No gunshot.

Haversume's confidence wavered. Joshua should have fired. It made him freeze.

Luckily for Haversume, he did not seem to be alone. For some reason Michael and Liam seemed rooted to the spot. It left all of their followers without leadership. Without direction.

Twenty armed men, facing each other in the clearing. All needed to know their next move. Needed to know if they were to fight or to flee. Needed someone to make a decision.

In the hills above them, someone did.

EIGHTY-THREE

Haversume's raised arm movement could not have been clearer. It was a signal, and that signal could only mean one thing.

Michael had known that the moment would come. He had thought he was prepared for it. But to stand and watch the signal that could end his life? To be so utterly helpless in that moment? So totally reliant on Dempsey's success? He had not been prepared for *that*, and so he had not known how to react when instant death did not come.

The sound of shots rang out from the hillside, breaking everyone's reverie. There was no stopping what would happen now.

With Sarah and Harry so exposed, Michael's instincts kicked in.

He broke into a sprint. Haversume was just ten yards away. Clearly he hadn't anticipated Michael's charge. He started to raise his pistol, but had no time to use it.

Michael's punch was thrown as he still ran. His movement made the blow clumsy, but his momentum made it powerful. It landed on Haversume's jaw before he could pull the trigger and sent him stumbling to the floor.

There was no time to follow up on the blow. Michael scooped Harry into his arms, grabbed Sarah and hauled them both into the nearby foliage.

From behind the cover of an oversized tree trunk Michael turned and looked back into the clearing. And he was not happy with what he saw.

Both groups had fallen back to their own vehicles for cover. From there they were firing wildly in each other's direction, each bullet having just the barest chance of hitting its target. What they had hoped would be a quickly won battle was already becoming a hopelessly entrenched war. One from which Haversume could easily escape.

Michael would not allow that to happen.

He turned back to Sarah and Harry and took a moment to free them from their restraints. He then carefully removed Harry's gag, before finally turning back to Sarah. There was no time for Michael to explain what was happening around them. No chance to reassure them. If they were to survive then Liam would need every one of his men. Including Michael.

'Stay here and stay down.'

It was all that Michael could say.

Without another word he pulled the 9mm Smith & Wesson M&P he had been given by Liam and moved back through the surrounding undergrowth until he was level with the three off-road vehicles. A group of Haversume's men were behind the first, safe from the guns of Liam's men. But not safe from Michael. To them he was invisible.

From here Michael could break the deadlock.

He tightened his grip on his weapon as he moved the final few yards, to where he would have the clearest shot. Just the wrong side of the undergrowth, the spot left Michael more exposed than was ideal. But one final look back towards Sarah and Harry justified the risk.

It was their safety that most motivated him as he pulled the trigger.

One man went down from Michael's first shot. A stream of blood seeped from the open wound on the man's neck. He fired four more shots in quick succession, taking out a second man and causing a third to dive for cover.

It was an effective attack, but a hazardous one. With his attention on his own targets, there was no way Michael could have noticed as one of Haversume's men emerged from behind a second vehicle and opened fire.

In Michael's career he had heard pain described in many ways. Particularly the pain of a gunshot. He had heard recollections of a burning bite. And of a strange feeling where the victim's strength has been sapped, with their energy and even their ability to think clearly drained away. These sensations were exactly what Michael felt now as a single bullet passed through his shoulder and forced him to drop to his knees.

He looked up, his mind already hazy from the effect of the bullet. The shooter he had not spotted was now striding towards him, his weapon raised. No doubt ready to deliver a final barrage of lead.

But before he could do so a bullet burst through the skull of Michael's would-be killer. Michael saw two more bullets take the lives of two more of Haversume's men, and realised they were coming from the hillside, not the clearing.

Joe Dempsey.

Dempsey's lethal, long-distant shots were devastating Haversume's men. They had abandoned the cover of their vehicles, which had proved useless as protection against the trained sniper. This had in turn made them easy prey for Liam's people, and so what had been a battle was fast becoming a massacre.

The clearing was a vision of hell. Michael saw that as he turned a full 360. All around it were bodies, cut down with bloody abandon. Horrific sights that Michael hardly registered.

His focus was both absolute and elsewhere, looking for one man and one man only.

And then, through the smoke and the gore and the darkness, Michael found him.

Haversume was crouched behind the five-foot stump of what must have once been a vast Irish oak. He seemed to be paying no attention at all to the death of his men, concentrating only on keeping his body behind the oak, out of the line of fire.

The sight released even more of Michael's adrenaline, sending renewed energy surging through his veins. It dulled the pain of his open wound.

He would not let Haversume escape unscathed.

Michael ignored the danger that was all around him. The lessening but still heavy gunfire. He strode through it, his Smith & Wesson aimed ahead of him and his finger repeatedly squeezing its trigger.

Four times Michael fired before Haversume knew he was there. Each bullet had dug into the trunk behind which Haversume had hidden; the most effective shield the clearing had to offer.

The fourth shot had come close, thudding to a halt just inches from Haversume's head. But it had also caught his attention. Peering around the trunk, Haversume saw Michael's approach.

Michael would never know what cold mental calculation compelled Haversume to do what he did next, but he would always regret it nonetheless. Because Haversume did not choose to fire from his hiding place. And nor did he choose to wait until Michael was close, to allow for a better shot.

What he chose to do was run. Full sprint, in the direction of the cabin.

Haversume took off with a speed Michael had not anticipated, firing behind himself as he did so. Bullet after bullet, all fired over his shoulder at a rate that denied him any accuracy but which nevertheless forced Michael to dive for cover, stopping him from firing back.

He forced himself back to his feet, ignoring the pain from his wound, in time to see Haversume enter the cabin and close its door behind him. Where the rest of the Lawrence family still were.

Michael ran towards the cabin. Haversume would not hurt anyone else he cared about.

Liam spotted his blood-soaked brother through the gun smoke.

Luck had drawn Liam's gaze to Michael's lumbering, injured figure as he slowly rose from the floor in the distance. At the same moment – in the same line of sight – he caught a glimpse of Haversume, gun in hand, as he entered the cabin.

Instinctively, Liam followed after his brother, knowing the danger he was about to step into. Liam ignored the final shots being exchanged around him, got to his feet and left the safe cover the cars had provided. As he ran he could feel the heat of bullets as they passed him. He was now a moving target, drawing fire as his steps turned into a sprint.

Liam moved faster than he had in twenty years, driven by the need to catch Michael before *he* could reach the cabin door. For an instant Liam thought he might fail. That he might lack the legs to cover the distance. But as Michael stumbled on the cabin's first step he felt a final rush of adrenaline and found one more gear.

There was no hesitation. Michael reached the cabin first. Dazed, exhausted and losing blood fast, he pushed open the unsecured door without a thought to his own safety.

Liam was not so naive.

EIGHTY-FOUR

Michael's eyes had no time to adjust to the cabin's darkness before he was pushed to the floor by an impact from behind. A shot rang out. His first thought was that he had been hit a second time. Mentally examining himself for the wound, Michael stopped when he registered that the impact that had taken him down had come not from the front. It had come from behind.

The realisation increased his panic. Terrified, he forced himself to look towards the doorway.

'Get up, Michael.'

Haversume might as well have not spoken. His words had no effect on Michael, whose eyes were fixed in horror on Liam, motionless on the cabin floor.

'I said, get up!'

This time Haversume shouted. Every last vestige of the calm, sophisticated conspirator had been abandoned. He manhandled Claire ahead of himself at gunpoint, pushing his one remaining advantage.

None of which registered with Michael.

It was several seconds before he could move. His body refused to obey the orders it received from his brain. Shock had shut him down. The paralysis did not last, but it was not external stimulus that broke it. It was the need to reach his brother.

Michael dragged his own failing body to Liam's side and carefully rolled him onto his back.

Blood was seeping from a single hole in Liam's chest, with a deep red pool of it now on the floor where he had lain. Michael refused to acknowledge either thing. All that mattered was that Liam was alive.

'Michael, I have Claire.'

Haversume's voice was now desperate. Almost pleading for a response.

He did not get one.

'Liam, you're gonna be OK.'

Michael ignored Haversume's interruptions. His only thought was his brother.

'Don't worry. You're gonna be OK.'

'No, Mikey. No I'm not.'

Liam's words were strained. Almost not there. They were pushed out between irregular, painful breaths. And yet they were more realistic than any Michael could muster.

'I'm finished.'

'No. No, Liam, you're not. You're going to be fine.'

Michael spoke through a mask of tears. Common sense was beginning to defeat his refusal to accept the inevitable.

'You get up now. Get up.'

Liam smiled and slowly lifted his hand to his brother's face. He gently wiped the tears from Michael's cheek. It said what neither brother could. And it used up the very last of Liam's strength.

Michael felt his brother's callused hand against his skin and it blocked out the rest of the world. He did not notice that the gunfire outside had died. That the cabin entrance was beginning to fill with Liam's men. That none of them – not even the immediately devastated O'Neil – could bring themselves to come closer. Michael noticed none of this. All that mattered was the dying body he held in his arms.

His rational mind told him they had little time. But, for all his eloquence, he did not have the words.

'Liam, I, I.' Michael had no idea of what he was trying to say. 'Liam.'

Unable to say what he wanted his brother to know, Michael joined him in silence. He was content just to feel the heat of Liam's hand on his face. But even that comfort could not last; Liam's arm was weakening, his hand beginning to falter. Michael took it in his own palm and pressed it to his cheek, where tears streamed through Liam's fingers as the light disappeared from his eyes.

As he felt the final strength disappear from Liam's hand, Michael pulled his brother's heavy body towards him and hugged it with all of his own. An embrace he wanted to last for ever.

For Haversume this seemed to be a step too far. Gripping Claire more forcefully by the nape of her neck, he turned his gun on Michael.

When he spoke it was with a voice that could no longer be ignored.

'Enough is enough,' he shouted, his self-control gone. 'Get to your feet and tell these fuckers to get out of my way before I put a bullet in her head. Pull yourself together and do as I say. Now!'

Michael looked up, almost quizzically, as if seeing the scene around him for the very first time. He registered Haversume's threat, and then noticed what was left of Liam's men crowded around the cabin door.

It made Haversume's demand clear.

With Liam's body still warm in his arms Michael could no longer feel the anger – the passion – that had been driving him on. What was left was an empty shell with nothing left to fight for.

He looked first at Claire, held at Haversume's mercy. Then at Sarah, now standing with O'Neil but who had been in Claire's position less than ten minutes before. And finally at Liam, dead against his chest.

He knew that he could lose no one else.

'Let him go.'

Michael's voice was full of impotent, defeated rage; the words of a man whose world had been ripped away.

'Just let the bastard go.'

With that his eyes returned to Liam's face. He did not watch as Haversume pushed his gun into Claire's neck, preparing to exit through a crowd of men who wanted him dead. Nor did he look up as that crowd parted, in obedience to Michael's instructions. He did not look up at all. And so he missed the last sight that Haversume would ever see.

Haversume steeled himself to move as Liam's men parted. It left a channel through which he and Claire could pass. He took a step towards it, but stopped at the sight of a figure who until now had stood unseen behind the crowd.

It was possibly the greatest shock of Haversume's life. And as Dempsey pulled his trigger from thirty feet away to send a single round into the front of his skull, it was certainly the last.

Haversume was thrown backwards by the force of the bullet. He was dead long before he hit the ground.

What remained of Liam's men watched as Dempsey strode through the channel they had opened for his victim and stopped directly over Haversume's lifeless corpse. The hole in

'Stanton's' forehead removed any doubt that the shot had done its job.

'I told you I'd find you.'

With those words, Dempsey turned and walked away.

It was over.

EIGHTY-FIVE

It was unusual for the world's press to cover the funeral of a mere backbencher of the British Parliament. But Anthony Haversume had come so close to being so much more. He had become the voice of the British majority, the man of the people who had stood up to the liberal elite. Haversume had challenged the weakness of the British government and in doing that he had caught the world's attention. Or at least that was the memory.

Haversume's message may have been false, but it had also been popular. It was a message now carried forward by Britain's new prime minister, Jeremy Ross. And it was to Ross that every camera now turned.

The world waited to hear his views on the new dawn.

'I stand before you today thanks to the efforts, the beliefs and the sacrifice of one man. I stand before you because Anthony Haversume, the man who deserved my position and the man Britain deserved as her leader, cannot. Anthony was taken from us by an act of the very violence he tried so hard to fight. I stand before you as a believer and as a supporter. And I give you my word that I will do everything in my power to live up to the ideals of this truly great statesman.

'As you all know, Anthony Haversume gave up a ministerial position to languish on the back benches. He did so because he was one of us. Because he objected to the government's capitulation to terrorism. Because he objected to its failure to support the men and women who fought and died for our ongoing security. That Anthony should have made such a sacrifice is a testament to the man's character. But there was so much more to him than just that.

'Anthony was, by anyone's standards, a true one-off. Not only was he possessed of a morality and patriotism that centred his political beliefs, he was also gifted with the determination of the soldier he once was. With a mind of which we could all be envious. He was, without question, the best of us—

Dempsey hit the off button before Ross could eulogise Haversume further. The myth they were now spinning was inevitable. He knew that. But that did not mean that he needed to listen to it.

He got to his feet, walked to the door of Liam Casey's office and stepped into the corridor. It would lead him back to the packed front rooms of the 32 Counties Bar. For now, though, Dempsey was alone. He stood for just a moment, motionless and silent. Thoughts ran through his mind. Hundreds of them. But first among them was disgust. Disgust that the establishment – terrified of what could happen if Haversume's actions were discovered – had chosen to cover them up and allow the man to die a populist hero.

It was not worth his time or concern. Dempsey knew that. It was the way that the political world worked, and he could do nothing to change it.

Dempsey stepped through the door that marked the border between the bar's public and private quarters. On its other side was the bustling crowd of black-clad mourners. At least a hundred. Probably a lot more. All celebrating the life of Liam Casey in a way that only the Irish could.

All around him was singing and dancing. It made Dempsey shake his head. He was bemused by how these people dealt with death. It was certainly not the English way. The dead man's family and friends were dancing with abandon to the sound of traditional Irish music while their emotions flitted from laughter to tears and then back again. All of them ably assisted by the content of the 32 Counties' cellar, which was being drained as the wake continued. It was perhaps a healthier approach than the stoic stiff upper lip, Dempsey thought. But still not a celebration of life that he could join. As he looked around he realised that he was not alone in this.

Michael stood behind the bar that had been his father's and then his brother's. Framed pictures of both were hanging on the wall behind him. His right arm was in a sling and his facial injuries were healing well. Dempsey thought that Michael looked remarkably healthy for all he had suffered.

'Are you not joining in with the singing?' Dempsey's sympathy went out to the one man who had lost more than he had lost himself.

'No. Never really been my thing.'

Michael tried to smile as he spoke, but the sadness in his eyes betrayed him. Dempsey recognised it. He had seen it often enough and he knew it would need to come out through proper mourning. This would not begin until Michael was finally alone. Until then he would need a distraction.

'Sarah seems to have settled into it well.'

Michael followed Dempsey's gaze. He smiled again. Wider this time. And genuine. Sarah and Anne sat at a table alone. They laughed, cried and even sang as they nursed what was left of a bottle of Irish whiskey.

'Yeah. Those two seem to have bonded. I'm glad she's been here for Anne.' Michael hesitated a moment before changing the subject. 'And back in England? How was everything?'

'The way I said it would be. The people who need to know

about Haversume know. And it's terrified them. Too many important people jumped on his bandwagon after Trafalgar Square. The truth coming out would damage them – ruin some of them – and so they're covering it up. The public will never know what he did.'

'And Sarah's role?'

'She did as she promised, Mike. For you and for Anne. Once I explained that there were still people out there who'd worked for Haversume – including whoever killed McGale – there was no way she was going to push things further. Not if it put you at risk.'

'You think she'll hold that against us?'

Dempsey glanced in Sarah's direction, then back towards Michael with a smile.

'I don't think there's anything that could make her resent *you*. Besides, she still got to file the fake story – the cover story – instead of the real one. It might not be the perfect start for a campaigner for truth and all that sort of thing, but with an exclusive like that, her career's made. So it's not so bad a result.'

Michael nodded. Dempsey had warned him of how things would need to be dealt with in London to ensure Sarah's, Anne's and his own safety from whatever might be left of Haversume's organisation. And he had been proved right.

Michael was just pleased that at least Sarah would benefit from the necessary lies.

It left only one question.

'What about Turner?'

'Time will tell,' Dempsey replied. 'He's hanging on, somehow. Christ knows what he's made of.'

'And if he lives?'

'If he lives he won't be going to any court you'd recognise.

They've got different rules for men like him. Different prisons, too.'

Michael nodded. He seemed satisfied that – dead or alive – Turner's crimes would not go unpunished.

'So what about you?' Dempsey finally asked, breaking into Michael's thoughts. 'What do you plan to do now?'

'I'll need to stay here for now,' Michael replied. 'Just for a short time. I need to help Anne clean up Liam's affairs. There's a lot of money there that she stands to inherit, but a whole lot of murk around it. Plus I want to make sure she's OK in every other way, too. After what she's lost.'

'What about what *you've* lost?' Dempsey asked. Once again his glance flicked to Sarah. '*And* what you might have gained? You can't put your life on hold for ever.'

Michael smiled. Dempsey's meaning might have been unspoken, but it was hardly unclear.

'I don't intend to,' he replied. 'Sarah has to go back soon, otherwise she risks losing the momentum this will give her career. And I've got some serious trials lined up to the end of next year. Which means we both need to get back to work.'

'So it's a "we" now, is it?'

'It is for me,' Michael replied, with a lightness in his voice as his eyes found Sarah across the room. 'And I hope it will be for her.'

'I don't think you have to worry about that, Mike.'

The two men smiled at Dempsey's words. A temporary silence fell as they both considered their meaning. Finally Michael spoke again.

'And you? What happens to you after all this?'

'That's complicated.' Dempsey's answer was all he had thought about since his return from London. 'They're going to disband the DDS. It'll be made official next week. Inevitable, I suppose, after Callum McGregor's involvement in everything that happened.'

'So you're out of a job?'

'Not exactly. It turns out that what happened has convinced the powers-that-be that a more unified approach to security and intelligence is needed. They think they need something beyond the usual domestic agencies, so they're forming a new department that'll be based in New York. The International Security Bureau they're calling it. God knows if that name will stick.'

'Do they want you?'

'As their first recruit, yeah. And they've promised I'll get to pick my own team from various agencies around the world. It seems my stock's fairly high these days.'

'But you'll be based in the States?'

'That hardly makes a difference, Mike. I've been based in London since joining the DDS and I've spent two weeks at home in all that time. Besides, the ISB's remit is worldwide. So I could end up anywhere.'

'Sounds like you're planning to take it?'

'I already have,' Dempsey replied. 'But that's all for another day. Tonight I'm helping my friend mourn his brother. Now pass that whiskey and get us both a glass.'

Acknowledgements

There is an old saying: it takes a village to raise a child. It's a cliché and it may or may not be true, but as I now sit down – still a little disbelievingly – to write the acknowledgements for my first novel, there is one thing I know: it took a village to write this book.

It was an unexpected discovery. When I began *Killer Intent* I foolishly believed that it was me and the page. I could not have been more wrong. The help I have received in the creation, marketing and publication of this novel has been invaluable. Without it, your hands would now be empty. The very least I can do in return is to say thank you.

First, the two women whose drive – and, at times, flat out cheerleading – kept me going. My wife, Victoria, and my mother, Elizabeth.

Mum was the first person to read *Killer Intent*, in bits and pieces as I wrote. She endured long phone calls, rambling questions and maybe the occasional need for some unearned praise, and through it all she gave me the reassurance and confidence I needed to keep going. Mum's advice was insightful, her encouragement vital. She was my first editor. She was my first critic. And she was my first fan. This book is entirely hers. Thanks, Mum.

Victoria came to *Killer Intent* much later, at a time when my focus was back on the day job. It was Victoria's instant enthusiasm, her support and her sheer drive that brought me back to this book. My brilliant, beautiful wife reignited my writing ambitions and pushed me to achieve publication. I would not be here without her.

The rest of my family, too, have played their part. Whether it was a detailed critique from a long-term reader of the genre (my brother Derek), the inspiration for various characters (my brothers Joe and Jimmy), sheer enthusiasm (my sister Kate) or even just a willingness to listen about the tortuous path to publication without telling me to shut up (my dad), everyone offered something and I realise how vital each 'something' was.

Moving from one family to another, I cannot write another word without recognising Lorne Forsyth, Jennie Condell, Pippa Crane, Angela McMahon, Anthony Keates and everyone at Elliott & Thompson for believing in an untested writer and for taking the risk to back me. The dedication and skill that Jennie and Pippa collectively brought to bear on the main edit, on the final preparation *and* on the publication of *Killer Intent* has been staggering; this is the book that it is because of them, and it is infinitely better for their attentions. Combined with the PR and marketing expertise of both Angela and Anthony, the E&T team have allowed me to jump into the deep end without fear of drowning. I could not ask for more effort, professionalism or skill from the people I have behind me.

And Lorne in particular deserves the utmost praise for championing the book you now hold and those that will follow. His extraordinary faith has changed my life.

My sincere thanks is also owed to Gill Richardson – a true champion of *Killer Intent* – Sarah Anderson and their incredible sales team at Simon & Schuster. I cannot thank them enough for everything they have done to make this book a success.

Next are Annalise Fard, Michael Ward and Virginie Duigon, for all of their amazing efforts in launching the hardback. They have truly gone above and beyond to give *Killer Intent* a start in life that was beyond my wildest dreams, and 'thanks' seems so woefully insufficient. And the same is true of Daniel Gedeon, whose determined support from his receipt of our first proof has been invaluable.

All of which brings me to Neil Speight, the friend whose skilled advice turned the first draft of *Killer Intent* from an amateur manuscript into something more. Neil spent weeks reading and editing what I foolishly thought was already a finished novel, and I realise how incredibly lucky I was for that attention. He added the finishing touches to my writing style, and his impact on every book I will ever write cannot be overstated. *Killer Intent* would have caught no one's attention without Neil's influence and advice. We each get very few true friends in life, and Neil has proved that he is one of the best.

So those are the big ones in terms of creating this novel, but of course there are many more. And so thank you to Scott Ewing, Jeremy Newell and everyone at Ewing Law for helping me to wear two hats; without their efforts and understanding it would be impossible to combine the Criminal Bar with crime writing. To my former pupil-master Craig Rush and to everyone at the Chambers of William Clegg QC, for introducing me to and educating me about the world of criminal courts and criminal lawyers that provides the backdrop for *Killer Intent*. To Craig again, this time for being the pedantic nuisance whose factual corrections to my earlier drafts were sometimes less than graciously received. To Lucinda Boon and to Jane Oldfield, for their character and plot suggestions that helped develop *Killer Intent* from draft to draft. To John Lawrence, for providing some of the inspiration – and all of the surname – for a key character. To David Charters, Clementine Rainey-Brown and Orla Constant, for the 'Rolls-Royce' of introductions which ultimately put me in touch with Lorne and therefore with Elliott & Thompson. And to my friends David French, Charlie Langley, Michael Epstein, Stephen Ferguson and Libby Ferguson, all of whom tried to help me achieve publication at times when – unknown to them and to me – the book was not yet ready. I truly appreciate the efforts they all made.

And finally to the readers. Those who have read and hopefully enjoyed *Killer Intent* at various stages in its development. Thank you, then, to my aunt Angela Gray; my uncle Michael Gray; my father-in-law Clive Christian OBE; his partner, the lovely Frances Falconer; my brother-in-law Stef Humphries; my self-appointed big sister Jacqueline Carey; and my good friends Grant Benjamin, Carolyn Lawrence, Shauna Bush, Helen Ding and Michelle Edelson.

It's a small village, but each and every one of you has been indispensable. Thank you all.

If you loved *Killer Intent*,
look out for the next book in the series:

MARKED FOR DEATH

by

TONY KENT

Coming soon

ONE

Phillip Longman was not woken by the sound of breaking glass. That would have required sleep, and sleep was something his elderly body no longer seemed to need.

A metal rail hung from a reinforced section of the ceiling. Longman's frail hands gripped it as tightly as they could and, using all of his strength, he pulled his body upright. The automated mattress followed, designed to support him if that strength gave out. Longman was a proud man; too proud to be raised by a mechanical bed, too proud for a panic alarm, even. But pride would not keep him vertical; the mattress was Longman's concession to his body's decay.

The sound of his exertion filled the room. Grunts, groans, heavy breaths. In his younger days Longman had been an active man. Even into his sixties his physical fitness had marked him out from his peers. But his sixties were long gone. Now he could barely climb out of bed.

The mattress finally caught up and pressed against Longman's back, taking the brunt of his weight. He released his grip on the metal rail and silence returned to the room.

Longman listened carefully. The sound had been unmistakable. Shattering glass makes a distinctive noise, one he recognised immediately, even with his diminished hearing. But identifying its source was much harder. Was it the sound of a dropped ashtray? A wine glass? Or of a broken window, smashed to admit the uninvited? Not that it really mattered. In the otherwise empty house of an eighty-five-year-old widower, every one of those possibilities was a cause for concern.

Longman strained to listen. At first there was nothing. At least nothing *he* could hear.

The house was big; much *too* big now that his wife had passed away and his children had moved on. But Longman had been unable to bring himself to leave the family home of fifty years. He knew it inside out.

And it was that familiarity that made the next sound an unintentional alarm. The creak of the first step on the main staircase.

It was a feature of the house that went back decades. In the daytime – during the housekeeper's working hours – it would be the most natural sound in the world. But when the bedside clock read 3 a.m.? At *that* hour it was terrifying.

As the sound of footsteps continued up the stairs, Longman threw back the duvet in a panic, freeing his frail legs from its weight and swinging them to the floor. The pain was excruciating; crippling arthritis meant he had not moved so fast in five years, back when his hips did their job. But he ignored the agony and climbed to his feet, one hand on the solid bedpost for support.

His breathing was out of control, his heart a piston. But Longman pushed himself on, staggering to the walk-in closet in the far corner of the room. For the first time in years he made the distance without a stick or a frame for support. Exhausted, he stumbled as he reached the door. Only adrenaline kept him upright.

Regaining his balance, Longman gripped the closet door's handle and then paused, holding his breath in an effort to hear. Nothing could stop the thumping pulse that filled his inner ear, or the fear that his overworking heart would not keep the pace. Still, it was quiet enough to hear the ever-approaching footsteps.

The closet opened easily and, fumbling in the dark, he found the light-switch. Momentarily blinded by the light, he frantically scanned the shelves as his eyes slowly adjusted, looking for something, anything to defend himself. He wasn't sure what he expected to find. What weapon would have been of use anyway, to a man crippled by age? But the wardrobe contained nothing that would have been any help to anyone. As his hope disappeared in a single breath, he realised the sound of footsteps had stopped.

Longman had not heard the door open, but that sixth sense that humans possess – that feeling that tells us when we are not alone – had not diminished with age. The bedroom was no longer empty. Longman already knew that as he turned around. But he wasn't expecting the sight he was met with as he stared at the figure in front of him in disbelief.

'You!' Longman's exclamation was more an accusation than an expression of shock.

It was the eyes. The most soulless Longman had ever seen. He would recognise them anywhere, even now, all these years later.

'You remember me.'

The reply was a statement, as sinister as the speaker. A predator born and bred.

'Some things one never forgets.' Everything about the man was as Longman remembered. 'And some people.'

A smile formed on the predator's lips, though his pale eyes remained cold. It was a smile of triumph, not happiness.

'True.'

The man moved closer, his pace slow, deliberate. A viper finding its range.

'It's good you've kept that mind of yours,' he said. 'Even at your age.'

'What does that matter?'

The old man spoke with defiance. His fate was sealed: he saw it in those pale, merciless eyes. But he would not face it on his knees.

'Oh, it matters.'

For the first time there was life in the voice, filled with an unmistakable venom that sent chills through Longman's veins.

Only inches now separated their bodies as he felt a vice-like grip constrict his wrist.

'Because it means you'll feel every second of what's coming.'

To hear all the latest news about Tony, his
writing and his events, visit www.tonykent.net
or follow him on Twitter: @TonyKent_Writes,
and Facebook: Tony Kent – Author.